A former au pair, bookseller, marketing manager and seafront trader, **Jessica Gilmore** now works for an environmental charity in York, England. Married with one daughter, one fluffy dog and two dog-loathing cats, she spends her time avoiding housework and can usually be found with her nose in a book. Jessica writes emotional romance with a hint of humour, a splash of sunshine and a great deal of delicious food—and equally delicious heroes!

USA TODAY bestselling and RITA® Award–winning author **Marie Ferrarella** has written more than two hundred and seventy-five books for Mills & Boon, some under the name Marie Nicole. Her romances are beloved by fans worldwide. Visit her website, www.marieferrarella.com.

D0682225

Discover more at millsandboon.co.uk

BABY SURPRISE FOR THE SPANISH BILLIONAIRE

JESSICA GILMORE

THE FORTUNE MOST LIKELY TO...

MARIE FERRARELLA

MILLS & BOON

All rights reserved including the right of reproduction in whole or in part in any form. This edition is published by arrangement with Harlequin Books S.A. This is a work of fiction. Names, characters, places and incidents are either the product of the author's imagination or are used fictitiously and any resemblance to actual persons, living or dead, business establishments, events or locales is entirely coincidental.

This book is sold subject to the condition that it shall not, by way of trade or otherwise, be lent, resold, hired out or otherwise circulated without the prior consent of the publisher in any form of binding or cover other than that in which it is published and without a similar condition including this condition being imposed on the subsequent purchaser.

® and TM are trademarks owned and used by the trademark owner and/ or its licensee. Trademarks marked with ® are registered with the United Kingdom Patent Office and/or the Office for Harmonisation in the Internal Market and in other countries.

First Published in Great Britain 2018
by Mills & Boon, an imprint of HarperCollinsPublishers,
1 London Bridge Street, London, SE1 9GF

Baby Surprise for the Spanish Billionaire © 2018 Jessica Gilmore
The Fortune Most Likely To... © 2018 Harlequin Books S.A.

Special thanks and acknowledgement are given to Marie Ferrarella for her contribution to the Fortunes of Texas: The Rulebreakers continuity.

ISBN: 978-0-263-26476-0

38-0318

MIX
Paper from
responsible sources
FSC™ C007454

This book is produced from independently certified FSC™
paper to ensure responsible forest management.

For more information visit: www.harpercollins.co.uk/green

Printed and bound in Spain
by CPI, Barcelona

BABY SURPRISE FOR THE SPANISH BILLIONAIRE

JESSICA GILMORE

For Katy!
That was fun! Let's do it again some time…

CHAPTER ONE

ANNA GRAY CLASPED her coffee cup in both hands, stepped gingerly out onto the creaking veranda and stared around in dismay. The island resort had looked charmingly ramshackle in the purple of twilight when she'd first arrived last night, but daylight revealed a very different picture. The low, white bungalows dotted around, each in its own private grove, should have made a beautiful scene, but even the mellow sun of an early May morning couldn't paint La Isla Marina in flattering colours.

From her vantage point Anna could see all around right to the very tip of the island. The administrative buildings, including her mother's living quarters, were here at the palatial villa that marked the island's centre point, the swimming pools, tennis courts and relaxation areas all interspersed amongst the bungalows. If she stood on her tiptoes, Anna could just see the deep blue of the sea and the friendly waving of the palms that marked the beach boundaries. It was all so very nearly idyllic.

Very nearly... Until she looked a little closer and saw the reality behind the charm; the paint peeling off the whitewashed bungalows, the green shutters battered and hanging at odd angles. La Isla Marina was known for its lush greenery and profusion of flowers, but right now it resembled a jungle, not an upmarket resort. What had happened? True, everything had been a little faded when she was last here for her *abuelo's* funeral three years ago, but the hotel had still been recognisable as the idyllic magical place where she had run free every childhood summer.

The old familiar guilt prickled through her. She knew how disorganised her mother was, she should have foreseen this, not needed a tearful phone call begging her to come and help out.

The guilt intensified. It wasn't the unusual panic in her mother's voice that had persuaded her, it was Anna's own need for an escape, for time to think. If she hadn't been nearing crisis point would she have stayed in Oxford and allowed her mother to struggle on alone? She knew the answer to that. Every time they spoke her mother asked when she'd have time to come and visit, and Anna always found an excuse to put her off. Visiting La Isla Marina knowing neither grandparent would be there to greet her had been too hard to contemplate—and it wasn't as if she and Sancia were close. Nor, she knew, did Sancia have any intention of making an effort to come and visit Anna.

No, she'd responded to her mother's pleas for her own selfish reasons, thinking a few weeks of relaxing in the sun, away from the pressures of Oxford, were just what she needed. Her heart sank as she looked around at the wild and untamed bushes. Relaxing was the last thing she was going to be able to do.

'Good morning, *querida*, how did you sleep?'

Anna turned at the sound of her mother's voice. 'Great, thanks. I was tired after my journey.' She eyed her mother critically, noting the extra grey threading through Sancia Garcia's thick dark mane, the lines around her mother's eyes, lines which hadn't been there three years before. 'How are you?'

'Everything is wonderful.' Anna stiffened as her mother

flung her arms around her, pulling her in close. 'I'm glad you're here, *querida*. It's been too long.'

'Yes, well…' Stepping back, Anna attempted to extract both herself and her miraculously unspilt coffee. 'I've been busy, you know. With the book and teaching… What's happened, Mama?'

'Happened?'

Anna bit down on her irritation as her mother looked vaguely around the resort. This was how Sancia Garcia operated, floating through the world in a time and space of her own. She'd never seen why her daughters needed to be at school on time, or even why they needed to *attend* school if the sun was shining, why dinner should be planned and at a set time, the point of timetables. Anna hadn't yet turned ten when she realised that if they were to be like other families she needed to take charge, to be responsible for both herself and her sister, Rosa. Her chest tightened. Nothing had changed; she was a fool to hope it ever would.

Sancia had even managed to separate from her husband in such a slow, dreamy way it almost seemed unintentional. And she never panicked, which was why her call for help was so out of character. Why Anna had booked the next flight over, leaving her father, her responsibilities, her teaching behind in Oxford. Not that Sancia seemed even slightly stressed now. Anna's grip tightened even more, the heat from the cup almost scalding her; no doubt as soon as Anna had shown up Sancia had thankfully abdicated all responsibility to her once again. 'To the hotel, Mama. It doesn't look like there's been any upkeep at all for goodness knows how long. How did it get to this stage?'

Sancia shrugged. 'You know Pedro retired when your *abuelo* died, then Bonita retired also and they both ran this place like clockwork. It's been hard to get staff to replace them, people who care, who stay. And everything happens at once, *querida*, one light breaks then another, then a toilet then the swimming pool filters and I just can't keep on top of it all.'

'No wonder bookings are down.' The real wonder was that anyone had booked to stay here at all. 'Why didn't you ask for help before?'

'You're so busy, you have your own life, Anna, as does your sister. I didn't want to worry you. I knew something would turn up and it has. This wedding will fix everything.' Her mother clasped her hands. 'The money, the publicity! The glamour! We can restore La Isla Marina to the way it was when I was young, when your grandparents first built the resort.'

The wedding. The magical ingredient on which her mother was banking all her hopes. The wedding she had agreed to host in exactly one month's time despite the island not being anywhere near ready. It would be bad enough, Anna thought, if this were any normal wedding. Only her mother would blithely take on the exclusive wedding of a supermodel and her millionaire fiancé. These people looked down on five-star luxury, and right now the island would barely scrape two stars.

'We have a lot of work to do before then. No one is going to want to have their dream wedding here, especially not some Internet sensation who posts every detail of their life online.' Anna looked behind her, peering through the half-opened door that led into the office. A career spent researching in libraries, a life of compiling footnotes and organising sources meant Anna had some pretty kickass admin skills. Her mother most likely needed budgets, accounting, marketing and day-to-day working rotas as soon as possible and Anna was just the girl to sort that out for her.

Of course there was the little question of fifty-two bungalows needing a lick of paint, a damn good clean and some DIY. Hopefully there was no need for Anna to get her hands dirty; DIY was not her forte. Luckily her sister was handy with a toolkit. 'When is Rosa getting here?' Anna's stomach clenched apprehensively as she waited for her mother to reply. She hadn't seen her sister in several years either, only in her case there weren't any weekly phone calls, not even the odd tag on social media. If Sancia had mentioned earlier that she had also begged Rosa to come and help, would Anna have agreed to come too? The truth was she had no idea. Three years was a long time, but she hadn't forgotten a single one of the bitter words she and her sister had exchanged back then. She wasn't eager for a repeat performance.

'As soon as she can. She's on an important assignment, you know. She said she wouldn't be able to get here in the next two weeks but she'll do her best to get here as soon as possible after that.'

Anna compressed her lips. Of course, whatever Rosa chose to do was important as far as their mother was concerned. She was always far more impressed by Rosa's unconventional approach to life than by Anna's achievements and qualifications. At twenty-eight she should be too old to be hurt by her mother's lack of interest in all Anna had worked so hard for. But Anna hadn't been able to help noticing that her mother's apartment was filled with framed copies of Rosa's photos—and she hadn't seen one copy of *her* book anywhere.

'Two weeks?' Anna looked back over the half of the resort visible from the terrace and swallowed. There was no way they would be able to wait two weeks before starting the practical work. Which meant, unfamiliar as she was with a paintbrush, Anna had little choice. She was going to need to learn—and fast.

'First things first,' Anna muttered. With two cups more of her mother's excellent coffee buzzing through her veins, she was almost raring to go. First they needed a list. Lists. Lists of repairs, lists of things they needed to make the bungalows suitable for a supermodel's wedding guests, lists of everything that needed repairing. Which meant inspecting every bungalow, every path, every deckchair and table, the beach bars, the tennis courts... She needed another list of all the lists she needed to make.

She left Sancia in the kitchen checking all the crockery for chips, dents and suspicious stains, glad of the solitude after spending a whole morning alone with her mother for the first time in more years than Anna could remember. The hotel used to be so vibrant; filled with her grandparents, their long-time staff, visitors and guests. Now it was a ghost of its old self, just one cleaner, one groundsman and a cook in residence, a couple of maids journeying over from the mainland. No guests at all. Anna suppressed a shiver. It was too quiet. Maybe she would head over to the mainland today after all, even if she only went to the small village just a few hundred metres away across the narrow strip of sea to have lunch.

The island wasn't very big, less than a mile from one end to the next, and it didn't take Anna long to reach the sheltered beach overlooking the mainland. Palms fringed the delicate yellow sand and Anna paused, taking in a deep breath, tasting the salt of sea, the lemon wafting over from the citrus trees. The sea was so blue it almost hurt, a deep turquoise that tugged at her, enticing her closer and closer. She shucked off her shoes, stepping onto the soft sand, wiggling her toes into the warm grains. When had she last been barefooted outside? Holding out her arms, she closed her eyes, feeling the sun penetrating every atom, every cell, warming her straight to her bones. The dark hair and olive skin she had inherited from her mother never really felt warm enough in Oxford; they craved this contact with the Mediterranean sun, even an early May sun better than none.

She took another deep breath, her bones aching as they absorbed the longed-for heat, inhaling the scents that always conjured up the island. For the first time in a long while she felt as if she was home.

She jumped, pulled back to the job at hand as the sound of a vacuum cleaner buzzed through the air. She wasn't on holiday, she was here to help her mother—and more importantly she was here to forget her troubles. A month away from her classes, from her research, from expectations, might give her overtired mind the reboot it so desperately needed.

Anna pulled out her notebook. She might as well start off by checking the seaworthiness of the boats. The jetty was in the next cove along, situated by the natural rock harbour, which separated the gentle, sheltered mainland-facing beaches from the more rugged sea-facing ones. The wide wooden jetty housed all the small kayaks and rowing boats kept for guests who wanted to venture out in the safe strip of sea.

Pushing her refreshed feet back into her pumps, Anna followed the narrow path as it wound round the corner and past the trees until, pushing her way through a particularly overgrown fern, she emerged, blinking, onto the boardwalk, her hair falling over her eyes.

What is that? She skidded to a stop, staring at the jetty in disbelief. In addition to several kayaks pulled high onto the pebbly beach and the boats moored tightly to the wooden posts, a white and chrome boat sat proudly in the deeper water. It was large enough to be an ocean-going boat, but this was no practical craft. Every gleaming rail, every white sail, every fitting she could see screamed 'rich man's toy' at her.

An equally gleaming dinghy was tied onto the jetty, a clear sign that someone had come ashore.

The island was private property, but occasionally day-trippers or passing boats did stop—and if they had money to spend were usually welcome. Anna looked around. She hadn't seen anyone on the main path. *'Hola!'* she called. 'Hello. Can I help you?'

No answer.

She hesitated. The sign on the jetty clearly instructed visitors—in six different languages—to head straight along the main path to Reception. Not that there was any-one actually on Reception...

'Dammit, as if I don't have enough to do.' What was her mother thinking? How could she possibly think a staff of four enough to get the island into shape for the season, let alone prepare for the wedding of the year? Sancia's airy assurances that she had enough seasonal staff ready to start soon rang hollow. They should be here by now, painting, cleaning and making sure the island was in tip-top condition.

Swivelling, Anna looked around, sucking in her breath as she saw a tall, broad figure casually strolling around the nearest bungalow, peering in through the shutters as if he had every right to be there. She thrust her shoul-ders back, indignation filling her. The signs were quite clear—this was private property. Without stopping to think twice she marched over to the bungalow by the straightest possible route, pushing her way through the overgrown trees and shrubs, barely noticing the branches scratching her skin.

'Excuse me.' Her Spanish completely escaped her as she reached hailing distance of the bungalow. 'What on earth do you think you're doing?'

Indignation had carried her within touching distance before common sense reasserted itself and she stopped abruptly, catching her breath as she took in the intruder. This was no over-entitled, overweight businessman out for a gentle sail. This was a pirate. Over six feet of muscled pirate. There wasn't an inch of fat—no, not a centimetre of fat—on him; his bare torso, exposed by his open white shirt, could have served as the model for Michelangelo's David. His dark hair was cropped short, his even darker eyes raking her up and down with an arrogance that made her tremble with rage.

Rage and awareness of just how grubby she was, no make-up, a crumpled old T-shirt, hair bundled hastily up. She resisted the urge to straighten her top, to shake out her hair and did her best to ignore the zing that shot straight through her traitorous body as his gaze travelled over her.

'Doing? I'm wondering if this is a hotel or a film set for a disaster movie,' he replied in heavily accented English.

'We haven't finished preparing for the opening of the season yet,' she said as loftily as she could, the heat mounting in her cheeks at the contempt in the dark depths of his eyes.

'Finished? You haven't even started. I don't know what kind of scam you're running here, *señorita*, but my sister will not be part of it.'

'Your sister?'

'Rest assured she will find somewhere else for her wedding.' He turned, his business clearly done, setting off along the overgrown path leading back to the jetty.

Anna's brain tried to unscramble the words. The big wedding, the model, the event that had sent her mother into such a spin she had summoned both her daughters to her side, the event her mother was counting on to restore the hotel's fortunes. The mess the island was in might be down to her mother's mismanagement, but how could Anna let the idyllic playground of her childhood, her beloved grandparents' legacy, fade away? Whoever this man was she had to try and persuade him not to give up on the island. 'You're the bride's brother?'

He barely paused. *'Sí.'*

Casting a look around for help and coming up blank, Anna realised with a sinking heart that it was up to her to persuade him not to tell his sister to cancel the booking. Breaking into a light jog, she followed him up the path, breathlessly braking as she reached his side. 'Look, *señor*, I know the island is in a bit of a state, but, I promise you, it will be perfect for your sister's wedding.'

Halting, he turned a scathing look on her. 'How? You have an army of elves?'

'No. No army.' How did one get an army of elves? Maybe some could write her book for her while they were here. 'We're a little behind, I admit, but I always meet my deadlines, *señor*, and this is no different. Give us the opportunity and I promise your sister will have the wedding of her dreams.'

Her words echoed round her head. 'I always meet my deadlines', her stomach lurching with the same sickening jolt it always gave when she thought about her agent's increasingly urgent emails. But she held her head high and met his thoughtful gaze, that same unwanted zing zipping through her body as his attention focussed on her. 'Please,' she said again, not too proud to beg, holding her breath while she waited for him to reply. 'Just give me a chance to prove it to you.'

Leo stared at the tall woman as she stood imploringly opposite him, hands clasped before her. He'd been surprised when she'd spoken to him in English, her accent so clear cut she could only be a native of that damp island. With her thick mass of dark hair and clear olive skin she looked like some kind of mythological Mediterranean nymph, her eyes, fringed with long dark lashes, the colour of the sea, her lips the pink of a summer sunset.

'Are you the owner?' Not that it made any difference. He needed to get back to the boat, phone Valentina and warn her this venue was a no go.

It wasn't as if his half-sister had no other choices for her wedding. Her fiancé's mother had offered the couple her Victorian house on Martha's Vineyard, but his sister had nixed that suggestion in no uncertain terms. 'She wants to make the wedding all *preppy* and tasteful,' she'd complained, scorn in her voice. Valentina's brand was all about exuberance and she wanted to make sure her wedding reflected that—and what Valentina wanted she usually got. That determination had propelled her from part-time model and socialite to online queen and supermodel. Her willingness to share every instant of her life, complete with the perfect filter and hashtag, was partly what had elevated her above all the other pretty-girl wannabes, but it was hard work and a cool business brain that had turned her into a global brand.

Leo didn't understand how Valentina could bear to live her life through millions of screens, but he didn't have to. All he wanted was for her to be happy, to make up for her childhood, for the neglect from his side of her family.

Which was why, after he'd heard that a fire had destroyed her previous choice of wedding venue, he offered to head to La Isla Marina and check out why they could accommodate a lavish wedding at such short notice.

It had taken approximately five seconds to reach an answer. The island was completely unsuitable—and yet here he still was. Gaze still fixed on the sea nymph, feet still fixed to the ground, still wondering exactly what shade of pink her plump lips were.

'No, I'm not the owner, I'm her daughter. Look. I know it doesn't seem like it, but everything is under control.'

But her eyes couldn't quite meet his as she said the words. Leo folded his arms and regarded her sardonically, watching the faint blush of colour spread over her cheeks. 'You're an experienced wedding planner? Or maybe you're an events co-ordinator? A hotel manager? A plumber and builder? All of the above?'

She blinked. 'Well, no…'

'No? What do you do?'

'I'm a lecturer, I don't see…'

'A lecturer? In plumbing?'

Her colour heightened. 'In European history. I mostly look at history from a feminist perspective…' She caught his eye and stopped.

'That will be very useful, I'm sure. I don't think I need to see any more.' There was no point in staying, no matter how pretty the help. He turned, ready to leave when his phone buzzed. He pulled it out. Valentina. *'Hola.'*

'Is it amazing? I wish I could be there with you. I have to fly to Japan tomorrow, and then I'm off to Australia for a week and there's a shoot booked in here in New York after that so it's impossible for me to get there before the wedding, but, Leo darling, I am so grateful that you are

there making sure everything is perfect. Is it perfect? Just
as I remember?'

'Valentina.' He tried to interrupt her, but his sister bab-
bled on.

'This feels right, Leo. It is such a shame about the villa,
but I spent such happy summers on La Isla Marina, that
has to be a good omen, doesn't it? It will be like coming
home in some ways. Todd won't know what's hit him,' she
added. 'I know the Vineyard is beautiful, but I want this
wedding to reflect me, to be as un-New York as possible.'

Leo paused. Valentina was extremely well off now, and
she was marrying into serious old New York money, but
she had been brought up on the edge of poverty thanks to
his father's nasty habit of discarding his mistresses and
their offspring as soon as their demands got too incon-
venient. While Leo had been brought up in the solitary,
austere luxury of the *castillo*, she had spent her childhood years in a tiny apartment in the rougher side of the
city. Who could blame her for wanting to live the fairy
tale she'd been denied? She was the daughter of a *conde*
after all, even if the illustrious Lord refused to acknowledge her.

Leo looked around, assessing the island with fresh eyes.
It was battered, sure, but it didn't need a fortune to bring
it up to scratch; it needed some time and care. Leo could
easily make that happen. It could be his wedding gift to
the sister he had spent too many years not knowing. 'It
needs some work, but nothing that can't be easily fixed.
Don't panic.'

'How can I panic when you're there taking care of
things for me, *mi hermano*? Will you keep an eye on it
until I can get there? I don't need it to be perfect for the
sponsors or all the people who will be watching and judging. I just want it to be perfect for me. For Todd.'

'It will be,' Leo promised. He snapped his phone shut. His options were clear: find his sister another whimsical Spanish island wedding venue able and willing to accommodate over one hundred bright young things in a month's time or make sure this place was transformed into the venue of her dreams. Besides, what else did he have to do? He fixed the nymph with a hard stare. 'Pass me that notebook,' he said. 'We have a lot of work to do.'

CHAPTER TWO

THE NYMPH CLUTCHED her notebook tightly and glared. 'We?'

'We,' Leo confirmed. 'Right now this hotel is only fit for a Halloween-themed wedding. I'm sure your knowledge of European feminist history will be very useful when it comes to sorting out the dripping showers, but just in case it isn't I am intending to stay and oversee.'

'Really?' The bright blue eyes were hard. 'And *you* know how to fix a dripping tap, I suppose?'

'I can fix a tap, tile a wall, paint woodwork. Can you?' It was all true, not that many people knew that. It would ruin his carefully cultivated, trust-funded euro-playboy image if anyone knew just how handy he was with a spanner, just as no one knew that every penny that slipped so seemingly carelessly through his fingers he had earnt. His father had cut him off at eighteen expecting a repentant and obedient son to beg for the purse strings to be reinstated. He was still waiting.

It drove him mad, not having the financial control he yearned for over his son, drove him to distraction that he had no idea where or how Leo obtained the funds for his extravagant lifestyle. And the lifestyle he saw his only son, the future Conde de Olvares, choose to lead drove him craziest of all. Every photo of Leo at another party, in a new casino, with a new model on his arm guaranteed it, Leo made sure of that. In the Conde de Olvares's rulebook appearances were everything, vices were to be hidden away.

Leo had taken his father's rule and reversed it. Every vice on the surface for everyone to see, the virtues hidden far beneath. Truth was he barely attended any parties any more—and when he did usually stayed just long enough to be photographed. Valentina had taught him well. Perception was everything.

The nymph tilted her chin defiantly. 'I'm sure I can learn. I can follow instructions.'

'That's good to know,' Leo said softly and her cheeks burned a deeper red.

'Look. I can see why you're worried.' Her gaze slid over to the nearest bungalow. 'But I have assured you, repeatedly, that everything is under control.'

Leo followed her gaze. The bungalow was dirty, the white paint peeling off the external walls, the trees and flowers growing so close it was only a matter of time till nature recolonised the building. It needed nails in the roof, a lick of paint and a damn good clean. Hot, sweaty, hard manual work.

His eyes narrowed. Maybe the work would help fix the melancholy he couldn't quite shake. Leo wasn't sure he'd ever experienced real, unadulterated happiness, but for the past twelve years he had managed something resembling content; always on the move, always making money, always his own man. But ever since Valentina had announced her engagement, that contentment had become elusive, her glowing happiness a sharp contrast to his darkness.

Leo had always thought that they were cut from the same cloth, but now his baby sister was proving braver—

or more foolhardy—than him. Either way Leo was left in her wake. It was an uncomfortable place to be.

His original intention had been to make a few phone calls and get a team of labourers despatched to La Isla Marina then return in a month's time to enjoy the wedding, but maybe a few weeks getting his hands dirty on a beautiful island with a beautiful girl was exactly what he needed. Time out from his usual regime.

Turning, he held out his hand. 'Leo di Marquez y Correa,' he said and braced himself. There was no flare of recognition in her blue eyes, no rise of her straight, no nonsense brows. Nearly everyone Leo met had already formed an opinion of him. Most people either disapproved of him, wanted to party with him or wanted to sleep with him. A very few, those in the know, wanted his investment. He rarely, however, met with blank politeness bordering on disdain.

It would be an interesting challenge to turn that disdain to desire. His blood stirred at the very thought; he did have a few weeks with no plans after all...

'Anna Gray,' she said after a moment, making no move to take his hand. 'Dr Anna Gray.'

'A doctor as well as an expert on feminism in Europe's history?' He smiled to show he was joking, turning on the full force of his charm to see if he could tempt those pink lips to smile.

She didn't respond in kind, folding her arms defensively. 'I have a PhD from Oxford, not that it's any of your business. Look, Señor di Marquez...'

'Leo.'

'I appreciate that things look a little ramshackle right now, and I know your sister's wedding is going to get a lot of publicity...'

'Publicity which will benefit you.'

'But I assure you, we are quite capable of getting everything ready in plenty of time…'

'Then I'm very sure another pair of hands will come in very useful. I'll make it easy for you, Dr Gray. I'll sleep on my boat and work for food alone. I won't even tell my sister just how much needs to be done here. Tell me, are you really in a position to refuse?'

Anna hugged her notebook tighter, her mind working furiously. She should be snatching Leo's offer with both hands, but something held her back. She didn't know whether it was the sardonic look in his dark eyes, the smirk playing about his mouth or the teasing tone in his voice. It didn't help that he was one of the most insanely handsome men she had ever seen in the flesh. Oxford wasn't exactly short of over-confident men thinking they could win using their charm alone, but the city didn't run to Spanish pirates, nor was she used to conducting conversations with practically bare-chested men.

It also didn't help that her knees weakened every time he fixed that intense gaze on her, that she could feel her pulse speeding up faster and faster. Her friends had been telling her to get out and date more. This must be her body's way of agreeing if one hard-eyed, hard-chested man could have this effect on her.

Anna dragged her thoughts away from Leo's chest and back to the matter at hand, her eyes narrowing as she considered his far-too-good-to-be-true offer. 'Don't you have a job to go to? How will you manage to take a month off work with no notice?'

'I work for myself and I am a famously forgiving boss.'

Lucrative boss if that boat was anything to judge by. 'It's not up to me,' Anna said finally. 'My mother owns the island.'

'Then lead on. I'll present my credentials to your leader.'

Anna tried to hold his amused gaze, but to her frustration her own dropped first. She could stand up in front of a full lecture theatre without breaking a sweat, turn overly confident undergraduates into shaking shadows of their former selves with one disbelieving arch of an eyebrow, but in front of this man her defences crumbled. 'Fine,' she said tightly. 'Follow me.'

As she led him along the overgrown paths, Anna was aware of Leo's keen gaze taking in every crack, every break in the path and the surrounding buildings and worry shivered through her once again. Had the resort been on the road to such dilapidation when her grandparents were still alive? They had been pretty old, after all, their staff of a similar age. It would have been too easy for things to start to slide unnoticed by them. Her mother, though, had little excuse. She'd been living here for nearly a decade, ever since she had drifted away from the family home for a holiday, a holiday that bled into an extended stay, which in turn became a separation. The same old frustration bubbled up and Anna curled her hands into loose fists. No doubt her mother had just employed her usual mantra of *mañana*, never worrying that one day she would have to deal with the rapidly escalating problems.

Well, she wasn't dealing, was she? Anna was here dealing for her. As usual.

Only, who was she to cast aspersions? Wasn't she doing exactly the same thing with her book? Hoping that somehow something miraculous would happen and it would all fall into place. Running away from her problems...

'So tell me, what does being a Professor of European history with a feminist slant entail these days?' Anna started, guiltily. It was as if Leo had read her mind. 'You seem very young to be a professor.'

'You're not the first to say that.' Although most people also snidely insinuated her renowned historian father had helped her climb the academic ladder faster than usual, that her name was responsible for her success, not her credentials. Or they looked down at the success of her first book, convinced a popular history book couldn't be as well-researched, as important, as an academic paper read only by other specialists in her field. It had been easier to hold her head high when she hadn't doubted herself, when she had been sure that the academic life was all she needed.

'I'm sure I'm not. Is it all libraries and lectures?'

'Mostly,' she admitted. 'There's a huge pressure to publish papers as well as teach.'

'And do you?'

'Papers, books. A book,' she amended, trying not to think about the mess that was book number two.

'An author? How impressive. Would I have read your book?'

'Only if you're interested in a rehabilitation of Joanna the Mad from a feminist standpoint, looking at how difficult it was for intelligent women to thrive in a male-dominated world.'

'I definitely missed that one. Joanna the Mad? Is she the one who carted her dead husband's body all over Spain?'

'That's one of the myths my book works to dispel.'

'Pity, I've always felt that if I got married I'd want my wife to love me enough to keep my corpse by her side at all times.' Anna shot him a quick glance. Joanna's husband had been famously known as Philip the Handsome, but surely even he would have paled into plainness next to the rugged good looks of Leo di Marquez. She caught his eye and felt her cheeks heat up yet again. What on earth was wrong with her? She'd never been a blusher before.

If she carried on at this rate they could save money on an electrician and use her face as a lamp.

To Anna's relief they finally reached the villa. Leo looked at the ornate, white building, more like a Moorish palace than a hotel reception and office, and whistled. 'Nice.'

Despite herself Anna felt the old ripples of pride. As a child she had always felt so special, so chosen, to be part of the island's heritage, to spend her summers in her little turret room surveying the island like some kind of medieval queen. 'It's not as old as it looks. It's a turn-of-the-last-century reproduction built by my great-grandfather as a wedding gift for his bride,' she explained. 'This was their own private island, but when my grandfather inherited, he couldn't afford to keep it as a second home. He and my grandmother turned the island into a resort. At one time, back in the fifties, this was one of the most exclusive resorts in the Mediterranean.' Anna looked up at the veranda's cobweb-infested ceiling and tried not to sigh. It was hard to imagine the island in its glamorous heyday right now.

'And now?'

'It's been a while since I visited,' Anna admitted. 'Things are a little less glamorous than they used to be.'

The problem was the island was expensive to run. Her grandfather had often bemoaned the price of labour and food, all of which needed shipping out; the mainland might be just a few hundred metres away, but the island was still only accessible by boat. Maybe they needed to think differently, turn the island into an event destination rather than a hotel, for weddings and other special occasions?

They? She pursed her lips. There was no way her mother would be capable of running that kind of business, and it was unlikely Rosa would want to stay in one place and help. Maybe, much as the idea broke Anna's heart, her mother should sell the island to someone who could look after it.

She'd broach the subject after the wedding. There was no point getting embroiled in a family drama before.

She led Leo through the grand hallway, now a hotel reception area, a board behind the huge desk holding the big iron keys that still unlocked the bungalow doors— no flimsy key cards here—and along the wooden panelled hallway until they reached the vast kitchen where her mother was still sorting crockery.

'*Mama?*'

Piles of brightly painted terracotta plates, bowls and cups covered every surface and most of the floor. In the middle of the chaos Sancia stood swaying, her hair falling out of its customary loose bun, her eyes closed as she sang along to the ear-piercingly loud music blaring from the radio. Anna winced, unable to even glance in Leo's direction.

The scene was all too reminiscent, a flashback to her teenage years. She'd soon stopped bringing friends home, no idea what would greet them once they walked through the front door into the untidy hallway. Sancia was usually at home, but she would be preoccupied with her current fad; dancing, painting, sculpting, cooking. Whatever it was tended to take over the whole house, a chaotic tangle of colour and mess. It was all about the creative journey, Sancia would say, whenever Anna or her father suggested she keep her artistic endeavours confined to one room. Which was a good thing as usually the end result was good for nothing at all. Anna preferred to spend her after-school time at her friends' houses instead, in ordered, peaceful homes where everything had its place and routines ruled.

'Mama!' she said again, this time loudly and sharply,

and Sancia's eyes flew open, fastening onto her daughter reproachfully.

'*Querida*, there is no need to shout.' She switched her gaze over to Leo and her dark eyes widened, her still-full mouth curving into a smile. '*Hola.*'

Anna's heart sank; she recognised that particular flirtatious smile. It was her mother's default smile for any reasonably attractive man and Anna had seen it used, always to great effect, on friends of her father's, and on her own friends' fathers. No girl should have to grow up seeing grown men reduced to red-faced boys by her own mother. Anna knew it wasn't conscious, that warm smile of appreciation, it wasn't meant with malice or intent or even deliberate flirtatiousness, but it was all the more devastating for that.

Leo didn't seem to be immune, his own smile wide as he bent over Sancia's outstretched hand. '*Hola,*' he answered, his voice so low it was a cross between a purr and a growl, a deep rumble Anna suspected was used as often as her mother's smile and with a similar effect—only she was pretty sure Leo di Marquez knew exactly what he was doing.

Sancia preened. 'Who is your charming *amigo*, Anna?'

Anna made a concerted effort not to grind her teeth. 'Mama, this is Señor di Marquez, he is Valentina's brother and he's come to check the island is suitable for his sister's wedding.'

Sancia turned her smile up another watt. 'What a lucky girl to have such an involved brother.' She gazed up at Leo as if he were edible and Anna tried not to follow her mother's gaze, especially as she seemed fixated on Leo's half-bared chest.

'Your resort is beautiful, *señora*,' Leo said, a smile still playing around his beautifully sculpted mouth.

'*Gracias*, and please, call me Sancia. *Señora* always makes me feel so old. I trust you're happy with everything? We are so looking forward to welcoming Valentina and her fiancé in a month's time.'

Anna stared at her mother in disbelief. Did she really think anyone would be *happy* with the state of the island? After all, it wasn't as if she didn't know what a huge task she had in front of her—she had called both her daughters to beg them to drop everything to come and help. Maybe now Anna was here Sancia considered her own job done. She had always relied on Anna to look after the dreary practicalities in the past. 'That's my sensible, organised girl,' she would say, as if sensible and organised were things to be tolerated, to be pitied, not to emulate.

By the way Leo's mouth quirked he was evidently amused by Sancia's blind optimism. 'Obviously you are not quite ready for the season,' he said. Why was he being so diplomatic with Sancia when he hadn't minced one of his words with Anna? 'As you know Valentina needs everything to be perfect and so I have promised to help you prepare the island for her wedding. I trust this is acceptable?'

If Sancia's eyes grew any wider they would fall right out of her head. As it was she was currently resembling a cartoon character more than a real human being. 'That is so kind of you.'

Anna couldn't stop her toe tapping impatiently on the tiled floor. Was her mother going to look at this practically in any way? Check that Leo was who he said he was, that Valentina wanted his input and, most importantly, that his presence here for a month wouldn't result in any reduction of the lavish payment Valentina had offered in return for a week's exclusivity? She took her mother's arm and steered her through the piles of bowls and plates to the open back door, lowering her voice and doing her best to ignore Leo's sardonic glance. 'Mama, don't you think you should check with your client first, and make sure this doesn't mean there will be any renegotiation on the price? That Leo is who he says he is.' But she knew she was wasting her breath.

'*Querida*, the fates have brought you a handsome young man and you want to check his references? Live a little, Anna. You're getting hunched, all that time over a keyboard, and you look positively sallow. A few weeks in the sunshine with some agreeable company is exactly what you need.'

'I'm not here for my health, Mama. I'm here to help you...'

'And thanks to Señor di Marquez your job will be a lot easier. After all, Anna, you're not the most practical of people, are you?' And while the gobsmacked Anna was still trying to formulate an articulate response her mother stepped away, turning back to Leo. 'We have plenty of space here in the villa, Señor di Marquez. I would be very happy to accommodate you.'

'Señor di Marquez has his own accommodation,' Anna interjected quickly.

Her mother's smile barely wavered. 'But we will feed you, I insist, it's the least I can do. Lunch will be served in just a couple of hours so shall we meet back here at two? I'm really looking forward to getting to know you better.'

Uh-oh. Anna knew exactly what that meant. At least four courses, wine and two hours of the day wasted. Then, no doubt, her mother would suggest a siesta and before Anna had had a chance to make even one list the day would be over. 'There's no need for a formal lunch. There's far too much to do. We can easily just grab a roll and some cheese and work through. It's only early May. It's not as if the sun will be too unbearable,' she finished a little doubtfully as she glanced out of the window at the perfectly blue, cloudless sky.

'Oh, Anna…' Her mother couldn't have sounded more reproachful if Anna had suggested drowning kittens, but her sorrowful protestation was drowned out by Leo, who leaned against the huge scrubbed table, arms folded and a sardonic gleam in his eyes.

'Skip lunch? Absolutely not. I'm looking forward to it, *señora*—I mean, Sancia. What's life without time out for good food and good conversation?'

Narrowing her eyes, Anna stared over at the insouciant Spaniard. 'I thought you wanted everything to be perfect for your sister's wedding?'

'I do, it will be, but there's no reason we can't have a little fun while we're working, now, is there?'

CHAPTER THREE

LEO TOOK A small sip of his coffee and grinned over at Anna. She had become increasingly, obviously impatient as lunch had meandered from course to course: fish soup followed by an excellent soufflé, chicken with garlic-roasted potatoes, and a cheese course, all washed down with a rather good rioja. Sancia García might not know how to run a hotel, but she did know how to employ a good cook and right now, sitting on a sheltered patio with a view of white beaches and an azure-blue sea, Leo felt a stir of that elusive contentment for the first time in months.

Sure, there was an entire island to be renovated and made fit for Valentina's arrival in just under a month, but the sense of urgency was lessened by the rich dark coffee, the richer wine and the last sliver of cheese temptingly within reach. Lessened by the knowledge he could make a phone call and an army of labourers would be despatched forth to take care of every detail. But mostly lessened by Dr Anna Gray's palatable disapproval. She had only eaten soup and a little cheese, had refused wine and was very obviously making copious lists proving just how busy she really was.

It was quite adorable. Not that Leo looked for adorable in women. He didn't really look for anything beyond the very, very superficial. What was the point when he had no intention of getting into anything deeper than casual? He chose carefully, ensuring the women he dated were as uninterested in his inner life as he was in theirs. He needed to be sure that they wouldn't be looking too closely at him. Too closely into him. That all they were interested in was his blue blood and deep pockets.

Of course here, out of the public eye, the usual rules didn't apply. It would be an interesting challenge to see just what it took to make Dr Anna Gray put down her pen and notepad, wipe those frown lines off her forehead and smile. Interesting, but all too risky. He'd known Anna for less than three hours and he already knew that she was the type who would always dig deeper—and that made her dangerous. Besides, he was pretty sure she didn't understand the 'good time' rule and *that* made her absolutely off-limits.

'Hit me.' He pushed his coffee cup to one side, propping his elbows on the table as he turned towards Anna. 'What's first?'

Anna brushed a lock of dark hair away from her forehead and Leo froze, awareness of her every movement shivering through him. For one endless second she was imprinted on him, her long graceful neck, her sweep of long, wavy hair, the shrewd expression in her clear blue eyes, and the vulnerability he saw behind them, a vulnerability he sensed was usually kept well hidden.

'First?'

Leo nodded at the notebook Anna carried like a talisman. 'On your list.'

'Oh.' Her hand lay over the page protectively. 'I've put together a list of supplies we need before we can really get started so I think I need to take a trip over to the mainland today. There really isn't any time to waste.' She glared meaningfully at his plate. 'Mama, I'll need to take your dinghy. Is that okay? Is the car still kept in the same place?'

'No need to borrow your mother's boat. I'll sail you over.' Leo sat back in his chair and watched Anna try and come up with an excuse to avoid his company.

Anna blinked. 'There's no point taking your boat such a short distance.'

'No, but my dinghy is at your dock.'

Sancia glanced from Leo to Anna, her expression amused. 'The car is parked in the harbour lot as always, *querida*. There's a big store on the outskirts of town, about five kilometres from the harbour. You can't miss it.'

'Right.' Anna pushed her chair back and stood up. 'Let's go.'

Leo didn't move.

She tapped her foot, her eyes gleaming dangerously. 'In your own time, *señor.*'

Sancia sighed, shaking her head at her daughter. '*Querida*, you are in Spain now. The store will be closed for siesta. There's no point in going now.'

'A siesta sounds like an excellent suggestion.' Leo winked at Anna. 'I'll see you at the jetty in two hours, Dr Gray. Bring your lists.' And he stood up. 'Thank you, Sancia, that was delicious.' He bowed over Sancia's hand and tossed another wink in Anna's direction before sauntering away, fully aware that Anna was glaring at him. His back prickled with awareness; he could almost feel the burn as her eyes bored into him.

Funny to think he had had no agenda this morning beyond popping over to what he had assumed to be a perfectly run luxury resort in order to reassure his sister. Now he had a month's work ahead of him and a hostile colleague. He couldn't wait to get started.

* * *

Anna stared down at the bucket of tepid, dirty water resentfully. She'd decided not to waste the two hours her mother and Leo were choosing to spend sleeping and instead had got started scrubbing down the outside of a couple of bungalows. Not that she had got very far. Right now getting the island into any kind of order seemed like a Sisyphean task—especially if long lunches and longer siestas were going to be the order of the day.

Still, at least she had made a start. She would get the groundskeeper and chambermaid to continue while she was on the mainland; but she really needed to talk to her mother and find out when the seasonal staff were due to start, and how many they were expecting. Without adequate staffing they would never get the island ready in time. Luckily the interiors of the bungalows were in a better state than she'd expected. They needed some cosmetic work, a good clean, taps and showers fixing, a quick paint, but the furniture was still good, simple, but well-crafted. A few luxurious touches, new cushions, rugs and accessories should bring them up to date. After all, if Valentina wanted marble and gilt she would have booked a hotel. She was after an authentic Spanish touch and that, at least, La Isla Marina could provide.

Picking up the bucket, Anna tipped the water down the drain. She'd worked her way through several buckets of water, lugging them to the desired spot, sloshing water down her legs as she did so. Her hands were red, two nails already broken. She made a mental note to add gloves to her list.

Had it really only been half an hour of work? It felt like eternity and she had barely started. This morning she'd been full of a sense of purpose, if a little daunted. Now she just felt like Cinderella, toiling away while the rest of the household slumbered, and just because she had volunteered for domestic drudgery didn't mean she couldn't help feeling resentful. She wouldn't mind so much if Rosa weren't swanking about somewhere, carefree, on the other side of the world, if her mother didn't look at her as if she were being fussy, if Leo di Marquez hadn't shown up…

Anna pushed her hair off her forehead, grimacing as she realised just how sweaty she was. What was Leo's deal anyway? What kind of man just decided to put a month aside for his sister's wedding with no planning, no notice? Placing the bucket on the floor, Anna tried to stop her mind dwelling on the planes of Leo's chest, the strong, sensual mouth, his mocking eyes. He knew how attractive he was all right—and there was nothing Anna distrusted more than a man convinced of his own worth, his own desirability. After all, she'd been taken in before, been badly burnt before.

She'd mishandled him from the first, allowing him to put her on the back foot even though he was the trespasser. It wouldn't—couldn't—happen again. She needed weapons, she needed armour, she needed control, she needed facts.

Her mother and sister might rely on intuition and spontaneity, but there was much more comfort in knowledge and plans. That was why she had become an academic, not because of her father's pre-eminence or because it was expected of her, but because she liked to dig deep, to find out the facts, to draw her own interpretation. If Leo's sister was some kind of media star then it shouldn't be too hard to find out exactly who he was, what he was. And then she would be prepared.

Mind made up, Anna headed back to the villa, letting herself through the hidden door that separated the public spaces from the family's private rooms. The wooden staircase was narrow and dark as she climbed all the way to the top floor and the turret bedroom that had been hers since she was a baby. Nothing had changed: the same iron bedstead stood in the corner, the same pictures hung on the whitewashed walls, the same colourful blankets were heaped on the bed. It was sparse and small, but Anna liked the memories of when they had been a proper family, Rosa in the other turret, her parents nearby, her grandparents still alive.

A pang of guilt hit her at the thought of her father home alone, rattling around their huge Oxford house. She'd left him a schedule, all his pills laid out ready, labelled meals in the freezer for the evenings he didn't dine in college. And she'd promised to text him reminders every day—he probably wouldn't even notice she was gone. She bit her lip, his lined, grey face clear in her mind. The only time he had ever relaxed was here on the island, when he would push his research and work aside for a few days, sometimes even weeks. When had he last taken a real holiday? Not since Sancia had left him. Left them.

Her laptop was already set up on the desk, her notebooks stacked neatly by its side, colour-coded by theme. Anna averted her eyes from the notebooks, an all too visual reminder that she still had no book, not even the bare bones of one. The usual wave of nausea swirled low in her stomach, the age-old fear that she would be revealed as an imposter, a fraud, whispering in her mind. Had she really thought that if she ran away to the island her doubts would stay meekly in Oxford? They were just as strong as ever—except when she had been engrossed in painting. Except when she had been sparring with Leo di Marquez… Pushing her notebooks to one side, she switched on her laptop, typed in Valentina's name and began to read.

Half an hour later Anna sat back and stared at the

screen; she still had no idea what Valentina did or why she was famous. Sure, the curvy brunette modelled, but she'd started modelling *after* she had got famous; for all her prominence she was a little shorter, a little bustier than the usual top models. Valentina seemed to spend her time photographing herself, her friends, her clothes and her food and posting the pictures up for comment. And she received them in their thousands, more, hundreds of thousands. Anna frowned as she looked at the photo posted just this morning, a photo of breakfast laid out on a patio table, every colour popping off the screen. How on earth was this a job? Judging by the lavish apartment, the designer clothes, the parties, it was lucrative even if it made no sense.

Most of the recent posts and tweets focussed on the forthcoming wedding. Anna's stomach clenched as she read through them; Valentina's expectations were high and the results would be instantly seen around the world. If they could make it a success then the island's fortunes would turn around overnight, but if they failed then they would fall very publicly. She had no choice; if there was to be any chance of pulling this off she simply had to work with Leo.

Except not once had she seen his name mentioned. Valentina made reference to growing up on the Barcelona coast, to working in a beach bar, to her mother, who had died a few years back—but there was no mention of a brother or a father. Not one.

Okay, then more research was needed. Anna poised her fingers over the keyboard for a second and then typed in *Leo di Marquez y Correa.*

'Bingo,' she said softly. The picture on the very first link looked very familiar indeed. The same close-cropped dark hair, the same sharp cheekbones set off by stubble too perfect to be completely natural. This Leo was dressed a lot more formally, in a light grey suit, a smiling blonde in a skin-tight dress hanging off his arm. Anna read the caption. 'Leo's new model'. Hmmm, it looked as if he was as at home in the gossip pages as his sister.

'He's not a pirate, he's a playboy,' she muttered as she brought up article after article. Leo on his boat, bare-chested in the sun, Leo in a casino, on a superyacht surrounded by the most glamorous people Anna had ever seen, Leo spraying champagne. Her stomach tightened. 'Spoilt, rich boys.' She could taste the contempt, bitter on her tongue.

The facts were there in clear black and white. Not just spoilt, not just rich, but Spanish aristocracy. The only son—only child—of the Conde de Olvares, a haughty grey-haired man, and his even haughtier-looking wife, Leo had been a fixture on the party scene since he was eighteen years old. No job, no occupation beyond sailing, gambling, drinking and women.

Anna stood up and stalked over to the window. From her vantage point high in the tower she could see the jetty and the gleaming boat moored out in the sea. A boat he hadn't worked to buy, a toy for a pampered princeling. Disappointment twisted her chest and she had no idea why. She didn't know Leo, and it wasn't as if she had liked what she had seen after all. Well, not beyond the physical at least. It was just she hadn't expected anything quite this shallow.

Anna knew the type all too well. They weren't as prevalent at Oxford as they had once been, but there were still plenty of entitled lordlings, their places secured by their name, their lineage, their education, their futures assured no matter what. They didn't care what anyone thought about them, didn't care what the consequences of their actions might be. At eighteen she might have been stupid enough to mistake that arrogant confidence for magnetism, found the frivolity and extravagance glamorous, but not any more. Now she valued work, reliability, sense. Old-fashioned values maybe, but her values.

And not only was Leo di Marquez a playboy, he was a liar. Valentina wasn't his sister, he was an only child. So what on earth was he doing here?

Of course he was late. Anna had known he would be and yet she had still arrived at the jetty at the agreed time, her shorts swapped for light cotton trousers, her T-shirt for a loose shirt, her notebook tucked away in a waterproof bag.

She'd deliberated sailing across alone and not waiting for Leo, but she wanted answers. Nothing added up. Why did a party playboy want to spend a month doing DIY on a tiny island with barely any inhabitants, no nightlife, no fun? And why had he claimed Valentina was his sister when she clearly wasn't?

She squinted over to the boat, lounging out in the flat sea like the embodiment of entitlement, blowing out a frustrated breath when she saw a tall figure swing over the side and climb down to the dinghy bobbing alongside. *Finally.*

It didn't take her long to walk to the end of the jetty, arriving there just as Leo executed a perfect, stylish turn to bring the small open boat alongside. 'Hop in,' he called. 'Unless you need me to help you?' He held out a hand, which Anna ignored as she stepped gingerly into the boat, seating herself at the furthest end away from Leo. He barely waited until she was seated before releasing the throttle and, with a roar, the boat sped off towards the mainland.

Despite her trepidation Anna found herself relaxing on the short trip, leaning against the back rail enjoying the sun on her face, the splash of the water on her outstretched hand as the boat cut through the sea. In Oxford, she saw students punting or kayaking all the time and yet never made time to get out onto the water herself, which was odd when she remembered just what a water baby she had always been on the island; surfing, windsurfing, boating, swimming until her skin wrinkled, her hair thick with salt.

Steering the boat towards the public harbour, Leo found a mooring spot right next to the main jetty. Small boats bobbed all around, larger cruisers and yachts moored further out in the deeper water. Anna could see the perfect curve of the beach to one side, deserted despite the sun, and the cheerful fronts of the bars and restaurants that lined the shore road behind it. Cala del Mar had seemed like the height of sophistication when Anna was in her teens. Now she saw it as the sleepy, provincial seaside village it was, all the fonder of it for its simplicity.

Leo killed the engine then turned and eyed Anna quizzically as she stayed seated, making no attempt to climb out of the boat. 'Are you stuck?'

'Why are you here?'

'That's a very philosophical question. Why are any of us here?' But the laughter drained out of his dark eyes despite the easy smile on his face.

'You know what I mean. Why have you decided to stay on the island? Why announce your intention of helping? What does the son of the Conde de Olvares want with a tiny island resort? There's no casino, no nightclub, no supermodels to entertain you.'

'Someone's been doing her homework.' The smile still played around his mouth, but there was an edge to his voice.

Anna raised her chin. 'It's all a matter of public record, as is the fact you're an only child. So why did you tell me Valentina was your sister?'

The smile disappeared, his eyes hardening to flints. 'Because she is. And she wants the perfect wedding and I am going to make sure that happens. Any other questions, Sherlock Holmes, or shall we get on with the matter at hand?' And without looking at Anna he climbed out of the boat and started along the jetty, head high, back ramrod straight. Anna stared at the set shoulders, the jerky stride. Somehow she had touched a nerve without getting any of the answers she sought and although Leo was the one lying, or at least omitting information, Anna felt as if she was the one in the wrong.

She blew out a frustrated breath before getting carefully to her feet and stepping out of the boat onto the dusty jetty. This wasn't over and she would get her answers. Leo di Marquez was playing some kind of game and Anna wasn't going to stop until she had worked out just what he was up to.

CHAPTER FOUR

LEO STEPPED BACK and surveyed the wooden wall, an unexpected pride swelling his chest. If he said so himself it looked rather professional. Sanding, filling and painting were proving to be unexpectedly soothing, each finished wall or window frame a tangible achievement in a way a successful deal or investment no longer seemed to be. Maybe that was because money was such an abstract thing. He didn't exactly sit counting gold coins, had more than enough, even for his fairly lavish needs.

Leo put the paintbrush back on the tray and stretched before reaching for his task list, a wry grin curving his mouth as he scanned the typed list, complete with timings and required equipment. Anna had, with the help of her trusty notebook, worked out a plan. A plan, Leo had not failed to notice, which kept him at one side of the island and her at the other. Nor could he help noticing that she no longer broke for lunch, and although she joined Sancia, himself and the staff for dinner she was usually distracted, spending the meal making even more lists or researching fixtures and fittings rather than joining in the conversation. He had a strong suspicion she was avoiding him.

Como sea. Let her keep her distance. Sure, he had enjoyed the brief one-sided flirtation, had thought it might be amusing to—metaphorically at least—unbutton the

terminally uptight doctor, but there were limits to even
his amusement and those limits had been reached when
Anna had rounded on him with a scornful expression he
knew only too well. It was the same expression he saw
on his parents' faces. The expression he sometimes saw
in the mirror.

Still, over the last few days he had almost reached a
state of contentment. It was repetitive work, this wash-
ing, sanding, filling and painting, but it had an end goal.
Each task added up to a whole, a newly restored bungalow.
Well, an almost restored bungalow because along with the
repainting of the outside Leo was making a list of all the
more specialised tasks that needed doing: the dripping
taps, the under-performing showers, the broken tiles, the
holes in roofs.

Right now it was just he and Anna with their buckets
and ladders and paintbrushes. At the start of next week
they would be joined by the seasonal staff including three
more groundsmen and, for a week, a plumber, a joiner and
a builder. That would leave two weeks for any internal repainting, replacement of furniture and adding in all the
extras Valentina and her friends would expect to find in a
luxury hotel. Anna seemed to spend any time she wasn't
painting flicking through lifestyle blogs and upmarket
magazines, every session resulting in even more copious
notes and yet another list.

The full-time groundsman and maid were equally hard
at work on the public and communal areas. With three separate beach bars as well as the main bar and restaurant,
two lounges and the beautiful central pagoda, where the
marriage ceremony was to be carried out, they had their
work cut out and Maria, the maid, was volubly looking
forward to the arrival of her seasonal counterparts to help
share the load. The island might shut over the winter, but it

still seemed like a particularly sparse skeleton staff when the off season was surely the time to refresh and repair?

How on earth had this place survived over the last few years? Sancia swung from relaxed to mildly concerned—on the surface anyway—but Leo occasionally saw a flash of worry in the dark eyes when yet another dozen items were added to Anna's seemingly inexhaustible lists.

'Here, Sancia sent this for you.'

A soft voice pulled him away from his thoughts and Leo turned, list still in hand, to see Anna standing under the shade of the overgrown copse of trees. His breath caught. Her mass of dark hair was pulled up into a ponytail, she wasn't wearing a scrap of make-up and her cut-off denims and simple navy T-shirt were strictly utilitarian yet a quiver of attraction still ran through him.

His gaze dropped to the tray she clasped tightly in her hands. It held a plate heaped with a roll, sliced meat and fresh tomatoes and a bottle of beer.

Anna held it out towards him. 'You missed lunch.'

Leo glanced at his watch. Sure enough it was nearly three. 'I got a little carried away.'

'Obviously.' She took a step nearer, eyes crinkled as she looked critically at the walls. 'It's looking good though.'

'Does that surprise you?'

'Yes,' she said and, jolted by surprise, Leo looked at her.

'Okaaaay…' he said slowly.

'I thought you'd get bored after a couple of days, or you would spend most of your days lounging around on your boat, spend an hour with a paintbrush in your hand and expect us to fall at your feet in gratitude. But, you have more than pulled your weight.' She took a visibly deep breath. 'I was wrong.'

'*Si.*' But he couldn't bring himself to labour the point. She had good reasons for her misconceptions, reasons Leo himself had planted. He couldn't blame her, just because for some reason he wanted her to look deeper. Wanted her to look beyond the playboy image and see what lay underneath—if anything lay beneath. He doubted it, but if there was anything there then surely Dr Anna Gray was the kind of woman to excavate it.

'So.' She hefted the tray up awkwardly. 'Are you hungry?'

He was ravenous, he realised. Nothing like sheer physical labour to get a man's appetite going. *'Sí,'* he said again, taking the tray from her and heading over to the wrought-iron patio table each bungalow was furnished with, perfect for al-fresco dining. This particular table was positioned to take advantage of the sea views and to get shelter from the midday sun and as Leo lowered himself onto the cool seat he realised how very hot and thirsty he was.

Anna shifted from foot to foot. 'Okay, then, enjoy. I'll just...'

'Join me,' he said, without realising he was going to extend the invitation. 'Unless you have a pressing appointment with a paintbrush, that is?'

She pulled a face. 'I am *dreaming* about paintbrushes.'

'Then a break is probably just what the doctor ordered.'

She hesitated for a long moment before, with a nod, more an acknowledgement to herself than to him, she walked over to the table. 'Probably.'

As she sat herself in the other chair Leo realised this was the first time they had been alone together in nearly a week, the first time since they had gone shopping for supplies and she had called him a liar.

'I shouldn't stay too long.' She leaned forward, her head drooping into her hands, shoulders sagging in weariness. 'I want to get the bungalow I'm on finished, and then I need to go through all Valentina's plans and make sure we have ordered everything we need.'

'Anna, have you ever heard the word delegate? Do you really think you can single-handedly renovate the entire island *and* be a wedding planner?'

She looked up at that. 'Who else is there, Leo? If everything isn't perfect then the island will be ruined, completely finished. God knows, it's on its last legs as it is. But if we—if I—can pull this off then we can save the island, save my grandparents' dream.' She looked down at her hands. 'It's an incredible opportunity, but it's so daunting. This is the most public wedding of the year, people are betting on which designer is making her dress and whether Valentina will wear a veil—it's insane.

'Add in one hundred and fifty guests, all arriving at once, the wedding that very evening followed by a huge party and then a week of celebrations. It's a lot to deal with.' She heaved a gusty sigh. 'I know we still have three weeks, and thank goodness most of the seasonal staff are able to arrive a week earlier than Mama had originally asked them to, but there is still so much to do, just to make the island look presentable, let alone the actual wedding itself. Thank goodness Valentina paid a huge deposit. We need every penny.'

'What was your mother thinking? To say yes to a wedding she clearly wasn't ready for?'

Her face closed. 'She *didn't* think. She never does. She acts spontaneously and then expects someone else to sort out all the details. Me. She expects me to sort out the details while she pats my shoulder and tells me to relax and why can't I be more like my sister?'

'You have sisters?' How had he not known this?

'One sister.' Her voice was tight. 'Rosa. She's a photographer. Travels around being all bohemian and socially conscious and doing exactly what she wants whenever she wants.'

Leo blinked, taken aback by the anger in Anna's voice—the anger and the hurt. 'You don't get on, then?' He'd always dreamed of a sibling growing up, of someone to share the burden of being a di Marquez. He adored Valentina, but they hadn't been raised together, their relationship unknown to anyone outside their immediate family—and Anna. Leo didn't know why he had blurted out the information to her. Not that it mattered; she hadn't believed him anyway.

'We're very different. Right now Rosa is on a beach somewhere in South America being artistic and free while I have taken leave from my job—my respected and important job—to help out. But when Rosa does finally waltz up, my mother will treat her like the prodigal daughter. A calf is probably being fatted right now.' The anger had faded. Now Anna just sounded sad. 'I haven't spoken to her in three years. Not since my grandfather's funeral. Much as I could do with her help, I have to admit I'm dreading her actually being here.'

Leo took a swig of the beer then pushed the bottle over to her. 'What happened?'

Taking the bottle with a faint smile, Anna set it before her, her fingers pulling at the label. 'We've always seen the world differently, never been close. Things just came to a head when I was invited to spend a semester at Harvard as a visiting teacher. Rosa was in England for a few weeks following the funeral and I asked her to stay on in Oxford while I was away It was only for a few months. Dad had—has—some heart problems. They were talking about the possibility of surgery. But she said she had her own commitments. That he was an adult. That he had to slow down and take responsibility for himself.'

'What did you do?'

'What could I do? I couldn't leave him. I said stuff, she said stuff, she left, we don't speak. That's it. Nothing exciting.'

'He's better now? You're here after all.'

'I text him every night to remind him to take his pills.' She shook her head. 'Maybe Rosa is right. Maybe I do have some kind of martyr complex. Look at me. Twenty-eight and I'm spending my leave working—unpaid and unthanked—for my mother. I spend my few leisure hours as my father's PA and carer. It's months since I went on a date, years really. I barely see my friends, spend most of my evenings working.' Her voice was so quiet he could barely hear her, her eyes fixed on the sea. He wondered if she had forgotten his very existence. 'Sometimes I wonder if this is it. This will be my life. In one way I'm so lucky, have achieved so much so young and yet even that doesn't feel right. It wouldn't matter if the new book was going well. At least I could be the academic *wunderkind*.'

Now she just looked defeated, her face almost grey, and Leo remembered how he'd felt when he first saw her. How he'd wondered what it would take to make her have fun, take that tired look off her face, make those blue eyes light up with laughter.

He'd also wondered what it would take to make those blue eyes light up with lust, how her face would look softened with desire. His blood began to thunder in his veins even as he shook the thought from his mind. Hands off, remember? Not his type—and he most definitely wasn't hers.

'Don't you think that maybe you expect too much from yourself? Life isn't about working from the moment you get up. It's not just the achievements that count...'

'It's not just about partying either. Not everyone has a title and a trust fund. Not everyone values those. There's more to life than casinos and boats and selfies, Leo. I couldn't bear to live such a shallow existence.'

As soon as she said the words Anna wanted to recall them. After all, Leo had given up a week to help her, had shown no sign of being the playboy the papers made him out to be. And even if he was, her anger wasn't with him, it was with her sister for blithely walking away, her mother for expecting her to take up the reins once more, with her father who sat at home, so wrapped up in *his* life he barely noticed what she had given up—what she had lost. With herself for allowing herself to be cast as the sensible, reliable one again and again. But she knew all too well what happened if she didn't step up—everything crumbled.

'I'm sorry,' she said.

Leo sat back and raised his hands in mock surrender. 'No need to apologise, Dr Gray.'

'It's just so hard to know what the right thing to do is. I mean, should I leave Dad alone to take his pills or not, like Rosa would say? Or leave Mama to flounder here alone?' Anna twisted her fingers together. 'They say opposites attract, but what no one mentions is what happens afterwards. What it's like living in a house where two people are so incompatible. My father likes everything in its place, he likes rules and routines and plans.'

'And notebooks?' Leo cast a meaningful glance at Anna's current notebook placed, as ever, within easy reach.

'And notebooks,' she agreed, unable not to answer his knowing smile with one of her own. 'Whereas Mama, well, you've met Sancia…'

He nodded, amusement dancing in his dark eyes. Anna didn't want to notice how good it felt when all his attention was on her, that direct gaze filled with warm approbation and something else, something hotter. Something that made her want to sit up, wish her hair weren't messily tied back, wish that she were wearing something other than a paint-splattered T-shirt and cut-off old shorts.

'I'd have thought that the law of averages should have meant that Rosa and I would have ended up somewhere in the middle,' Anna continued, reaching for the beer and taking a sip of the light, slightly bitter liquid. 'But although neither of us are quite as extreme, we definitely ended up on one side or the other.' She glanced back across, her whole body tingling as she saw he was still looking at her with the same unnerving intensity. Laughing a little nervously, she ducked her head down to avoid meeting his gaze head-on. 'Anyway, that's ancient history.'

But she could still feel his gaze burning into her, hotter than the afternoon sun. 'Let me get this straight. So you have no Sancia in you at all?'

'Not a drop.'

'You're never spontaneous?'

'Never. At least,' she amended, as thoughts of her student folly, her intense crush on Sebastian, and the nearly catastrophic consequences flashed through her mind, leaving a wave of hot shame in its wake, 'I have been, but it didn't end well.' Which was the understatement of the year.

He sat back, eyes alight with mischief. Anna tried to ignore the churn low down in her abdomen, mixed with an anticipation she didn't want to admit to. After all, there was nothing *to* anticipate.

'I'm all for making a plan every now and then, Anna.'

Her stomach tumbled as he drew out her name, his accent caressing each syllable, adding a slight stress on the first. 'Aaan-na.'

'That's good to hear.'

'But,' he continued as if she hadn't spoken, 'spontaneity is what gives life its spice, don't you agree?'

'I'm English.' No way was she going to let him see the swirl of excitement the dark caress of his voice invoked in her, let him see how the thrill of the unknown possibilities spiralled through her. *What was wrong with her?* She didn't do spontaneous, remember, especially not with playboys.

Leo raised his eyebrows. 'English. And?'

'We're not an island known for our spice,' Anna said, ruthlessly pushing away thoughts of steaming curry, fresh falafel, her favourite tapas bar. 'Nice, plain food, that's the English way. Preferably boiled.' Nothing like a stereotype to win an argument.

'Ah, but you're half Spanish,' Leo reminded her. 'Heat runs through your veins no matter how much you may try to dampen it.'

He spoke truer than he could have known. Heat did flare up at his words, flickering through her veins and along her arteries as if he had lit a fuse. Anna swallowed, dragging her eyes away from Leo's hypnotic gaze, down the contour of his throat, only to stutter to a stop as she reached the bronze breadth of his chest. Did the man never put a shirt on?

'I thought we already established that I'm a clone of my father.'

His voice dropped, low and suggestive. 'I don't believe that, Anna. And I don't think you do either.'

Where was the quick response, her smart put-down? She'd belonged to a debating team throughout university, for goodness' sake, she ate overconfident undergraduates for breakfast and *still* had space for elevenses, but for once Anna was utterly lost for words. Lost and floundering. She was hyper-aware of her surroundings, of the sun beating down relentlessly, the tart scent of lemons, the tang of salt drifting in on the sea breeze. Hyper-aware of colour; of the gleaming white of the freshly painted bungalow, the faded green of the shutters and low tiled roof, such a contrast to the lush greens of the overgrown trees and bushes surrounding her, the clear turquoise of the sea, fringed by the creamy yellow crescent of sand.

And overpowering it all she was hyper-aware of Leo di Marquez. Sitting almost insolently as he lounged on his chair, muscles gleaming under the sun's caress, his eyes laughing, promising something she didn't want to comprehend. Anna had felt a connection to him the day they met, unwanted, unlooked for, unknown—that was why she kept her distance. But like a greedy child she had allowed her curiosity to lead her into the gingerbread house and now she was trapped.

'Don't you think it's fun to be just a little spontaneous every now and then?' Leo continued, his voice still low, still mesmerising.

No, Anna's mind said firmly, but her mouth didn't get the memo. 'What do you have in mind?'

His mouth curved triumphantly and Anna's breath caught, her mind running with infinite possibilities, her pulse hammering, so loud she could hardly hear him for the rush of blood in her ears.

'Nothing too scary,' he said, his words far more reassuring than his tone. 'What do you say to a well-earned and unscheduled break?'

'We're having a break.'

'A proper break. Let's take out the *La Reina Pirata*—' his voice caressed his boat's name lovingly '—and see where we end up. An afternoon, an evening, out on the waves. What do you say?'

Anna reached for her notebook, as if it were a shield against his siren's song. 'There's too much to do...'

'I'm ahead of schedule.'

'We can't just head out with no destination!'

'This coastline is perfectly safe if you know what you're doing.' He grinned wolfishly. 'I know exactly what I'm doing.'

Anna's stomach lurched even as her whole body tingled. She didn't doubt it. 'I...' She couldn't, she shouldn't, she had responsibilities, remember? Lists, more lists, and spreadsheets and budgets, all needing attention.

But Rosa would. Without a backwards glance. She wouldn't even bring a toothbrush.

Remember what happened last time you decided to act like Rosa, her conscience admonished her, but Anna didn't want to remember. Besides, this was different. She wasn't trying to impress anyone; she wasn't ridiculously besotted, she was just an overworked, overtired young woman who wanted to feel, to be, her age for a short while.

'Okay, then,' she said, rising to her feet, enjoying the surprise flaring in Leo di Marquez's far too dark, far too melting eyes. 'Let's go.'

CHAPTER FIVE

WHAT WAS SHE DOING?

Anna tried to quell the rising panic as Leo helped her into the dinghy and pushed off the jetty, rowing in sure, strong strokes towards his boat, moored just fifty yards away at the mouth of the island's tiny natural harbour. She didn't do spontaneous and she certainly didn't do spontaneous with an insanely handsome man who seemed to have a hard time locating a shirt and convincing it to stay on his impressively toned body. Although, it was hard to be too irritated by the lack of shirt when rowing showcased just how effective said muscles were, obviously both use *and* ornament.

Looking up, Anna caught Leo's eye and her cheeks burst into flame at his knowing look. She tore her gaze away and stared fixedly at the white crests of the small rippling waves, ignoring his snort of laughter.

It only took a few minutes to reach the side of *La Reina Pirata*, Leo throwing a rope to moor the dinghy alongside with practised ease. 'After you,' he said, gesturing at the narrow ladder on the side of the boat.

It wasn't easy to be graceful scrambling up a ladder that was more footholds than treads. Of course Leo bounded up after her with a careless ease born of practice and a natural athleticism. 'Welcome aboard.'

'Thank you.' But all she could do was gaze around, aware her mouth was hanging open in awe. 'This is quite something.'

The deck was ridged teak, gleaming as if freshly oiled, and ran from the cockpit, through the glass enclosed galley and the open-air seating area to the open deck at the back of the boat. Inside the galley wide padded bench seats surrounded a dining table, a state-of-the-art television and sound system dominated the other side of the cabin, and next to that a small but perfectly formed kitchen. A hatch was open, steps leading down into the interior of the boat.

'Drink?' Leo strolled over to the full-sized fridge. 'I have wine, beer, *cava*?'

'Water please,' Anna said hastily. The boat was already going to her head; the last thing she needed was alcohol discombobulating her further.

Leo handed her a glass filled with ice, fresh fruit garnishing the drink. Even the drinks were fancy on this boat. 'I'm just going to stow the dinghy. Have a look around, make yourself at home.'

Leo kept the boat suitably shipshape, not an item out of place, everything gleaming as if it had been recently waxed or polished and yet there was nobody else on board. Not what she would have expected of a careless playboy at all. His toys might be of the very best quality, but at least he looked after them.

The almost clinical tidiness continued as she made her way down to the lower deck. She'd expected it to be dark and a little claustrophobic but the glass-sided walls were tinted so that although outsiders couldn't see into the cabins, the sunlight flooded through. There were three rooms, a master suite with a perfectly made king-size bed, a second double bedroom and a study equipped with a desk and not one, but three computers, a satellite phone and a printer. 'Curiouser and curiouser,' she murmured as she scanned the room. Why on earth did Leo need so many computers?

The sound of the engines starting stopped her in her tracks. She was really doing this. Going for a trip with no planning, no foresight, nothing on her except the clothes she stood in—the dirty, paint-splattered clothes which, she was uneasily aware, made her the grubbiest thing on the boat.

She paused, fear thundering through her veins, the urge to yell out and tell Leo to stop almost overwhelming. Anna took a deep breath, and then another. Life as she knew it wasn't working; nothing was how she had thought it would be. Order and sense weren't bringing her the contentment they usually did. Taking one day—one afternoon—out to try a different path wasn't going to hurt her. And that was all this was. One afternoon. Tomorrow she would get out her lists and be Dr Anna Gray once more.

As soon as Anna reappeared on deck Leo knew something about her was different. It wasn't just that she had loosened her dark mane from its clasp, nor that she had removed her T-shirt to expose a remarkably pretty red bikini top. It was more the way her whole being seemed more relaxed, the pinched look wiped off her face, the habitual worry gone from her eyes. This was exactly what he had intended; he just hadn't expected the transformation to be so quick. Or for every atom in his body to stand up and take notice. *Easy, she's just a girl in a bikini. You've seen many girls in skimpier bikinis than that.*

But none that looked quite as sensational as Anna.

She wandered over to stand next to him, staring at the dashboard with wide eyes. 'Can I do anything?'

'Have you ever driven a boat? No? Come here, then. This is the steering wheel...'

'I have worked that one out,' she said drily.

'And this is the throttle here, and here is the gear control. Okay...' He continued to talk her through how to speed the boat up, how to slow down, brake and steer the powerful vessel, enjoying standing behind her, one arm loosely around her as he guided her hand on the throttle. The warmth of her burned into him, the subtle floral scent of her hair filling his senses. 'That's good,' he said, swallowing, aware just what an effect her proximity was having on him. 'Keep her going exactly like that.'

Stepping away was both an exquisite relief and an even more exquisite torture. He wanted to keep that arm around her, to touch the smooth skin on her back, exposed now to his gaze, only the thin red strings of her bikini contrasting with her olive skin. Her waist dipped in then flared out at the denim waistband of her shorts. Was she wearing matching bikini bottoms? *No*, he reminded himself. This afternoon might be about having fun, but it wasn't about having *that* sort of fun.

Leo swallowed. He knew there were several good reasons why, right now, he was struggling to remember them. He took another step back.

'This is great,' Anna called out, her face intent as she steered the boat through the sea. 'Where am I going?'

'Wherever you want. We can't get lost, not around here, and the tank's full.'

'Seriously? Just head off with no destination in mind?'

'Anna, that's half the fun.' It almost physically hurt as he backed further away, her scent continuing to tease his senses. He could still feel the imprint of her body against his. Leo swallowed hard, curling his hands into fists to stop himself reaching back out to her. He didn't remember ever wanting to touch someone quite so badly before.

'Just keep going, yell if you get bored. I'm off for a siesta.' He stepped back again and then again, turning to make his way out of the galley to the padded upper deck, aware of the puzzled, slightly hurt look Anna gave him as he retreated. Suddenly this trip didn't seem like the best idea he'd ever had. In fact it felt downright foolish, the two of them cooped up on a boat that usually felt so spacious, but right now seemed cramped, claustrophobic even, although he was breathing in the salt-tanged sea breeze, nothing overhead apart from blue sky and hot afternoon sun. What was going on?

Leo took a deep breath. *Let's be rational here.* He was attracted to Anna, good old plain and simple lust. It just seemed odd because he was usually careful not to get close to people of substance, of intellect. Didn't allow himself to forge ties that might have any durability. He didn't know how to handle a woman who made him sit up and think, who made him want to challenge not just who he allowed himself to be seen as, but who he truly was.

He grabbed a pair of sunglasses before lying down on the comfortable padded sun deck, folding his hands under his head and staring up at the sky. This ennui wasn't new, but it was getting more and more pervasive. It had followed him around for the last few years, tainting every success, cheering the occasional failures. After twelve years his nomadic life seemed hollow, meaningless, making money no longer gave him the same thrill—but he knew no other way.

Somehow this last week, painstakingly painting and repairing, was the most satisfying week he could remember in a long time.

Leo shifted uncomfortably. The ennui might not be new,

but it had certainly intensified ever since Valentina had announced her engagement. Like him she was very careful about what she revealed to the public gaze, like him she was all myth and mystery masquerading as reality. She didn't create, she didn't sing or act or dance, her fame solely concentrated in what she wore, where she was photographed and with whom, and she elevated what could be seen as vacuous existence to an art form. Not that he judged her, no, his little sister who had grown up knowing only poverty and deprivation deserved every moment of her success. But she *had* changed over the last year, both sharpened and softened by love. She was canny enough to use her wedding and her fiancé's connections to promote her own career, to turn herself into a serious supermodel, push her brand upmarket, but she truly loved Todd. She had lowered her defences where he was concerned, had allowed him to see the sweet young woman behind the polished, posed exterior. What had that cost her?

He'd never know, because he would never make himself so vulnerable. What if he allowed someone in and they saw that he was exactly who he thought he might be: a sharp-minded, money-making machine with no real soul? All Leo knew was that he didn't want to find out— and whether that was self-preservation or fear he had no idea. No idea at all.

He sat back up, impatient with the dark thoughts clouding what was supposed to be a carefree afternoon. He didn't do introspection, remember? He did what he pleased. And right now what he wanted was to cool off, to slew the self-doubt right off.

Anna had kept the boat going in a fairly straight trajectory, the coastline visible on the far horizon. Leo scanned it. There. Perfect. Jumping to his feet, he sauntered back to the cockpit, careful to keep his face as insouciant as possible, to ensure none of his indecision was written anywhere on his body. 'How's it going?'

'Good, as long as I don't need to change direction or speed and nothing gets in my way.' Anna turned and smiled and Leo's heart stuttered to a stop for one long moment as he drank her in, the tousled waves falling over her shoulders, the bikini revealing more than it concealed and the new, relaxed glint in her eye, the natural smile, the confidence in the way she stood. Funny, he had spent the last few moments questioning who and what he was, whereas Anna seemed to have slewed off her uptight and organised persona with the casting off of the boat.

He stood a good foot away, not sure he wanted to be within touching—or smelling—distance of Anna, not until he felt a lot more like himself. 'Fancy a swim?'

'Here?'

'Close. There's a bay just ahead. We can anchor at the mouth to it and swim off the boat.'

'Won't the water be cold?' she said, screwing her face up doubtfully. 'It's still early in the season.'

'We'll find out when we get in. Where's your sense of adventure, Dr Gray?' he added and saw the doubt clear off her face as if it had never been.

'If I get frostbite I'm suing you,' she said. 'Okay, Captain, guide me in.'

Leo took a deep breath. It would be all too easy to walk over and help her steer into the harbour, to lean against her, to put his hands against hers, to feel the suppleness of her waist, to inhale her scent, but that kind of thinking was why he needed this cold swim in the first place. It was all his own fault. He'd wanted to see Dr Gray unbuttoned—he just wasn't expecting her bikini top to show off quite so many enticing curves when she did so.

'Okay.' He leaned against the window, arms firmly

folded, not allowing himself to step within touching distance. 'You need to relax your grip on the throttle and turn the wheel like that, yes, that's good, a little gentler. Keep her on that course...'

It didn't take long for Anna to steer the boat into the mouth of the cove. It was deserted, the turquoise sea lapping against the volcanic rocky shore, the cliffs rising up ensuring that the only people to enter the cove would be doing so via the sea. 'What a gorgeous spot.' Anna stood, staring out at the view, spellbound.

'I'm going to anchor the boat. It's calm today, but we still don't want it to drift off and leave us marooned here.' Although there would be worse people to be marooned on a desert island with. She would be bound to come up with a plan for food, shelter and rescue within twenty minutes of a shipwreck.

Anna followed him out onto the deck and watched as he unwound the sea anchor, casting it out, calculating just how much chain it needed this close to shore. 'Do you live on this boat all the time?' she asked as he straightened.

'Not continuously. I have an apartment in Barcelona, but I do spend most of my time on here.'

'Doesn't it get scary? Alone at sea at night?'

'I'm not often alone,' he said deliberately and watched her cheeks flush. Leo didn't want to analyse just why he was pushing his playboy credentials so hard when the truth was he hadn't actually slept with a woman in over a year. 'Nor do I moor out at sea. It can be dangerous, even with warning lights on. I'm usually in a harbour somewhere.'

'It doesn't get claustrophobic? Living in such a small place?'

'She's bigger than an average studio apartment in London or New York. Besides, who can get claustrophobic with the sky overhead, the sea all around and the knowledge that as soon as the scenery palls I can pull anchor and go wherever I wish? Cannes, Monte Carlo, Ibiza…'

'Anywhere as long as it has a coastline,' Anna pointed out.

'Anywhere I want to go does have a coastline.' Leo peered over the side of the boat, one hand on the anchor cable checking for stability. 'This looks fine. Okay, Dr Gray, let's see just how spontaneous you can be.' He flashed a smile at her as he shucked off his shorts, turned and jumped off the boat, gasping as he dived cleanly into the sharp cold.

Anna stood by the rail, laughing as Leo surfaced spluttering. 'Is the temperature good for you?' she called.

'It's perfect, come in and try it,' he called back, flipping on his front to shoot through the water with bold strong strokes. Anna couldn't stop her gaze lingering on his dark, muscled limbs, on his clean lines, the moment he had stood in front of her bare except for his swim shorts emblazoned clearly on her mind. He looked good for someone who apparently spent his life at parties, and it wasn't as if there were a gym on-board.

Strange he actually lived on a boat, even a boat as luxurious and spacious as this. It didn't look like a home; there were no photographs, no knick-knacks, nothing to personalise it at all.

Leaning over the rail, Anna looked down at the dazzling blue sea, aware how deceptive its welcoming was. Even paddling was cold; here in deeper water the temperature would be decidedly chilly. Still, she was supposed to be spontaneous, wasn't she? Remembering that she was on holiday as well as working. Rosa would already be in the water, swimming after Leo, flirtatiously instigating a water fight. In fact, she probably would just jump straight in either with her clothes on or with no clothes at all. At least Anna was wearing a bikini...

It would be spontaneous if she weren't...

A smile curved her mouth as she pictured the shock on Leo's face, the way his brown eyes would darken to black. She'd been so aware of him as he had showed her how to drive the boat, so very close she could have leaned back just a little and pressed against him. He'd been aware of her too, she knew it. If she dived in next to him, in her bikini or out of it, would that awareness be sharpened, heightened? Probably.

Did she want that? Could she handle it?

Anna shivered, her skin goosebumping despite the heat in the late spring air. What was she doing? Leo was flirty, sure, but he probably flirted more with Sancia, with Maria the maid, than he did with Anna. They had barely spoken over the last week.

Barely spoken maybe, but she had been aware of his every move, every look. And she knew he had been equally aware of her.

She should stop thinking and start doing. Have some fun for the first time in a long, long time.

And with that thought memories hit. Another swim, another man. An outdoor swimming pool, a glass of champagne or two. Memories of clothes discarded recklessly, of the way she had dived in, turning to smile provocatively, knowing he would follow. Knowing, wanting, welcoming what would happen next.

Only she hadn't been in any way prepared for what happened next. It turned out that spontaneity had consequences, that a playboy couldn't be reformed.

Almost without intending to Anna folded her arms around herself, as if she could cocoon the hurt, the memories safely inside, almost shaking with grief, with embarrassment for the naïve girl she had once been. Her hand slipped down to her stomach, pressing hard against the flatness as if she could keep all the hurt, the memories contained within. But she would never forget the scorn in Sebastian's eyes the moment before he turned and walked away from her.

Anna swallowed, her throat thick with tears. Spontaneity wasn't for her, she knew that all too well, and playboys who lived on boats were definitely not for her. Let Leo have his swim. Then she would demand he turn the boat around and take her back to La Isla Marina, back to safety and sense. Where she belonged.

CHAPTER SIX

By the time Leo finished his swim Anna had composed herself, sitting at the galley table, a glass of water before her, scrolling through her phone, barely looking up as he strode in, a towel around his shoulders, drops falling from the sleek dark head.

'You didn't want a swim?'

'Not really.' She couldn't look directly at him in case he saw through her casual tone. 'Leo, this is lovely, but...'

'You want to go back?'

'Yes, I think that's best.' She raised her eyes to his face then, but his expression was utterly inscrutable.

'Before or after dinner? Only if I remember rightly there's a great seafood restaurant along this coast, not too far along. Shame not to try it.'

Home, now, her instincts screamed, but her good manners won out. 'Dinner would be nice. Thank you.'

Anna returned her attention to her phone, glad of the ever-present excuse of emails to occupy her, to stop her watching Leo towel himself dry. Her agent and editor had both sent impatient if encouraging questions about her progress, her father had sent a brief, terse message asking what the password was for their online supermarket account and, in the space of just a few hours, her mother had managed to send her several emails, complete with many exclamations and emojis denoting goodness knew what, Anna certainly didn't.

She reread the first of her mother's lengthy missives and couldn't help exclaiming, 'Oh, brilliant!'

Leo paused. Anna did her best not to notice how the white towel set off his tan, how the casual way it was draped over his shoulder emphasised every sculpted muscle. 'What is?'

With an effort she tore her gaze back to her phone. 'Sancia's received a huge delivery, all the wedding decorations including fairy lights, tablecloths, candles—everything we need apart from the flowers, which are apparently coming on the actual wedding day. Valentina has sent everything labelled and ready to go. That's a huge amount of work saved.'

'Val mentioned it was on its way. That reminds me, she was hoping that her favourite restaurant in Barcelona will be able to cater the actual reception. Will that cause any problems?'

'Actually it's a relief. The kitchen staff can concentrate on producing the food for the rest of the week. I know the day after the wedding Valentina wants paella on the beach, but they still have five more dinners to plan, plus all the breakfasts, lunches and snacks. Every dish has to be traditionally Spanish with vegetarian, vegan, nut-free, dairy-free and gluten-free options as well—which does make the traditionally Spanish part a little tricky.'

'I'm surprised that's all the options she's asked for. You wait till you meet her guests—and start meeting their demands. You will be earning every cent, believe me,' Leo said darkly.

Anna pushed her hair out of her eyes as she leaned back against the comfortably padded bench. 'I can't help wondering why the short notice for the wedding—and why hold it somewhere she hasn't even seen? It seems odd for someone whose life is so public to be so hands-off with something so important—my most down-to-earth friends are completely consumed by their weddings. I can't imagine any of them getting married somewhere they haven't actually been to!'

She still wasn't sure why Leo was here on Valentina's behalf. He obviously cared enough about her to consider her to be like a sister to him, but apart from their nationality they appeared to have nothing in common. Valentina lived in New York, was an Internet princess and hung out with a group of privileged, beautiful, fashionistas; Leo lived in Spain and his social group, although equally privileged, was much wilder. And nothing Anna had come across on social media linked them in any way. Not one photograph, not one friend in common, nothing except they were both Spanish, both hailed from near Barcelona.

'La Isla Marina wasn't the original venue,' Leo said, pulling on a T-shirt, to Anna's equal relief and disappointment, before he slid onto the opposite bench, grabbing her glass of water and taking a long sip. 'She was planning to hold the wedding at the villa in Ibiza where she met Todd.'

It all began to make a little more sense. 'What happened?'

'Fire, catastrophic apparently. There was no way the villa could be repaired in time. She needed somewhere here, in Spain, able to host one hundred and fifty guests for the week on just over a month's notice...'

'Where better than a resort so down on its luck, they had no guests for the start of the season at all? Lucky for her, lucky for Mama. But she knows nothing about us *or* La Isla Marina. I know she's busy, but I can't believe she hasn't visited yet to check everything out.'

'She spent several summers on the island when she was

a child. She has very fond memories of it. That's why she was so keen to relocate the wedding to it. Why I'm so keen to make sure it's ready for her.'

'She was a guest on La Isla Marina? When?' Not recently, obviously, but if Valentina had spent a holiday when the island was in its heyday then it was no wonder she had switched the wedding over; when it was at its best there was nowhere more magical. More romantic.

Leo shook his head. 'Not a guest. Her mother worked for your grandparents for two or three summers starting when Valentina was around eight. That's why she knows it so well. She lived there too over those summers.'

Anna thought back, but there was no niggle of recognition. Her grandparents had often hired couples as seasonal workers and as a result there had usually been a small gaggle of workers' children running around the place. Families were housed in small apartments in and around the villa, the children looked after at the same holiday clubs as those set up for island guests. 'When she was eight? She's what? Twenty-one now? That means she would have been there when we still went for the whole summer. Only I doubt I would have taken much notice of her,' she added.

'Si, I'm sure a maid's daughter was far too below the owners' granddaughter to be noticed.' His voice was cutting.

'No.' She sat up, indignation crashing through her at Leo's scathing tone, her face hot. 'Not at all, but if she was eight I was fifteen and at that age that's an entire generation gap. The different ages didn't mix, but that was the only barrier. Some of my best summer friends had parents who worked on La Isla Marina, only a few were visitors. That was really uncalled for.'

'I apologise. It's just people can be...' he paused '...rigid, about things like class.'

'Well, I'm not and nor were my grandparents. Mama will remember her, I'm sure. So the wedding is a homecoming?' That made a difference, somehow. Welcome as the money would be to Sancia, making this effort for one of the island's daughters seemed right somehow.

'A homecoming?' he echoed. 'Maybe it is. Lucky Valentina, to have a place she considers home.' He slid out of his seat, his face shuttered. 'I'll go and haul in the anchor. Let me know if you want to try that restaurant or head straight back. I don't mind either way.'

With a deep sigh Anna slumped onto the table. Even though her aim had been to put the brakes on whatever might or might not be simmering between Leo and her, she still couldn't help feeling that she'd blown it. Not just ending the new accord between them, but reverting to type. Sensible Anna didn't sail away with handsome pirates, sensible Anna didn't leave chores undone, sensible Anna didn't swim in cold seas. Sensible Anna didn't get hurt; she didn't have much fun either, but that was the trade-off she made. That was what kept her safe.

Somehow the knowledge didn't give her the same satisfaction it usually did. Safe was a book unwritten, a father who couldn't even order his own shopping, a mother content to leave Anna to sort out her problems for her, a sister she didn't see or speak to. A sister who would never waste an afternoon on a boat with a handsome man checking emails and worrying about the future.

What would it be like when Rosa finally turned up? Anna could already see the amused scorn in Rosa's face, how she would love the knowledge that Anna had spent so much time with a gorgeous, occasionally charming man and spent it doing chores. How satisfying would it be if she and Leo were on friendly terms when Rosa did deign to rock up?

By the time they got back the light would be almost gone; they wouldn't be able to do any more work today. So why not extend the trip for a few hours? Continue with careful spontaneity. Yes to a sail and a meal, both civilised activities. No to the intimacy of swimming, no to reacting to his every light touch, no to lingering glances.

Just because Leo discombobulated Anna, just because he made her want things she knew weren't good for her to want, made her feel fusty and stuffy and dull, just because every quirk of his mouth dared her to take risks she had no intention of taking didn't mean they couldn't be friends.

Besides, it still stung that he thought she was the kind of person who would stand on her dignity, that she would consider a maid's daughter her inferior. What they needed was a new start. She would be her most charming through dinner and Leo di Marquez y Correa would have no choice but to see that there was more to her than notebooks and efficiency.

Pushing back his chair, Leo stretched and glanced at his watch. Two hours had disappeared in a flow of emails and reports and he had barely made a dent. Over the last week he'd neglected his business and his out-of-control inbox reflected it. There were still far too many decisions to be made, reports to read, to be commissioned, to be acted upon. Funny to think he'd once got such a thrill from moving such huge sums of money around, from creating wealth, bestowing it. Now it just seemed nebulous, more like playing a video game than work. Not like painting and repairing. Maybe he should give it all up and become a full-time groundskeeper? He smiled wryly. Would his father consider that a step up or a step down from a professional playboy and gambler? He suspected a step down.

He glanced at his watch again; another hour until the

restaurant opened. They'd moored at the little seashore village's small wooden harbour earlier that afternoon, but Anna had turned down Leo's offer of a walk, preferring her emails and making even more of her interminable lists. She'd erected another layer of protection around herself while he swam, the laughing girl who'd driven his boat once more replaced with the cool, organised woman with a large *keep out* sign stapled to her forehead.

A sign he had every intention of respecting.

'Leo, I've just realised all I have is what I'm standing up in…oh, I'm sorry, I didn't realise you were busy. I didn't mean to disturb you.' Leo was so engrossed in his thoughts he didn't hear the door open. Anna peered around it, staring at his three computer screens with unabashed curiosity. 'What on earth are you doing?'

She stepped into the room, still transfixed by the screens. Leo shot them a brief glance, checking nothing incriminating or confidential was on display; one showed the day's open stock markets, another the report he was currently working on, the third his emails. Innocuous if peculiar for a man who supposedly did nothing but cruise the seas and party. *'Nada importante,'* he said quickly.

'No? It looks important. You were a hundred miles away. You didn't even hear me call you.' She stepped closer. 'I wondered why you had three computers in here.'

Turning on his best lazy smile, Leo moved slightly, blocking his email. 'It's important to know what's going on when sailing. I'm just checking the weather forecast.'

The lift of her eyebrows showed just how far short he was of convincing her. 'Funny, that looks far more like the FTSE than the Met to me.'

He turned up the wattage on his smile, adding a hint of roguish for good measure. 'Gambling takes more than one form, you know.'

'True, but stocks and shares are for some reason seen as a lot more respectable than the roulette wheel. Is that what you're doing? Trading? And what's that?' She nodded at the report.

Leo had hidden behind a faceless company name for so long, hidden behind a false image of a partying gambler for so long, he sometimes forgot why the charade had started. It was second instinct to keep pretending. Hiding. But the curiosity in Anna's sharp gaze tugged at him and he knew he wanted to see the change in her face when he told her exactly what he was doing, to see that faint, unconscious superiority she employed turn to respect. Hardly anyone beyond his employees, faceless anonymous employees working in virtual offices all around the globe, knew what he did. It would be nice for someone he respected to know.

'Leo?' She sounded concerned now. 'I'm sorry, am I intruding? I was only joking. It doesn't matter. My question can wait…'

'It's not the FTSE, it's the Dow Jones,' he said abruptly and watched the blue eyes widen.

'So you do gamble with stocks as well as at casinos?'

'No, I invest.'

'In shares?'

'At first, but now I invest in companies. Preferably in start-ups, although sometimes in companies who want to expand, or are in trouble and need to turn around. The term is angel, I believe. I put money in, usually with conditions, although that depends on the company, and then they pay me back with interest or I retain a share of the company.'

'But…how? Nothing I read said that you were interested in investments.'

'That's because nobody knows. It doesn't quite fit the image, does it? My company itself is the investor. I'm not publicly listed as the owner. Any investigator would have to look hard to find my connection to it—and why would they? We don't invest in controversial projects. We're an ethical investor. There's nothing to spark their interest.'

Anna's mouth was open, but no words were coming out, which, Leo suspected, was a first. She pulled out a chair and sat down heavily, staring at the rapidly changing screen displaying all the stock movements of the day. 'You are telling me that you are a playboy gambler with a secret identity? Like Batman? Do you have a cape as well? Does this boat turn into a plane?' She shook her head, her hair, once more respectably confined into a ponytail, swinging with the movement. 'I've heard of secret gamblers, but not the other way round.'

'No cape, no fighting villains, just investing. And despite the title I'm no angel. I do it all for profit.'

That wasn't entirely true, not any more. Sometimes he invested because a young company had such vision, such passion, he wanted to be part of it in some way. In the hope that passion, that belief would somehow rub off on him. He was still waiting.

Anna regarded him keenly, curiosity brightening her clear, blue eyes. 'Is this how you make a living? Not in casinos?'

'I've never gambled a penny I wasn't prepared to lose.' Leo shifted, her scrutiny making him uncomfortable. 'You had a question when you burst in here. What is it?'

'A question? Right. The trouble with spontaneity...' Anna tugged at her paint-splattered shorts and grimaced '...is the lack of planning. I have nothing suitable for a restaurant at all. I can't turn up in these and a dirty T-shirt. Maybe we should head home after all.'

'There are clothes in the spare bedroom.' He scanned her slim figure, trying not to let his gaze linger on the curve of her breasts. 'Valentina sometimes joins me here when she is in between jobs. I think you're not too dissimilar a size. Help yourself to anything. There's plenty of hot water if you want a shower.'

'Thank you.' She got to her feet, headed for the door then turned. 'Leo, why is it such a secret? Investing in start-ups is a great way to make a living. Why let the world think you're nothing but a party-going playboy when there's so much more to you?'

So much more? He might not make his living the way the world thought, but he wasn't sure that meant that he was worth anything. Anna might be intelligent, but she had missed the mark this time.

He pushed out of his chair, wanting, needing to shut the conversation down. 'Come on, I'll show you the clothes and how the shower works.'

Anna followed him out of the study, across the narrow corridor and into the guest cabin at the very front of the boat. The bed was made up. Leo tried not to look at the crisp white sheets, tried to push the thought of how Anna would look entangled in them from his mind.

He'd invited Anna for a sail on a whim, purely because he enjoyed discombobulating her. What he hadn't taken into consideration was how she might affect him. He was so used to always having the upper hand, it hadn't occurred to him that a smart, curious woman like Anna was more than capable of seeing through him, seeing into him.

She liked facts, knowledge and solving problems. She had a keen intellect. And when that scrutiny was turned on him, it was like a compulsion. He'd been more honest with Anna Gray than he had been with any other human being for a very long time, including himself.

'Wardrobe's there,' he said brusquely. 'And the shower is in here.'

Anna opened the folding doors and peered in at the tiny

but tidy en-suite bathroom. 'Very nice, not that I've come to expect anything else from this boat.'

'Press that button to activate the water. You can adjust the heat and power with those handles. Towels are in the wardrobe, and I believe Valentina has left toiletries in the bathroom cabinet. You should have everything you need.' Rattling off the instructions made him feel a little like Anna must with her lists, like restoring order to a suddenly disordered world. And her world was disordered for all her calm exterior; a mother who needed her, a sister she didn't speak to. No wonder she tried to restore order wherever she saw it. As long as she didn't try to restore him...

'Thank you. This is incredible.'

'Right.' He most certainly wasn't going to hang around, to imagine Anna pulling off her shirt, untying her bikini-top strings, slipping her shorts down her strong, toned legs, stepping into that shower. *Get a grip*, Leo told himself fiercely. This enforced abstinence wasn't good for him. He needed one of his no-strings, no-effort, short-term affairs and soon. Good thing there was a wedding coming up. They were usually good for a quick, fun fling. 'I'll leave you to...'

Leo stepped back and, at the same moment, Anna stepped back, straight into him, her warm body colliding hard with his. Instinctively Leo reached out, grabbing onto her, his arms pulling her close as she struggled to regain her balance. For one long second she relaxed against him, every slim curve snuggled into him, the scent of her enfolding him even as his body enfolded her.

Lust rushed through him, hard, fast, intense and all-consuming, his blood hammering through his veins, thundering in his ears. *Want. Need. Have.* His body was issuing demands, demands he wanted more than anything to accede to and Leo's arms tightened around her body, holding her closer for one incendiary moment.

Did she feel it too? Was lust shivering through her? Were her nerves humming with desire? Were her eyes dark, her mouth dry, every atom of her attuned to his? Leo didn't know what would be worse—if she did or if she didn't. If this lust was one-sided that would be humiliating enough, but if it burnt through them both then how much worse would it be when she discovered just how hollow he was? Leo spent a great deal of time making sure no one got close enough to reject him, making sure he was the first to walk away.

Letting her go, stepping back, finding the right, unconcerned smile, felt like a Herculean task and yet somehow he did. 'Careful,' he said in a voice that didn't sound like his, aware of the slight tremor as he spoke.

Anna's eyelashes fluttered down, shielding her eyes, allowing him to think he might have imagined the flicker of hurt, of disappointment in her eyes. But her voice was completely unconcerned, as matter of fact as ever. 'If I'm this clumsy when we're moored imagine what I'd be like in the middle of the ocean. I'd say a pirate's life is not for me.'

On these last words she turned, flashed him a quick smile, and disappeared into the bathroom leaving Leo standing in the cabin. Alone. The way he chose to be. The way he preferred to be. At least, that was what he told himself. One day he might even believe it.

CHAPTER SEVEN

ANOTHER LONG SILENCE fell over the table. Anna cast around for something to say and, in desperation, fell on platitudes. 'This is beautiful!'

It was a warm night and they'd been seated on the restaurant terrace overlooking the sea. The sun had already set, leaving just a few purple and grey traces in the starstrewn sky. A soft glow fell across the terrace from the tiny lanterns hanging from the flower-twined beams that connected the terrace to the building, candles illuminating the table. Blankets hung on the backs of their chairs in case the night chilled.

'Really beautiful,' she added. Leo had been practically monosyllabic since that moment in the cabin, the moment when their bodies had collided, when he had broken her fall. She'd never felt anything like the explosive attraction, as if his light clasp on her waist had ignited a fuse burning straight through her. Neither of them had moved for a long, sizzling second, their bodies perfectly melded together, their pulses beating in perfect harmony. If she'd turned would he have kissed her? All she knew was that she would have kissed him back. Only he had let go, stepped away, and since then had kept his distance physically and emotionally. Which was for the best—hadn't she decided to go for a cordial friendship, not heat-filled passion? After all, passion never ended well for her.

She couldn't help replaying that moment over and over though, and in the replay it never ended with Leo stepping away.

No, she wasn't going to think about that now, not when they were alone on this candlelit terrace, the sea serenading them. Summoning her best bright, friendly smile, Anna looked at Leo, only to find his eyes on her, not the view. 'Yes,' he said softly. 'Very beautiful.'

Heat flushed her cheeks and she glanced down at her empty plate, wishing for food, anything to occupy her hands. Truth was she *felt* beautiful tonight. Unlike herself. Valentina had left the kind of luxurious creams and cosmetics Anna didn't usually look at, let alone buy, in the small cabin and by the time she had washed her hair and applied a little make-up she already felt like the 'after' photo in a makeover.

Choosing an outfit had been a little harder. Valentina's tastes ran to skimpy and barely there, none of which fitted the friendly and cordial brief. In the end Anna had selected a silky slip dress, pleased with the way the deep, shimmering red gave a warm glow to her skin.

'Thank you for letting me pilfer Valentina's wardrobe,' she said, pulling at the gold, filmy scarf she had flung over her almost bare shoulders with nervous fingers. 'The clothes in that small wardrobe probably cost more than everything I have ever bought added together. Are you sure Valentina won't mind me wearing this?'

'She's probably forgotten she even owns it. She never wears the same outfit twice anyway, you know.'

Anna tried to imagine discarding clothes after just one wear and failed. She still had tops she'd bought while at school. 'Never? Wow. I live in the same clothes day in, day out. I can't imagine wearing something this lovely just the once.'

'She gets paid to wear them, or sent them for free.' Leo nodded at the menu. 'Have you decided what you would like to order?'

'I'm going to go with the fish of the day.' Anna put the simple, handwritten menu down onto the table and propped her elbows on it, resting her chin in her hands as she studied the man opposite. Today, she couldn't help feeling that she'd learned more about him than he usually let slip to anyone, but there were still unanswered questions nagging at her. And keeping up a flow of conversation would mean less time for meaningful glances, less time for traitorous thoughts. 'Leo?'

'*Si?*'

'What are you really doing spending so much time on La Isla Marina?' She glanced down at his tanned, capable-looking hands, noting the scratch he'd received from an over-enthusiastic chisel. 'Why spend a whole month getting your hands dirty?'

'For my sister,' he said.

There was something here she simply wasn't grasping. Anna frowned. 'Did you know her when you were little? How on earth does the son of a *conde* and...?'

'The illegitimate daughter of the same *conde*.'

Of course. Now it all made sense...

'She really is your sister? I assumed it was an honorary term.'

'No, there's nothing honourable about our relationship. My father seduced her mother with lies and promises he had no intention of keeping—and then when he found out she was pregnant he sacked her. She spent her winters juggling as many jobs as she could, her summers cleaning and waitressing and counting on tips to get her through

the leaner months. As soon as Valentina was old enough
to help she was working too. That's why I have given up
a month to give her a dream wedding. I couldn't help her
then, but I can and will help her now. No matter what I
have to do.'

'But, it's the twenty-first century! People have rights.
Didn't he have to at least pay maintenance? She should
have taken him to court or…'

Leo's smile was so cold Anna stuttered to an abrupt
stop. 'Assumptia, Val's mother, was too scared to fight.
You have to understand, my father is a very powerful man.
No one can force him to do anything he doesn't want to
do. He told her that if she chose to have the baby, it would
be her problem alone. Nothing to do with him. My father
always keeps his word,' he added, reaching for his glass
of rioja. 'In the end Assumptia decided that, hard as things
were, it would be better for her and Valentina to stay away
from my father. To be free.'

Anna swallowed, memories rising for the second time
that day, bitter and poignant. 'That poor woman, pregnant and alone.' She couldn't keep a melancholy knowledge from her voice and Leo looked at her sharply. She
didn't return his gaze, keeping her own focussed out to
sea. 'When did you find out that you had a sister? Or have
you always known?'

Leo paused as the waiter came over with bread and oil
and to take their orders. 'Assumptia, her mother, came to
work for us when I was seven or eight. My parents were
absent a lot, and even when they were home they didn't
spend much time with me. The house I grew up in was
very old, very large, a little frightening for a young boy
with an overactive imagination. I was left alone a lot. Most
of the maids didn't want to bother with a small, silent boy,
but Assumptia was kind to me. I loved her very much.'

Anna's heart ached as she pictured the scene, pictured the small boy alone with no one who really cared for him. Whatever her parents' faults they had loved Anna and Rosa. True, they argued, but they did their best to provide a stable, loving home. And when Anna was small, when their marriage had worked, life had been wonderful. Even when things began to fall apart, when she had become the peacemaker, she still had had the long summers with her grandparents where she was safe and free. Leo might look as if he had everything in the world—money, looks, a title—but he had grown up with nothing. 'What happened?'

'I got back from school and she was gone.' He shrugged. 'It wasn't the first time this had happened. After a while I forgot about her. There were so many different maids, you see, although not all were…kind.' He paused before he said the word, and Anna shivered in empathy, her throat thick as she listened. 'Ten years later I was at the coast and stopped at one of the beachside bars for a drink. She brought my beer to my table and I knew her immediately, greeted her as if she were my long-lost relation, which in a way she was.' His eyes were shadowed as he reminisced.

'Was she glad to see you?'

'No, not at first. She seemed cold, cagey, but you see…' He paused then, as if searching for the right words. 'The thing is, Anna, at that time I was used to people leaving, to being considered as little more than my name and heritage.' Anna blinked at the hollowness in his voice and realisation struck her, cold and true. Leo di Marquez y Correa still felt that way. Still assumed people were only interested in *who* he was, not what he was. Was that why he hid behind his playboy image?

'Valentina ran over and straight away I knew… The way she looked, her age. Maybe in some way I had always known. There must have been rumours and gossip at the time. Val was around ten, already helping wash dishes, collecting glasses, working while other children played on the beach. I vowed then that she would be able to play, that she would have her childhood, that I would take care of her.'

'You were eighteen,' Anna said softly. 'Not much more than a child yourself.'

'Old enough.'

She leaned forward, propping her elbows on the table, absorbed in the sad tale. 'What did you do? Did you talk to your father?'

'Despite how cold and critical he was, I thought maybe he didn't know. He always told me that to be a di Marquez was to have honour. That our family was very old, very revered, that I must never let it down.' His voice dripped bitterness and Anna shivered, reaching for her wine glass. 'I couldn't imagine that he would let a child of his wash up at a cheap bar by the shore, let a child of his go hungry. I was wrong. He told me never to mention her existence. Not to be a sentimental fool. That accidents happen, but what matters is keeping them quiet, that I'd learn that as long as I uphold the family name in public, I could do anything I liked in private, that's how it is for people like us.'

'Nice,' Anna murmured, the need to comfort him overwhelming her. She stretched a hand across the table and took his. Leo sat motionless for a second and then his strong fingers enfolded hers, as if she were a lifeline connecting him to the present.

'My eyes were opened then. The family name I had been brought up to revere was nothing but hypocrisy. My duty was to keep up appearances, to be seen to be responsible, a credit to the family, do the right degree, get the right job, marry a girl whose blood was as blue as mine, ensure there were several heirs, as soon as possible, and in return I would have money to enjoy any vice I wish as long as I was discreet. I wanted no part of it. I decided then that my vices would always be there for the world to see.'

Anna tightened her grip on his, wishing she could find that hurt, lonely boy and make it all right for him—and find his parents and tell them exactly what she thought of them. 'If we can't go crazy at eighteen, then when can we?'

Leo's eyes gleamed. 'Surely you were never crazy, not even at eighteen, Dr Gray.'

'Me?' She didn't have to think back, the past always with her. 'I fell in love, totally, wholly, lost myself in love. There's nothing crazier than that.'

A flicker of something dark passed over his face. For a moment Anna almost thought it was jealousy, although his voice was light and teasing. 'Love doesn't sound too bad.'

'Infatuation is a disease. I lost myself entirely. It was more than bad.'

'I take it he's no longer around?'

'I haven't seen him in years.' Truth was she avoided any situation where Sebastian Montague-Hughes might be seen. Even the sight of an arrogant profile resembling his was enough to make her nauseous, her chest tight.

'Replaced him with a sensible man who ticks every box on your list?'

Anna knew exactly the kind of man she wanted to settle down with one day. Someone reliable, someone with good morals and ethics. Someone safe. Not an entitled rich boy, nor, much as her heart sped up around Leo, an aristocratic Spanish pirate with issues deeper than the seas he sailed. But not yet. 'My work is my passion now.' She paused. 'At least it was.'

'Was?'

'I've had to be very dedicated to get this far so young. I just can't help wondering if this is it, can I carry on doing the same thing for the next forty years.' Sometimes, when Anna looked into the future, she could see the walls closing in, trapping her in a world she wasn't sure was for her at all. 'You know, when Mama called and begged me to come and help out I didn't say yes because I'm the good daughter who always does what's expected. I said yes because I needed to get away from Oxford for a while. I needed some space.' She searched for a change of subject, not wanting to think any more about her dilemma. 'So, number five on *Titles* magazine's *"Wicked Aristocrats We'd Like to Redeem"* list, how is the playboy lifestyle? As much fun as you hoped it would be?'

His smile was pure wickedness. 'Care to find out?'

Luckily for Anna the waiter brought out their food before she could formulate a response that didn't involve stammering, blushing, or turning into Dr Gray with a withering put-down. The fish and perfectly grilled vegetables were delicious and, by unspoken accord, they moved on to lighter topics, discussing the plans for the week ahead, how Valentina wanted the decorations to be displayed and how she had first met Todd.

Although Anna was mostly relieved by the change in intensity, part of her was a little frustrated. She sensed that Leo rarely let anyone in, that she was in a privileged position—and that every time he did more and more of her preconceptions were chipped away.

Her preconceptions were her armour, protecting her from a man she was no way equipped to handle. Leo's arrogance, his bearing, his confidence might in turn be his armour, but they were also part of him, forged while he was young, in anger and defensiveness. He might despise his parents and all they stood for, but there was a pride in his bearing, in his manner, that was all born of an old name, old money and a sense of knowing who he was and what he stood for.

But, like the expert researcher she was, she wanted more. Now he had opened the chink she wanted to reach further inside, to expose all he was, all he felt. She'd been here before—and she'd got it so horribly wrong last time. Was she just repeating the same mistakes? She had assumed there was more to Sebastian, that he had hidden depths, depths only she could find. Assumed she could reform him with love, make him into the man she dreamed he was. She'd been brutally, horribly wrong. If she allowed herself to fall for Leo and be wrong again then it might break her.

But somehow she knew it might be far too late.

Leo was silent as he escorted Anna back to the boat. It was ironic. Just twelve hours ago he had been looking at a painted wall with complete satisfaction. Now he felt as if he'd spent an hour in the confessional, scourged and empty. Not that he'd been to confession since he'd left his parents' house. His father still went every week. Did he feel absolved of his sins? Was that why he felt able to carry on with impunity? Leo preferred to carry his with him, companions on a long, weary road.

'You might as well get some sleep as we sail back,' he said a little brusquely once they were both safely aboard. 'It will take a couple of hours to sail back to La Isla Marina at this time of night. The spare cabin is freshly made up—you can sleep there.'

'It's very late though,' Anna pointed out. 'Why don't we just stay here and sail back first thing in the morning?'

'Won't your mother worry?'

Anna held up her phone. 'I can text her. The only prob-

lem is she will never believe that we're not, you know…
she'll probably hang out bunting to celebrate.'

Leo arched a brow. 'You know?'

Folding her arms, Anna threw him a scathing glare.
'You do know so don't pretend.'

He did know, and he didn't want to dwell on the thought.
Not when he could imagine it so clearly, could almost taste
the lushness of her mouth, feel the silk of her skin under
his fingertips. But Leo wasn't his father, he only slept with
women who wanted what he did—a momentary comfort.

He sought for the right tone of his voice, to keep his face
relaxed even as his blood heated. 'She'll hang out bunting,
not be waiting for me with a pitchfork?'

'With an entire band to welcome us back in style. My
mother thinks I'm boring. You probably agree.'

Boring he could handle. Right now he was yearning
for boring. 'Boring? No. Organised? Oh, yes.' He paused,
knowing he should leave the conversation there, but something about the evening's frank exchanges compelled him
to carry on. 'Afraid? Definitely!'

'Afraid?' Anna sounded indignant. 'Rubbish! Just look
at the last two weeks. I took a month's holiday with no notice to come and help organise a wedding, despite knowing nothing about weddings. I came sailing with you on a
moment's notice…'

'I take it back.' Leo held his hands up. 'You're a lioness.'

But Anna's expression clouded. 'There's nothing wrong
with being careful,' she said. 'That's all I am, not afraid,
careful. It's not fun having your heart broken, not fun
seeing your dreams evaporate. Believe me, I've tried it.'

With a jolt Leo realised that he hadn't. He'd never fallen
in love and so his heart was completely intact; he'd never
had a dream worth following. He'd made money without
aim or purpose, finding he was good at it. Maybe by in-

vesting in other people's dreams he tried to inhale them second-hand, but the satisfaction was as muted as the effort.

He laughed at Anna for her lists and caution, but at least she had put herself out there once. Who was the real coward here?

He pushed the unwelcome thought aside. 'So that's it, then, you tried it once, it didn't work and so now you're going to live your life according to to-do lists? No interruptions or deviations?' It seemed wrong. There was fire in Anna, he could see it, muted now, damped down, but there. Every now and then a gleam in her eye showed just how hot it could burn if she ever let go. It would be something to see if she ever did, definitely worth getting burned just to bask in her heat.

Moving over to the deck rail, Anna leaned on it, staring out at the starlit sea. 'I'm not saying I don't sometimes wish it could be different,' she said, so softly that he could only just make out her words. 'Mama and Rosa certainly seem to have more fun. Of course they do. Acting without thought, without consequences, letting someone else always pick up the pieces is by far the better way to live, if you're lucky enough to be able to.'

'Why can't you?' Leo wandered over and joined her at the rail, his hand lying next to hers.

She laughed. 'It's not in my make-up. I need facts, timetables, to explore every option, otherwise I worry and fret. But being the sensible one is exhausting.' Her voice lowered even more. 'Lonely.'

'It doesn't have to be.' Leo covered her hand with his, no idea of seduction in his mind, just the need to give comfort as she had comforted him earlier.

'I don't know any other way, not any more. I don't know

how to take a risk, how to let anyone in. You're right, I am a coward.'

'No.' His hand tightened over hers. 'You've just left no space in your life for you, that's all. I know you spent the hour before we went out for dinner ordering groceries for your dad. Your mother has just placed every decision about getting the island ready for the season on your shoulders, even though you have a job and should have a life of your own. You need to learn to say no, Anna.'

'It's that easy?'

'Worth a shot every now and then. What would Sancia have done if you hadn't come along?'

'She'd have been all right. A handsome pirate with some keen DIY skills happened to moor up in her harbour the very next day.'

'Handsome?'

She looked up at him then, a smile finally curving her full mouth. 'Oh, as if you don't know. No one spends that much time shirtless if he doesn't know full well he has swoonworthy abs.'

Leo's heart slowed, every nerve centred on the palm of his hand, on the warmth of Anna's slightly roughened hand under his, the delicacy of her bones. 'You know, I think I've told you more of my secrets in one day than I've ever told anyone else. That makes you a very dangerous woman, Dr Gray.'

'Me?'

'You,' he confirmed. Was it his imagination, or was the space between them shrinking? He couldn't see, wasn't aware of anything but Anna, the touch of her hand in his, those luminous eyes fixed so intensely on his. She'd dropped the scarf once they'd got aboard, her shoulders now almost bare except for the merest sliver of red silk, the dress caressing her like a second skin, swaying with every movement, emphasising the curve of her waist, the length of her legs, the swell of her breasts. He swallowed. 'It's most unfair,' he said hoarsely.

'Are you scared?'

The space had definitely shrunk down to just her, moon-bright under the midnight sky.

'Scared?'

'I am,' she whispered. 'Scared that I won't live with myself if I kiss you. More scared that I won't live with myself if I don't.'

'Anna.' He couldn't believe he was about to say this, that he wasn't tasting her, touching her right now. 'I don't do relationships. I might not be the party-going playboy the world thinks I am, but I'm a strictly no-strings man. Save your kisses for someone who deserves them.'

'Leo, relax. I'm not asking for an engagement ring. I'm not even asking for a date. I just want to be someone different for one night. No to-do lists, no plans.' She bit her lip, her cheeks flushed. 'I mean, obviously there's a few things we'd need to think about. Ground rules, contraception…'

'I thought,' Leo said slowly, trying to rein in the blood thundering around his body, to silence the voice in his head yelling at him to just kiss her already, 'you were talking about a kiss…'

The flush heightened. 'As a universally agreed starting-off point, but I'd be willing to see where it led. It's never too early to talk about contraception. We're both adults, aren't we?'

Dios mio. Did she have any idea what she was saying? Leo tried desperately to recall all the reasons he needed to stay away, but they had slipped beyond his reach. 'Anna.' It was a question and an entreaty all bound up in her name.

'I know what I'm doing. Do you want me, Leo?'

'I don't think there's a man alive who wouldn't want you tonight, Anna.'

'Then stop over-thinking. That's my role.'

Leo stood, fighting for control. He'd promised himself that Anna was safe with him—he hadn't expected her to be so upfront, so unafraid. 'You're sure?'

Her fingers curled around his as she nodded, and then his mouth was finally on hers, sweet, a little uncertain as she stood rigid for the first second until, with a small gasp, she yielded against him, her body pliant, moulding into his as the kiss intensified. Freed by her response, Leo crushed Anna closer, one hand sliding through her thick wavy hair, the other slipping around her waist. It was as if she was made to kiss him, every inch of her fitting him exactly, the softness of her breasts against his chest, her leg winding around his as she pressed ever closer.

He'd never been so stirred by a simple kiss, never been brought down by the merest touch, never been so undone by a woman's response. Leo didn't have a home, but somehow he knew that kissing Anna was the closest he would get. In a dim recess of his mind he knew that he needed to put a stop to this now, that he needed to walk away. But it was too late. He was lost.

She tasted like the sea breeze on a summer's night, like a citrus grove, like the best vintage wine, heading straight to his brain until Leo was consumed by her. His hands moved to her shoulders, caressing the silk of her bare flesh until he found those thin, tiny straps and pushed them down, over her shoulders. He wanted no barriers between them, nothing but flesh and touch, kisses and need, and, judging by the way Anna was impatiently working his buttons, she felt the same way. 'Got it,' she murmured against his mouth as she finally managed the last button, pushing his shirt off his shoulders with a ruthless abandon he could only admire.

Pausing, Leo caught her wrists as they moved with exquisite torture down his chest, his abdomen, towards his waistband. 'Anna, is this really what you want?'

She was panting as she pulled her wrists free. 'You said yourself I'm dangerous, Leo. If I was you I'd stop talking and help me get this dress off.'

And he could only oblige.

CHAPTER EIGHT

'MORNING, SLEEPYHEAD.'

Leo sounded disgustingly chirpy as Anna walked into the gallery. How did he manage that when she knew, to the second, just how little sleep he had had?

'Your English is very good. How do you know so much slang?' she said as she headed straight to the coffee machine, trying not to touch her swollen mouth, to ignore the faint soreness between her thighs, feeling as if both were lit up in neon, signalling exactly what she had got up to last night.

'English nannies, only the best for the son of the Conde de Olvares. I was brought up to have tea and supper, and to spend far too much time going on afternoon walks.'

'Poor Little Boy Fauntleroy,' Anna hadn't been entirely sure how to greet Leo, but now she was right next to him it seemed silly not to kiss his cheek, a kiss that all too easily slid to his mouth. 'Morning,' she added breathlessly.

'You look good in my shirts,' Leo said, looking at her with an undisguised approval, which heated Anna more than the coffee.

'You see, that's because I do this radical thing where I button shirts up,' she said, trying not to stare too hard at Leo's only half-covered chest and remember just how every part of that chest had tasted. 'How long have you been up?'

'An hour or so. We're only about twenty minutes away now,' he said and Anna instantly sobered up. The island, jobs, responsibilities, real life. She didn't regret for a second her boldness of the night before; she just wasn't sure how to act here in the morning after. It wasn't as if she had much practice. At least this time she had been sensible enough to talk about protection early—to control the spontaneity, to put sensible limits on the recklessness. 'Look, Leo, I'm not the kind of girl who usually has one-night stands,' she said, needing to keep some kind of control over the situation.

'Me neither,' he said to her surprise. 'I'm more of a "let's see where this goes until one of us gets bored" kind of guy.'

Anna narrowed her eyes. 'And do you usually get bored first? Quickly?'

'*Sí.*' She was sure he had practised that boyish grin in front of the mirror; it was far too disarming. 'Always. But then I have never had an opponent as dangerous as you before.'

'So what do we do, just pretend last night didn't happen?'

'Now that,' he said softly, eyes locked on hers, 'would be a shame. I suggest we try it my way. Have fun until one of us gets bored.'

'Such a smooth talker,' Anna said, but her heart was racing at the prospect of three more weeks with Leo. Three weeks with a man who challenged her, laughed at her, made her laugh at herself. It was probably exactly what she needed. Time out of her usual life, new experiences, new perspectives. 'But there is some logic in what you say, looked at objectively, I mean.'

'There is?'

'Well, we are kind of stuck with each other.'

'True.' The gleam in his dark eyes made her heart beat faster. She swallowed, aiming for cool and collected.

'Besides, I suppose last night wasn't too bad.'

'Ah,' he murmured. 'The English gift of understatement.'

The gleam intensified and her knees buckled at the suggestion in them. Not too bad wasn't just an understatement; it verged on slander.

'And everyone needs a hobby.'

'Anna.' He drew out the syllables of her name in the way guaranteed to make her putty in his hands. 'You are a very intelligent woman. I'm sure we can find many interesting ways to pass the time. Maybe...' his smile was piratical '...you should write them all down. I'd hate for us to miss anything out.'

Anna had been expecting, if not bunting, her mother to be waiting for her, eager for details. The year before Sancia left she would wait for Anna to get in from her dates with Ed, her painfully serious if very sweet sixth-form boyfriend. Sancia was desperate to be a cool, modern mother, to talk birth control and share confidences. Anna's refusal to disclose anything—not that there had been anything to disclose—had obviously disappointed her. At times Anna had been tempted to make up some torrid details just to make her mother happy.

Of course, when she'd needed her mother, when Sebastian had walked away and broken her heart, when her life was such a mess she couldn't see any way to make it right, her mother had already left for La Isla Marina and Anna had realised just how alone she was, that her pain was hers alone. Her father was so emotionally remote, and she'd wanted to spare Rosa the burden of growing up too soon, a burden she knew all too well. In some ways she didn't think she would ever forgive Sancia for not being there.

To her surprise the jetty was empty, no casually hovering figure awaited her return and when she walked back to the villa she saw no one other than Maria.

It was still early, the air refreshing, but with a sultry tinge that suggested a scorching day ahead. At least the paint would dry quickly. Anna tried not to grimace at the thought of all the work still ahead of her. She'd had an afternoon and evening playing hooky; that would have to be enough for now.

The back of the villa opened out into a beautiful stone courtyard, hung about with trellises, plants and huge tubs of bright flowers, the view to the shore uninterrupted. The courtyard was home to the island's more informal restaurant and breakfast was also served *al-fresco* on the wrought-iron little tables and chairs. The handful of staff, Anna, Leo and her mother had fallen into the habit of congregating there first thing for freshly fried *churros*, served with rich, melted chocolate, fresh fruit and coffee. Anna swung round the side of the villa heading for the unmistakeable smell of the sweet fried dough only to skid to a halt. One of the tables was occupied by a man who definitely hadn't been there yesterday. Around the same age as Anna, he was pale with dark hair and, she couldn't help noticing, incredibly sexy.

Not as sexy as Leo, of course. Anna didn't have that same instinctive pull that had gravitated her towards Leo the day they met; she noted it more in an objective way. His attractiveness was part of him, effortless, something to admire like a painting or a song. Sancia would be beside herself, Anna thought, grinning, two gorgeous young men to chat up.

Nodding a greeting at the unknown man—although

she couldn't help noting that he seemed awfully familiar—Anna looked around for her mother, blinking, then blinking again. Was she seeing things? 'Dad? What are you doing here?'

Was that really her father? Wearing shorts of all things, sitting at a table, *churros* in front of him, a coffee in hand, as if he had no cares or responsibilities in the world? And why was her mother sitting next to him, an excited warm smile on her face, one hand proprietorially on his arm? Had she actually sailed back into a different reality, one where her parents had not only never separated, but were actually happy?

'Your father arrived last night. He was worried about me. Isn't that sweet?'

Anna stared at her mother, trying to process her words through her admittedly tired brain. 'I didn't know you guys even talked,' she said lamely.

'I was worried when you abandoned your classes and work,' her father said. 'When your mother told me how much she has to do, I thought I'd offer my help.' Her parents shared an oddly conspiratorial look and unease whispered through Anna. What weren't they telling her?

'Oh.' So many conflicting replies flitted through Anna's mind she had no idea where to start. 'What use will you be? We need someone practical,' warred with, 'How have you not noticed how lost I am? Why do you never try and help *me*?' In the end she settled for, 'I just did you an online shop. I'd better see if I can cancel it.'

Her father gave no indication of having heard and, not for the first time, Anna couldn't help wondering if Rosa was right. If Anna should just let him try and look after himself; he wasn't just a grown man, he was a highly intelligent man, more than capable of remembering to take his pills and buy his own food. Probably. Anna narrowed her eyes. 'Hang on, didn't you have an appointment two days ago? What did the specialist say?' How could she have forgotten? She always accompanied her father, if only to make sure he actually obeyed the doctor's strictures.

The shifty look on her father's face told her everything she needed to know. 'She told you to rest, didn't she?' That was why he was here, not because he wanted to help, or had noticed that Anna was struggling, but to add to the workload.

'She said a change of scene might be helpful, that I could do with some sun and fresh air,' he admitted.

'Now, *querida*, don't nag your father.' Sancia stood up and her hand brushed the back of Anna's father's neck. 'We should just be glad that he's here, that Rosa will be here in less than a week and the whole family will be together. It's all too *maravilloso!*'

'Oh, yes, completely wonderful.' Was it too late for Anna to return to the boat and to instruct Leo to sail away anywhere but here and not come back? 'And who is your companion, Dad?'

'Hmm?' Professor Gray looked around as if a companion might have materialised on the spot beside him.

'Right there,' Anna whispered fiercely. 'Eating breakfast.'

'Oh, I never saw him before yesterday. We got the boat over together. He's staying here.'

'What?' Anna turned to her mother, eyebrows raised so high she could feel the strain in her forehead. 'I didn't think we had anyone booked in. How long is he staying?'

'Jude? Just a few weeks.' Sancia waved her hand as if to indicate that time didn't matter. 'He knows we're not fully open yet, but that's what he wants. Peace and quiet and some inspiring scenery.'

'A few weeks? But Valentina's wedding is in just three

weeks. He can't be here for that. She has reserved the whole island, remember?' Why was it Anna's responsibility to point this out? Years had passed, but nothing had changed.

'I know all this, *querida*. You really do worry too much. I've been running La Isla Marina for several years now. I do know how to sort out bookings. Jude is in Bungalow Five, that has been painted and according to your list didn't need any further work. If he is still here during the wedding then I'm sure Valentina will be happy for such a handsome boy to be part of the festivities.'

Anna rubbed her forehead, pretty sure that the ache in her temples had very little to do with lack of sleep and an awful lot to do with her mother's whimsical management style. 'But we haven't got in the new bed linen or towels or any of the extras to dress the bungalows up yet.'

'Anna, people have been holidaying here for many years, many of them come year after year, and they are all very happy with the simple look of the bungalows. The beds are comfortable, the sheets are clean—it's the views and the sport they come for, not scented candles.'

'This wedding is different, you know that. Every guest spends their life taking pictures and posting them online.' But Anna was a little mollified by her mother's words. If the man had chosen to take his holidays in a semi-closed resort then he would just have to take them as they were, ladders, paintbrushes and all. She smiled over at him as he stood and nodded politely in the family's direction, before ambling out of the courtyard, probably in search of that peace and quiet. He did look awfully familiar. What had her mother called him? Jude? Recognition teased her brain, but Anna still couldn't place him.

Rubbing her forehead again, Anna tried to push her parents out of her mind. She wasn't going to micromanage her father's health or take on her mother's responsibilities, not this time. Better to think about last night, to dwell on every second of the most wonderful night she had ever had—and to remember that there were more to come.

Best of all she already knew how this ended. There would be no unwelcome surprises, no heart broken, just a mutual parting of the ways. She could wave her pirate off into the sunset and resume her normal life with no regrets. Maybe she should see if Leo could help with her headache. He was bound to have some inventive cure up his sleeve, or at least a foolproof way of taking her mind off it.

'Your father is actually really handy with a paintbrush.' Leo leaned close to Anna as he spoke, enjoying the way she quivered as he touched her. Her hand crept into his as she leaned into him. Although he had no intention of analysing why, these moments were the highlight of Leo's day, the moments when they paused in their labours and simply gravitated towards each other. Luckily it was a small island, easy for Leo to track Anna down with minimal effort. Today she'd been helping her dad. Leo couldn't help noticing how reversed their roles seemed, Anna the patient parent with a particularly forgetful child. But he also saw the deep-rooted affection between them.

The same affection was evident between Anna and Sancia, despite Anna's issues with her mother. The last few days had been like living in the middle of a family—a quirky family, a family with problems, but a family with heart. Leo couldn't help wondering what it would be like to have parents he could tease, parents he could laugh with. Parents who loved him.

'Who would have thought it? I've never seen him do anything even remotely practical before. I didn't know he had it in him. What's more,' she added, 'I know it's only been a few days, but he looks a lot better than he has done for a long time, more relaxed, pink rather than that awful grey face I'm so used to seeing. I know how he feels. Despite all the cleaning and painting it's actually pretty peaceful here.'

'Enjoy every moment because it all changes tomorrow.' Leo wasn't looking forward to the influx of people due onto the island over the next couple of days, even though it would mean his own workload would be considerably lessened. The seasonal staff were all due and tomorrow the professional joiner, plumber and builders arrived to do a week's intensive work sorting out any jobs that had been beyond Leo, Anna and the groundsman. Not that their own workload would lessen too much, as Anna kept reminding him: the barmen would need help getting the three bars back up to scratch, the lifeguard would need a hand painting the boats and kayaks—and all fifty-two bungalows would need a post-repair intensive clean and to be dressed up in media-filter-friendly luxury. Every item ticked off on one of Anna's lists just seemed to generate another three. It seemed impossible that they would ever be done in time.

Leo had fully expected to be bored by now, to find an excuse to slope off for a few days' recuperation, but the combination of work and Anna kept him on the island. It wasn't all work either, he reflected as he ran his hand over her denim-clad hip. One of the tennis courts was in perfect condition, the sea was warming up nicely and the island's surfboards, windsurfs and pedal boats were all completely seaworthy. And of course there was Anna… Leo's throat dried as she pushed back against him, in a way he was sure she knew full well was calculated to drive him mad. Their agreement was working out very well. He wasn't at all ready to cut his losses, not nearly.

It would all feel so very different tomorrow. He now realised what an idyll the last two weeks had been, and how much he had needed it. Time out from his life, purpose.

'I can't believe that they start arriving so soon.' Anna's melancholy tone showed she shared his thoughts about the incoming invasion. 'We need them all, goodness knows, but I like it as we are. And Mama is expecting Rosa any day now.'

'You're not looking forward to seeing her? I know you're not close, but with your parents getting on so well...'

'Getting on suspiciously well, don't you think? They're always whispering in corners and I have no idea where Dad is sleeping, thank goodness. There are things no child needs to be privy to. And no, I don't see Rosa and I falling on each other's necks. I'm actually dreading it,' Anna confessed. 'She always brings out the worst in me. I get all defensive and prickly. I don't want you to see that side of me.'

'Then let's not be here when she gets here,' Leo suggested. 'You've left enough instructions for everyone to know what needs doing, and your father is more than capable of issuing out tools and work lists. I need to go to Barcelona to finalise the menu and instructions with the restaurant there. Come with me.'

'I can't just go off to Barcelona when there's so much to be done.' But she sounded tempted.

'Sure you can. In fact you should. The food is going to be absolutely key to the success of the wedding.'

She stilled under his embrace. 'It is, isn't it? You're right. When do we go?'

'Right now?'

'Now?'

'Look how well it turned out last time you decided to be spontaneous,' Leo said and she tapped his hand.

'The jury's still out on that one, thank you very much. How do you want to get there? Sail?'

'If only, but it would take us a few days. One day I think we should set off for a long sail with no distractions, but this is not that day. No, we shall fly. Can you be ready in a couple of hours? Oh, and, Anna? Bring something dressy. We'll hit the town tonight.'

CHAPTER NINE

COMING HOME WAS always bittersweet. On one hand Leo loved Barcelona, the city where he had first tasted freedom, where he had started his business, where he had got to know Valentina. On the other it was irredeemably tainted by his upbringing at the old *castillo* just a few miles out of the city environs. Even though Leo maintained an apartment in one of the modernist buildings that characterised the ancient, proud city, he rarely stayed there.

Truth was his life was so contained he could manage on his boat or in a hotel with little difficulty. All he needed was his laptop and a few changes of clothes; his music was digitalised, his books likewise. His living spaces were a stark contrast to the antique-filled *castillo*, all of which were strictly for looking at, not touching—including many of the toys.

Anna's initial enthusiasm to see his 'inner sanctum' as she termed it visibly dimmed when she set foot inside the huge apartment with its tiled floors and arched roof. Although she was clearly charmed by the many quirky modernist touches, by the huge terrace, the view out over the city and the leafy inner courtyard, she was much less enamoured of his sparse furnishings. 'This could be the most gorgeous apartment in the world,' she said after completing her tour. 'The bathroom is so perfect I want to move in and never leave, and as for the views…utterly incredible. But I've seen chain hotel rooms with more personality.'

'What can I say? I missed interior design week at school,' Leo tried to joke, passing her a freshly made gin and tonic and doing his best to steer her out to the terrace where the view more than made up for any deficiencies in the décor.

'It's just I don't see *you* in here.'

That could be because there was nothing of him to put into the apartment. Sometimes Leo thought that he and the old building had a lot in common—illustrious pedigrees housing something hollow.

Luckily it was easy to distract Anna with a tour of the city and she was obviously enchanted by the parks, by the wonderful array of Gaudí buildings topped off with the still not finished Sagrada Família, and by the tapas served with their drinks in the small, local bars. 'Don't eat too many,' he warned her as she tucked into the small bowl of spicy *patatas bravas*. 'We've got an entire wedding menu to sample yet.'

Her hand stilled, hovering in mid-air over the small fried potatoes, topped with a spicy tomato sauce. 'I love tapas,' she said dreamily.

'Keep that thought in your head,' Leo advised her. 'There are a lot of dishes to sample. You might never want to eat them again when we finish.'

But Anna was shaking her head. 'Never going to happen.'

She was right. Despite the magnitude of the task before them she didn't seem daunted. The restaurant occupied the bottom floor of one of Gaudí's distinctive curvy buildings and Anna and Leo were seated in the private dining room, a cave-like alcove with undulating walls and a co-lourful mosaic on the ceiling. The room could seat up to twelve people, but it didn't feel too big for two, not when the table was set with a huge variety of bowls and plates, each with a card propped up against it with the name of the dish written neatly on.

'Right.' Leo handed Anna a pen and a menu. 'Tick the ones you like best. Be sparing with your samplings though. This is just the first round.'

'You're going to have to wheel me out of here, or maybe roll me out.' But she didn't sound at all worried by the task ahead. 'This is my type of research. Why didn't I decide to write about the history of food in Barcelona rather than boring old queens? I'm sure I'd be much further along with the book-from-hell than I am now.'

Leo waited until she had filled her plate with a selection of stuffed olives, marinated anchovies and meatballs before taking his seat and pouring her a glass of wine. 'You don't seem very enthused by your current work,' he commented. When he had first met Anna he might have poked fun at her job, but secretly he'd been impressed. She had a real passion, something she was an expert in. Academia would never make her the kind of money that speculation and investment made Leo, but she was far richer in all the ways that mattered.

Yet all her enthusiasm seemed reserved for her older work. Every time Anna mentioned her new book, her forehead creased, a pinch of worry visible at the bridge of her nose, some self-deprecating comment ready.

'I am,' she said quickly. 'It's just a lot of pressure, that's all. We need to publish all the time, to build our reputations, to seal the university's reputation. And of course what we publish has to be really innovative and groundbreaking.'

'Like a feminist reinterpretation proving the sanity of Joanna the Mad?'

There it was, the enthusiasm missing from any conversations about her current book. Anna's eyes were immediately alight, the meatball on the end of her fork in danger of falling as she gesticulated widely. 'Poor Joanna, she had a really hard life. Every man in her life betrayed her, you know, her father, husband, brother, son. Then she was sent to a convent for the rest of her life. She was probably a little unhinged by all that, as any of us would be. That book was considered groundbreaking, although some people,' she added darkly, 'don't think it counts as research. They don't think that anything that's shelved in popular history and actually sells more than three copies can be academic enough to count. Other people think I'm all hype...'

'Hype?'

'I was only twenty-six when it came out, and the publishers went for this really moody black and white author photo, all bare shoulders and loose hair, playing on my Spanish heritage. It was a little controversial amongst my peers. When I got invited onto TV and radio to do interviews, and to book festivals, there was a lot of nasty talk. That I traded on Dad's reputation—which, despite his inability to remember to take his own medicine, is stellar— that I used my looks to get ahead. That I was a one-book wonder.'

'They were jealous.'

'Yes, but there is just enough truth in the accusations to sting. The photo probably *was* a little too sexy, and my name certainly didn't hold me back. Truth was I liked the photo, liked the image they created. That Anna looks fearless, so sure of herself. I just wish she was real.'

Leo had never heard her sound quite so self-doubting before. All he wanted to do was show Anna that she was wrong, that she was more than the success of one book. He swallowed, hand tightening on his fork. This overpowering need to comfort, to help, was uncharted territory, terrifying in its vastness. He fought to sound light, almost uninterested. 'Does it matter that much? If you don't write another groundbreaking book. After all, most of us don't even manage to write one.'

'Does it matter?' She stared at him, eyes huge with astonishment. 'Of course it matters. My reputation, my career, they are all I have. If I'm not an eminent historian then who am I? What have I achieved? What was it all for?'

Leo waited until the first courses had been cleared away and an array of seafood arranged before them—crispy, delicate fried calamari, prawns glistening with garlic and olive oil, sweet clams served with artichokes, and salt cod fritters, the whole thing served with a delicious selection of salads, rice and fresh bread. It all looked incredible, but his appetite had gone, chased away by the tumult in his mind. Why did he care so much about how Anna felt? They were just keeping each other company, turning what could be a dull few weeks into something more entertaining. Moreover, they were totally chalk and cheese. She was fun to be with in the short term—the very short term—but that organised, note-taking, sensible nature would drive him mad before too long.

His lifestyle might be a charade, but he was still used to pleasing no one but himself, his own needs, desires and whims paramount. Maybe it was selfish, but at least this way he could do no damage. He took a sip of wine and searched for a safe topic of conversation. 'What's the new book about?'

Anna didn't answer at once, busy staring at a huge prawn with fascinated wonder. She closed her eyes as she bit into it. 'Ohmigod, that is absolutely amazing. Tick this dish, several times.' She took another bite, swallowing slowly, eyes still closed.

'Do you want me to give you and the *gambas* some privacy?'

'Yes please, all I need is some music, candlelight and a plate of these bad boys.' She speared another prawn with a flourish. 'So, my new book is also about Spanish queens, not consorts, but rulers. It seemed to make sense, you know, after Joanna did so well. Unluckily for me the Spanish haven't been too keen on female monarchs, so I only have Isabella I of Ferdinand and Isabella fame, and then a mere three hundred years later another Isabella, Isabella II as she is originally known. They shared more than a name. They both had to struggle to be recognised as rulers in their own right; they lived in times of great uncertainty and change. But all I have is a series of anecdotes, a lot of dates. Nothing more than a plain biography. I can't see my way through to something new.' She looked at the prawns speculatively, before pushing the plate away.

'Then pick another topic.'

'It's not that easy. My editor, my agent, my college have all approved this. I've dedicated the last two years to research. I have an advance, a contract...'

Leo sat back. 'What drew you to Joanna in the first place?'

Anna paused, her eyes soft in the dim light. 'My grandmother used to tell me bedtime stories about her. The traditional ones, you know, the "carting her husband's corpse all over the country" one. I wanted to find out more.'

'So it was the story that attracted you, not finding something groundbreaking?'

Anna paused, laying her fork on the plate in front of her. 'I guess.'

'There you are. Look for the story first and then look for the facts. Find a story which sings to you.'

'I'm a historian, not a storyteller.' But she looked thoughtful.

Leo picked up his glass of wine. 'Can't you be both?'

Leo's words continued to echo around Anna's mind as they finished the seafood and moved on to meat and vegetables before finishing with a final course of sweet dishes and a platter of cheese and fruit. She'd always known who she was and what she wanted to be. But why? Because her father noticed her when she got top marks in history, liked her following in his footsteps?

No. Or at least, she conceded, not wholly. She had always loved the stories behind the facts, loved bringing the long-dead back to life with her words. Maybe Leo was right. Maybe she was looking in the wrong place at the wrong stories. All she knew was that she couldn't put off calling her agent any longer. Her book needed a profound rethink, maybe even her entire career. Just coming to that conclusion was like losing a huge burden she hadn't even known she carried, she was so used to the weight.

She smiled at Leo, but he didn't notice, sunk in thought, barely touching the incredible food, his shoulders a little slumped. Was his mood due to being back in Barcelona? He'd mentioned his parents lived just outside the city.

What would it be like to despise your parents? Anna freely admitted that hers exasperated her, frequently disappointed her, but she loved them, recognising that their flaws were a crucial part of them. She even envied them, wished she could have a little of her mother's insouciance, her father's certainty. Leo didn't mention his parents often but when he did anger was never far from the surface—and buried underneath the desolation of someone lost.

Maybe that was why his apartment was so impersonal, why he preferred to spend his time on his boat, never anchored down. He didn't know where he belonged.

The urge to fix him was almost overwhelming. But Anna had tried fixing people in the past. Tried to fix her father's health, her mother's unhappiness, her sister. She'd failed all three. The truth was she couldn't fix anyone who didn't want to be fixed. And that kind of involvement wasn't part of their deal anyway. She had to remember what their friendship was, remember what happened last time she'd started projecting feelings onto another human being, seeing truths that simply weren't there.

'Thank you,' she said, sliding, with some difficulty, off the bench. 'How many dishes did we tick?'

'You ticked nearly all of them,' Leo said with a ghost of a smile. 'Luckily I was a little more restrained.'

'They were all delicious. Do you know, now the decorations have arrived, now we've discussed the practicalities with the kitchen here, now the rest of the staff are due to arrive, I'm beginning to think maybe, just maybe, we can pull this wedding off after all.'

'I always knew you could do it.' The intensity in his dark eyes weakened her knees. 'The minute I met you, when you marched up to me, notebook in hand, wanting my name, rank and badge number. I almost saluted.'

'You did not. You were arrogant and supercilious, and downright annoying.' And sexy as hell, but she wasn't going to admit that.

'All I wanted to do was unbutton you. In every possible way,' Leo said hoarsely and Anna had to grip the table to prevent her legs from buckling, heat spreading from the pit of her stomach, scorching a path along every nerve.

She licked her lips, desperate for moisture in her suddenly dry mouth. 'How's that going for you?'

'I'd say not too bad. There's some ways to go…'

'Really?' She arched a brow, aiming for cool and casual, but all too aware of her heart hammering away.

'I'm just waiting till I have your full attention, *mi cariño.*'

The promise in his voice turned her insides molten, her grip tightening on the table. 'You have it.' Was that really her voice? So husky, so full of desire? How could Leo seduce her so completely with nothing more than words and eyes full of promise? Her whole body was pulsing with desire, swaying towards his as if he was her true north, her true south, her everything.

'No, part of you is still wondering what's going on on La Isla Marina, another part of you is thinking about your book, and I'm pretty sure you are still obsessing over those prawns. My task will be completed when you can think of nothing but me. Nothing but me and what I'm going to do to you.'

The noise that escaped her was purely involuntary, a mix between a gasp of surprise and a moan of pure need. The smug smile that spread across his face showed he'd achieved his goal. No way, she vowed, would Leo di Marquez get to have everything his own way. Summoning all her strength, Anna stepped forward, her eyes focussed directly on his.

'That's nothing compared to what I'm going to do to you before this is through,' she said. 'Consider this a challenge. And, Leo? Remember how much I like to win.'

Surprise flared in his eyes, wiping the slightly smug expression off his face. Surprise swiftly replaced by lust so pure it was as if the whole room seemed to smoulder with its heat. 'Challenge accepted.' He stepped back. 'I think we should go back to the apartment, An-na.' His voice lingered lovingly over her name. 'Don't you?'

He didn't take her hand as they exited the room, barely looked at her as they bid farewell to the manager, Leo promising to email the final menu choices through the next day. He didn't need to. They were connected by a rope of desire, binding them together, ensuring she was aware of his every move, every word, moving with him like the steps of an ancient dance. This wasn't what she'd signed up for. This went beyond a good time, crossing a barrier she knew neither of them were ready to cross and yet they had no choice. It felt foreordained and she welcomed her fate, however it fell.

The formalities over, they walked slowly, in perfect time towards the door. There was no need to hurry. They might as well savour every single second of this night. Somehow Anna already knew it would be the kind of night she would relive in her dreams, the kind of night she would look back on as on old lady and know that she had lived.

'Leo?' A sharp, surprised voice cut through the atmosphere that surrounded them and Leo halted, a curiously blank expression immediately descending onto his face. The deep breath he took was so quick Anna might have thought she'd imagined it, if she hadn't seen his hands curl into quick, tight fists before relaxing again.

He turned, slowly, and looked at the corner table where a well-heeled couple sat. 'Madre, Padre. What a surprise.' He'd switched to Spanish, she realised. Her own was fluent enough that the transition wasn't too much of a problem, although he immediately reverted to English. 'I'd like you to meet Dr Anna Gray. Anna, these are my parents, the Conde and Condessa de Olvares.'

Should she curtsey? It almost seemed as if the haughty woman, her hair in the kind of sleek chignon Anna could never manage, her outfit a marvel of devastating understatement and wealth, expected it. Anna reined in the urge, smiling instead. *'Encantado,'* she said with a nod instead. 'Leo has told me so much about you. It's a pleasure to meet you.'

There was no answering smile, just a swift, sweeping look, which quite clearly summed Anna up, found her wanting and dismissed her. All in less than three seconds. Impressive.

'How long are you back?' The Conde had at least switched to English, even if he didn't acknowledge Anna outright, his cold attention focussed on his son.

'One night only.'

'How lucky we ran into you, then.'

'Lucky indeed.'

'Please, join us for a coffee and a drink.' His sharp gaze switched to Anna. 'If it's agreeable to your companion? We so rarely get the pleasure of our only son's company.'

'Coffee will be lovely,' Anna said as the silence stretched on.

Leo didn't react in any way and she couldn't tell if her acceptance annoyed him or not. He stood, unmoving, a beat too long for comfort and then inclined his head. 'How can I turn down such a civil invitation?'

'You've been very quiet, Leo,' his mother said once their plates had been removed and coffee and brandy supplied to the whole table. Anna rarely drank spirits, but she clutched her glass gladly, aware she needed some help to get her through the next few minutes. 'I don't think I've seen your picture in the paper for months.'

'How are you making ends meet? Don't tell me you're looking for a job? More than time you settled down, in every way.' The Conde swirled his brandy as he spoke.

'I've been doing this and that. In fact, right now I'm working with my hands. That's how I met Anna. She's employed me to do some painting and decorating, haven't you, Dr Gray?'

'I wouldn't say employed.'

'Bed and board only. Still, I'm grateful.' Leo lounged elegantly, his own glass in one hand, turning it into the light.

'Leo's very kindly helping out.' Anna didn't know why she was trying to explain, why she was once again taking up the mantle of peacemaker, a mantle she had worn through most of her childhood. 'I'd be lost without him.' The last bit was true enough.

'Señor di Marquez, you're still here?' At this opportune moment the manager bustled up, phone in hand. 'One more thing I need to confirm. Señorita Valentina has asked for a small discount in return for the attention generated by her forthcoming wedding. We don't usually court such publicity, and as you know we have little need to advertise, but as Señorita Valentina is a well-loved daughter of the city and we wish her all the best for her wedding, we are happy to acquiesce on this occasion. I hope the *señorita* will be happy with the final quote.'

Anna couldn't help watching the Conde and his wife's faces throughout the long-winded speech. Their usual expressions of bored condescension betrayed into a horrified surprise. The manager had no sooner backed away when the Conde rounded on his son.

'You're involved in that girl's wedding?'

'That girl is my sister.'

'Valentina's holding the wedding on the island my mother owns,' Anna interjected, not knowing whether she was making things better or worse, just knowing she needed to defuse the rapidly building tension. 'It's going to be very traditional, but very beautiful, I think.'

'And she would like you there.' Leo gazed steadily at his father. '*Dios* knows why, but she does.' And then, when the Conde failed to respond, 'She has asked me to accompany her down the aisle.'

'What?' The exclamation came from the Condessa and, glancing over, Anna saw her knuckles were white.

'She wants a male member of her family to walk with her.'

'This nonsense has gone on long enough!' Anna stared at the Conde. She had never seen such palpable yet controlled anger. The Conde hadn't raised his voice, no one looking over would guess that this was anything but a cordial discussion, yet the air throbbed with his rage. Was this how Leo had been raised? Under this measured anger?

'You are a disgrace to the family name, to your mother and to me. Your life is frivolous and meaningless, your friends worthless and your insistence on flaunting your relationship with that girl an embarrassment. It stops now, Leo. You will return to the *castillo* with your mother and I, get a proper job, start shouldering some of your responsibilities and marry someone suitable. Do you understand me?'

'And if I don't?'

Anna couldn't believe the nonchalance in Leo's voice, didn't believe his father's outburst hadn't affected him, no matter how easily he lounged, how amused his smile.

'I'll disinherit you. You'll get the title, but nothing else.'

Leo didn't bat as much as an eyelash. 'Such a shame the inheritance laws preclude you from doing that. But don't worry, Padre, I don't need a penny of your money.'

'I find that hard to believe. Oh, you may scrape by, sponging off your friends and gambling, but don't tell me you're not short of money, a wastrel like you.'

That was it. She'd heard enough. 'I have only known Leo a few weeks, but I knew within a week that he was so much more than he portrayed himself to be. And I am ashamed, *ashamed*,' she repeated, proud that her voice wasn't wobbling, 'that it took me that long. I was prejudiced, I admit. But I should have seen within the first hour just what a good, loyal man he is. Just how principled he is. How hardworking. It took me a week. But you? You have had a lifetime and you still don't see him at all. Shame on you.' Anna pushed her still-undrunk brandy away and got to her feet. 'Thank you for the drink. Leo? I believe we have unfinished business to conclude. I wish I could say it was nice meeting you both, but I was brought up to be honest.'

And without looking to see if her words had any effect, without looking to see if Leo was following her, Anna swept out of the restaurant.

CHAPTER TEN

LEO KNEW THAT when he looked back on this moment he'd regret not taking the time to enjoy the identical shocked expressions on his parents' faces. But all he could do was get to his feet, nod to them politely and follow Anna out of the restaurant, thoughts and feelings whirling so fast he was amazed he could walk in a straight line.

No one had ever spoken about him with such passion, such tenderness, such understanding before. Leo was used to disdain, used to amusement, used to contempt. Understanding was beyond him and, he suspected, when he processed how he felt about Anna's intervention he would be undone—which was why he wasn't going to process it just now.

Anna stood waiting outside the restaurant, her expression anxious. 'I'm sorry. I shouldn't have…'

Tilting her chin, Leo stared into her eyes for one long second, drinking in the still-simmering anger mixed with contrition before bending his head to hers and kissing her. Hard. It wasn't the seductive kiss he had planned, not a teasing romantic gesture. It was passion, gratitude, need, lust all mixed together in one intoxicating mixture—and she kissed him back equally fiercely, her hands snaking into his hair, pulling him closer and closer until they were almost fused into one.

'Let's go back,' he breathed finally, reluctant to break the contact, and Anna nodded. But he couldn't let her go, not yet, his arm around her shoulders holding her close. Leo didn't usually hold hands with anyone, but tonight he wanted everyone to know the blue-eyed girl in the demure black dress belonged with him. To him.

'I didn't mean to say anything,' Anna said after a moment, her arm tight around his waist. 'I hope I didn't make things worse.'

He laughed at that, low and deep. 'I don't think they could be made worse.'

Anna didn't join in the laughter. 'Why do they speak to you like that?'

'You heard them, my life is frivolous, a waste. They see what they want to see. They catch a few photos, a few headlines and to them, that's the truth. I embarrass them, and if there is one thing my parents can't take it's public humiliation.'

'You do know that you're not the person they think you are, don't you? I meant every word I said in there.'

Did he? He tried to tell himself that, but somehow he never quite managed to convince himself. The intensity in Anna's voice went some way to soothing the pain in his soul. He tightened his grip on her waist. 'They've known me for thirty years. You've only known me for a couple of weeks…'

'I look for the truth behind the story, remember?' She stopped and turned towards him, her hands cupping his face as she looked into his eyes. 'You need to let them go, Leo. You need to move past them. Find a way to be happy.'

'If only it was that easy.'

'It's not, but I believe in you. Believe in yourself.'

Finally they reached his apartment building and Leo guided Anna up the three flights of stairs, their steps in perfect unison, hands clasped tight. Half an hour ago he had been anticipating this moment, this arrival back at the apartment, how charged the atmosphere would be between them, how ready they would be. He had planned to kick the door shut behind them, turn to her, capture her mouth, explore her body right there in his apartment hallway, couldn't imagine having the patience to carry her to the sofa, let alone the bedroom, passion thrumming so hard it was barely contained. The passion was still there, but the meeting with his parents had dimmed it somewhat, and he didn't want their eventual coming together to be tainted by anger and spite.

The doors to the terrace were still ajar and wordlessly they walked over, stepping through the doors, and leaned on the balustrade, staring out at the city below.

'I grew up thinking that my parents' approval was within my grasp,' Leo said eventually. 'I tried to be the perfect son, to not demand anything, to be no trouble, to make them proud, and yet they always went away again, I always messed up. Disappointed them. I broke something, didn't know my lessons well enough, wasn't still enough during Mass, talked at the theatre, didn't answer their friends' questions quickly enough. Whatever I did, no matter how hard I tried, I never lived up to their high expectations. I used to get sick when I knew they were due home, with excitement, with tension, promising myself this time would be different, that I wouldn't fail. But I always did.'

'It's not failing to be a child, to act like a child. You must see that now.'

'The thing is, Anna, it wasn't just them. Everyone went, everyone left, every maid, every nanny. No matter how small I tried to make myself, how good, it never worked.' He swallowed, memories bitter in his throat. 'I couldn't understand it. Then, when I was maybe about ten, after Valentina's mother had left, I heard my nanny talking to her friend. About me.'

Anna leaned in close, her warmth a balm to his soul. 'What did she say?'

Leo couldn't look at Anna, couldn't bear to see pity on her face. Or worse, agreement. 'That I was no trouble, but I was too quiet to be true. It was creepy, she said. I wasn't natural. There was something missing.' He took a deep breath, the memory of that night so clear it was as if he were still there, standing frozen by the door, the night falling, too stunned to move. That was the night his heart had broken, the night he had realised what was wrong with him. Realised why no one stayed, why no one loved him.

There was something missing.

'That's a terrible thing to say.'

'She was right though, wasn't she? There had to be a reason, Anna. Most parents don't ignore their only child. Most parents don't dislike their son, spend as much time away from him as possible. It had to be me. I knew it, as soon as she spoke. Knew it was all my fault.'

'No.' Her voice was sharp as she turned to him. 'I wish I could tell you that every parent loves their child, that all childhoods are happy, but it isn't true, Leo. There's no test for new parents, no training. And some people are simply lousy parents. Through active cruelty, or neglect, or because they're too selfish to put their children first. Your parents made sure you were fed, looked after, educated, but they still neglected you. And that's on them, will always be on them, will never be on you. And shame on that nanny for not seeing it, for not helping you.'

What was that lump in his throat? That swelling in his chest? Leo swallowed, willing the surge of emotion away, not sure he could cope with the consequences if he allowed it to overwhelm him. All he could do was speak, carry on unburdening his soul to the bright-eyed girl next to him—although he knew he would regret his confidences by the time dawn lit the terrace. 'By the time I was eighteen I told myself I'd given up, but I hadn't, not really. I still wanted their approval. To be worth more than the continuation of a name, a title. But then I found out about Valentina... I'd spent all those years wanting to be someone my parents approved of, were proud of. Overnight I wanted the opposite. I wanted to shame them the way they shamed me.'

'Hence the pretence? Hiding behind your reputation?'

He nodded. 'Ironically my father showed me the way. He took me to a club on my eighteenth birthday. Men only, apart from the hostesses, men of breeding like us, men with money, power. The kind of man he expected me to be. Fortunes changed overnight at this club, men gambled, bought sex, took drugs, but, crucially, it was exclusive and therefore respectable. That was the first time he made it clear—all vices could be indulged as long as they were hidden, as long as publicly I followed the rules. I knew the only way to hurt him was to drag his precious name through the dirt as often, as wildly as I could.'

Anna moved a little closer, her arm brushing his, burning, branding him. 'How long did the novelty last?'

'Just a few weeks,' Leo confessed. 'I was bored within days. I had also promised Assumptia I would help them out so I got a job, on a building site. The son of the Conde de Olvares nothing but a common labourer by day, masquerading as a playboy by night. Luckily I made a small sum of money that very first time I went to a casino. I invested some of my profits in shares, and some in a business a friend was setting up. Both prospered and so I reinvested the profits and then again and again until I could give up the job and set up my own business.' It sounded so easy, as if it were luck, not maths and formulae, and business plans and gut instinct. 'There have been losses of course, failure, but generally I have been lucky.'

'And they still have no idea? What you really do?'

'None,' Leo confirmed. 'Truth is I stopped partying almost straight away, but the seeds were sown. I show my face at just enough parties, the odd famous casino and they believe the headlines and gossip columns. They think I live from one spin of the roulette wheel to the next when the reality is I could probably buy the family fortune twice over.'

'What about your trust fund?'

'There is no trust fund. Not until I settle down, run the family estates and marry. My parents keep hoping to starve me into submission. They've been waiting a long time. They'll wait a lot longer. I have no intention of giving them anything they want. I won't be taking over the family estates, I won't marry, I will never father an heir.' It wasn't just a case of thwarting his parents; what did Leo know of marriage, of love, of fatherhood? He saw Valentina, so fearless in her love for Todd, and envied her, even as he shrank from the trust she handed her fiancé along with her heart. Leo only trusted himself. It was safer that way.

'Don't let them take that away from you as well, Leo. They took your childhood. You should own the rest of your life. Be happy. Isn't that the best punishment for them? Your happiness?'

'I can't, Anna. I can't risk it. I don't know what happiness is—and I would never pass that legacy on to a child.'

'Oh, Leo.' Anna reached up, drew a finger down his cheek. He closed his eyes at the touch, so light and yet so very right. 'It must get very lonely being you.'

Leo paused, her words softly spoken and yet hitting him right in the heart. He didn't like to admit any weakness and loneliness was the biggest weakness of all. He was thirty, rich by any calculation, he could walk into any city in Europe and bump into an acquaintance, be invited to a party, surround himself with people. But, Valentina aside, who truly knew him?

And did Valentina even know him? He cast himself as her protector. Showed her no weakness. She needed that from him. Somehow Anna saw through all his defences, saw deep within him. That wasn't in their agreement, wasn't something he wanted and yet here they were.

No, these thoughts weren't for tonight. Tonight was the cityscape glittering below, the stars glittering overhead. Tonight was Anna, so close to him he could feel her breathing. He turned, his hands on her bare arms, and felt her quiver, the movement shuddering through him. 'Now then, Dr Gray,' he said softly and with satisfaction he watched her pupils flare, heard her breath hitch. 'We were in the middle of something when my parents so rudely interrupted us. Let's remind ourselves where we were, shall we?' Leo bent to kiss the hollow of her throat and as he tasted the soft saltiness of her skin the rest fell away. There was only her and for tonight there was nowhere else he would rather be.

It was late when Anna finally stretched and opened her eyes. The sun slatted in through the blinds, casting a warmth on the bed, the air already ripe with heat, but the space next to her was cool. Leo must have got up some time before. She sat up, pulling the sheet with her, wrapping it around herself, aware of her nakedness, here in this strange apartment in this strange city.

She shivered as memories of their lovemaking returned. The sex had been good—really good—from the start. Leo was a skilled and generous lover and the chemistry between them added an extra heat to their activities. But last night had been intense, almost dark at times, as if Leo had been trying to lose himself in her. As if she had been trying to heal him. But she knew that she couldn't heal him, the damage was too deep, too ingrained. Leo would have to try and heal himself. Only she was pretty sure he never would.

Why did the thought of that hurt her so much? Was it because the easy days and easier nights they had promised themselves had twisted into something darker? Or was it because she was beginning to forget her promise to herself not to fall for him?

'Buenos dias.'

'Morning.' She pulled the sheet higher, suddenly, unaccountably shy, brightening when she saw the paper cup in Leo's hand. 'Oh, coffee.'

'And pastries,' Leo confirmed, tossing a paper bag onto the bed. 'And these...' Another bag followed the pastries. Anna grabbed it, her cheeks heating up when she saw the contents. 'I'd hate for us to run out. And the rate we're using them...'

'It's important to be safe,' Anna said with as much dignity as she could muster, putting the bag filled with packets of condoms back onto the bed.

'I expect nothing less from you. I'm surprised you haven't given me a list of ways to make sure we use them correctly.' She ducked her face at his teasing tone. 'Hey, what did I say?'

'Nothing. You're right. I do want to be safe.' She knew all too well the catastrophic consequences of taking a chance with contraception, how easily a spontaneous moment could ruin a life. She had no intention of repeating the same mistake, no matter how romantic the setting, how seductive the man. She looked up and forced a smile, but he wasn't fooled.

'What's wrong?'

'Nothing. I'm fine.' She grabbed the bag of pastries. 'These look amazing, thank you.'

Leo's eyes darkened. 'You don't have to tell me, Anna, but neither do you have to pretend. Don't lie. Not to me. I thought we were honest with each other.'

He was right. She didn't have to tell him anything. But last night he had bared his soul to her. Didn't she owe him a secret in return? A balancing of the scales between them? 'I wasn't always careful,' she said eventually. 'I believed someone when he said it would be fine. Although I was old enough to know better. I just wanted to be the kind of person who took a risk. A different Anna.' She couldn't look at him, all her focus on the paper bag, the pastry crumbling under her nervous touch.

'There's nothing wrong with this Anna. You don't need to change a thing. And if he thought so then he didn't deserve you.'

The controlled anger in his voice steadied her, and for the first time in a long while Anna wanted to confide in someone. Maybe then she could finally heal. Finally move on. And this man who had shared so much with her, who she would never see again once their time was over, was here, asking for her trust. She swallowed, putting the pastries to one side and finally looking up to meet his eyes. 'His name was Sebastian. You remind me of him in some ways. He was rich, entitled, arrogant, supremely confident. I thought he was Mr Darcy and every Georgette Heyer rake and Lord Peter Wimsey all rolled into one.'

'Is he the man you fell in love with?'

He'd remembered. 'The man I was so infatuated with,' she corrected him. 'I'd spent my whole life being careful, Leo. Sensible. Things were great when I was little. Dad found Mama's scattiness endearing, and Mama loved the way he looked after her. But at some point they stopped being amused by each other. Rosa was still small, so I stepped into the role of peacemaker. I tried to make sure things were organised at home so Dad wouldn't get cross, to cover up for Mama. I was so used to doing it that when she left I just carried on. I didn't even leave home when I started university, still looking after Rosa, not that she wanted me to, or thanked me for it. And then I met Sebastian.' Her voice faltered.

'Your knight in shining armour?'

'He swept me off my feet. Truth was he was unreliable, could behave appallingly, but I thought I could reform him. I might have been book-smart, but when it came to men I was a naïve fool. For three months I followed him around like a lapdog, did everything he wanted, never allowed myself to question how he treated me, how he acted with other people. Told myself I was living a more glamorous, exciting life, even though at heart I think his arrogant disdain for people not as privileged as him made me uncomfortable. Then I forgot to be careful...'

'You got pregnant?'

'I got pregnant.' She stared at the sheet, remembering how terrified she had been, and yet so hopeful. Even excited. 'I stupidly thought it might all be fine. That he loved me and that we could make a life together, that he would welcome me into his gilded world. Truth was he was already bored. I just didn't want to see it. He walked away. A month later I miscarried.' She took a deep breath as the memory of the darkness swirled through her mind. 'I went to pieces. Blamed myself for it all. It took me a long time to get my life back, to forgive myself. I swore I would never be that foolish, that gullible, that reckless ever again.'

She took a deep breath. Last night she had wanted Leo to face some unpalatable truths; now it was time to face some of her own. 'That time left its scars. I nearly lost my place at university, so I dug in, hid behind my studies. Became a scholar because I didn't know who else to be, didn't trust myself, trust my judgement. Told myself Dad needed me to stay at home. Truth is I needed him just as much. More.'

Leo sat down next to her, taking her hand in his. 'You're so brave, Anna, a survivor.'

'I'm not.' Was that really what he saw?

'Brave, dangerous, compassionate. I'm so sorry that happened to you. That he happened to you.'

'It was a long time ago.' But she had been living with the consequences ever since, hiding away, behind her book, her title, her father's illness. Who would she be if Sebastian hadn't tainted her life?

Anna had no idea, but maybe it was time she found out.

CHAPTER ELEVEN

ANNA HEADED TOWARDS the villa, unable to believe it was time for the final checklist. Thanks to all the outside help and some truly Herculean efforts by the staff, every bungalow was ready. Fresh paint gleamed white in the late spring sun, the shutters and doors a fresh green contrast. The outside areas were all weeded, the greenery trimmed back to lush from jungle-like, and new cushions and umbrellas had been added to the cleaned and repaired outside tables. Inside looked just as good, every bungalow scrubbed surgically clean and dressed with new gossamer-thin white curtains, fresh white cotton bedding, crockery and artfully arranged mirrors and flower arrangements, keeping the look as simple as possible while adding the luxurious feel Valentina and her guests would expect from their living quarters. More importantly every toilet flushed, every shower worked perfectly and there wasn't a single dripping tap anywhere on the island.

Although the guests could order food at any of the island's three bars or two restaurants at any time of the day or night, Anna had also stocked the tiny kitchenettes with coffee machines and a range of exclusive herbal teas. Work was still continuing on the public areas, the last few boats and kayaks needed to be checked, the third tennis court to be resurfaced and Anna was still waiting for the cushions and throws she had ordered for the biggest bar, but the beach bars were rethatched and restocked, the breakfast courtyard was ready for their guests' arrival, and the pagoda and central courtyard where the wedding and reception were to be held were nearly ready, fairy lights already strung through the surrounding trees.

They'd done a good job, she and Leo. Anna smiled just at the thought of his name, even though she knew she was heading for a fall. Attraction had turned to lust to trust and now she was already in far, far too deep, but she couldn't, wouldn't get out now even if someone threw her a lifeline.

She leaned against the doorframe to steady herself. God help her she was falling in love with Leo di Marquez. It was beyond foolish and she had no doubt it would end in her heartbreak, but some things were just meant to be and for once she wasn't going to borrow trouble, she was going to enjoy every minute she had with Leo and let the future take care of itself.

But one thing she knew was absolute: Leo mustn't know. She wasn't his salvation, this wannabe bad boy's redemption. They had made an agreement and she was going to stick to it. The only person to break her heart this time would be Anna herself. She had sworn that nobody else would ever have that power over her again.

'You're looking all doe-eyed. Does Señor Tall, Dark and Handsome have anything to do with that?' A sardonic voice from the office made Anna stop and grit her teeth. They'd arrived back on La Isla Marina to find Rosa had breezed onto the island while they had gone and, true to form, was already right at home—Anna had seen her sister in a couple of intense conversations with their mysterious guest from which she'd emerged with flushed cheeks and sparkling eyes. It never took her sister much time to stake out her territory.

Not, Anna reflected, that it had taken too much time for *her* to get close to Leo. Not that her sister needed to know that. She smiled as sweetly as she could. 'None of your business.'

Rosa appeared at the office door and Anna's teeth ground down even harder. How did her sister manage to look so effortlessly cool no matter what she was wearing? Her thick dark hair might look like Anna's to the untrained eye, but Anna had never managed to get the hang of braids, let alone the thick fishtail plait Rosa had confined her glossy tresses in, strands hanging just so, as if it had been designed by some boho hairdressing genius. She was casual in jeans and a T-shirt, but still managed to look chic enough to walk into the ritziest party, Anna's own shorts and T-shirt suddenly looking dowdy by comparison.

'How's the paperwork? Sorted out the wedding guests into rooms yet?'

It was Rosa's turn to set her jaw. 'I don't understand why you're being so stubborn. You love spreadsheets and solving problems. I love being outside and fixing things. We should just swap...'

'If you'd hadn't arrived over two weeks late then you could have had your pick of jobs. As it was I had to get on and do what needed doing most. You keep going with the wedding planning and helping Mama with the office. It'll do you good to stretch yourself.' Back then Anna would have jumped at the chance to swap responsibilities with Rosa, now she wanted to see the repairs and decorating through, proud of what she and Leo had achieved.

'Of course you dropped everything and rushed straight here.' The scorn in her sister's voice hit Anna right in the gut, just where it always did.

'It's a good thing I did. Look at what your *stand back*

*and let them make their own mistake*s plan has achieved. This place was chaos…'

'Chaos until St Anna turned up and fixed it all?'

'Yes. Actually.' Besides, Rosa had turned up eventually; she must have felt a little guilty to have put her plans to one side.

'Dragging Dad with you? Couldn't trust him on his own for a month?'

'Dad turned up on his own.' Anna folded her arms. 'You do know he nearly died?' she said almost conversationally.

'What?' The smug look disappeared off Rosa's face. 'Nonsense, he looks fine.'

'He looks fine now. He looks fine because he has no stress outside work, his meals are prepared, he takes his pills, he gets reminded to take regular walks. Not because I'm a saint, not because I'm a martyr, but because someone has to do it— and no.' Anna raised her hand as Rosa tried to interrupt. 'Don't tell me he's an adult, I know that. I also know that when he wants to be he's the most organised man alive. But his health isn't a priority, work is. And he would forget, just like Mama forgot to take care of the basics here. So what do I do, Rosa? Swan off to Harvard and let him get ill and Mama sink? Is that your answer?' The offer for a semester at the prestigious university had recently been renewed, not that Anna had allowed herself to consider it, worry over her book, over her father making the move an impossibility.

'I don't understand.' Rosa paled—as much as she could with a truly enviable tan. 'I was ten before I realised other families didn't get given their own individual holiday itineraries and checklists two weeks before they went on holiday, and most families didn't stock check their cupboards monthly. How can he not remember to take his pills?'

'Things changed after Mama left.' Anna blew a frustrated breath. 'You were still at home then, Rosa. I know how self-centred you are, but surely even you noticed?' But then again maybe she hadn't; after all, hadn't Anna stepped in to run the household, juggling A-levels with housework and trying—trying and failing—to motivate her sister.

'I know you got bossier and more self-righteous than ever. I know you refused to move into halls during term time, staying at home to prove what a good daughter you were. At least until you started seeing that guy, then suddenly we saw another side of Anna...until he dumped you, that is. Then you got even more boring than before.'

Anna's chest tightened at the smirk on her sister's face. Would things be different if she had confided in Rosa then? Confided in anyone? When had she decided it was safer keeping the rest of the human race at arm's length, caring more about the lives of people long dead than those who walked next to her? Until the last couple of weeks, that was. Somehow she had found herself allowing Leo further in than anyone ever before. At least he was upfront with her. He always walked away. He didn't want marriage, children, any emotional ties. That was fine with her. She wasn't equipped for any of that either. How could she be when she had barely lived?

'It's always lovely catching up with you, Rosa, but I have a lot to do. Good luck with those spreadsheets.' Anna turned, refusing to let the memories Rosa had stirred taint the sweet island air, the short time she had left with Leo. It would be nice if she and Rosa could spend ten minutes together without reverting to the squabbling children they had once been. It would be nice to have a sister, not an adversary.

'I'm just worried about you, Anna.' Rosa's voice stopped her in her tracks. 'Leo di Marquez isn't the kind of man you're used to...'

'I'm more than capable of handling Leo, thank you,' but even as she said it, Anna knew she wasn't being completely honest. Not with her sister and certainly not with herself.

'I just don't want a repeat of the Sebastian situation. I mean, he was an utter idiot, and Leo doesn't appear to be quite so arrogant, or as sleazy, but he broke you, Anna. I don't want that to happen again.'

Anna swallowed as the tears rose up, hot and ready. She had sworn never to cry over Sebastian again, but it was harder not to cry for the girl she had been, the naïve little idiot who believed in love and happy ever afters. 'Sebastian didn't break me, Rosa. I did that all by myself.'

It all looked so beautiful it almost hurt Anna to walk across the island, knowing all this was just temporary, that her life would soon revert to libraries and lecture halls. Over the last few weeks Anna had been probably the happiest she had ever been and that happiness wasn't just because of Leo. It was because the island felt like home. She loved putting it back together, planning for the future, knowing that everything she did made a difference. The thought of leaving physically hurt her.

But, if the island was home, then what was Oxford? Her old goals made no sense any more; she didn't care about being a youthful success or how many papers she could author. She wanted something real. Leo was right: she needed to find her story, not try and create one.

Not much of Valentina's lavish deposit was left, but the advance publicity had done wonders for bookings and it looked as if this would be the best summer for several years. Anna just hoped Sancia would be able to cope. At some point she would need to broach the island's future with her mother, but not till after the wedding, not while she was still this Anna, the Anna who went sailing out into the sea every evening once work finished, the Anna who had actually swum nude the other evening, the Anna who fell asleep wrapped around a shirtless pirate.

'Hey…' Speaking of shirtless pirates.

'Hey, yourself,' Anna said, unable to stop the smile spreading over her face as she drank Leo in. His tan had intensified over the last few weeks, his muscles gleaming under his golden olive skin, his hair grown out so it flopped over his forehead, adding a boyishness to his good looks, a boyishness that in no way diminished his aura of danger. 'Forgot your shirt again?'

'I know you like me half naked.'

Anna's knees weakened at the gleam in his eyes. She did prefer him like this, sweaty from the sun and manual labour, so different from the polished, fashionable playboy the world knew. 'You do add a certain aesthetic appeal to the island.'

Leo's grin broadened. 'You look remarkably empty-armed. I thought you went searching for the Final Checklist Clipboard.' Anna could hear the capitals in his teasing tones. Maybe she had put a lot of emphasis on just how important the checklist was.

'The clipboard? Oh, yes. That. You know, I think we can just as easily do the last walk through in the morning.'

'Oh?' Leo arched an eyebrow. 'You've changed your tune. I thought it was imperative we did that this afternoon or the whole timetable would go up in flames. What did you have in mind for the rest of the afternoon instead?'

'We—ell. I was thinking we could be spontaneous…'

'Spontaneous?'

'You, me, the boat.'

'Oh, that kind of spontaneous, *mi cariño*. Much as I was looking forward to inspecting every single one of the fifty-two bungalows, maybe I could be persuaded.'

Stepping closer, Anna ran a hand down his arm, enjoying the play of muscles under her fingertips, how soft his skin was, hot under her touch. 'Not in public,' she said softly. 'Boat first, persuasion later.'

His eyes darkened, flickering lust heating her through. Anna loved how her words, how her touch could elicit this response, how powerful Leo made her feel. 'Is that a promise, Anna?'

'A definite promise—and you know I always keep my word.'

'In that case,' Leo said, taking her hand in his, 'let's go. Right now.'

Just a few more days... Anna intended to make the most of every single moment.

Leo knew that Valentina's arrival would change things, he just hadn't realised how much, nor that he would find himself wishing for those halcyon days when it was just Anna and himself most of the time. Even though the main body of guests were still to arrive the island felt alive, buzzing, and it was impossible now to wander around and not see a living soul. Instead the maids bustled around, keeping the bungalows and public areas pristine, the groundsmen worked full time taming the greenery and ensuring the pools and courts were safe and inviting, and Leo couldn't sit down without a smiling server offering him a drink and snack. It was all very impressive, but not a patch on the informal friendliness of the island out of season.

But his happiness wasn't the point and his sister was delighted with everything. For a self-made millionairess who was marrying into old money Valentina had relatively simple tastes, and the lush green island ringed with beaches, the charming, white bungalows and the friendly staff captured her heart immediately. Especially when she

had shyly outed herself to Sancia as Assumptia's daughter
and been warmly embraced and welcomed home.

'Oh, Leo, it's perfect, even more perfect than I remembered. No wonder you couldn't tear yourself away. Or was
it a certain hotel manager who kept you here?' she asked
slyly. It hadn't taken her more than a few moments of
watching Leo and Anna together to ascertain their situation, even though they had both been completely discreet,
not a single lingering glance or touch in front of the guests.

'I just wanted to make sure everything was the way you
want it,' Leo said, refusing to be drawn on his relationship
with Anna, no matter how his sister teased him. 'How did
I do?' He leaned back in his chair, smiling at his sister, her
happiness so palpable she glowed.

Valentina had the biggest bungalow of all and Anna had
worked hard to make sure it looked as bridal as possible,
with sweet-smelling flowers in every room, and plenty of
space for the bridal party to gather. Despite her intention to
have a traditional Spanish wedding, Valentina had agreed
to her husband's requests for a few American touches such
as including bridesmaids and groomsmen and reception
speeches. In return Todd had agreed to be escorted down
the aisle by his mother and to an early evening ceremony,
which would be followed by a party lasting well into the
next morning.

'I can't wait for Todd to get here,' Valentina said for
the twentieth time that day as she wandered around the
elegant sitting room. 'This is beautiful, but it's far too big
for one person.'

'Your mother would be really proud of you,' Leo said,
guessing that his younger sister was thinking of her
mother. At times like this Assumptia was never far from
either of their thoughts. It was only four years since she
had died; sometimes it felt like yesterday.

Valentina smiled. She didn't look like a media queen tonight, her thick mane of hair pulled back and her heart-shaped face free of any make-up. 'I hope so. She would love Todd, wouldn't she?'

'If you love Todd, she would love Todd,' Leo reassured her.

'I just want to be married. To be a wife and have a husband. To be part of a real family at last. Not that you're not an amazing brother, Leo, but I want to belong to someone, for someone to belong to me.'

Leo stared down at his bottle of beer. Valentina and he had almost instinctively decided to keep their relationship secret. She had wanted no connection to the father who rejected her, and Leo hadn't wanted the world knowing about the one good thing in his life. Valentina's knack for spin and brand management had ensured that any childhood stories she told began after Leo had introduced stability into their lives—tales of surfing and beach volleyball, fashion and fun. Her father, she claimed, had died before she was born. Her request for Leo to be part of her wedding would invite speculation, interest he had shied away from. But Anna was right. He needed to find his own way to be happy.

'Val, I want to walk you down the aisle. If you still want me to.' He wanted to be at her side on such an important occasion. Valentina's capacity for love, for forgiveness, for optimism, were the things he loved most about her. The things he envied most about her. His little sister was far braver than he was.

Valentina looked up, her eyes sparkling with tears. 'Leo? Really? Oh, thank you. It's the only wish I had left unfulfilled.' She leaned across and into him, as fragile as a bird, her bones clearly visible at her throat, the delicate blades at her back. She'd barely touched any food all day,

Leo remembered, turned down wine for water; she hadn't even been tempted by the home-made lemon sorbet the cook had asked them to sample.

'I hope you start eating after this wedding,' he scolded her.

'Me too.' She squeezed his hand. 'It's just I have no appetite at all at the moment. Leo, don't tell anyone, it's too early, but I'm pregnant. You're going to be an uncle!'

CHAPTER TWELVE

'PREGNANT?' ANNA HAD curled up on the sundeck like a lazy kitten, basking in the sun, and at Leo's news she turned onto her back and stretched out. 'Is she happy?' For the first time in a long time Anna could hear the word without a pang of regret. Maybe she was finally moving forward.

'Ecstatic. Of course, this explains why she wouldn't postpone the wedding after the fire. For all her attitude and fashion sense there's a strong sense of traditionalist in Valentina. She will want to be married when the baby is born, for it to have the father she was denied.'

'Does she feel up to a big wedding if she isn't eating?'

'She says so. She says that she was dizzy for a couple of weeks, that she has been really nauseous and doesn't want to eat much, but she feels fine. She's really looking forward to the wedding, even if she will be toasting her husband with fruit juice.'

'And you'll be an uncle,' Anna teased. 'How do you feel about that? Don't worry,' she said as his face clouded. 'Every child needs an irresponsible uncle who buys them too much ice cream and lets them stay up far too late. I'm sure you will fill that role perfectly.'

'Is that my fate?'

'Afraid so.'

Anna looked up at the darkening sky, that same melancholy that had been chasing her all week shivering through her. Lucky Valentina, she thought. Marriage to a guy she adored, a baby on the way. She didn't seem to be worrying about her future, to be caught in a place she wasn't sure she wanted to be. Anna had been expecting a self-obsessed starlet demanding perfection from every tiny detail, creating drama for drama's sake, instead she had found Leo's sister to be a warm, intelligent young woman far more focussed on the marriage she was entering into than the wedding itself.

Pregnant. Anna's hand drifted down to cover her own belly, memories of the brief weeks she too had carried life within her floating back. She had thought she was in love, yes, but she hadn't been secure. She'd been torn apart with fear over her future, how she'd manage work and a baby, worried about what Sebastian would say—and then once he knew she had had to deal with the crushing reality that she was on her own. That the man she thought she was in love with was just a fantasy, the reality someone completely and devastatingly different.

But within all that despair and pain there had also been excitement, a sense of wonder that somehow she was creating something real and tangible, not just words on a page. That she would have someone on her side, someone to really love, someone to love her unconditionally. Until that morning she had woken up writhing in pain and she'd known, long before the doctor had confirmed that the baby was no more.

She had never told anyone about her miscarriage until last week, until she found herself so unexpectedly confiding in Leo. Sebastian hadn't asked what happened, and she had spent the next two years avoiding anywhere she might see him. Her father had been oblivious, Rosa too wrapped up in her own affairs, Sancia gone. No one noticed that Anna was slowly unravelling in a toxic mixture of guilt, self-loathing and heartbreak. Guilt thanks to that momentary glimmer of relief that the decision of whether or not to have the baby, to raise the baby, had been taken from her, that her life could continue on its foreordained path with no deviation. Self-loathing at her folly, at how easily she had been fooled, how easily she had fallen. Heartbreak that the man she loved didn't exist. She'd skipped lectures and tutorials for Sebastian, handed essays in late and badly researched. She still couldn't believe just how close she'd been to being 'sent down', expelled temporarily, or even expelled altogether. It had taken months to put herself back together, and to this day she knew that part of the girl she had been was still left back there in that damp Oxford winter.

It must be so different to be pregnant and to know that the baby was wanted by both parents, to celebrate every milestone, to have someone to sympathise with aching breasts, nausea, the extreme tiredness…

Hang on a second. Anna sat bolt upright, ice-cold fear flooding her. *She was a week late.* She was never late…

'Anna, have you got a minute?'

A minute? She didn't even have a second. She needed to get on a boat, get over to the mainland and drive to the nearest pharmacy straight away. 'Not now.'

Rosa took no notice. 'It's Jude. Valentina has asked him to the wedding and he wants me to be his plus one. Will that be a problem, I can still oversee the seating charts and things, and you'll be there with Leo anyway…'

What on earth was Rosa chattering on about? Anna pushed her hair out of her eyes. 'Leo hasn't mentioned me accompanying him to the wedding,' she said slowly.

'We're not, I mean, it's not serious.' Oh, God, Leo…no, she couldn't even think about Leo until she had taken the test and knew either way.

'Oh, come on, I've seen the way he looks at you.'

'It's not serious,' she repeated, Leo's words echoing through her. He didn't want anything permanent, had no interest in children. She would be on her own, just as she had been all those years ago.

'If you say so. So you don't mind? It turns out Jude knows Valentina quite well. He used to go out with one of the bridesmaids—the redhead who complained that the bed is too hard and that we haven't provided the right range of herbal teas—and it ended, well, horrifically. Long story short, she was involved with the book, so it's a pride thing to accept the invite and bring a date, I guess. But what with the way we left things, I think…'

Anna held up her hand to silence her sister and slowly counted to ten. 'Rosa, fill me in later. I have to go over to the mainland and I hate sailing over in the dark. Yes, go to the wedding. It's fine.' At any other point she would have wanted to know why Jude had asked Rosa to be his plus one, why Rosa was acting as if they were old friends, not new acquaintances, what book had sent Jude into such a spin and why Jude looked so damn familiar, but right now she didn't care. Let Valentina invite who she wanted to the wedding with just three days' notice. They'd deal.

'What's so urgent?' Rosa's voice sharpened. 'Are you okay? You're very pale. Do you feel ill?'

'Rosa, don't fuss. I just have to do something.'

'I really think you should wait till morning.' Then, as Anna shook her head, 'In that case I'm coming with you. I'll drive the boat. The way you look you won't be able to get it out of the harbour!'

Her first instinct was to refuse. She wasn't one for

company at the best of times and now, with fear running through her veins, all she wanted was dark, brooding solitude. It wasn't as if she and Rosa were confidantes Anna knew more about some of her students' hopes and dreams than she did about her sister's. But somehow the decision was taken from her, Rosa not waiting for an answer, simply taking the boat key out of Anna's hand and leading the way down to the jetty. Leo's boat was clearly visible, the warning lights gleaming bright. At least he wasn't on there, having been bid to dinner with his sister and bridesmaids; at least Anna wouldn't have to pass him on her stealthy trip to the mainland.

Despite her desire for solitude Anna found herself surprisingly grateful for her sister's company. Rosa seemed to sense that she didn't want to talk and didn't press her for details, concentrating instead on steering the dinghy over the short distance as speedily as possible. She pulled up alongside the jetty on the mainland with a smooth flourish. 'Right, where next? Anna, I'm coming with you. Don't argue.'

Anna opened her mouth to protest and then shut it again. What was the point? Right now, someone else taking charge was blissful. Pulling the key to Sancia's ancient rusty small car from her pocket, she handed it to her sister, barely registering the moment Rosa's hand closed over hers with a reassuring squeeze. 'The town,' she said, her throat sore with suppressed tears. 'The pharmacy. There's one on the retail park this side of town. It's not far.'

The roads were deserted and it didn't take long to clear the small village and head towards the town. Rosa drove with the same careless confidence that characterised her every move, accelerating around every bend like a racing driver, her foot pressing the accelerator right to the floor so the car was almost vibrating as it sped along. Normally

Anna would tell Rosa to slow down, to insist she stop the car and let Anna take over, but this evening she was glad of the speed. The sooner she got her hands on that test, the better.

Think logically, she told herself. She was probably overreacting. Definitely overreacting. Just because she had only ever been late once before didn't mean there wasn't a perfectly reasonable explanation this time. Look at all the stress she had been under with her parents, Rosa, the wedding and her book. It made complete sense that her body would react in some way. It was only three weeks since she and Leo had sailed away to the mainland, three weeks since she had worn that little silk slip of a dress, three weeks since he had peeled it off her. It was far too soon for her to think she was pregnant. So what if, now she thought of it, her breasts were a little sore? So just the whiff of wine turned her stomach? There were one hundred explanations, none of which meant she was pregnant. And they had been careful, hadn't they? Of course they had.

They'd been careful, she reassured herself.

She had promised herself that she wouldn't make the same mistake twice, but Anna knew all too well that not every promise could be kept.

Bright, neon lights broke the darkness. They'd arrived. Rosa swung the car into a free space and killed the engine. 'Do you want me to come in with you?'

'No. Thanks.' But now she was here Anna didn't think she could move.

'Anna, let me go.' Rosa had never sounded so gentle, so understanding. 'Do you need me to buy you a pregnancy test? Is that what's happening here?'

She was frozen, unable to form any words, to nod, to do anything but stare straight ahead and wonder how on earth she had managed to get herself into this situation again, how she could have been so stupid again. Did she have some kind of self-destruct button? A bat signal audible only to unsuitable men, instructing them to impregnate her then walk away, leaving her in pieces.

'Leo doesn't want a family.' That wasn't what she had intended to say. 'He'll think I've betrayed him.'

'Anna, honey, it takes two to make a baby. Leo's a grown man. If you are pregnant, he'll understand.'

'No, he won't. He told me from the start, no promises, no commitment. It's bad enough I've fallen in love with him. How could I be so stupid as to get pregnant too? It's like Sebastian all over again, only much, much worse. I only *thought* I loved Sebastian.'

'You were pregnant back then? Why didn't you tell me? Why do you never let anyone help, Anna?' To Anna's surprise Rosa sounded like she was close to tears. 'You don't have to do it all alone. You don't have to be perfect. You can ask for help...'

'Last time I needed your help you walked away.'

Rosa bit her lip. 'Things were complicated then. I'm sorry. But I'm here now and I promise you, you're not alone. Now let me go and get the test for you and then, if you are pregnant, we'll figure out what to do. And if you're not then you and I need to have a long, overdue talk. Deal?'

'Deal.' Anna squeezed her sister's hand tightly then sat back and watched Rosa jog over to the store. When had her little sister got so wise? So strong? At least it looked as if Anna wasn't alone. That was something. It had to be something. Right now it was all she had.

Leo had never been quite so grateful to leave his sister before. She'd been joined by her bridesmaids, all intent on turning their first night on the island into an impromptu hen party. A beautifully choreographed, much photo-

graphed hen party, but one he had rapidly realised was
no place for a red-blooded Spanish male. Especially not
a red-blooded Spanish male who wanted to keep his dignity intact.

Wandering along the track that led to the villa, he realised he had no idea where to find Anna. Usually he
found her almost by instinct, drawn to her wherever she
was, but tonight her whereabouts eluded him. She'd been
happy enough, lying on the sundeck on the boat, and then
she'd gone strangely quiet before disappearing on some
mysterious errand. He hadn't seen her since.

Her absence shouldn't bother him. After all, their idyll
was nearly at an end. In three days' time Valentina would
be married and his time on the island at an end. Time to
sail on, to Nice or Monte Carlo, or maybe around the is-
lands. Time to actually read some of the reports piling up
in his inbox and move some money around. Time to resume his life.

The thought shouldn't feel so hollow.

But it did.

Leo exhaled, willing the negative feelings back into
the box where he usually kept all emotions. What was the
alternative? Anna would be returning to Oxford, burying
herself back in her library, searching for the story to set
her alight, the kernel she could turn into another book.
That was where she belonged, Dr Anna Gray in her but-
toned-up shirt. So different from his Anna, a sheet wound
round her naked body, hair tumbling over her shoulders.

He always got bored with relationships first, that was
what he'd told her—and he had been telling her the truth.
He'd fully expected to be ready to leave her without a single pang of regret—which just showed what an idiot he
really was. Right now all he felt was regret; their time together didn't seem finished.

But his biggest regret was knowing he would do nothing to prolong the relationship. Knowing that he would just let her walk away and not lift a finger to stop her. Knowing he was too scared to try for something real, too scared to let her in, too scared to feel.

He deserved regret.

The courtyard was just ahead, lit by hundreds of small lamps, and as Leo turned towards it he glimpsed a silhouetted figure leaning on the archway, her slim build as familiar as his own reflection. She turned as he neared. 'Hey.'

'Hey yourself.' That leap of his heart, that lightening in his chest, they didn't mean anything other than his libido springing into life. *Keep telling yourself that, di Marquez.* 'You've been elusive this evening.'

'I had an errand to run.' Anna didn't return his smile, her eyes solemn in the lamplight. 'Leo, can we sit? I need to talk to you.'

'Sure, do you want a drink?'

'No, I'm not thirsty. Let's go find somewhere quieter, less busy.' She cast a quick look at the far table where her parents sat with Rosa and Jude, a board game set out on the table. Usually Leo would scoff at so cosy a scene, but tonight he was filled with a desire to walk over, pull up a chair and join in the teasing game, accuse Sancia of cheating with the rest of her family and challenge Professor Gray on every obscure academic word he insisted was within the rules.

It was a good thing their idyll was nearing its end. He was getting soft, weak, reverting to the needy boy he had once been.

Anna led the way through the trimmed-back greenery to the small beach at the furthest end of the island. There was no jetty here, no boats, no bar, the nearest bungalow a five-minute walk away. It had always been her favourite spot, she'd told him once, because it was quiet, facing out towards the sea, only the horizon in sight. It was so dark she had to use a torch to guide them there, but once they were on the beach the moon shone down and the tiny cove was illuminated by a thousand stars. Leo inhaled sharply, the beauty of the night cutting straight through the layers of cynicism, of irony, of humour with which he protected himself.

'There's no easy way of saying this.' Anna didn't make a move to sit down on the wooden loungers, invitingly laid out on the soft sand. Instead she stood on the very edge of the beach, her hands twisting together. The moon shone down, transforming her into a naiad of the night.

Foreboding stole into Leo, strong and knowing. Their idyll was over.

'Anna, what's wrong?'

She swallowed, but when she spoke her voice was clear. 'I'm pregnant. I'm sorry, Leo, but it's yours. I'm having your baby.'

CHAPTER THIRTEEN

FOR ONE SECOND, one tiny split second, Leo was aware of nothing but joy. Of hope, of redemption. But before he had a chance to register the feeling reality crashed back, cold and bitter.

What did he, Leo di Marquez, know about being a father? He, an unwanted son, an unworthy brother, untrustworthy lover? What did a man who couldn't commit to a home know about family? A man who knew nothing about love. Nonetheless, he knew his duty. 'Are you sure?'

The moment he spoke, the moment he saw Anna flinch—at his cold words, his cold tone—Leo knew the die was cast. In a way he was relieved; after all, it couldn't be any other way.

'I wouldn't tell you otherwise.' No, she wouldn't want to share fears or worries with him. They weren't a team after all. 'Turns out even I can't be careful enough. I don't know how it happened…' She swallowed, her eyes glistening in the moonlight before she snapped them shut, and when they opened her face was set. Determined. 'Don't worry, Leo. If you don't want to be involved you don't have to be. I'm quite capable of doing this alone. It's not the first time after all.' She looked so sad, standing alone in the moonlight, that Leo had to clench his fists to stop himself from heading over to comfort her. He had no right. He wanted no right. He could do this, but it had to be on his terms.

'I told you, Anna. I don't want a long-term relationship. I don't intend to have children. The family name dies with me.'

'You should have thought of that before. I didn't impregnate myself,' she snapped back and a small part of him applauded her courage, her fire. But he carried on as if she hadn't spoken.

'However, I know what has to be done, what has to be right. We will be married of course. You and the child will be under my protection.' He stood, straight and tall, and willed her to understand. This was all he had. All he was. But it was everything.

She didn't say anything for a long while and all Leo could do was stand and wait, trying to quell the myriad emotions jostling for prominence inside him, trying to shut them all down. Finally Anna sighed, a deep, bone-weary sigh, and wandered over to the nearest lounger, perching on it like a wary bird who knew it might need to escape at any time. 'I can't believe that this has happened again. That despite every precaution...' She paused, visibly fighting for control. When she spoke again, however, her voice was steady. 'I told myself all those years ago that I would never allow myself to be vulnerable again. That I would be focussed and strong. That I would never deviate from the plan, because I knew that way lay heartbreak. And then I met you...'

Silence fell and Leo welcomed it. Let every second excoriate him. He deserved it.

'I knew you were trouble. A poor little rich boy masquerading as a pirate, but I was so bloody sick of doing the right thing, I thought a few weeks out of the rigid life

I allow myself wouldn't hurt, not if I was careful, not if I weighed up every risk and mitigated for it. I'm a fool.'

Every word fell straight onto his heart and left its own scar. How could he contradict her? She had put her faith, her trust in him and he had nothing for her except a tarnished name.

'But, you know what, Leo? I'll be fine this time. I will do everything I can to nourish and carry this baby to term, and if I manage that, then I will love it and raise him or her to have compassion along with confidence. To dare to reach out for what they want, but not to trample others while they do it. And I'll teach them to love. Because that's the greatest gift I can give them. I'm sorry that you weren't given that gift. I'm sorry that you feel it's too late.'

She got to her feet and looked directly at him and Leo shivered at the sadness in her gaze, sadness for him, not because of him, and all the more devastating for that. 'Goodbye, Leo.'

She turned as if to leave. Had she not heard? 'Anna? You don't have to do this alone. I will marry you. I will be a father to your child.'

'Do you love me, Leo?' Her voice was so soft he could barely make out the words above the roar of the waves.

Love? He didn't even know what love was. But he owed her too much to lie. 'Love isn't what's important here...'

She shook her head, dark tendrils caressing the nape of her neck. 'Love is all that matters, Leo. My parents couldn't make it, couldn't overcome all their differences even *with* love. How can we be a family without it? We'll fail before we start. I appreciate the offer, I really do. I know what it has cost you. But you're off the hook, Leo. I'm setting you free.'

And then she was gone and all he could do was stand alone in the moonlight and listen to the waves crash on the shore and wonder why, when Anna had made it so easy for him to walk away, he was rooted to the spot.

It was finally the night before the wedding. Earlier that day they had welcomed Todd, the groom, to the island, along with his family and groomsmen, and hosted a Spanish-style lunch for the entire wedding party. Four courses over several hours followed by much-needed siestas had made for the perfect introduction to the island, and Rosa had planned for beach games and a much more informal supper to be served at the beach later that evening. The informal evening would not only be fun, but crucially it gave the island staff plenty of time to prepare for the next day when another hundred guests were due to arrive and for the wedding ceremony itself, which would begin in the early evening.

Everything looked perfect. Every bungalow was ready, every tree had fairy lights threaded through it, the pagoda and central area were set up for the ceremony and party. Valentina's dress had arrived that day, escorted by a dressmaker who would stay until Valentina was dressed, and the chefs from Barcelona were already set up in the kitchen, working remarkably amicably with the island's own cooks. Valentina seemed delighted, her groom's wealthy parents approving and the bridesmaids—most of them—full of nothing but praise. If they could provide this level of service to the rest of the guests then the island's future would be secure. For now at least.

Four weeks of hard work coming to a climax. And all Anna could feel was limp relief. That was all she could allow herself to feel. Opening up the floodgates would come later, when she allowed herself the indulgence. For now all she could do was look at the unexpected turn her life was taking and do what she did best: plan. Notebooks filled with lists, budgets, ideas.

She hadn't seen Leo alone since two nights ago, keeping herself busy behind the scenes, but she knew he hadn't come to look for her once. He'd caught her eye today, at the lunch, when Anna had come out from the kitchen to check everything was okay. Her gaze had flown straight to him, despite herself; he'd sat with Todd's parents, but it was as if he had sensed her the second she stepped into the courtyard, his eyes instantly finding hers. Nausea hit her, swirling deep, as she did her best to calmly meet his gaze, trying to summon up a polite smile from somewhere. Trying not to read too much into his expression, trying not to tell herself that he looked haggard, as if he hadn't slept. Trying not to tell herself that he looked like a man facing into hell with no idea how he'd got there.

Anna knew she had to speak to him and tell him she understood. That she had met his parents. That she had held him while he slept, heard the muttered groans, enough words to know just how lost he truly was. That she knew he considered himself no more than the playboy he presented himself as, that he didn't believe he was worthy of love. That she loved him nonetheless, but had no intention of allowing him to destroy her life or their child's. But she couldn't bring herself to say the words yet. That she wasn't able to marry him, but he should be in their child's life regardless. That somehow they would make it work.

It was all so different this time round. She'd been so terrified before, unsure of herself, wanting someone to tell her that everything would be all right, desperate for Sebastian to be the man of her dreams, not the cold reality. She had no such illusions where Leo was concerned. He couldn't offer her what she needed and she loved him too much to accept less.

Raising a child alone wouldn't be easy, there were no guarantees, no certainties and all the lists in the world wouldn't change that, but she was strong. She could do this. She had to.

And she had to start by taking control of her life, of her happiness.

Anna took a deep breath and stepped into the large sitting room. 'Mama, Dad, have you got a moment?'

'What is it, *querida*?' Yet again her parents were sitting together. For a couple who had separated a decade ago and barely spoken since they were awfully cosy. If Anna had one brain cell to spare on them she would be consumed with curiosity.

'I am going to make some changes, and I want to talk them over with you. Is now a good time?' She felt a little guilty. They had all been working flat out for days and this hour, while the guests took their siesta, would be the last peace they would know for the next week—but that was why she needed to talk to them now. She couldn't go into the next week without having some idea where she would be at the end of it.

'Of course,' her mother said. Professor Gray didn't say anything, but Anna hadn't really expected him to. He'd never been the curious type where his family were concerned. Sometimes she had been desperate for him to ask, just once, what was wrong.

'Okay, then.' She curled up on the padded window seat next to them. How many times had she sat here, in the tiled private sitting room, the family's only space on the entire island where they could just be themselves? It hadn't changed since she was a child, the same flower pictures on the walls, the same wicker side tables, the same comfy seats, the same stove in the corner for the brief but chilly winter. This was as much her home as the large house in

Oxford—more so. The house belonged to her father's college and when he retired some other professor would move in, no matter that Anna and Rosa's initials were carved into the apple tree trunk in the garden, that Anna had recovered from her heartbreak in the attic bedroom.

'I need to make some changes in my life. I haven't been happy for a long, long time. I see that now. I thought work, success, might change that, but the harder I work, the higher I climb, the less I feel like me. It's as if the more lists I have, the more notes I take, the more control I think I have. But over the last few weeks I've realised I've been so busy chasing other people's stories I've forgotten to look for my own. And I think my story is here, at least, at the moment. Mama, I'd like to stay here, and help you run La Isla Marina. How do you feel about that?' Anna held her breath as identical shocked expressions crossed her parents' faces.

Explanations could come later.

Professor Gray broke the silence first. 'What about your teaching? Your work? The offer from Harvard?' Anna looked keenly at her father. She hadn't realised he knew about the offer. Did he know she'd turned it down before—and why? 'You're doing so well, your book was so well-received, why throw it all away?'

'I stayed in academia, in Oxford, for you, not for me,' Anna admitted, the truth in her words bitter on her tongue. 'After Mama left you were so sad.' She shot a quick look at her mother, and flinched at the raw pain on Sancia's face. 'I just wanted to make you proud. Then I was so worried about you I couldn't bring myself to move out. I know, you're a grown man, you're the parent, Rosa and Mama told me that all the time. I think I just needed to be wanted, wanted to be needed. I like teaching, I like researching, but I'm only twenty-eight. The thought of doing nothing

else for the next forty years fills me with fear, not anticipation. The truth is if I really wanted Harvard nothing
would keep me away.'

'Is this just more of the same, *querida*?' Sancia asked,
her dark eyes fastened on Anna's face. 'You think I need
you to look after me now?'

'I did,' Anna admitted. 'Things were in a bad way here,
and, I admit, I'm a little concerned that you're not cop-
ing.' She searched her mother's face in turn looking for
clues. She should have asked what had happened earlier,
not stormed in and taken over. 'But my original plan was
to talk to you about selling, or bringing in a manager. I
wouldn't even consider moving here if I didn't truly want
to. I'll still write. Not the book I intended to. I'm thinking
about writing about the island, the people who have lived
here, how its fortunes have waxed and waned along with
Spain's, a social history of Spain seen through La Isla Marina. We'll be independent, Mama, have our own tasks.
Our own quarters. But only if you want me...'

Suddenly she was a child again, desperate to know she
mattered, that she was wanted. Sancia's eyes softened. 'Of
course I want you, *querida*. More than you could know.'
Her voice broke on those words, and Anna's father took
her hand. 'I haven't been much of a mother to you recently,
have I? You just seemed so capable, Anna. You were always so much more in control than me. Things were difficult back then and I didn't feel like you needed me any
more. That you could look after your father and Rosa so
much better than I ever did.'

'I'll always need you, Mama.' Anna's voice broke as
she felt the tears thick in her throat, burning her eyes. 'I
needed you then, I need you now. Things were so hard and
you weren't there.'

She'd never make the same mistakes, she vowed as her

mother enfolded her in her arms, and for once Anna allowed her mother to bear her weight, to comfort her. She would always be there for her child, no matter what. Never let pride, or unhappiness or a misunderstanding drive them apart.

Sancia released her and wiped her eyes. 'I would love you to live here with me, to help me run La Isla Marina, *querida*, but only if you're sure this is what you want. Take your time, Anna. Go back to Oxford after the wedding and make sure you're doing what's right for you—and if so, we'll look at turning some of the unused rooms into an apartment for you.' Anna could tell her mother was teeming with unasked questions, about Leo, about what had really brought about this change in direction and she was glad her mother decided not to ask them just yet—although she knew Sancia wouldn't be able to keep silent for long.

In one way her decision had everything to do with Leo, and with the baby she was carrying. The baby she couldn't bring herself to mention to her parents, not just yet, not until after the wedding, until Leo had sailed away. But it went deeper than that. She liked the Anna she was here, even if she had messed up. She liked waking up to the smell of citrus and salt, she liked how every day was different, brought its own challenges and successes. She liked how her organisational skills were honed and used. She belonged here; she always had. It had just taken a couple of wrong turns to get here. And she couldn't imagine anywhere better to raise her baby.

'That sounds sensible.' Anna did her best to keep the surprise from her voice; she wasn't used to hearing sense from her mother. 'But the decision feels right. I won't change my mind.'

Getting to her feet, she leaned over to give both her parents a kiss, ignoring Rosa's quizzical look as she entered the room, a checklist in her hand. How long since they had all been together—and relatively amicably at that? The tension between Rosa and Anna had considerably lessened since the trip to the pharmacy. In fact Rosa had turned into somewhat of a confidante, never judging, always supportive. Maybe they'd never be best friends; they didn't need to be. They were sisters and they had a long-lasting bond no matter how different they were—and Rosa had promised to be an awesome aunt. Anna believed her.

'It all looks very cosy in here. Everything all right?' Rosa asked, looking directly at Anna. She knew of Anna's decision to wait until after the wedding to tell their parents about her pregnancy and was being, for Rosa, incredibly discreet. Probably because she seemed to be spending most of her time with Jude. Anna hadn't quite got to the bottom of what was going on there. All she knew was that they had dated a few years ago and for one reason or another it had fizzled out. They didn't look particularly fizzled right now—in fact the air practically sizzled whenever they were in the same space.

'Everything's good,' Anna said. 'I was just discussing the possibility of staying on the island. After all, it's never been one person's job to run it before.'

Rosa's eyes widened, a hundred questions clearly jostling for attention while she tried—and failed—to choose one. 'But… Oxford… Book… Dad… Here?'

'Quite,' Anna said enigmatically. 'Did you put the volleyball net up, Rosa? Don't worry, I'll go. I could do with some fresh air.' And she slipped out of the room aware her whole family were staring after her. She'd taken the first step towards deciding her future. All she had to do was let Leo know what she had decided. She couldn't avoid him for ever and she had to tell him how she felt. She knew it wouldn't change anything, she knew he had offered her all that he had, but she owed the truth to her baby—and she owed it to herself.

CHAPTER FOURTEEN

THE MID-AFTERNOON SUN was fierce, and Anna envied the guests, all sleeping off their lunch in the cool air-conditioned bungalows. 'Hats,' she muttered. She needed sun hats, a much bigger summer wardrobe if she really was planning to live here. Far fewer sensible pairs of trousers, more shorts. Vest tops and trainers instead of blouses and heels. The more she thought about it, the more sense her decision made on every level. Not least because she was itching to get started on her new book, to excavate all the island's secrets. She hadn't felt this fizz about her work since Joanna had been published. She'd missed it.

The beach games were to be played on the wide seafacing beach on the far side of the island. Cricket, volleyball, boules and beach croquet had all been set up; the rules of at least three of the activities would be a mystery to most of the mainly Spanish and American guests. Anna walked briskly along the path with a new sense of ownership, of purpose. Every hour she put in here was an investment in her future, in her child's future. Hopefully. Her hands curled into fists; she knew all too well not to take anything for granted.

What was surprising her was how optimistic she was about the future. About the choices she was making. Of course she wanted things to be different, wanted Leo involved—*wanted Leo*—but she was strong. She had a family who weren't perfect, but who she now knew would support her, each in their own way.

'*Hola.*'

Anna jumped. She'd been so wrapped in her thoughts she hadn't even sensed Leo, let alone seen him. 'Hi.'

He fell into step beside her and they walked in silence. Funny, even when she had been actively hostile she had had things to say to him, any silences comfortable. Now, when there was so much to discuss, she didn't know where to begin. 'Todd seems nice.' Great, start with inanities.

'He is. He'll look after Valentina. Anna...'

Anna's heart stuttered as he said her name, that slow, languorous drawing out of syllables she loved. Her name, so prosaic, so boring, always sounded exotic when he said it.

'We need to discuss our situation. Marrying me may not be what either of us want, but it's the sensible thing to do. The right thing.'

'Leo...' How she wanted to tell him yes. To marry him, and hope that time would thaw him, that her love would be enough for the both of them. But she was too old and too wise to believe that was true. She couldn't do it to any of them; she had to be strong for all their sakes. 'I can't.'

He nodded, curtly, as if he had expected nothing less. 'In that case then I wanted to tell you that I will be leaving tomorrow. After the wedding.'

'Tomorrow? But the wedding is so late...'

'After the dinner, and the speeches. Before midnight.'

'Like Cinderella,' and she cringed at the startled look he gave her. 'I'm staying,' she blurted out, her throat swelling with the realisation that this really was it. He was leaving. Just as he had always said he would. She wasn't enough for him. The truth was nobody was. 'On the island. I'm going to help Mama run everything and write from here. Look for the story, not the most impressive display of research.'

'You'll need a new notebook.' Leo's smile didn't go anywhere near his eyes.

'Several.'

'Here.' He handed her a card. Anna turned it over, trying to make sense of the type. An email address—not his—a number. 'This is the best way to contact me, through my business manager. If you need anything, get in touch. I'll arrange for a monthly allowance…'

'I don't need your money.' The words came out more harshly than she intended and as he flinched she felt a moment of victory. 'Please. You can still be involved, even if we're not married.'

'I don't know how, Anna. I need some time.'

Anna stopped and turned to him, raising her hand to cup his cheek one last time, closing her eyes as she felt the rasp of his skin against hers, breathed in the scent of him. 'You do know how, if you'd just let yourself feel. You're so much more than you allow yourself to be, Leo. I think you've been playing a part so long you've forgotten who you really are. The sad truth is, the only person you have ended up hurting is yourself, even if you don't see it.'

She dropped her hand, instantly aching to touch him again. 'The sad truth is…' she repeated, taking a deep breath, knowing she would regret not saying the next words, even if they scared her. 'I like who I am with you. Like who you are with me. I think we're good together. You challenged me, made me step back from my path and take a look around, re-evaluate who I was and what I wanted. And I think you were real with me, you were honest. Which is why you're running. Because that scares you. Honestly? It scares me too. I didn't expect this, didn't want it, but here we are.'

'You seem to be forgetting,' he drawled, 'that you are the one who turned me down. I offered to marry you, Anna. You said no.' The shutters were up now. He was the bland playboy of the photos, not the pirate who had captured her heart, not the confidant who made her think and challenge herself. Anger flared up; this was her life he was messing with now, her happiness he spurned.

'I don't need marriage, Leo. All I need is your heart. Because you have mine. I love you, Leo.' A flare of something she couldn't read in the dark eyes at her words—anger, passion? Before she could get a handle on the heat it faded and he was back to bland. She pressed on. 'I know that wasn't the deal, wasn't what you wanted, but I couldn't help it. I'm in love with you, Leo. Not with your father's title, or the playboy, or the money, or the looks. With the man who spent a month fixing up an island for his sister. With the man who refuses to play his family's games. With the man who puts integrity before an easy life. With the man who listens to me. With the man who makes me feel beautiful.'

'You are beautiful,' he said hoarsely.

Anna stood there, knowing her heart was in her eyes, on her face, knowing she had nothing else to say, to give, hoping it was enough. And for one moment she thought it might be, her heart speeding up as Leo took her hand in his, only to drop it and step away. 'I'm sorry,' he said and then he was gone, leaving her alone on the path.

'There you are, *mi hermano*.' Leo hadn't even realised that he had ended up at Valentina's door until she stood before him, worry etched on her picture-perfect face. 'Do you know I have barely seen you over the last three days? I was hoping we could spend some time before the wedding together.'

'I'm sorry.' Lately he seemed to spend a lot of time apologising to women he had let down. 'I've been busy.' Looking at his sister, he frowned. She was dressed in a bright orange bikini top and white shorts, her hair twisted up in a complicated braid. He recalled the extensive itinerary which Anna—his heart stuttered, of course it was Anna—had ensured each guest had copies of. 'You're off to the beach games? It's a bad time. I'll let you get on...'

'No, Leo.' Valentina caught his hand. 'I'm not playing. I know it's silly superstition, but I don't want Todd to see me before the wedding...'

'You might have thought about that before choosing to get married on a small island where you're never less than fifteen minutes from each other.'

'True, which is why I've arranged for Todd to spend tomorrow on a boat trip. By the time he gets back I'll be getting ready in here, so we'll be quite safe. It's just to-night, and I don't mind missing the games, especially if it means we get the chance to catch up. You've not been yourself, Leo.'

Of course she'd noticed. She was wasted on modelling. His little sister would make a great detective.

'I'm fine.'

'Hmm?' Valentina raised her eyebrows at him. 'Come in, sit down. There's some bottled water, want some?' She waited until he was safely sitting on the sofa, a cold drink by his side, before pouncing. 'You've been avoiding the pretty manageress.'

'Anna? I'm not avoiding her. It's just complicated.'

'How? You like this girl, Leo! I've seen you with her. You're like a different man. No masks, no pretending...'

Each word hit home. He had been a different man this last month. A happier man. But happiness didn't last. 'She's pregnant, Val.'

His sister stilled. 'What?' and to Leo's horror her eyes filled, one large tear rolling—in the most photogenic way—down her face. 'Leo,' she breathed, reaching for his hands and clutching them. 'That is wonderful. Our children will be cousins, will be friends. They will grow up with family around them, not like us, huh? Better than us.'

'It's very early, Val, don't tell anyone.'

'No, no, of course. Oh, but, Leo. This is what I have prayed for. I am so happy and now you have happiness too.'

The only way Leo managed to get through every long second was by staying numb. It was something he had a lot of practice in, he'd learned long ago to school his face, his very thoughts, but Valentina's sheer delight in his news tore through his defences. 'We're not together, Anna and I.' The words were wrenched from him.

'You're having a child together. What else do you need?' The certainty in Valentina's voice would almost be comical in any other situation. There was the grit that had helped her rise to the top of her profession.

'Val, I asked her to marry me and she said no.' Saying the words allowed hurt in a way he had never imagined possible. But then Anna had just poured her heart out to him. Had given him her heart and he had done nothing. He deserved the pain.

'She turned you down? Why?'

'I'm not enough. Not to be a father, or a long-term father. Anna deserves better, she deserves more. I don't know how to love her. To love anyone.' To his shame his voice cracked as he said the words. She did deserve more, but how he wished he were the man to provide it.

Taking his hand in hers, Valentina sat next to him, leaning in, giving him her warmth and support. Leo had always been the big brother, the one who took care of her, proud to hand over his pay checks to help with rent; when had his little sister got old enough to start taking care of him? 'Mama always said you were the saddest child she'd ever known. She said leaving you broke her heart. She'd never known a child who stood so stiffly when she cuddled him before. She was so happy when you came back into her life. Our lives.

'Leo, you gave up university and got a job to help pay our rent. I know you spent that first year working on a building site until your investments paid off because of us. You looked after me when I was a child. You were the one who held me when Mama died. You were the person I needed to give Todd his seal of approval. You are the person I want by my side tomorrow. My child is so lucky to have you as an uncle, and that baby Anna is carrying is lucky to have you as a dad—and me as an aunt,' she added with a cheeky grin. 'The only person who doesn't believe in you is you. How does she make you feel? In here?' She tapped his chest, right over his heart.

'She makes me feel...' Anna's words came back to him with devastating clarity. *All I need is your heart. Because you have mine.* Was that what they had been doing? Exchanging hearts during those long, hot nights? Those intense conversations? That baring of souls?

Leo closed his eyes and all he could see was Anna. Anna standing there with that notebook in her hands, blue eyes blazing as she ordered him off the island. Anna dirty and hot, paint all over her shorts, determined to make sure every single inch of the bungalow she painted was perfect. Anna glowing as she told him once again how misunderstood Joanna the Mad was. Anna icier than he imagined possible confronting his parents. Anna, hair tumbling over her shoulders, wrapped in a sheet. Anna supine on the sundeck of his boat in nothing but a tiny bikini and an inviting smile.

He liked every single Anna, wanted every single Anna. Wanted to possess her, protect her, make her laugh, tease her, provoke her, seduce her. Was that love? How did a person know?

'Leo? Do you love her?'

'How can you bear it, Valentina? Putting your trust in one person? Your heart?' The words were torn from him.

'How can I bear not to?' she said simply. 'Leo, I would much, much rather give it my all and let it all go horribly wrong than never try. There's no guarantees. I was luckier than you, I know that. We had no money, but I always knew I was wanted, knew I was loved. And if I lose all this...' her expansive gesture took in all the trappings of success littering the sitting area: the deceptively simple cashmere cardigan, the flip-flops and beach bag that cost more than a second-hand car, the luxury hand lotion on the table, the huge diamond glittering on her hand '...I can cope. I know how to work. But I can't live without love. I don't want to. So tomorrow I put my faith, my trust in Todd. I wish you could have the same faith, *mi hermano*.'

Leo stayed with Valentina for the rest of the evening. She'd arranged for a simple salad to be delivered to her bungalow, and the two ate, sharing stories of Assumptia as they did so. 'I wish she had met Todd,' Valentina said wistfully. 'Wish she was here to celebrate tomorrow, wish she could meet the baby. But I know she would be so happy you are here by my side, Leo. And I know she would want you to take a leap of faith. To believe in love, to believe you are worthy of love. Because you are, more than you know.'

Leo kissed his sister goodnight, promising to be back in the morning, and set off down the lantern-lit path towards the dock and his boat. He had sailed it to the mainland for cleaning and restocking just a few days before, but if he was setting off with no known destination tomorrow then he needed to give it a quick check-over. But as he reached the dock he found himself rooted to the jetty, unable to climb into the small dinghy. This would be the last time he would sail over to his boat knowing he would be returning to the island, to Anna. Tomorrow he wouldn't simply fasten the dinghy to the boat, but would stow it and when he pressed the throttle it would be to sail away for ever.

Staring out at the moon-kissed waves, Leo didn't feel the usual sense of freedom, of adventure. Did he really think his absence was better for Anna and for the baby? That a loveless marriage of convenience was the only other answer? Or was he just too afraid to put his heart on the line? He who was so contemptuous of his father's fear of public dishonour was just as afraid himself. Not of being publicly humiliated, but of being found wanting. Far easier to steer clear of intimacy than risk rejection.

Truth was, he hadn't intended to leave quite so soon, hadn't intended to break things off with Anna. Not yet. Not until fear had precipitated his decision. If there were no baby then he would be looking forward to tomorrow, to dancing with her, steering her into a secluded corner, sweeping her away from the festivities and back to the boat. Thoughts of her consumed him—would those thoughts disappear with the miles or would she continue to haunt him?

And there was a baby. Right now just a vulnerable bunch of cells, but a bunch of cells that would divide and grow into a child. Would it have Anna's blue eyes or his own brown ones? What would it think of him? Would it resent him for not being there? Despise him for being a coward? Ironic, he'd spent his childhood desperate for his father's love and approval. Valentina had just wanted a father to acknowledge her. Did Leo really think that throwing money Anna's way would make him a better man? He of all people should know that money solved nothing.

He'd told Anna that she was the bravest person he knew. Anna who used her notebooks and lists as a shield. Anna who had been hurt by her family, but who had the courage to love them regardless, to keep trying, keep loving. Anna who had been so scarred by her last pregnancy yet who faced this new one with resilience and with hope. Anna who loved him, who believed in him, who wanted nothing from him except what she was prepared to give in exchange. Anna who was stronger than he could ever be.

Did he love Anna? And if so did he have the courage to be vulnerable before her, with her? All Leo knew was that he couldn't carry on this way. Couldn't be this lonely and survive. Something had to give before he broke and the only person he wanted, the only person he needed was right here on La Isla Marina. If he was brave enough to find her. Brave enough to let her in. Brave enough to love.

CHAPTER FIFTEEN

IT WAS A perfect evening, as if Valentina had ordered the weather along with the tiny cakes, the *piñatas* hanging from the tree, the tasteful wedding favours. Not a cloud marred the pristine blue sky, the late spring sun warm rather than scorching. The day had been manic with last-minute wedding preparations, checking in the hundred-plus guests who'd arrived that day, and taking care of the myriad tiny problems that popped up, from a blocked shower to a loose tile, the wrong brand of herbal infusions to forgotten toiletries. It was all going to be worth it though. Most of the guests, on Valentina's side anyway, were young, beautiful and had thousands of social-media followers. The island had been photographed hundreds of times—the trees, the fairy lights, the boats, the beach, the bathrooms. No detail was apparently too small for a filter and a fitting hashtag: *#valwedding #spanishheaven* and the ubiquitous *#blessed*. They wouldn't have been able to buy that kind of publicity with an unlimited budget and a crack PR team.

The best thing about being so busy was that Anna didn't have time to think about Leo or his imminent departure. To feel upset or humiliated that Rosa was attending the wedding with Jude while she stayed firmly in the background as staff, dressed in the same black skirt and white blouse as the rest of the female staff, hair tied back, a world apart from the glamour of the guests.

She just had to get through today and then Rosa would take over for the week of post-wedding festivities, all already planned and organised, the departure of the wedding guests next week and the resumption of normal holiday guests. Usually they would have a couple of months at half capacity before the summer madness, but thanks to the Valentina effect they were fully booked right through to October and Anna had a list of brides wanting exclusive use of the island next year.

Next year... Her hand crept to her stomach. Things would be very different next year. She crossed her fingers. *Please let this one be healthy.* Anna had never quite forgiven herself for that momentary sense of relief ten years ago when she realised nothing need change, that she could go back to university and resume her life. The guilt contributing to the depression that had dogged the rest of her first year and still flared up if she wasn't careful to heed the warning signs. Guilt and grief a toxic mixture.

Sometimes she wondered how her life would have turned out if she hadn't miscarried. Would she have the career she had now or would ambition have been sacrificed to the demands of single motherhood? Either way there would be a nine-year-old running around now. When Anna closed her eyes she could picture her—it was always her—a skinny dark-haired child with Sebastian's green eyes. She'd never forget her ghost baby, never not love her, never not want forgiveness.

Which was why she had to concentrate on this baby. Not allow Leo's departure to send her spiralling, to stay strong and healthy and to count her blessings every single

day. Be grateful Leo had been in her life even for so short
a time, had helped her see a new way.

The sound of the traditional Spanish band starting up
a lively tune pulled Anna back to the here and now and
she straightened, pulling at her skirt to neaten it. She had
elected to stand with the rest of the staff at the back of
the tree-lined clearing where the wedding and party were
being held. The official stood waiting, due solemnity on
her face, and the guests were sitting in lines facing the pagoda, an aisle separating the two sides, wide enough for
the bridal party to proceed along.

Valentina had kept the bridal party outfits simple with
cream linen suits for the groomsmen and red knee-length
dresses for the bridesmaids, the full skirts and hint of
ruffle a nod to Valentina's Spanish roots. The six couples
proceeded along the aisle, lining up along the front, either side of the pagoda, ready to welcome the bride and
groom. First Todd, his mother on his arm, solemn faced
and nervous. Anna loved the Spanish custom of letting the
groom's mother walk him down the aisle, a lump forming
in her throat when Todd kissed his mother's cheek as he
handed her into her seat, then turned to watch his bride
proceed down the aisle.

Valentina looked glorious. The bodice clung like a second skin, accentuating her tiny waist and curves before
flaring out into a full knee-length skirt. She'd opted for
white rather than the traditional Spanish black, with a sheer
overdress embroidered with bold, beautiful red flowers,
her hair loose and unfettered except for the matching
flower in her hair. Anna's eyes skimmed over the breath-
taking bride, all her attention on the man accompanying
her down the aisle. Leo, devastating in a cream linen suit.
Anna drank him in, imprinting every detail on her mem-

ory. How the dark hair fell over his forehead, the broad shoulders, the unconscious grace with which he carried himself. She blinked back hot tears. Four weeks of memories weren't enough. Not nearly. But they were all she had.

Leo looked preoccupied, all his attention on the ceremony, the vows, the readings. Anna knew that Todd and Valentina had actually married quietly in New York earlier in the week to cut down on the paperwork, but considered today their real wedding day, Valentina openly crying as she made her vows and the couple presented each other with *arras*, coins that represented their commitment to each other, and the wedding rings, which Valentina wore on her right hand, as was usual in Spain, and Todd on his left.

And then it was done. They were married. Time to swing into action, make sure the drinks and canapés were circulated, put out the tables and chairs while the photos took place, and check on the kitchens and the performers who had been booked to entertain the guests. Anna stepped back into the trees. Leo still hadn't looked at her. Not once.

The ceremony was over, the food had been eaten, drinks drunk, bands had played, speeches made, the *detalles* handed out and the bride and groom had taken to the floor to perform a very sexy and perfectly choreographed tango. Now Jude had taken centre stage and, accompanied only by his guitar, was serenading the happy couple with a ballad Leo vaguely recognised. Couples swayed to and fro under the lantern-lit scene, Valentina and Todd right in the centre, eyes locked as they danced. Leo swallowed. This was when he had been planning to slip away, all his duties done.

He looked around, but there was no sign of Anna. He

had caught glimpses of her during the evening, like a ghost at the wedding, unobtrusive in her staff uniform, her hair pulled severely back. Every time he had gone to intercept her she had slipped away. He couldn't tell if she was purposefully avoiding him; he did know that she hadn't once caught his eye.

Rosa was sitting near the pagoda, her gaze fixed on Jude. Leo swallowed his annoyance. Anna's sister hadn't been carrying drinks or trays of food; she hadn't sponged marks off dresses or attended to torn hems or got more ice because the water wasn't chilled enough. No uniform for her, instead a lemon-coloured dress that set off her tan, her hair intricately braided as it fell down her back. Leo pulled a chair up next to her. 'Where's Anna?'

The hostility in Rosa's eyes was a shock. Was this a forewarning of the reception he could expect from Anna? 'I thought you were leaving.'

'I need to speak to Anna.'

'Maybe she doesn't want to speak to you.'

'Maybe,' Leo acknowledged. 'It's important, Rosa, please.'

Rosa sat staring at the stage, her face set. 'She'll be back at the villa. She's overseeing the clean-up and packing.'

'Packing?'

'She's heading back to Oxford tomorrow.'

'I thought she was staying here?'

'Mama wants her to go back and think about it. It's a huge change. Everyone just wants her to be sure. To make sure she's doing it for the right reasons.' The glance she slanted at him was unreadable.

'Thanks.' He got to his feet.

'Leo? She's actually doing really well. If you are going to make matters worse then stay away or I'll make you sorry you ever messed with my sister.' And she turned her attention back to the stage, clearly dismissing him. Leo stood for a second, staring at her slim, determined form.

'Warning understood,' he said and walked away.

The whole island thrummed with activity, the music permeating every corner, lights illuminating every path and cove. There were no hidden corners; people seemed to be everywhere in groups or couples, dancing, talking, embracing. It wasn't midnight yet; the party would go on for hours, probably until dawn. A couple of times people tried to intercept him, to draw him into the festivities, but Leo's attention was focussed on the ornate villa at the centre of the island and the woman within it.

The reception area was quiet, although he could hear a hubbub from the kitchen, and Leo looked around before slipping through the door that he knew led to the personal family rooms. It looked as if an entire wing of the villa was for family use. The wide hallway he stood in led to a huge sitting room, a study and a small kitchen, stairs winding up from the far end. Leo headed for the stairs and the next floor. Bedrooms, bathrooms, all unoccupied, and another staircase, winding up to the turret. Of course Anna's bedroom would be up here. A princess in a tower dreaming of kings and queens and adventure. The door was open and he stepped in.

The small, octagonal room was a contrast to the luxury of the bungalows. A simple rug on the tiled floor, an iron bedstead covered in bright blankets, a trunk filled with clothes. But there were windows on three sides looking out over the island and a certain quirky charm to the room, which suited Anna. She'd been sitting on the bed when he stepped in and she stood up slowly, the colour draining from her face.

'Leo, what are you doing here? I thought we'd said all there was to say.'

'Rosa told me where you were. You're leaving?'

'You don't have the monopoly on running away.'

'Is that what you're doing?'

'Yes, no—I need time to think. To sort my affairs out. To sort myself out. I *am* coming back though. I've made my mind up. This is where I belong.'

Leo looked at her. At the dark shadows under her blue eyes. She'd lost weight over the last few days, her cheekbones a little more prominent. Anger rose in him, hot and thick. He was responsible for all of it.

'What does Sancia think about you staying?'

'Thanks to Valentina we're booked up well into next year. I'm not sure there will even be an off season this year. If we can heat the bungalows properly we might be able to open all year round. Mama is relieved, I think. Surprised, but relieved. We've come to a new understanding. I think there is more to be said, but we're in a good place. I think we'll work well together.' Leo recognised the matter-of-fact tone, the way Anna looked at the list lying on the bed. She was protecting herself with facts. Protecting herself from him.

Regret burned deep, regret and apprehension—and hope. 'How would she feel about a full-time painter and decorator living on the island too?' His heart hammered as he said the words, his pulse beating louder than the drums on the stage outside.

Anna just stared. 'We have the groundsman. I guess if we need another person we could hire them...'

'I mean me.'

Her eyes flew to his, hope mingling with wariness and a hint of anger. 'What do you mean *you*?'

'I mean I could stay on full time.'

'Is this the next stage in the *annoy your parents* crusade? Full-time gambler to handyman? Because the only teen rebellion I'm interested in will be happening in around thirteen years' time.'

There was so much he needed to say. Wanted her to hear, but he didn't want to do it here surrounded by her suitcase and piles of clothes. Her lists and notebooks. He needed neutral ground. Leo held out a hand. 'Walk with me? Please?'

It hurt to see how long it took her to decide, to see the conflicting emotions pass clearly across her face before she finally nodded, although she made no move to take his hand. 'Ten minutes. I have a lot to do.'

Silently they left the room, heading back downstairs and slipping out of the side door back into the moonlit night. The sound of the band wafted clearly across the night air, along with the hubbub of over one hundred people enjoying themselves. Without speaking they turned away from the noise, heading to the far end of the island, to the cove where just three nights ago Anna had turned his world upside down—and he had broken her heart.

Leo searched for the right words to show her he was serious, to tell her what was in his heart. He had no practice, no experience at this type of honesty, at laying himself bare—and the stakes had never been higher.

'My wish to stay here has nothing to do with my parents. Anna, I turned up here lost. So lost I could just sail across to La Isla Marina and know that no one, nowhere would miss me. So lost I could just stay for a month knowing no one would even notice. I came here with no agenda, no expectations and yet I was happier than I think I've ever been. Every day I achieved something, made something, did something. And then there was you.'

'Me?' Her voice a whisper.

It was now or never. All Leo knew was that he had to try. That he had to convince Anna, show her that he loved her. That even if she still didn't want to marry him he would be the best father possible for the baby. Their baby. That she had changed his life, changed him. He just needed to find the words. Tell her that he had always thought he was no one, nothing, but Anna made him realise he knew he was someone worth being. 'You. Infuriatingly organised, superior, sexy as hell you. You took one look at the façade I presented and dismissed me as being beneath your notice—and then you took a second look and I was defenceless.'

Anna didn't know what to say or where to look. She'd reconciled herself—well, she was doing her best to reconcile herself—with Leo's departure, with knowing that all foreseeable future contact would be via a business manager, that she couldn't save him after all. And now here he was, by her side, telling her everything she wanted to hear. But how real was he? Hope rose, treacherous and seductively sweet, no matter how she tried to clamp down on it. 'You want to stay here and what? Be the handyman?' she said, trying to make some sense out of the senseless and failing.

His mouth quirked into a smile. 'I want to be with you. I'm just trying to sell it to you in practical terms, because I know you'll want to make a pro and con list and so I thought I'd get straight in there with the practical reasons. I can run my business from here, but I can also help you run this place, help it grow, be the place you want it to be. The place your grandparents wanted it to be.'

'You are pretty handy with a paintbrush.' She couldn't believe she'd just said that, but she had no idea what else to say, what to think. Not quite believing this was happening despite the sincerity in Leo's eyes, in his voice.

'When I asked you to marry me I expected you to turn me down. Why would a woman like you marry me? You're not impressed by money, by titles and I thought I had nothing else to offer. I was too scared to look deeper.'

'I wanted to say yes,' Anna whispered. 'More than you'll ever know. But how could I marry you when you wouldn't let me in? Once I might have thought that was okay, despite my parents' break up, despite my own instincts. But I'd glimpsed more—and I couldn't settle for less. I can't settle for less. Not once I realised just how much I love you. It's not fair on me or you.'

'I'm sorry, Anna. I let you down. I reacted badly. I was so used to expecting nothing from my life and then there you were and I had this vision of a whole other life. Of a family and a place in the world. It was all I ever wanted once, but I gave up on that hope many years ago. I don't know how to be a father. How to be a husband. But I've realised that's okay. I just need to try. To trust in you. In us.'

They had reached the cove and Anna sank thankfully onto a bench, trying to quell the trembling in her legs, her hands, to make sense of it all. She wanted to believe that Leo was here, was trying again because he had realised he was head over heels in love with her, but he hadn't spoken of love. He wanted to do the right thing by her—and that was laudable, of course it was, but how could she say yes when she loved him? When nothing had changed? She remained convinced of one thing: a one-sided marriage would never work.

She stared out at the dark vastness of the sea, the whisper of the waves calming her, giving her the strength to turn to him. 'Leo, listen to me, you don't have to marry me for the baby. We can raise it together. And it's still such early days. I know what can happen, how wrong things can go, how quickly it can all change. Don't make promises... don't change your life for what might be.'

'I know it's early, and I know you're scared that you might lose it, and I can't make you any promises except I will be here no matter what, and that I want to marry you no matter what. I love you, Dr Anna Gray. I made a list...'

The shaking in her hands intensified. Had he just said love or were her ears hearing what they wanted to hear? 'You made a *what*?'

'I didn't think you'd believe me otherwise. I know you're a great believer in a good list. I was talking to Valentina yesterday, about all the reasons you're too good for me, and I went home and wrote them down. And that's when I realised. They're not just the reasons why you're too good for me. They're also why I love you. And why I would be a fool to let you go. My life had no meaning, Anna, has no meaning without you. I need you and I love you and I want to marry you.'

She had no idea what to say, what to think, her mouth was dry, her blood thumping, hope tantalising her every breath. 'Do you have the list?' She needed proof, evidence, something tangible to believe in.

A smile curved his mouth, seductive and wicked. 'It's back on the boat, but I know it by heart.' Leo knelt by her side, capturing her hands in his as he looked into her eyes, his own shining with sincerity, with hope. With something that looked a lot like love. 'I love how you pretend to be so sensible, but then you can be so spontaneous. I love the way you eat *gambas* with no inhibitions. I love the way you look after your parents even though they drive you mad. I love the way you talk about people who are long dead as if you met them yesterday. I love every notebook, every list. I love the way you spent every hour making sure

Valentina had the perfect wedding. I love how patient you are with the most unreasonable guest. I love how dangerous you are when riled. I love the way your eyes get hazy just before I kiss you. I love your mouth and your eyes and your hair. I love your determination. I love you, Anna.' His voice broke and he was looking at her with an intensity, with a passion she had never seen before. An intensity that called to her, completed her. 'I don't deserve you, but I promise to learn to. Please, Anna, *mi corazón*, will you marry me? For the right reasons. Because I love you and you love me and I want us to be a family, together.'

'Leo.' The words wouldn't come; all she could do was hold onto his hand as if it were a lifeline and let the hot tears flow. Tears of relief, of happiness, of love. 'Are you sure?'

'I couldn't be surer. I've spent my whole life sailing from place to place, searching for something, someone to make me feel, to believe in myself, never believing I would find it. Too scared to put my faith in anyone, too scared to trust, terrified of always being alone, but never seeing another way. I knew as soon as I saw you, a sea nymph on the shore, that my life would never be the same again. I love you, Anna. You make me a better man. Let's build a life together here, raise our children here and continue your grandparents' legacy.'

Anna searched his face, looking for traces of the bland playboy, the practised mask, but all she could see was love. Love mingled with hope and resolve and finally she began to believe. Believe that Leo loved her as she loved him, believe that happiness might be in her grasp if she was brave enough to trust in him, believe that she could take a chance on the unknown. 'Yes,' she said, her grasp tightening on his. 'Yes, Leo. I will marry you.'

If she had any lingering doubts, the joy on Leo's face

instantly dispelled them. *'Mi amor,'* he breathed, pulling
her to her feet and enfolding her in his arms, and as his
head bent to hers, in a kiss of infinite tenderness, of love,
Anna knew it wasn't only Leo who had finally come home.
She had as well, and right here, in his arms, was where
she belonged.

* * * * *

THE FORTUNE
MOST LIKELY TO…

MARIE FERRARELLA

To
Susan Litman,
with thanks
for her
patience

Prologue

It was time that he finally faced up to it. He had never gotten over her.

Sitting on the sofa in his living room, Dr. Everett Fortunado frowned as he looked into the glass of expensive whiskey he was sipping. The single glass, two fingers, was his way of winding down. Not from a hectic day spent at his successful, thriving medical practice, but from the stress of terminating yet another less-than-stellar, stillborn relationship.

How many failed relationships did that make now? Ten? Twelve? He wasn't sure.

He'd honestly lost count a number of years ago.

Admittedly, the women in those incredibly short-lived relationships had all become interchangeable. Now that he thought about it, none of them had ever stood out in his mind. And, if he was being honest about it, Everett couldn't remember half their names.

As for their faces, well, if pressed, he could give a general description, but there again, nothing about any of them had left a lasting impression on his mind. Strictly speaking, he could probably pass one or more of them on the street and not recognize them at all.

A mirthless laugh passed his lips. At thirty-three he was way too young to be on the threshold of dementia. No, that wasn't the reason behind this so-called memory loss problem. If he were being entirely honest with himself, he thought, taking another long, bracing sip of whiskey, this cavalcade of women who had been parading through his life for the last thirteen years were only poor substitutes for the one woman who had ever really mattered to him.

The only woman he had ever been in love with.

The woman he had lost.

Lila Clark, the girl he'd known since forever and had barely been aware of until he suddenly *saw* her for the first time that day in Senior English class. Though a straight A student, Everett had found himself faltering when it came to English. Lila sat next to him in class and he'd turned to her for help. She was the one responsible for getting him through Senior English.

And somewhere along the line during all that tutoring, Lila had managed to make off with his heart. He was crazy about her and really excited when he found out that she felt the same way about him. Not long after that, they began making plans for their future together.

And then it had all blown up on him.

When he'd lost her, his parents had told him that it

was all for the best. They had pointed out that he was too young to think about settling down. They wanted their brightest child to focus on his future and not squander his vast potential by marrying a girl from a working-class family just because he'd gotten her pregnant. To them it had been the oldest ploy in the world: a poor girl trapping a rich boy because of his sense of obligation.

But Lila really wasn't like that. And she hadn't trapped him. She'd walked out on him.

Everett sat on the sofa now, watching the light from the lone lamp in his living room play across the amber liquid in the chunky glass in his hand. He would've given anything if he could go back those thirteen years.

If he could have, he wouldn't have talked Lila into giving up their baby for adoption.

Because that one thing had been the beginning of the end for them.

He'd been at Lila's side in the delivery room and, even then, he kept telling her that they were doing the right thing. That they were too young to get married and raise this baby. That they could always have more kids "later."

Lila changed that night. Changed from the happy, bright-eyed, full-of-life young woman he'd fallen in love with to someone he no longer even knew.

And that was the look in her eyes when she raised them to his. Like she was looking at someone she didn't recognize.

Right after she left the hospital, Lila had told him

she never wanted to see him again. He'd tried to reason with her, but she just wouldn't listen.

Lila had disappeared out of his life right after that.

Crushed, he'd gone back to college, focusing every bit of energy entirely on his studies. He'd always wanted to be a doctor, ever since he was a little boy, and that became his lifeline after Lila left. He clung to it to the exclusion of everything else.

And it had paid off, he thought now, raising his almost-empty glass in a silent toast to his thriving career. He was a doctor. A highly successful, respected doctor. His career was booming.

Conversely, his personal life was in the dumpster.

Everett sighed. If he had just said, "Let's keep the baby," everything would have been different. And his life wouldn't have felt so empty every time he walked into his house.

He wouldn't have felt so empty.

Blowing out a breath, Everett rose from the sofa and walked over to the liquor cabinet. Normally, he restricted himself to just one drink, but tonight was different. It was the anniversary of the day Lila had ended their relationship. He could be forgiven a second drink.

At least, he told himself, he could fill his empty glass, if not his life.

Chapter One

"Your problem, brother dear," Schuyler said after having listened to him tell her that maybe he'd made a mistake talking Lila into giving up their baby all those years ago, "is that you think too much. You're always overthinking things and making yourself crazy in the process."

"Says the woman who always led with her heart," Everett commented.

"And that seems to be working out for me, doesn't it?" Schuyler asked.

He could hear the broad smile in her voice. It all but throbbed through the phone. Everett had no response for that. All he could do at the moment was sigh. Sigh and feel just a little bit jealous because his little sister had found something that he was beginning to think he never would find again: love.

"By thinking so much back then about how everything would affect your future," Schuyler went on, "I think you blew it with Lila. You were so focused on your future, on becoming a doctor, that you just couldn't see how badly she felt about giving up her baby—*your* baby," she emphasized. "And because you didn't notice, didn't seem to feel just as badly as she did about the adoption, you broke Lila's heart. If it were me, I would have never forgiven someone for breaking my heart that way," Schuyler told him.

"Thanks for being so supportive," Everett said sarcastically.

This was *not* why he'd called his sister, why he'd lowered his guard and allowed himself to be so vulnerable. Maybe he should have known better, he thought, about to terminate the call.

"I *am* being supportive," Schuyler insisted. "I'm just calling it the way I see it. I love you, Ev, and you know I'm always on your side. But I know you. I don't want you to get your hopes up that if you just approach her, she'll fly back into your arms and everything'll be just the way it was back then. Not after thirteen years and *not* after what went down between the two of you back then. Trust me, Lila is not going to get back together with you that easily."

"I know that and I don't want to get back together with Lila," he insisted defensively. "I just want to talk to her." Everett paused because this next thing was hard for him to say, even to Schuyler, someone he had always trusted implicitly. Lowering his voice, he told his sister, "Maybe even apologize to her for the way things ended between us back then."

He could tell from Schuyler's voice that she felt for him. But she was far from optimistic about the outcome of all this. "Look, Everett, I know that your heart's in the right place, but I really don't want to see it stomped on."

"No worries," Everett assured her. "My heart is not as vulnerable as you think."

What he'd just said might have been a lie, but if it was, it was a lie he was telling himself as well as his sister.

He had a feeling that Schuyler saw it that way too because he could hear the skepticism in her voice as she said, just before she ended their call, "Well, I wish you luck with that. Maybe Lila'll listen to reason."

Maybe.

The single word seemed to throb in his head as Everett decided to find out as much as he could about Lila and what she was doing these days.

It had all started two months ago when he'd taken the day off, gotten another doctor to cover for him and had driven the 165 miles from Houston to Austin to pick up his sister, Schuyler. At the time, he was supposed to be bringing Schuyler back home.

Given to acting on impulse, his younger sister had initially gone to Austin because she had gotten it into her head to track down Nathan Fortune. The somewhat reclusive man was supposedly her cousin and the ever-inquisitive Schuyler was looking for answers about their family tree. The current thinking was that she and the rest of their brothers and sisters were all possibly related to the renowned Fortune family.

It was while Schuyler was looking for those answers that she decided to get closer to the Mendoza family whose history was intertwined with the Fortunes. She managed to get so close to one of them—Carlo Mendoza—that she wound up completely losing her heart to him.

Confused, unsure of herself for very possibly the first time in her life, Schuyler had turned to the one person she was closest to.

She'd called Everett.

Listening to his sister pouring out her heart—and citing her all uncertainties, not just about her genealogy investigation but about the direction her heart had gone in—he had decided he needed to see Schuyler and maybe convince her to come home.

But Schuyler had reconciled with her man and decided to stay in Austin after all. Everett returned home without her. But he hadn't come away completely empty-handed. What Everett had come home with was a renewed sense of having made a terrible mistake thirteen years ago. And that had come about because while he'd been in Austin, he had run into Lila.

Sort of.

He saw Lila entering a sandwich shop and it had been a jarring experience for him. It had instantly propelled him back through time and just like that, all the old feelings had come rushing back to him, saturating him like a huge tidal wave. At least they had in his case.

However, he'd been struck by the aura of sadness he detected about her. A sadness that had *not* been there when they were in high school together.

He'd thought—hoped really—that when he got back to Houston, back to his practice, he'd be able to drive thoughts of Lila back into the past where they belonged. Instead, they began to haunt him, vividly pushing their way into his dreams at night, sneaking up on him during the day whenever he had an unguarded moment.

He began wondering in earnest about what had happened to her in all those years since they'd been together. And that sadness he'd detected—was *he* responsible for that? Or was there some other reason for its existence?

He felt compelled to find out.

Like everyone else of his generation, Everett turned to social media in his quest for information about Lila Clark.

He found her on Facebook.

When he saw that Lila had listed herself as "single" and that there were only a few photographs posted on her page, mainly from vacation spots she had visited, he felt somewhat heartened.

Maybe, a little voice in his head whispered, it wasn't too late to make amends after all.

Damn it, Everett, get hold of yourself. This is exactly what Schuyler warned you about. Don't get your hopes up, at least not until you talk to Lila again and exchange more than six words with her.

Who knows, she might have changed and you won't even like Lila 2.0.

Everett struggled to talk himself out of letting his imagination take flight. He tried to get himself to go slow—or maybe not go at all.

But the latter was just not an option.

He knew he felt too strongly about this, too highly invested in righting a wrong he'd committed in the past. Now that he'd made up his mind about the matter, he needed to make Lila understand that he regretted the way things had gone thirteen years ago.

Regretted not being more emotionally supportive of her.

Regretted not being able to see the daughter they had *both* lost.

Still, he continued to try to talk himself out of it for two days after he found Lila on Facebook. Tried to make himself just walk away from the whole idea: from getting in contact with her, from apologizing and making amends. All of it.

But he couldn't.

So finally, on the evening of the third day, Everett sat down in front of his computer, powered up his internet connection and pulled up Facebook. Specifically, he pulled up Lila's profile.

He'd stared at it for a full ten minutes before he finally began to type a message to her.

Hi, Lila. It's been a long time. I'm planning on being in Austin soon. Let's have lunch together and do some catching up. I'd really welcome the chance to see and talk with you.

Those four simple sentences took him close to half an hour to settle on. He must have written and deleted thirty sentences before he finally decided on those. Then it took him another ten minutes before he sent those four sweated-over sentences off into cyberspace.

For the next two hours he checked on that page close to a dozen and a half times, all without any luck. He was about to power down his computer for the night when he pulled up Lila's Facebook page one last time.

"She answered," he announced out loud even though there was no one around to hear him.

Sitting down in his chair, he read Lila's response, unconsciously savoring each word as if it was a precious jewel.

If you're going to be here Friday, I can meet you for lunch at 11:30. I just need to warn you that I only get forty-five minutes for lunch, so our meeting will be short. We're usually really swamped where I work.

Everett could hardly believe that she'd actually agreed to meet with him. He'd been half prepared to read her rejection. Whistling, he immediately posted a response.

11:30 on Friday sounds great. Since I'm unfamiliar with Austin, you pick the place and let me know.

After sleeping fitfully, he decided to get up early. He had a full slate of appointments that day. Best to get a jump on it. But the minute he passed the computer, he knew what he had to do first.

And there, buried amid approximately forty other missives—all of which were nothing short of junk mail—was Lila's response. All she'd written was the name of a popular chain of restaurants, followed by its address. But his heart soared.

Their meeting was set.

If he'd been agile enough to pull it off, Everett would have leaped up and clicked his heels together.

As it was, he got ready for work very quickly and left the house within the half hour—singing.

The second Lila hit the send button on Facebook, she immediately regretted it.

What am I thinking? she upbraided herself. Was she crazy? Did she actually *want* to meet with someone who had so carelessly broken her heart? Who was responsible for the single most heart-wrenching event to have happened in her life?

"What's wrong with you? Are you hell-bent on being miserable?" she asked herself as she walked away from her computer. It was after eleven o'clock at night and she was alone.

The way she was on most nights.

Maybe that was the problem, Lila told herself. She was tired of being alone and when she'd seen that message from Everett on her Facebook page, it had suddenly stirred up a lot of old memories.

"Memories you're better off forgetting, remember?" she demanded.

But they weren't all bad, she reminded herself. As a matter of fact, if she thought back, a lot of those memories had been good.

Very good.

For a large chunk of her Senior year and a portion of her first year at community college, Everett had been the love of her life. He'd made her happier than she could ever remember being.

But it was what had happened at the end that outweighed everything, that threw all those good recollections into the shadows, leaving her to remember that awful, awful ache in her heart as Emma was taken out of her arms and she watched her baby being carried away.

Away from her.

She'd wanted Everett to hold her then. To tell her that he was aching as much as she was. That he felt as if something had been torn away from his heart, too, the way she felt it had for her.

But all he had said was: "It's for the best." As if there was something that could be described as "best" about never being able to see your baby again. A baby that had been conceived in love and embodied the two of them in one tiny little form.

Lila felt tears welling up in her eyes even after all this time, felt them spilling out even though she'd tried hard to squeeze them back.

She wished she hadn't agreed to see Everett.

But if she'd said no to lunch, Everett would have probably put two and two together and realized that she hadn't the courage to see him again. If she'd turned him down, he would've understood just how much he still mattered to her.

No, Lila told herself, she had no way out. She *had* to see him again. Had to sit there across from him at a table, making inane conversation and proving to him that he meant nothing to her.

That would be her ultimate revenge for his having so wantonly, so carelessly, ripped out her heart without so much as a moment's pause or a word of actual genuine comfort.

"We'll have lunch, Everett," she said, addressing his response that was posted on her Facebook page. "We'll have lunch, and then you'll realize just what you lost all those years ago. Lost forever. Because I was the very best thing that could have ever happened to you," she added with finality.

Her words rang hollow to her ear.

It didn't matter, she told herself. She had a couple of days before she had to meet with him. A couple of days to practice making herself sound as if she believed every syllable she uttered.

She'd have it letter-perfect by the time they met, she promised herself.

She *had* to.

Chapter Two

Half the contents of Lila's closet was now spread out all over her bed. She spent an extra hour going through each item slowly before finally making up her mind.

Lila dressed with great care, selecting a two-piece gray-blue outfit that flattered her curves as well as sharply bringing out the color of her eyes.

Ordinarily, putting on makeup entailed a dash of lipstick for Lila, if that. This morning she highlighted her eyes, using both mascara and a little eye shadow. She topped it off with a swish of blush to accent her high cheekbones, smoothed her long auburn hair, then sprayed just the slightest bit of perfume.

Finished, she slowly inspected herself from all angles in her wardrobe mirror before she decided that she was ready to confront a past she'd thought she'd buried—and in so doing, make Dr. Everett Fortunado eat his heart out.

Maybe, Lila thought as she left her house, if she took this much trouble getting ready for the occasional dates she went out on, she might not still be single at the age of thirty-three.

Lila sighed. She knew better. It wasn't her clothes or her makeup that were responsible for her single status.

It was her.

After breaking up with Everett, she had picked herself up and dusted herself off. In an all-out attempt to totally reinvent herself, Lila had left Houston and moved to Austin where no one knew her or anything about the past she was determined to forget and put totally behind her.

She'd gone to work at the Fortune Foundation, a nonprofit organization dedicated to providing assistance to the needy. Through hard work, she'd swiftly risen and was now manager of her department.

And because of her work, Lila's life went from intolerable to good. At least her professional life did.

Her personal life, however, was another story.

Sure, she'd dated. She'd tried blind dates as well as online dating. She'd joined clubs and had gone to local sporting events to cheer on the home team. She'd gone out with rich men as well as poor ones and those in-between.

It wasn't that Lila couldn't meet a man, she just couldn't meet *the* man.

And probably even if she could, she thought, that still

wouldn't have done the trick. Because no matter who she went out with, she couldn't trust him.

Everett had destroyed her ability to trust any man she might become involved with.

Try as she might, she couldn't lower her guard. She just couldn't bear to have a repeat performance of what had happened to her with Everett.

Rather than risk that, she kept her heart firmly under lock and key. And that guaranteed a life of loneliness.

At this point in her life, Lila had decided to give up looking for Mr. Right. Instead, she forced herself to embrace being Stubbornly Single.

As she took one last look in the mirror and walked out the door, she told herself that was what she really wanted.

One day she might convince herself that was true.

Her upgraded appearance did not go unnoticed when she walked into the office at the Fortune Foundation that morning.

"Well, someone looks extra nice today," Lucie Fortune Chesterfield Parker noted the moment that Lila crossed the threshold. "Do you have a hot date tonight?" she asked as she made her way over toward Lila.

"No, I don't," Lila answered, hoping that would be the end of it.

Belatedly, she thought that maybe she should have brought this outfit with her and changed in the ladies' room before going to lunch instead of coming in dressed like this.

Lucie and she were friends and had been almost from

the very first time they met at the Foundation, but Lila really didn't want to talk about the man she was having lunch with.

Initially from England, Lucie was married to Chase Parker, a Texas oil heir who had been her teenage sweetheart. Because of that, Lucie considered herself to be an expert on romance and she felt she had great radar when it came to the subject.

Her radar was apparently on red alert now as she swiftly looked Lila over.

Studying her, Lucie repeated, "Not tonight?"

"No," Lila said firmly. She never broke stride, determined to get to her office and close the door on this subject—literally as well as figuratively.

"Lunch, then?" Lucie pressed. "You certainly didn't get all dolled up like that for us."

Lila looked at her sharply over her shoulder, but her coworker didn't back off. The expression on her face indicated that she thought she was onto something.

When Lila made no response, Lucie pressed harder. "Well, *are* you going to lunch with someone?"

Lila wanted to say no and be done with it. She was, after all, a private person and no one here knew about her past. She'd never shared any of it. No about the child she'd given up for adoption or the man who had broken her heart. However, it wasn't in her to lie and even if it were, Lucie was as close to a real friend as she had in Austin. She didn't want to risk alienating her if the truth ever happened to come out—which it might, likely at the most inopportune time.

So after a moment of soul-searching, she finally answered Lucie's question.

"Yes."

Lucie looked at her more closely, obviously intrigued. "Anyone I know?" she asked.

"No," Lila answered automatically.

Not anyone I know, either. Not really, Lila silently added. After all, it had been thirteen years since she'd last been with Everett. And besides, how well had she known him back then anyway? He certainly hadn't behaved the way she'd expected him to. It made her think that maybe she had never really known Everett Fortunado at all.

"Where did you meet him?" Lucie wanted to know, apparently hungry for details about her friend's lunch date.

"Why all the questions?" Lila reached her office, but unfortunately it was situated right next to Lucie's. Both offices were enclosed in glass, allowing them to easily see one another over the course of the day.

"Because you're my friend and I'm curious," Lucie answered breezily. "You've practically become a workaholic these last couple of months, hardly coming up for air. That doesn't leave you much time for socializing."

Pausing by her doorway, Lila blew out a breath. "It's someone I knew back in high school," she answered. She stuck close to the truth. There was less chance for error that way. "He's in town on business for a couple of days. He looked me up on Facebook and he suggested having lunch to catch up, so I said yes."

Lila walked over to her desk, really hoping that

would be the end of it. But apparently it wasn't because Lucie didn't retreat to her own office. Her friend remained standing in Lila's doorway, looking at her as if she was attempting to carefully dissect every word out of her mouth.

"How well did you know this guy—back in high school, I mean?" Lucie asked, tacking on the few words after a small beat.

Lila stood there feeling as if she was under a microscope.

Did it show, she wondered. Did Lucie suspect that there had been more than just high school between her and Everett?

"Why?" she asked suspiciously, wondering what Lucie was getting at. It wasn't that she didn't trust Lucie, it was just that inherently she had trouble lowering her guard around *anyone*.

"Well, if someone who I knew back in high school suddenly turned up in my life," Lucie said easily, "I don't think I'd dress up in something that would make me look like a runway model just to go out to lunch with him."

Lila shrugged, avoiding Lucie's eyes. "I'm just showing off the trappings of a successful career, I guess."

"Are you sure that's all it is?" Lucie asked, observing her closely.

Lila raised her chin, striking almost a defiant pose. "I'm sure," she answered.

Lucie inclined her head, accepting her friend's story. "Well, if I were you, I'd remember to take a handkerchief with me."

Lila stared at the other woman. What Lucie had just said made absolutely no sense to her.

"Why?"

Lucie's smile was a wide one, tinged in amusement. "Because you'll need a handkerchief to wipe up your friend's drool once he gets a load of you looking like that."

Lila looked down at herself. Granted, she'd taken a lot of time choosing what to wear, but it was still just a two-piece outfit. "I don't look any different than I usually do," Lila protested.

Lucie's smile widened a little more as she turned to leave. "Okay, if you say so," she answered agreeably, going along with Lila's version. "But between you and me, you look like a real knockout."

Good, Lila thought. That was the look she was going for.

There were mornings at work when the minutes would just seem to drag by, behaving as if lunchtime would never come. Lila would have given anything for that sort of a morning this time around because today, the minutes just seemed to race by, until suddenly, before she knew it, the clock on the wall opposite her office said it was eleven fifteen.

She'd told Everett that she would meet him at the restaurant she'd selected at eleven thirty.

That meant it was time for her to get going.

Lila took a deep breath, pushed her chair away from her desk and got up.

When she stood up, her hands braced against her

desk, her legs felt as if they had suddenly lost the power of mobility.

For a moment, it was as if she was rooted in place.

This was ridiculous, Lila told herself, getting her purse from her drawer.

She closed the drawer a little too hard. The sound reverberated through the glass walls and next door Lucie immediately looked in her direction. Grinning, Lucie gave her a thumbs-up sign.

Lila forced herself to smile in response then, concentrating as hard as she could, she managed to get her frozen legs moving. She wanted to be able to leave the office before Lucie thought to stick her head in to say something.

Or ask something.

This was all going to be over with soon, Lila promised herself.

Once out of the building, she made her way to her car. An hour and she'd be back, safe and sound in the office and this so-called "lunch date" would be behind her, Lila thought, trying to think positive thoughts.

It would be behind her and she'd never have to see Everett again.

But first, she pointedly reminded herself, she *was* going to have to get through this ordeal. She was going to have to sit at a table, face Everett and pretend that everything was just fine.

She was going to have to pretend that the past was just that: the past, and that it had nothing to do with the present. Pretend that those events from thirteen years ago didn't affect her any longer and definitely didn't get in the way of her eating and enjoying her lunch. Pretend that the memory of those events didn't impede her swallowing, or threaten to make her too sick to keep her food down.

Reaching her car, Lila got in and then just sat there, willing herself to start it. Willing herself to drive over to the restaurant and get this lunch over with.

Not a good plan, Lila. This is not a good plan. You should have never agreed to have lunch with Everett. When he wrote to you on your Facebook page, asking to meet with you, you should have told him to go to hell and stay there.

You've got no one to blame but yourself for this.

Lila let out a shaky breath and then glanced up into the rearview mirror.

Lucie was right. She looked fantastic.

Go and make him eat his heart out, Lila silently ordered herself. *And then, after you've finished eating and he asks if he could see you again, you tell him No!*

You tell him no, she silently repeated.

Taking another deep breath, she turned the key in the ignition.

The car rumbled to life. After another moment and a few more words of encouragement to herself, Lila pulled out of her parking space and drove out of the parking structure and off the lot.

The restaurant she'd selected was normally barely a five-minute drive away from the Foundation. Even with the sluggish midday traffic, it only took her ten minutes to get there. Before she knew it, she was pulling into a space in the restaurant's parking lot.

Sitting there, thinking of what was ahead of her, Lila found that she had to psych herself up in order to leave the shelter of her vehicle and walk into the restaurant.

To face her past.

"No," she contradicted herself through gritted teeth. "Not to face the past. To finally shut the door on it once and for all and start your future."

Yes, she had a life and a career, a career she was quite proud of. But she also needed to cut all ties to the woman she had once been. That starry-eyed young woman who thought that love lasted forever and that she had found her true love. That woman had to, quite simply, be put to rest once and for all.

And she intended to do that by having lunch with Everett, the man who had taken her heart and made mincemeat out of it. And once lunch was done, she was going to tell him goodbye one last time. Tell him goodbye and make him realize that she meant it.

Lila slowly got out of her car and then locked it.

Squaring her shoulders, she headed for the restaurant. It was time to beard the lion in his den and finally be set free.

Chapter Three

This was absurd, Everett thought. He was a well-respected, sought-after physician who had graduated from medical school at the top of his class. Skilled and exceedingly capable. Yet here he was, sitting in a restaurant, feeling as nervous as a teenager waiting for his first date to walk in.

This was Lila for God's sake, he lectured himself. Lila, someone he'd once believed was his soul mate. Lila, whom he'd once been closer to than anyone else in the world and had loved with his whole heart and soul. There was absolutely no reason for him to be tapping the table with his long fingers and fidgeting like some inexperienced kid.

Yet here he was, half an hour ahead of time, watching the door when he wasn't watching the clock, waiting for Lila to walk in.

Wondering if she wouldn't.

Wondering if, for some reason, she would wind up changing her mind at the last minute and call him to cancel their lunch. Or worse, not call at all.

Why am I doing this to myself? Everett silently demanded. Why was he making himself crazy like this? So what if she didn't show? It wouldn't be the end of the world. At least, no more than it was all those years ago when Lila had told him she didn't ever want to see him again.

The words had stung back then and he hadn't known what to do with himself, how to think, what to say. In time, he'd calmed down, started to think rationally again. He had decided to stay away from her for a while, thinking that Lila would eventually come to her senses and change her mind.

Except that, when he finally went to see her, he found out that she was gone. Lila had taken off for parts unknown and no one knew where. Or, if they did know, no one was telling him no matter how much he asked.

That was when his parents had sat him down and told him that it was all for the best. They reminded him that he had a destiny to fulfill and now he was free to pursue that destiny.

Not having anything else to cling to, he threw himself into his studies and did exactly what was expected of him—and more.

He did all that only to end up here, sitting in an Austin restaurant, watching the door and praying each time it opened that it was Lila coming in and walking back into his life.

But each time, it wasn't Lila who walked in.

Until it was.

Everett felt his pulse leap up with a jolt the second he saw her. All these years and she had only gotten more beautiful.

He immediately rose in his seat, waving to catch her attention. He had to stop himself from calling out her name, instinctively knowing that would embarrass her. They weren't teenagers anymore.

Lila had almost turned around at the door just before she opened it. It was only the fact that she would have been severely disappointed in herself for acting like such a coward that forced her to come inside.

The second she did, she immediately saw Everett and then it was too late to run for cover. Too late to change her mind.

The game was moving forward.

She forced a smile to her lips despite the fact that her stomach was tied in a knot so tight she could hardly breathe. It was the sort of smile that strangers gave one another in an attempt to break the ice. Except that there was no breaking the ice that she felt in her soul as she looked at Everett.

All the old heartache came rushing back to her in spades.

"I'm sorry," she murmured to Everett when she finally reached the table. "Am I late?"

"No," he quickly assured her. "I'm early. I didn't

know if there was going to be a lot of traffic, or if I'd have trouble finding this place, so I left the hotel early." A sheepish smile curved his lips. "As it turned out, there was no traffic and the restaurant was easy enough to find."

"That's good," she responded, already feeling at a loss as to what to say next.

She was about to sit down and Everett quickly came around the table to hold out her chair for her.

"Thank you," she murmured, feeling even more awkward as she took her seat.

Having pushed her chair in for her, Everett circled back to his own and sat down opposite her. He could feel his heart swelling just to look at her.

"You look really great," Everett told her with enthusiasm.

Again she forced a quick smile to her lips. "Thank you," she murmured.

At least all that time she'd spent this morning fussing with her makeup and searching for the right thing to wear had paid off, she thought. Looking good, she had once heard, was the best revenge. She wanted Everett to be aware of what he'd given up. She wanted him to feel at least a little pang over having so carelessly lost her.

The years had been kind to him, as well, she reluctantly admitted. His six-foot frame had filled in well, though he was still taut and lean, and his dark hair framed a handsome, manly face and highlighted his dark-blue eyes. Eyes that seemed to be studying her.

"But you do seem a little...different somehow," Everett said quietly a moment later.

She wasn't sure what he meant by that and it marred her triumph just a little. Was that a veiled criticism, she wondered.

"Well, it has been thirteen years," she reminded Everett stiffly. "We knew each other a long time ago. That is," she qualified, "if we ever really knew each other at all."

He looked at her, wondering if that was a dig or if he was just being extremely touchy.

It seemed there were four of them at the table. The people they were now and the ghosts of the people they had been thirteen years ago.

The moment stretched out, becoming more uncomfortable. "What's that supposed to mean?" Everett asked her.

"Just an observation," Lila answered casually. "Who really knows who they are at that young an age?" she asked philosophically. "I know that I didn't."

He sincerely doubted that. "Oh, I think you did," Everett told her.

Seeing the server approaching, she held her reply. When the server asked if he could start them out with a drink, Lila ordered a glass of sparkling water rather than anything alcoholic. Everett followed her example and asked for the same.

"And if you don't mind, I'd like to order now," Lila told the young server. "I have to be getting back to the office soon," she explained.

"Of course."

After he took their orders and left, Everett picked up the thread of their conversation. "I think you knew just what you wanted years ago," he told her. "I'm the one who got it all wrong."

Was he saying that out of pity for her, she wondered, feeling her temper beginning to rise as her stomach churned.

"On the contrary," Lila responded. "You were the only kid who was serious when he said he wanted to play 'doctor.' If you ask me, 'Dr. Fortunado' achieved everything he ever dreamed about as a kid."

Everett's eyes met hers. Longing and sadness for all the lost years filled him. For the time being, he disregarded the note of bitterness he thought he detected in her voice.

"Not everything," he told her.

This was an act. She wasn't going to fall for it, Lila thought, grateful that the server picked that moment to return with their drinks and their orders. Everett wasn't fooling her. He was just saying that so that she would forget about the past. Forget her pain.

As if that were remotely possible.

Silence stretched out between them. Everett shifted uncomfortably.

"So, tell me about you," he finally urged. "What are you doing these days?"

Lila pushed around the lettuce in her salad as if the fate of the world depended on just the right placement. She kept her eyes on her plate as she spoke, deliberately avoiding making any further eye contact with him. She had always loved Everett's dark blue eyes. When they'd been together, she felt she could easily get lost in those eyes of his and happily drown.

Now she couldn't bear to look into them.

"I'm a manager of one of the departments at the Fortune Foundation. My work involves health outreach programs for the poorer families living in the Austin area."

That sounded just like her, Everett thought. Lila was always trying to help others.

But something else she'd said caught his attention. "Did you say the Fortune Foundation?"

"Yes," she answered. Suspicion entered her voice as she eyed him closely and asked, "Why?"

"Well, it just seems funny that you should mention the Fortunes. My family just recently found out that our last name might very well be 'Fortune' rather than 'Fortunado.'" He pulled his face into a grin. "Crazy coincidence, isn't it?"

Coincidence. Lila had another word for it. Her eyes narrowed as she pinned him with a look. "Is that why you wanted to get together for lunch?" she wanted to know. "To ask me questions about the Fortunes and see how much information you could get?"

He stared at her, practically dumbstruck. What was she talking about?

"The fact that you work for the Fortune Foundation has absolutely nothing to do with my wanting to get together with you," Everett insisted. Thinking over her accusation, he shook his head. "I'm not even sure if the family *is* connected to the Fortunes. It could all just be a silly rumor or a hoax.

"And even if it *does* turn out to actually be true, my family's not positive if we want to reveal the connection. It sounds like there are a lot of skeletons in the

Fortune closet. Actually," he confessed, backtracking, "maybe I spoke out of turn, talking about the possible connection. I'd appreciate it if you didn't say anything to anyone at the Foundation."

Did he think she was going to go running back after lunch and act like a human recording device, spilling every word that had been said between them? Just what sort of an image did he have of her?

Lila found herself struggling to tamp down her temper before she said anything.

"Well, obviously not everyone at the Foundation is a Fortune," she pointed out icily. "And anyway, the Fortunes are a huge family. I don't think anyone would be surprised to find out that there's another branch or two out there. There've been so many that have been uncovered already."

Everett nodded. "Makes sense," he agreed, even though he still felt a little leery about having the story spread around that the Fortunados believed that they were really Fortunes. Trying to steer the conversation in a different direction, he asked, "I'm curious—what do you think of the Fortunes?"

Lila's smile was reserved. She remembered hearing a great many unnerving rumors concerning the Fortune family before she began working at the Foundation. But most of what she'd been told turned out not to be true. For the most part, the stories were just run-of-the-mill gossip spread by people who were jealous of the family's success as well as their money.

"In my experience," she qualified in case he wanted to challenge her words, "they're a great family. A lot of people hold the fact that they're rich against them, but the family does a lot of good with that money. The Fortunes I've met aren't power hungry or self-centered. A great many of them have devoted their lives to the Foundation, to doing as much good as they can," she emphasized.

"Power-hungry and self-centered," Everett repeated the words that she had used. "Is that the way you think of most rich people?" he asked. Then, before Lila could answer, he went on to ask her another question—the question he *really* wanted the answer to. "Is that how you think of me?"

Her eyes narrowed again as she looked at Everett intently. Rather than answering his question, she turned it around and asked Everett a question of her own. "Did I say that?" she asked pointedly.

"No," he was forced to admit. She hadn't said it in so many words, but he felt that Lila had implied it by the way she'd structured her sentence.

"Then let's leave it at that, shall we?" Lila told him.

It was obvious to Everett that he was going to have one hell of a rough road ahead of him if he ever hoped to win her over. And despite what he had told his sister to the contrary, he really did want to win Lila back.

He admitted to himself that Lila was the missing ingredient in his life, the reason that every triumph he had had felt so hollow, so empty. It felt that way because Lila wasn't there to share it with him.

For now, he changed the subject to something lighter. "You know," he said as he watched Lila make short work of her Caesar salad, "as a doctor I should tell you that eating your food that fast is really not good for your digestion."

"And being late getting back from lunch isn't good for my job approval," Lila countered tersely. Finished, she retired her fork.

Was she really serious about needing to get back so quickly? Initially, he'd thought it was just an excuse, a way to terminate their meeting if she felt it wasn't going well. Now she seemed to be waving it in front of her like a flag at the end of a marathon.

"I thought you said that you were the manager of your department."

"I am. And as manager, it's up to me to set a good example," she told him.

If she really wanted to leave, Everett thought, he couldn't very well stop her. "Can't argue with that, I guess."

"No, you can't," she informed him, a stubborn look in her eyes as they met his.

He gave it one last try. "I suppose this means that you don't want to order dessert. I remember that you used to love desserts of all kinds," he recalled.

"I did," she acknowledged. "But then I grew up," she told him crisply. "And right now, I'm afraid I have no time for dessert."

He nodded. "Maybe next time, then."

Lila was about to murmur the obligatory, "It was good seeing you again," but his words stopped her cold. "Next time?" she echoed, surprised and stunned.

She sounded far from happy about the prospect. Everett did his best to ignore the coolness in her voice. Instead, he explained his comment. "I might be spending more time in Austin over the next few months."

"Oh?" She could feel the walls going up around her. Walls meant to protect her. She could feel herself struggling with the strong desire to run for the hills. She forced herself not to move a muscle. "Why?"

"Well, with Schuyler engaged to Carlo Mendoza and living here, I thought I'd be the good brother and visit her from time to time to make her transition here a little easier for her." This was harder than he thought it would be and it took him a few moments before he finally said, "I was wondering if it's all right with you if I call you the next time I'm in Austin."

His question was met with silence.

Chapter Four

Despite the fact that the restaurant was enjoying a healthy amount of business with most of the tables taken, the silence at their table seemed to wrap tightly around Everett and Lila.

Lila realized that Everett was waiting for her to answer him. And unfortunately, the floor hadn't opened up and swallowed her, so she was forced to say *something*. At a loss and wanting to stall until something came to her, Lila played dumb.

Clearing her throat she asked, "Excuse me? What did you say?"

Everett had a sinking feeling in the pit of his stomach as he repeated, "I asked if it would be all right with you if I called you the next time I was in Austin. You know, so we could get together again," he added and then watched her, waiting for an answer.

Again? Lila thought, astonished. *I'm barely surviving this time.*

She debated just shrugging her shoulders and saying, "Sure," with the hopes that if and when Everett called, she would have been able to come up with some sort of a viable excuse why she couldn't see him again.

But if she didn't put him off now, there was the very real possibility that she'd be doomed to go through another uncomfortable meeting in the near future.

Gathering her courage, Lila told him, "Um, I'm not sure if that's such a good idea."

If he were being honest with himself, Everett had half expected her to react this way. Still, actually *hearing* Lila say the words was very difficult for him.

Nodding grimly at her rebuff, he told her, "I understand."

But he really didn't understand because he didn't think it was a bad idea. He thought it was a perfectly *good* idea, one that would allow him another chance to convince her that they should try making their relationship work again after all these years.

Because they *belonged* together.

"Well, I really need to get going," she told Everett, rising to her feet. When he began to do the same, she quickly said, "Oh, don't leave on my account. Stay," she urged. "Have that dessert," she added. And then she concluded coldly, "I wish you luck with the rest of your life."

Then, turning on her heel, she quickly left the restaurant without so much as a backward glance.

Lila didn't exhale until the restaurant doors closed behind her.

Her heart was hammering hard and the brisk walk to her car had nothing to do with it. Lila didn't come anywhere close to relaxing until she reached her vehicle and got in.

Then she released her breath slowly.

She'd done it, she thought. She'd survived seeing him again.

She really hoped that Everett hadn't realized just how affected she was by his presence. With that in mind, there was just no way she could see him again, Lila thought. She was certain that she wouldn't be able to endure being face-to-face with Everett a second time, even if it was only for a couple of minutes.

But she'd done it. Lila silently congratulated herself as she started up her car. She'd sat across from Everett Fortunado and she hadn't bolted. She'd held her ground until she announced that she had to be getting back.

And now, having made it through that and gotten it out of the way, she could go on with the rest of her life.

Everett left the restaurant a couple of minutes after Lila did. There seemed to be no point in staying. He'd only mentioned having dessert because he remembered how fond of sweets she had always been. The thought of dessert had no allure for him, especially now that Lila had left. So he paid the tab and walked out.

He had barely managed to get into his car and buckle

up before his cell phone rang. His first thought when he heard the phone was that it was Lila, calling to say she had changed her mind about having him call her the next time he was in Austin.

But when he answered the phone, it wasn't Lila. It was Schuyler.

"So how was it?" his sister asked in lieu of a hello.

Trying hard not to sound irritated, he asked her, "Why are you calling? I could have still been at the restaurant with Lila."

"I took a chance," she told him. "If you were still with Lila, I figured you wouldn't have answered your cell. But you did," she concluded with a resigned sigh. "So I take it that she really did have a short lunch break."

He didn't have it in him to lie or make something up, so he just said vaguely, "Something like that."

He should have known Schuyler wanted to know more. "What was it like *exactly*?" she asked him.

Everett sighed. There was no point in playing games or pretending that everything was fine. He'd been pretending that for the last thirteen years and it had just brought him to this painful moment of truth. And he knew that Schuyler would just keep after him until he told about lunch.

"I think Lila might hate me," he said to his sister. He'd said "might" because stating it flatly just hurt too much.

"Hate you?" Schuyler questioned in surprise. "Why? What happened at lunch?" Then she chuckled. "Did she try to set you on fire?"

Everett laughed dryly. "No, she stopped short of that.

But when I asked if I could call her again the next time I was in Austin, she told me she didn't think that was such a good idea."

"Wait, back up," Schuyler told her brother. "You *asked* her if you could call?"

"Yes." Schuyler was making it sound like he'd done something bad, but he had just been trying to be thoughtful of Lila's feelings. He didn't want Lila thinking he just presumed things. He was proud of the fact that he was first and foremost a gentleman.

He heard his sister sigh in disbelief. "Everett, you are a brilliant, brilliant doctor and probably the smartest man I know, but what you know about women could be stuffed into a walnut shell with room for a wad of chewing gum. You don't *ask* a woman if you can call her. You just call her."

He didn't operate like that. "What if she doesn't want me to call?"

"Then you'll find that out *after* the fact," Schuyler told him. "Believe me, if she doesn't want you to call, she'll let you know when she answers the phone. But if you hold off calling because she said she doesn't want you to, then you might wind up missing out on an opportunity."

This was making his head hurt. "Nothing is straightforward with you women, is it?"

"That's where the aura of mystery comes in," Schuyler told him with a laugh. And then her voice sobered. "*Are* you planning on seeing Lila again?"

Lila had as good as told him not to—but he couldn't bring himself to go along with that. Not yet. Not while he felt that there might be the slimmest chance to change her mind.

"I'm going to try," he confessed.

"When?" Schuyler questioned. "Now?"

"No." He was still smarting from Lila's rejection. "I think I'm going to give her a little time to mull things over. I'll probably talk with her the next time I'm in Austin."

"Talk with her about what?" Schuyler wanted to know.

"I want to make things right," Everett explained simply. "Maybe even tell her—"

Schuyler cut him off before he could say anything further. "Ev, not even *you* can bring back the past, you know that, right?"

"Yes, I know that," he said impatiently, "but I just want Lila to know that I wish I'd handled things differently back them. Schuyler, you have your happy ending in the works," he pointed out, "but I wound up driving away the best thing that ever happened to me and I'll do anything to get her back."

"Oh Everett," Schuyler said, emotion in her tone, "that is deeply, deeply romantic—and deeply, deeply flawed. You're going to wind up failing and having your heart broken into a thousand little pieces, and then ground up into dust after that."

"I don't want to hear about it, Schuyler," he told his sister with finality. "I don't need you to tell me how I can fail. I need you to tell me that I'll get her back. I *need* to get her back," he emphasized.

He heard Schuyler sigh, as if she was surrendering.

"Okay. Just please, *please* don't do anything stupid," his sister warned.

"I already did," Everett told her. "I let Lila go in the first place."

"Everett—"

"I'll be in touch, Schuy," he told her before he terminated the call.

Everett gave it to the count of ten, then opened his phone again. He had a call to make and then he had to get back on the road if he wanted to reach Houston before nightfall.

Lila didn't need to get back to the office that quickly. She'd just told Everett that she did so she had a way to end their lunch. She'd estimated that half an hour in his company was about all she could take.

She had a feeling that if she came back early, the people she worked with, the ones who seemed to take such an inordinate interest in her life, would be all over her with questions.

Especially Lucie.

But if she timed it just right, she could slip into the office just as they were coming back from their own lunches. That way she stood a better chance of avoiding any questions.

She thought it was a good plan and it might have actually worked—if it hadn't been for the flowers. Two dozen long stemmed red roses in a glass vase to be precise. They were right there, in the middle of her desk, waiting for her when she walked into the office an hour after she'd left.

And there, right next to the vase, was Lucie. With a broad smile on her face.

"You just missed the delivery guy," she told Lila. "I signed for them for you."

"Um, thank you," Lila murmured, although what she was really thinking was that Lucie shouldn't have bothered doing that.

"No problem," Lucie answered cheerfully. Her eyes were practically sparkling as she looked from the flowers to her friend. It was obvious that she had barely been able to curtail her curiosity and keep from reading the card that had come with the roses. "Who are they from?"

"I have no idea," Lila murmured, eyeing the roses uneasily, as if she expected them to come to life and start taunting her.

"You know a really good way to find out?" Lucie asked her innocently. When Lila glanced in her direction, Lucie told her with great clarity: "Read the card."

Lila nearly bit off that she *knew* that. Instead, resigned, she said, "I guess I'll have to."

"Boy, if someone sent me roses, I'd sound a lot happier than that," Lucie commented.

"Want them?" Lila offered, ready to pick up the vase and hand it over to her friend.

"I'd love them," Lucie said with feeling. "But I can't take them. They're yours. Now who sent them?" Her eyes narrowed as she looked directly into Lila's.

Steeling herself, Lila reached over and plucked the small envelope stuck inside the roses. Slowly opening it, she took out the off-white rectangular card.

Till next time. Everett.

Her hand closed around the card. She was tempted to crush the small missive, but something held her back.

Damn it, why couldn't the man take a hint? Why was he determined to haunt her life this way? Why couldn't he just stay away the way he had done for the last thirteen years?

"Well?" Lucie asked, waiting. She tried to look over her friend's shoulder to read the card. "Who sent the flowers?"

"Nobody," Lila answered evasively.

"Well 'nobody' must have some pretty deep pockets," Lucie commented, eyeing the roses. "Do you know what roses are going for these days?"

"I don't know and I don't care," Lila answered defiantly. She was debating throwing the card into the trash.

"Well, 'nobody' certainly does. Care, I mean," Lucie clarified. "By any chance, are these flowers from the guy you went out to lunch with?"

Lila closed her eyes. She really did wish she could convincingly carry off a lie, but she couldn't. Absolutely no answer came to her, so she found herself having to admit the truth.

"Maybe."

Lucie gave a low whistle as she regarded the roses. "All I can say is that you must have made one hell of an impression at lunch."

"No, I didn't," Lila replied. "He asked if he could call me again and I told him I didn't think that was such a good idea."

Taking in the information, Lucie nodded. "Playing

hard to get. That really turns some guys on," she confided. "They see it as a challenge."

"I'm not playing hard to get," Lila stressed between gritted teeth. "I'm playing impossible to get."

"Same thing for some guys," Lucie responded knowingly. "What you did was just upped the ante without realizing it. Play out the line a little bit, then tell him that you've had a change of heart because he's so persistent. Then reel him in."

She felt like her back was up against the wall and Lucie was giving her fishing analogies. She looked at the other woman in disbelief. "You're telling me I should go out with him?"

"What I'm telling you is that you should give him another chance," Lucie told her.

Another chance. She knew that was what Everett wanted as well, even though he'd started out by acting as if he didn't, Lila thought. But there was no other reason why he would want to call her the next time he was in Austin *unless* he wanted another chance. It certainly wasn't because they'd had such a spectacular time today at lunch and he wanted to continue that.

They hadn't been spectacular together in a long, long time, Lila thought.

She tried to close her mind off from the memories, but they insisted on pushing their way through, punching through the fabric of the years.

Echoes from the past both softened her and squeezed her heart, reminding her of the pain she'd gone through at the end.

How could she willingly open herself up to that again? She'd barely recovered the last time.

Lila blinked. Lucie was standing in front of her, waving her hand in front of her eyes.

"Hey, Earth to Lila. Earth to Lila," Lucie called out.

"What?" Lila responded, stopping short of biting off an angry cry.

"I was talking to you and you seemed like you were a million miles away. Where were you just now?"

Lila blew out a quick breath and pulled herself together.

"You called it," she told the other woman. "I was a million miles away. And now it's time to come back and get to work," she announced. "I've got a stack of reports to review so I can make the rounds tomorrow."

Lucie inclined her head. "I can take a hint."

"I certainly hope so," Lila murmured under her breath.

Hearing her, Lucie added, "For now," as she left the room.

Lila suppressed a groan. Glaring at the roses, she moved the vase to the windowsill.

It didn't help.

Chapter Five

"Have you given 'Mr. Roses' any more thought?" Lucie asked her a few days later completely out of the blue.

They were each preparing their input to submit for their departments' monthly budget and, taking a break, Lucie had peered into her office to ask about Everett.

Surprised by the unexpected salvo—she'd thought she was out of the woods since Lucie hadn't brought the subject up for several days—Lila answered, "None whatsoever." She deliberately avoided Lucie's eyes as she said it.

"You're lying," Lucie said.

This time Lila did look up. She shot her a look that was just short of a glare, but Lucie wasn't intimidated.

"You know how I know?" Lucie asked her.

Lila braced herself inwardly. Her outward countenance didn't change. "Please, enlighten me," she requested coolly.

"You're blushing," Lila pointed out triumphantly. "Every time you say something that you're not entirely comfortable about—like a little white lie—you start to blush."

Lila drew herself up. "I do not," she protested. But even as she said it, she could feel her cheeks getting warmer.

"Got a mirror?" Lucie asked. She appeared to be serious. "I'll show you."

Lila sighed, dropping her head back. "Okay, so I've thought about him, but the answer to your next question is still 'no.' I'm not going to be seeing him again anytime soon—*or ever.*"

Lucie shook her head. It was obvious by her expression that she thought Lila was turning her back on a golden opportunity.

"I think you're making a mistake," Lucie told her in no uncertain terms.

"My mistake to make," Lila informed her cheerfully. And then, because she knew that Lucie was only looking out for her, she relented. "No offense, Lucie. I know you're a romantic at heart. I'm aware of your story," she went on. "You and Chase were teenage sweethearts who, despite a few bumps on the road—"

"Big bumps," Lucie emphasized, interjecting her own narrative.

"—were meant to be together," Lila continued, pushing on. "But not everyone is like you. Most teenage sweethearts usually outgrow each other and are meant to be apart."

"Aha," Lucie exclaimed. "So you two were teenage sweethearts."

Lila stared at her. That had been a slip. "I didn't say that," she protested.

"Not in so many words," Lucie countered. "But you definitely implied it. Lila," she said, lowering her voice as she put her hand over her friend's. "The heart wants what the heart wants and it doesn't always make perfect sense. But old loves imprint themselves on your heart and on your brain. Take it from me. They *always* stay with you."

"That might have been your experience," Lila granted. "And I know that you and Chase are extremely happy—"

"We are," Lucie assured her.

Lila forged on. "—but not everyone is like you," she concluded. "As a matter of fact, I'm pretty sure that very few people are like you."

Apparently her remark didn't satisfy Lucie, who went on. "Why don't you give this guy another chance and see if you belong to the 'very few?'" she suggested.

Lila went back to looking over her notes and figures for the budget. "Not going to happen."

Lila might have wanted to drop the subject, but Lucie obviously didn't. The subject of reunited lovers was something that was near and dear to her heart.

"Why?" Lucie asked her. "What are you so afraid of, Lila?"

Lila's eyes met her friend's. "I'm afraid of not getting my budget done in time," she said in a crisp voice.

"Seriously," Lucie coaxed.

"Seriously," Lila insisted, refusing to be distracted from the subject any further.

Just then, she saw a movement out of the corner of her eye. She looked toward the doorway. For a split second, she was afraid that Everett had found his way up to the office, but then she realized, as the man drew closer, that it was a deliveryman—and he was carrying another vase filled with flowers.

Not again!

"Oh, look, more roses," Lucie announced gleefully. "Just in time to replace the ones that are beginning to wilt," she added, grinning at Lila.

"How do you know they're for me?" Lila asked almost defensively. "There are plenty of other people who work here."

"Oh, I just have a feeling," Lucie told her, her eyes sparkling as she looked at her.

Her grin grew wider as the deliveryman came over to Lila's office where they were working.

"Ms. Clark?" the deliveryman asked, looking from one young woman to the other.

"That would be her," Lucie said, pointing toward Lila.

With a nod of his head, the deliveryman offered Lila what looked like a rectangular, brown Etch A Sketch.

"Would you sign here for the flowers, please?" the man requested.

Though she was strongly tempted to refuse the

flowers, Lila didn't want to create problems for the deliveryman, so she did as he had said.

Then he indicated the flowers. "Where do you want them?" he asked her.

"Be nice, Lila," Lucie cautioned, as if she could see that her friend was tempted to tell the man exactly where she wanted him to put the roses.

Resigned, Lila told the deliveryman, "I'll take them."

When she did, she realized that this vase felt even heavier than the last one had. Looking closer, she saw that the vase appeared to be cut crystal.

"Have a nice day," the deliveryman told her cheerfully, retreating.

"With those roses, how could she do otherwise?" Lucie asked, calling after him.

"You like them so much, here, you take them," Lila said, trying to hand the vase over to the other woman.

But Lucie raised her hands up high, putting them out of reach and thus keeping the transfer from being carried out.

"You know what this means, don't you?" she asked Lila.

"That the price of roses is being driven up even higher?" Lila asked sarcastically.

Lucie shook her head. She looked very pleased with this turn of events.

"No. It means that you might think you're done with this guy from your past, but he clearly is *not* done with you."

Lila had another take on the situation. "Maybe he's

just not used to taking no for an answer," she countered, frowning, then insisted, "All these flowers don't mean anything."

"You know, you still haven't answered my question," Lucie said, watching as Lila placed the flowers on the windowsill beside the other vase.

Lila didn't bother fussing with the newest arrangement. Instead, she sat down at her desk again, still trying to focus on the budget that was due. "What question is that?"

Slowly, enunciating each word for emphasis, Lucie repeated, "What are you afraid of?"

"I thought I answered that," Lila told her. "I believe I said I was afraid of not getting my budget done in time."

Lucie's eyes met hers. "You know I'm just going to keep after you until you tell me what's up with you and this guy."

And she knew very well that Lucie would, Lila thought. This had to stop. It was bad enough she was trying to get Everett to back off and leave her alone. She did *not* need her friend championing Everett's cause as well.

"Lucie, I love you like a sister—but butt out," she told Lucie in no uncertain terms.

"Sorry," Lucie replied, looking at her innocently. "That doesn't compute."

Lila rolled her eyes. "*Make* it compute," she told Lucie and with that, she ushered the woman out and closed the door to her office because, all distractions and two dozen roses aside, she really *did* have a budget to hand in before the end of the week. Which meant that she had no time to think about Everett Fortunado and his attempts to get her to give him another chance to shatter her heart.

The roses on the windowsill were beginning to drop their petals. They fell sporadically, drifting like soft pink tears onto the industrial beige floor covering in her office.

There was something sad about watching the flowers wilt.

Or maybe she felt that way because, despite the two separate deliveries of long-stem roses, she had not heard from Everett since she'd left him in the restaurant on their one and only lunch date—if it could actually have been called that.

Lila told herself that she was relieved. If Everett didn't call, then she didn't have to come up with an excuse not to see him.

But amid all that so-called relief, she had to admit that there was just the slightest tinge of disappointment as well. She really hadn't thought that Everett would give up so easily, or so quickly.

But he obviously had.

He'd moved on and he was off her conscience—not that she'd ever done anything to feel guilty about when it came to Everett, she silently insisted. Everett, on the other hand, had a lot to atone for—

What was wrong with her? she suddenly upbraided herself. Why was she wasting time thinking about Everett or trying to figure out why he'd behaved the way he had? She didn't have time for all that, she admonished herself. Less time than usual.

She was in the middle of a very real health crisis.

Everyone at the Fortune Foundation was. They had been stricken by an unseasonable, full-fledged flu epidemic that was laying everyone low. As a result, they were understaffed, with almost a third of both the volunteers and employees alike calling in sick.

Being short-staffed when it came to the workers was one thing. But now two of the doctors who regularly volunteered their services, making the rounds and tending to the people in her district, had fallen sick and were out of commission as well.

What that meant in the short run was that there weren't enough doctors to administer the flu vaccines or to treat the people who were down with it.

This directly affected Lila, who oversaw the department that made certain poor families in her area had access to flu shots and to medical care.

She needed replacement for the sick doctors. STAT.

Lila had spent half the morning on the phones, calling every backup physician she could think of in the area. All the calls yielded the same results. The doctors were either up to their ears in patients—or they were sick themselves.

The cupboard, Lila thought, exasperated, was appallingly bare. There weren't any doctors in or around Austin left to call.

Frustrated, she closed her physicians' file on the computer. The people whose trust she had painstakingly worked to gain and whom she had gathered into the fold now needed help, and they were counting on her to come through. They weren't going to believe her when she said that she couldn't find any doctors to make house calls.

But it was true. She was totally out of doctors to call. Totally out of options…

Except for one, she suddenly realized as the thought zigzagged through her brain.

She hated to do this. Hated to have to call him and sound as if she was begging.

But this wasn't about her, Lila reminded herself. This was about the sick people who were counting on her. People who were in desperate need of medical care. Otherwise, some of them, the very young and the very old, might not make it.

Telling herself not to think about what she was doing, Lila took out the card Everett had handed her during the less than successful lunch. The card with his phone number on it.

Not his cell phone. She didn't want this to sound personal, although *that*, she had a feeling, might get the fastest results.

Lila squared her shoulders and rejected the thought about using Everett's cell phone number. She was going to try his office phone number first—and pray that she got through that way.

Tapping out the number on her landline, Lila found herself connected to a recording with a list of menu options.

Feeling unusually short-tempered, Lila nearly hung up at that point. But she forced herself to stay on. This was about the kids, she reminded herself. The kids, not her. She needed to try every available possibility.

After dutifully listening to the selections, she pressed "Number 4 for Dr. Fortunado."

That connected her to yet another recording, which asked her to leave her name, phone number and a brief message. The recording promised her a return call within twenty-four hours. It didn't sound reassuring, but she supposed that it was better than nothing.

The second the "beep" went off, Lila began talking.

"Everett, it's Lila. I'm sorry to bother you like this, but we've been hit really hard with this flu epidemic. I'm down two doctors, not to mention a number of staff members. Every backup physician I've called is already handling too many patients—if they're not sick themselves. I'm totally out of options, otherwise I wouldn't be bothering you. I know you're an internist and not a family practitioner, but to put it quite simply, I'm desperate. A lot of the people I interact with are down with this flu and I need help.

"If you're too busy to return this call, I'll understand. However, I hope you'll consider it. You can reach me in my office, or on my cell." She proceeded to recite both numbers slowly. "I hope to hear from you soon, but like I said, if you decide you can't help, I'll understand."

With that, she hung up and desperately tried to think of some other course of action. Maybe she could try physicians' assistants in the area. The way she saw it, it was any port in a storm at this point.

But she just ran into wall after wall.

Lila was beginning to think that the situation was hopeless.

And then her phone rang.

Snatching the receiver up, she cried, "This is Lila Clark," as she literally crossed her fingers, hoping that one of the many, *many* doctors she had called today was calling back to tell her that after due consideration, they had found a way to spare a few hours to work with the needy families.

"Lila," the deep voice on the other end of the line said. "It's Everett."

Chapter Six

As the sound of his voice registered, Lila felt as if everything had suddenly ground to a standstill all around her.

But maybe her imagination was playing tricks on her, or she had just heard incorrectly and *thought* it was Everett calling her. Someone else might have said that wishful thinking was to blame, but she refused to call it that.

Rousing herself, Lila asked in a small, stilted voice, "Everett?"

"Yes."

She exhaled a shaky breath before saying his name, as if to make certain that it really was him calling. "Everett."

Had he gotten her message? Lila wondered. Or was

this just a coincidence and he was calling because she hadn't acknowledged the roses he'd sent her? Taking nothing for granted, Lila replied, "I called you earlier today—"

"Yes, I know," he responded. "About a flu epidemic you're having in Austin. That's the reason I'm calling back. If you still need me, I can be there by tomorrow morning."

Relief swept over her, drenching her like a huge tidal wave and stealing her breath. Lila was certain she now understood how lottery winners felt.

"Oh, I need you," she said with feeling, and then she realized how that must have sounded to him. Mortified, Lila immediately backtracked. "That is… I mean—"

She heard Everett laugh softly. That same old laugh that used to make her skin tingle and had warm thoughts flowing all through her, fast and heavy.

"That's okay, I know what you meant," Everett assured her. "Are you really that short-handed out there?"

Looking at the mounting stack of calls on her desk, almost all requesting help, she stifled a groan. "You have no idea."

"Well, you can give me a tour and let me see what you're up against when I get there tomorrow," he told her.

She knew that Everett had his own practice and that he was going to have to make arrangements on his end in order to accommodate her, even for one day. It didn't take a genius to know that that he was really going out of his way for her.

"I can't begin to tell you how much I appreciate this, Everett," Lila began.

Everett cut her short. "I'm a doctor," he replied simply. "This is what I do." She heard papers being moved around on his end. "I should be able to get in by eight. Where should I meet you?"

This was really happening, she thought. Everett was actually coming to her rescue, despite the way everything had ended between them the last time they saw one another. Relief and gratitude mingled with a sharp twinge of guilt within her.

"Why don't we meet at the Fortune Foundation?" she suggested to him. "And we can go from there."

Lila went on to give him the address of the building, although that would have been easy enough for him to look up if he wanted to. She told him which floor she was on as well as the number of her office.

"I can wait outside the building for you if that'll be easier," Lila added.

"That won't be necessary," Everett assured her. "They taught me how to count in medical school."

Had she just insulted him somehow? Afraid of saying something wrong, Lila felt as if she was stumbling over her own tongue. "Oh, I'm sorry. I didn't mean to—"

"Lila," Everett raised his voice as he cut into her words. When she abruptly stopped talking, he told her, "Stop apologizing."

She took a deep breath, trying to center herself and regroup. None of this was easy for her. Not when it came to Everett. "Um, I guess I'm just not used to asking for favors."

Everett read between the lines. "Don't worry. I'm not going to ask you for a favor back if that's what you're thinking," he assured her. There was another moment of awkward silence on her end and then he said, "All right, if I'm going to be there tomorrow morning, I've got a few things to see about between now and then. See you tomorrow," he told her.

Everett hung up before she had a chance to thank him again.

Lila slowly returned the receiver back to its cradle. "Well," she murmured, still feeling somewhat numb as she continued to look at the receiver, "that at least solves some of my problem."

She was still one doctor down, but one out of two was a lot better in her opinion than none out of two, she told herself. She could definitely work with one.

In the meanwhile, she needed to get the list of patients prepared for the doctors who *were* coming in so that they could start making those house calls.

Lila looked down at the various names and addresses she'd already jotted down. The number of people who were just too ill to get to a local clinic on their own was astounding, and growing rapidly. Some of the people, she thought, were probably exaggerating their conditions, but she couldn't really blame them. The free clinics were always positively jammed from the moment they opened their doors in the morning. Waiting to be seen by a doctor was exceedingly challenging when you weren't running a fever. Sitting there with a fever of a hundred or more and feeling too weak to win a wrestling match against a flea was a whole different story.

If she were in that position, she'd ask to have the doctor come to the house, too.

Oh, who are you kidding? You could be at death's door and you'd drag yourself in to see the doctor because you wouldn't want to inconvenience anyone.

Lila smiled to herself as she gathered her things together to meet with the physicians who were volunteering their time today.

The silent assessment rang true. She'd rather die than to surrender to her own weakness, Lila thought, going out the door.

Lila was exhausted.

Having stayed late, reorganizing supplies and hustling all over the city to beg, borrow or threaten to steal more vaccine serum as well as arranging for more lab tests to be done, she had finally dragged herself home after midnight.

Too tired to eat, she still hadn't been able to get right to sleep—most likely because part of her kept thinking about having to interact with Everett after she had summarily rejected him the last time they had been together.

But she had finally dropped off to sleep somewhere around 1:00 a.m., only to wake up at 4:30 a.m., half an hour before her alarm was set to go off.

She lay there for several minutes, staring at the ceiling, telling herself that she had half an hour before she needed to get up, which meant that she could grab a few more minutes of sleep.

She gave up after a couple more minutes, feeling

that there was no point in trying to get back to sleep. She was wired and that meant she was up for the day.

With a sigh, she got up, showered and dressed. A piece of toast accompanied her to her car, along with a cup of coffee that would have been rejected by everyone except a person who felt they had no extra time to make a second, better cup of coffee.

Sticking the thick-sludge-contained-in-a-cup into a cup holder, Lila started the car.

There had to be a better way to achieve sainthood, she thought cryptically to herself as she drove to the Foundation in the dark.

The streets were fairly empty at that time in the morning. The lack of light just intensified the pervasive loneliness that seemed to be invading every space in her head.

Snap out of it, damn it, she ordered. *He's a doctor and you need a doctor in order to help out. And that's all you need.*

However, ambivalent feelings about seeing Everett again refused to leave her alone. They continued to ricochet through her with an intensity that was almost numbing.

He's not Everett, she silently insisted. *He's just an available doctor who's willing to help you. That's what you have to focus on, not anything else, understand? Don't you dare focus on anything else.* She all but threatened herself.

It helped.

A little.

Arriving in the parking lot located behind the Fortune Foundation building, she found that there were only a few vehicles that pockmarked the area at this hour. Apparently the Foundation had a few early birds who liked to come in and get a jumpstart on the day and the work they had to do.

As she made her way toward the entrance, she saw that one of the cars, a navy blue high-end sedan, had someone sitting inside it in the driver's seat.

As she passed the vehicle, the driver's side door opened and Everett stepped out. A very casual-looking Everett wearing boots, jeans and a zippered sweatshirt with a hood.

She almost hadn't recognized him.

Her heart suddenly began to hammer very hard when she did.

"I got here early," he told her, nodding at Lila by way of a greeting. "Traffic from Houston wasn't too bad this time," he explained. He saw the way she was looking at what he was wearing. He looked down at his attire himself, just to be sure that he hadn't put anything on inside out. "I didn't want to look intimidating," he explained. "Someone told me that three-piece suits make some people nervous."

The way he said it, she felt as if he was implying she was the nervous person.

You've got to stop reading into things, she upbraided herself. Out loud she told him, "You look fine. We need to go in," she said, changing the subject as she turned toward the building. "I need to get a few things before we head out."

Everett nodded, gesturing toward the main doors. "You're the boss," he told her.

That almost made her wince. "This'll work better if you just think of me as your tour guide," she said, avoiding looking at him.

Holding the door open for her, Everett followed her into the building. "You told me that you manage the department," he recalled.

"I do," she answered cautiously, wondering where he was going with this.

"Then that would make you my boss for this," Everett concluded. "At least for now."

This had all the signs of degenerating into a dispute. But Everett *was* doing her a favor by coming in today and he was getting no compensation for it. She didn't want to pay him back by arguing with him.

"Whatever works for you is fine with me," Lila told him loftily.

He smiled at her as they headed toward the elevators. "I'll keep that in mind."

Was he just being agreeable, or was that some sort of a veiled warning, she wondered. This was all very exhausting and they hadn't even gotten started, Lila thought.

The next moment, as she got into the elevator, Lila told herself that any way she looked at it, this was going to be one hell of a long day.

But then, she had her doubts that Everett was going to be able to keep up. Making house calls to all the people on her list was going to turn into a marathon as well as an endurance test, at least for Everett.

And maybe her, too.

Getting what she needed from her office, Lila led the way back out of the building. "We'll use my car," she told him.

"Fair enough," Everett answered agreeably. "You know your way around here a lot better than I do."

"At least in the poor sections," she answered. They had barely gotten out on the road when she said, "Be sure to let me know when you've had enough."

He thought that was rather an odd thing to say, seeing as how they hadn't even been to see one patient yet. "And then what?" he wanted to know.

She spared him a glance as she drove through a green light. The answer, she thought, was rather obvious. "And then we'll stop."

"For the day?" he questioned.

"Well, yes." What else did he think she meant? They weren't talking about taking breaks.

"You made it sound like you needed me for the long haul," he said. And to him, that meant the entire day— with the possibility of more after that.

"I do." However, she didn't want to seem presumptuous and she definitely didn't want to totally wear him out. "But—"

"Well, then that's what you've got me for," Everett said, interrupting. "The long haul," he repeated.

Was he saying that to impress her, or did he really mean it, she wondered.

"I just wanted to warn you," she said as they drove to a run-down neighborhood. "This isn't going to be what you're used to."

He looked at her then. "No offense, Lila, but we haven't seen each other for a very long time," he reminded her. "You have no idea what I'm used to."

Everett was right, she thought, chagrined. She had no idea what he been doing in the years since they had seen one another. She knew, obviously, that he had achieved his dream and become a doctor. She had just assumed that he had set up a practice where he tended to the needs of the richer people in Houston. It never occurred to her that he might concern himself with even middle-class patients, much less those who belonged to the lower classes: the needy and the poor. And she had no idea that he ever volunteered his time to those less fortunate.

"You're right," she admitted quietly. "I don't. I just know that your parents had high hopes for you and that you weren't the rebellious type."

Everett was only half listening to her. For the most part, he was taking note of the area they were now driving through. It appeared seedy and dilapidated. It was light out now, which made the streets only a tad safer looking.

He tried to imagine what it was like, driving through here at night. "How often do you come out here?" he wanted to know.

"As often as I need to. I usually accompany the doctors who volunteer at the Foundation. It wouldn't be right to ask them to come here and not be their go-between."

"Go-between?"

She nodded. "Some of the doctors have never been

to places like this before. They're uneasy, the patients they've come to treat are uneasy when they see the doctor. I'm kind of a human tranquilizer," she told him. "It's my job to keep them all calm and get them to trust each other enough so they can interact with one another," she explained.

"A human tranquilizer, huh?" he repeated with a grin, trying to envision that. "I kind of like that."

She laughed as she brought her small compact car to a stop in front of a ramshackle house that looked as if it was entering its second century.

"I had a feeling you would." Pulling up the hand brake, she turned off the ignition. "We're here," she announced needlessly. "You ready for this?" she asked, feeling somewhat uneasy for him.

Everett looked completely unfazed. "Let's do it," he told her, getting out on his side.

Lila climbed out on the driver's side, rounded the hood of her car and then led the way up a set of wooden stairs that creaked rather loudly with each step she took. Like the house, the stairs had seen better years and were desperately in need of repair.

Reaching the top step, she approached the front door with its peeling paint and knocked.

"The doorbell's out," she explained in case Everett was wondering why she hadn't rung it. "I've been here before," she added.

"That was my guess," Everett responded.

A moment later, the front door opened rather slowly. Instead of an adult standing on the other side, there was a small, wide-eyed little boy looking up at them. He was holding onto the doorknob with both hands.

In Everett's estimation, the boy couldn't have been any older than four.

Chapter Seven

Lila thought that Everett had dropped something when she saw him crouching down at the door of their first house call—single mother Mrs. Quinn. The next moment, she saw that what he was doing was trying to get down to the level of the little boy who stood across the threshold.

"Does your mom know you open the door to strangers?" Everett asked the boy.

The little boy shook his head from side to side, sending some of his baby-fine, soft blond hair moving back and forth about his face. "No. Mama's asleep next to my little brother."

"You're very articulate," Everett told the little boy. "How old are you?"

"Four," the boy answered, holding up four fingers so

that there would be no mistaking what he said. "What's ar-tic—, ar-tic—" Giving up trying to pronounce the word, he approached it from another angle. "What you said," he asked, apparently untroubled by his inability to say the word.

"It means that you talk very well," Everett explained. Then he rose back to his feet. Glancing toward Lila so that the boy would know she was included, he requested, "Why don't you take us to see them? I'm a doctor," he added.

That seemed to do the trick. The little boy opened the door further, allowing them to come in. "Good, 'cause Mama said they need a doctor—her and Bobby," the four-year-old tacked on.

Impressed at how well Everett was interacting with the boy, Lila let him go on talking as she and Everett followed him through the cluttered house.

"Is Bobby your brother?" Everett asked.

This time the blond head bobbed up and down. "Uh-huh."

"And what's your name?" Everett asked, wanting to be able to address their precocious guide properly.

"Andy," the boy answered just as he reached the entrance to a minuscule bedroom. "We're here," he announced like the leader of an expedition at journey's end.

There was a thin, frail-looking dark-haired woman lying on top of the bed, her eyes closed, her arm wrapped around a little boy who was tucked inside the bed. The woman looked as if the years had been hard on her.

Andy tiptoed over to her and tried to wake her up by shaking her arm.

"Mama, people are here. Mama?" he repeated, peering into her face. He looked worried because her eyes weren't opening.

Lila finally spoke up. "Mrs. Quinn?" she said, addressing the boys' mother. "It's Lila. I brought a doctor with me."

The young woman's eyelashes fluttered as if she was trying to open them, but the effort was too much for her. She moaned something unintelligible in response to Lila's announcement.

Before Lila could say anything either to the woman or to Everett, he took over.

Moving Lila aside, he felt for the woman's pulse. Frowning, he went on to take her temperature next, placing a small, clear strip across her forehead.

"No thermometer?" Lila asked.

"This works just as well," he assured her. Looking at the strip, he nodded. "She's running a low-grade fever." Checking the boys' mother out quickly, he told Lila, "I can't give her a flu shot because she already seems to have it. But I can lower her fever with a strong shot of acetaminophen."

As Everett spoke, he took out a syringe and prepared it.

Andy's eyes followed his every move, growing steadily wider. "Is my Mama gonna die?" he asked, fear throbbing in his voice.

"No, Andy. I'm going to make your mom all better. But you're going to have to be brave for all three of you," Everett told him. "Think you can do that?" he asked, talking to him the way he would to any adult.

The boy solemnly nodded his head. He held his breath as he watched his mother getting the injection.

"Good boy." Everett moved on to the woman's other son. "Looks like he's got it, too," he said to Lila. Turning to Andy, he asked him, "Andy, do you know how long your mom and brother have been sick?"

Andy made a face as he tried to remember. He never took his eyes off the syringe, watching as the doctor gave his brother an injection next.

"Not long," Andy answered. "We were watching *Captain Jack* yesterday when Bobby said he didn't feel so good. Mama carried him to bed and she laid down, too."

Everett turned to look at Lila. *"Captain Jack?"* he questioned.

"It's a syndicated cartoon," Lila told him. "I think it airs around eight or so in the morning. One of the women in the office has a little boy who likes to watch it," she explained in case he wondered why she would know something like that.

"So Mrs. Quinn could have been sick for a couple of days?" Everett questioned, attempting to get a handle on how long mother and son had been down with the illness.

Lila was about to narrow it down a little more. "Mrs. Quinn called my office yesterday, but I didn't have anyone I could send."

Everett nodded, taking the information in. "You can only do as much as you can do," he told her. He knew

Lila would beat herself up but it wasn't her fault. She couldn't make doctors appear out of thin air.

He performed a few tests on Mrs. Quinn and Bobby, and then he turned in Andy's direction. "It's your turn, Andy."

Andy looked totally leery as he slanted a long glance in the doctor's direction. "My turn for what?" he asked in a small voice.

"You get to be the one in your family to get a flu shot," Everett told him.

"But I don't want a shot. I'm not sick," Andy cried, his voice rising in panic.

"No, you're not," Everett agreed. "And if you let me give you a flu shot, you'll stay that way. Otherwise..." His voice trailed off dramatically.

Andy tried to enlist Lila to help him. She was just returning into the bedroom, bringing bottles of drinking water she'd brought with her in her car.

"But won't a flu shot give me the flu?" the boy asked, anticipatory tears of pain already gathering in his eyes.

"No, it acts like a soldier that keeps the flu away," Everett told him. "You don't want to get sick like your mom and your brother, do you?" Everett asked. "Someone's got to stay well to take care of them."

Andy looked torn, and then he sighed. "I guess you're right."

"Good man," Everett congratulated the little boy with hearty approval.

Lila set down the bottles of water as well as several pudding cups and bananas she'd brought in. "Attaboy," she said to Andy. "If you like, I'll hold you on my lap while Dr. Everett gives you that shot."

She didn't wait for the boy to answer. She gathered him up in her arms and held him on her lap.

"Okay, Dr. Everett. Andy's ready." She felt the little boy dig his fingers into her arm as Everett gave him the flu injection. She heard Andy breathe in sharply. "You were very brave," she commended the boy.

"I'll say," Everett said, adding his voice to praise the boy. As he packed up his bag, he looked around, concerned. "Is there anyone who can stay with the kids until Mrs. Quinn is well enough to take care of them?" he asked Lila in a low voice. "I don't like the idea of just leaving them this way."

"Mrs. Rooney comes by to stay with us sometimes whenever Mama has to go out," Andy said, looking from the doctor to Lila as if to see if they thought that was good enough.

"Do you know where Mrs. Rooney lives?" Everett asked Lila.

"I think that's the woman next door," she told him before Andy could respond. Shifting Andy off her lap, she rose to her feet. "I can go and knock on her door," she volunteered.

"We'll go together," Everett told her. When she looked at him quizzically, he said, "You shouldn't be out there alone."

In a low voice, she told Everett, "I've been dealing with people in this neighborhood and places *like* this neighborhood for several years now. You don't have to worry about me."

"No," Everett agreed. "I don't 'have to.' But since I'm here, I'd feel better going with you," he told her, adding, "Humor me."

Instead of answering him, she looked at Andy, who was rubbing his arm where he had received his vaccination. "Andy, do you know if Mrs. Rooney does live next door?" she asked.

Sniffing as he blinked to keep big tears from falling, Andy nodded. "Uh-huh, she does."

Lila smiled at Everett. "Problem solved. I'll just pop in next door and ask the woman to keep an eye on this family."

She glanced at her watch. They had spent more time here than she'd anticipated. She was glad that it had gone so well for Everett, but they did need to speed things up.

"And then we're going to have to get a move on," she told Everett. "Otherwise, we're not going to get to see all the people on my list unless we work through the night and possibly into the next morning."

He hadn't thought that there were going to be *that* many houses to visit. But as far as he knew, Lila had never been one to exaggerate.

"Then you'd better find out if Mrs. Rooney is willing to stay with Andy and his family," he urged.

That went off without a hitch.

After getting the woman to stay with the Quinn family, Lila drove herself and Everett to the second name on her list.

Again she was treated to observing Everett's bedside manner. She was completely amazed by how easily he seemed to get along with children. Not only get along with them but get them to trust him and rather quickly.

She smiled to herself as she recalled worrying that he might frighten the children because he'd be too stiff or too cold with them, but that definitely didn't turn out to be the case. Right from the very beginning, she saw that Everett knew exactly how to talk to the children.

Moreover, he acted as if he actually *belonged* in this sort of a setting.

Talk about being surprised, she mused.

As they drove from one house to another, Lila found herself wondering what these people who had so little would think if they knew that the man who was administering their vaccinations, writing out their prescriptions and listening so intently to them as they described their symptoms was actually a millionaire's son with a thriving, fancy practice back in Houston.

She laughed quietly to herself. They'd probably think that she was making it up because Everett seemed so down-to-earth, not to mention so focused on making them feel better.

As she continued observing Everett in setting after setting, Lila could feel her heart growing softer and softer.

It became harder for her to regard Everett in any sort of a cold light and practically impossible for her to keep the good memories at bay any longer.

Everett had grown into the good, decent man she had, in her heart, always felt that he was destined to become.

* * *

"How many more?" Everett asked her as they drove away from yet another house.

He and Lila had been at it for a straight twelve hours, stopping only to pick up a couple of hamburgers to go at a drive-through. They ate the burgers while driving from one patient to the next.

Keeping her eyes on the road as she drove, Lila smiled at his question. She didn't have to pull out her list to answer him. "That was the last house on my list."

"No more left?" Everett questioned, thinking that she might have accidentally overlooked one or two more patients.

"Nope, no more left," Lila told him. She flashed him a relieved grin to underscore her words.

"Wow." Everett leaned his head back against his headrest. "I was beginning to feel like we were going to go on with these house calls forever."

She laughed. "Does feel that way, doesn't it?" She spared him a glance as she came to a stop at a light. "Bet you're sorry now that you returned my call yesterday."

"No," Everett responded quite seriously. "I'm not."

After twelve hours of work on very little sleep, all she should be thinking about was getting some rest, nothing else. So why in heaven's name did she suddenly feel what amounted to an all-consuming hot tingle passing over the length of her body just because Everett had said that he wasn't sorry he'd called her back?

What was wrong with her?

Punchy, she was punchy. That had to be it, Lila decided.

Talk, damn it. Say something! she ordered herself. The silence was getting deafening.

Clearing her throat, Lila said, "Well, I have to admit that you surprised me today."

"Oh?" Everett responded. "How so?"

Lila was honest with him. She felt it was the best way. "I didn't think you had it in you to just keep going like this. And I really didn't think you knew how to talk to children."

"Why?" he asked. "Children are just short adults."

Lila laughed, shaking her head. "You would be surprised how many doctors don't really know how to talk to fully grown adults, much less to little children," she told him.

"That's right," Everett recalled. "When we started out today you told me that you were there to act as the go-between." He continued to look at her profile, curious. "So I guess I passed the test?"

The light turned green and Lila pressed down on the accelerator. Once they were moving again, she answered, "With flying colors." Again she felt she had to tell him how surprised she was by his performance. "I didn't think that you'd keep at it long enough to see all the people on the list." She struggled to stifle a yawn. The long day was catching up to her. "But it's kind of late now," she told him needlessly.

"It is," he agreed.

She glanced at the clock on the dashboard, even though she already knew what time it was. "Too late for you to be driving back to Houston tonight," she told him.

"Are you offering to put me up?" he asked, doing his best to keep a straight face.

That startled her. "What? No, I just—"

"Take it easy," he laughed. "You don't have to worry. I've already talked to Schuyler. She's expecting me. I'm spending the night at her place."

"So that means that you're not going back until sometime tomorrow?" Lila asked.

He laughed again. "I can see the wheels turning in your head. No, I'm not going back to Houston until the day after tomorrow. So, if you want me to make a few more house calls with you tomorrow, I'm available."

That would be a huge help. She was still down a few volunteer doctors and she still hadn't found any more replacements.

"Don't toy with me, Everett," she told him, casting a glance his way.

His eyes were smiling at her. "I wouldn't dream of it."

Her heart fluttered. She forced herself to face forward. "All right. If you don't mind putting in some more time, then yes, absolutely. I could *really* use you for however much time you can spare."

"All right, then, same time tomorrow?" he asked as she pulled into the Foundation's parking lot.

"Make it eight-thirty," she told him.

"I'll be there," he promised, getting out of her car.

"If you decide to change your mind," she began, feeling obligated to give him a way out. After the day he had put in today, she didn't want to force him to come in tomorrow.

But Everett cut her off. "I won't," he told her just before he walked over to his own car.

Lila caught herself smiling. She knew he meant it.

Chapter Eight

When Lila got up the next morning, she felt absolutely wiped out. If possible, she was even more tired than the day before. It was as if her get-up-and-go had physically gotten up and left.

"You're just burning the candle at both ends," she told the tired-looking reflection staring back at her in the bathroom mirror. "And maybe a little in the middle as well."

The shower did not invigorate her the way it usually did.

Dragging herself over to her closet after her shower, Lila pulled out the first things she found and got dressed. She was staring down the barrel of another grueling day, but at least she had a doctor for part of it, she thought. And after Everett left for Houston, maybe she would get lucky and be able to scrounge up another volunteer physician to conduct the house calls that were left on the list.

Determined to make herself look a little more human than what she saw in her mirror, Lila patiently applied her makeup. She succeeded in making herself look a little less exhausted—or at least less like someone who had recently been run over by a truck. The last thing she wanted was to have Everett take one look at her this morning and breathe a sigh of relief that he had dodged a bullet thirteen years ago.

Lila was still struggling to pull herself out of what was for her an atypical funk when she drove to the Foundation. This just wasn't like her, she thought. No matter how tired she felt, she never dragged like this, as if there was lead in her limbs.

C'mon, snap out of it! she silently ordered.

Just like the day before, when she drove into the parking lot, she found Everett sitting in his car, waiting for her.

When Everett saw her car approaching, he quickly got out of his vehicle. The cheery greeting on his lips didn't get a chance to materialize because he took a closer look at her as she got out of her car.

"Are you feeling all right, Lila?" he asked her.

So much for makeup saving the day, Lila thought. "I'm just running a little behind," she answered, deliberately being vague. Changing the subject, she asked, "Do I have you for half a day—or less?"

Rather than give Lila a direct answer, Everett told her, "Why don't we play it by ear and see?"

Lila put her own spin on his words. Everett was setting the stage so he could bail whenever he felt as if he'd had enough. Not that she blamed him, she thought. The man had already given a hundred and fifty percent of his time yesterday, far more than she had the right to expect, and she couldn't be greedy.

The hell she couldn't, Lila caught herself thinking. After all, this wasn't about her. This was about all those people who were counting on her to find a way to keep them healthy—or get them healthy—and at the very least, that involved having a doctor pay them a house call.

"Okay," Lila said with all the pseudo enthusiasm she could muster as she opened the passenger door for Everett. "Let's get started."

"How do you do this every day?" Everett wanted to know after they had made more than half a dozen house calls.

"Doctors used to do this all the time," she told Everett.

It took him a moment to understand what Lila was referring to. He realized that they weren't on the same page.

"I'm not talking about the house calls," Everett told her. "I'm talking about seeing this much poverty and still acting so cheerful when you talk to the people."

"I'm being cheerful *for* their sake. An upbeat attitude brings hope with it," she told him. "And hope and perseverance are practically the only way out of these neighborhoods," Lila maintained.

Everett was more than willing to concede the point. "You probably have something there." And then he blew out a breath, as if mentally bracing himself for round two. "How many more people are on that famous list of yours for today?" he wanted to know.

It was already closer to one than to noon. Did he know that, she wondered. They'd been at this for hours and she'd assumed that no matter what he'd said on the outset, she just had him for half a day.

"Don't you have a plane to catch or a car to drive?" she asked.

"Trying to get rid of me?" he asked her, an amused expression on his face.

"No, on the contrary, trying not to take you for granted and start relying on you too much," Lila corrected. And in a way, that was true. That had been her downfall all those years ago. She'd just expected to be able to rely on Everett forever. And look how that had turned out, she thought. Determined to pin him down, she asked, "How long did you say you could work today?"

"I didn't, remember?" he reminded her.

"Right. You said, quote, 'why don't we play it by ear and see,'" Lila recalled.

"Well, it still seems to be going, doesn't it?" he observed, his expression giving nothing away. "Who's next on the list?" he asked, redirecting her attention back to the immediate present.

Eyes on the road, Lila put one hand into the purse

she kept butted up next to her and pulled out the list of patients that she'd put right on top. All she needed was a quick glance at the page.

"Joey Garcia's next," she answered. "Joey's the baby of the family," she added, giving Everett an encapsulated summary of his next patient. "He's got two big sisters and two big brothers and he always gets everything after the rest of the family's gotten over it.

"However, according to my records," she said, trying to recall what she had entered on her tablet, "I don't think anyone in the family has had the flu *or* gotten the vaccine this year."

"Well, I guess we're about to find out, aren't we?" Everett speculated as she pulled the car up before another house that looked as if it might have been new over fifty years ago.

Lila got out on her side and immediately found that she had to pause for a moment. She held onto the car door for support. Everything around her had suddenly opted to wobble just a little, making her head swim and the rest of her extremely unsteady.

Realizing that she wasn't with him as he approached the house, Everett looked back over his shoulder. "Something wrong?"

"No." Lila refused to tell him she'd felt dizzy, especially since the feeling had already passed. She didn't want to sound whiny or helpless and she definitely didn't want him fussing over her. "Just trying to remember if I forgot something."

Everett thought that sounded rather odd. What could she have forgotten? "Did you?"

"No," she answered rather abruptly. "I've got every-thing."

He played along for her sake. She didn't look as if she was herself today.

"I don't know how you manage to keep track of everything," he told her as they approached the Gar-cias' front door.

"It's a gift," Lila told him wryly. She forced a wide smile to her lips as she fervently wished that she'd stop feeling these odd little waves of weakness that kept sweeping over her.

Taking a deep breath, she knocked on the front door. It swung open immediately. The next moment, she was introducing Everett to a big, burly man who appeared to be almost as wide as he was tall.

"Mr. Garcia, this is Dr. Everett Fortunado. He'll be giving you and your family your flu vaccinations," Lila told Juan Garcia and the diminutive wife standing next to him.

The couple went from regarding Everett suspiciously to guardedly welcoming him into their home.

"The children are in the living room," Mrs. Garcia said, leading the way through what amounted to almost railroad-style rooms to the back of the house.

As he walked into the living room, Everett was im-mediately aware of five pairs of eyes warily watching his every move.

Everett did his best to set the children at ease, talk-ing to them first and asking their names. He explained exactly what he was about to do and what they could ex-pect, including how the vaccine felt going into their arms.

When he was done, he surprised Lila by handing out small candy bars to each child. "For being brave," he told them.

"That was nice of you," Lila said as they left the Garcias' house twenty minutes later.

Everett shrugged. "Candy makes everything better." He got into the car. "I thought you said they called you."

"Well, sometimes I call them," Lila replied. She could feel Everett regarding her quizzically as she pulled back onto the street. "Mr. Garcia is very proud. He doesn't like accepting help. He's also out of work. I thought he and his family could do with a little preventative medicine so that if a job *does* come up, he won't be too sick to take it. He's a day laborer when he's not driving a truck," she explained. When Everett didn't say anything, she elaborated on her statement. "The man has five kids. If they all came down with the flu, it would be guaranteed pure chaos. This was a pre-emptive strike."

That was one way to look at it, Everett thought. Obviously Lila was focused on doing good deeds. "So when did you get fitted for the wings and halo?" Everett asked her.

"I didn't," she answered crisply. "They were left behind by the last department manager." She kept her eyes on the road, not trusting herself to look at him. Sudden movements made her dizzy. "I just try them on for size occasionally."

"Oh." He pretended as if what she'd just said made

perfect sense. "So, how many more house calls do we have left?" he asked, getting serious again.

This time Lila didn't have to consult her list. "We've got two more."

"Just two more?" he questioned. Yes, they'd been at this for a long time, but he'd just expected to keep going until almost nightfall again, the way they had yesterday.

"Just two more," Lila repeated. "And then you're free."

"Free, eh?" he echoed. He studied her profile. "How about you?"

"How about me what?" she asked. Had she missed a question? Her brain felt a little fuzzy and she was having trouble following him.

"Are you free?" Everett asked, enunciating each word clearly.

"Free for what?" she asked. She was still having trouble following him.

"Free for dinner," he asked, then quickly added, "I thought that maybe, since we've developed this decent working relationship, you wouldn't mind grabbing some dinner together."

Lila pressed her lips together. All she'd been thinking about the last few hours was going home and crawling into bed. But she was not about to tell Everett that. She didn't want to have to listen to a lot of questions.

So instead, sounding as cheerful as possible, she said, "I guess I do owe you that."

"I don't want you to have dinner with me because you 'owe' me," he told her. "I want you to have dinner with me because you want to."

Potato, po-tah-to, she thought. He'd come through for her, so she supposed that she could humor him. "I want to," she answered quietly.

"Great," he said. "Let's go see these last two patients."

The visits took a little longer than he'd come to anticipate, mainly because the second one involved more than just dispensing flu vaccinations to the two older children and their parents. Everett found himself tending to a pint-size patient with a sprained wrist that he didn't even know he had.

Afraid of being laughed at by his brothers for being clumsy, when it was his turn for the vaccine, little Alan had tried to hide his swollen wrist.

Drawing him over to Everett, Lila had accidentally brushed against the boy's wrist and saw him wince, then try to pretend he was just playing a game with her. The truth came out rather quickly.

"Never try to hide something like that," Lila told him as Everett bandaged the boy's wrist and then fashioned a makeshift sling for him. "They just get worse if you ignore them," she told him.

Alan solemnly nodded his head.

"He's been moping all day," Alan's mother told them as they were packing up their supplies. "Now I know why. Here," she said handing Lila a pie, which, by its aroma, had just recently left the oven. "This is my way of saying thank-you."

Lila declined. "As a Foundation worker, I can't accept payment," she told the other woman.

"Then take it as a friend," Alan's mother told her. "One friend to another. You will be insulting me if you don't accept it," the woman insisted.

The way she felt, Lila was not up to arguing. Pulling her lips back into a thin smile, she expressed her thanks, saying, "Dr. Everett will take it home with him. Maybe your gift will encourage him to return to Austin again soon."

The woman was obviously pleased to play her part in coaxing the good-looking doctor back.

"Maybe," she agreed, flashing a bright, hopeful smile at Everett.

"I wouldn't have thought of that," Everett told Lila when they were back in her car again. "That was quick thinking," he complimented her.

Lila was hardly aware of shrugging. "I didn't want to hurt her feelings, but I didn't want to set a precedent, either. Having you take it seemed like the only logical way out."

"Still wouldn't have thought of it," he told her.

"Sure you would have," she countered. "You're the smartest man I know."

No I'm not, he thought. He could cite a time when he'd been downright stupid.

Like thirteen years ago.

Everett studied her quietly as she drove. In his opinion, Lila had blossomed in the intervening years. She was no longer that stricken young girl who'd told him she never wanted to see him again. She'd become a self-assured woman who obviously had a mission in life.

A mission she was passionate about, and that passion made her particularly compelling and exciting.

He found himself being attracted to Lila all over again and even more strongly this time than he had the first time around.

"Can you clock out once we get back to the Foundation?" he asked suddenly, breaking the heavy silence in the car.

"This actually is the official end of my day, so yes, I can clock out."

"And we're still on for dinner?" he asked, not wanting to come across as if he was taking anything for granted. He knew that winning Lila back was going to take time and patience—and he very much intended to win her back.

"If you still want to have dinner with me, then yes, we're still on," she answered cautiously. She made a right turn, pulling into the parking lot. "Are you sure this won't interfere with you getting back to Houston? I feel guilty about keeping you away from your practice for so long."

"Nothing to feel guilty about," he assured her. "The choice was mine. And my practice is part of a group. We all pitch in and cover for one another if something comes up."

"And this qualifies as 'something?'" she asked him, a touch of amusement entering her voice.

"Oh, most definitely 'something,'" Everett assured her.

My lord, she was flirting with him, Lila realized. She really wasn't herself.

The next moment, there was further proof. "Lila, you're passing my car," Everett pointed out.

Preoccupied and trying to get a grip on herself, she hadn't realized that she had driven right by the navy blue sedan.

"Sorry," she murmured. "Just double-checking the schedule in my head."

"Schedule?" he questioned. But she'd said there was no one left on today's list, didn't she? Was there some secondary list he didn't know about?

"The list of patients," she clarified.

"Did we miss anyone?" he asked, wondering if she was going to find some excuse to turn him down at the last minute.

She wished she didn't feel as if her brain had a fog machine operating right inside her head. It was getting harder and harder for her to think straight.

"Lila?"

She realized that Everett was waiting for her to answer him. "Oh, no, we didn't. We saw everyone on the list. I was just thinking about tomorrow," she lied. "Let's go have dinner."

"Sounds good to me," he replied, silently adding, *Anything that has to do with you sounds good to me.*

Chapter Nine

"On second thought, maybe I should drive," Everett said to her just as Lila started her car up again.

Putting her foot on the brake now, Lila looked at Everett, confused.

"Why?" she wanted to know. "I know the city better than you do. You said so yourself."

"True, but I've been able to find my way around without much trouble and I don't mind driving. To be honest, you look like you're rather tired and you don't want to push yourself too hard," Everett stressed.

He was right. She *was* tired, Lila thought, but her pride kept her from admitting it. Her self-image dictated that she was supposed to be untiring, with boundless energy.

"Is that your professional opinion?" she asked.

"Professional and personal," Everett replied quietly.

There was that calming bedside manner of his again, Lila thought. But she wasn't a patient, she reminded herself.

"Tough to argue with that," she responded. "But you'll have to drive me back here after dinner so I can pick up my car."

Everett had already taken that into account. "No problem," he assured her. Getting out of her car, he took a few steps, then stood waiting for her to follow suit.

After a moment, Lila sighed, surrendering. Since she hadn't pulled out of the parking space yet, she left her car as it was and got out.

Crossing to his car, Everett unlocked it and then held the passenger side door open for her. After Lila got in, he closed the door and got in behind the wheel. He looked at her and smiled just before he started his car.

Was that smug satisfaction she saw, or something else? Lila wondered. "What?" she asked him.

"I thought you'd put up more of a fight," he confessed as he started up his vehicle. Within moments, they were on the road.

Lila lifted one shoulder in a careless shrug. She realized that her shoulder felt heavy for some reason, like someone was pushing down on it. After dinner, she was heading straight for bed, she promised herself.

"I guess I'm more tired than I thought," she told Everett.

He accepted her excuse. "You in the mood for Chinese or Italian?" he asked, offering her a choice of the first two restaurants he thought of. He favored both.

"The Italian place is closer," Lila told him.

And in this case, he thought, closer seemed to mean better, otherwise she would have cited a different criterion first.

"Italian it is." He spared her one quick glance, coupled with a grin. "Now all you have to do is give me the address."

Lila dug in just for a second. "I thought you said you knew your way around."

"I do," he assured her, then added, "Once I have an address."

She laughed shortly. "That's cheating," Lila accused.

"I'd rather think of it as being creative," he told her, then asked again, "The address?"

She was much too tired to engage in any sort of a war of resistance. With a sigh, she rattled off the address to the Italian restaurant.

Everett immediately knew where it was. "You're right, that is close," he acknowledged.

They were there in less than ten minutes. As luck would it, someone in the first row of the parking lot was just pulling out and Everett smoothly slipped right into the spot.

Shutting off his engine, he quickly came around to Lila's side.

Aware that Everett had opened the door for her, she felt a little woozy and it took her a moment to focus and swing her legs out. She really would have rathered that Everett wasn't holding the door open for her so he wouldn't see just how unsteady she was.

"You know, I have learned how to open my own door," she told him defensively.

If she was trying to antagonize him, Everett thought, he wasn't taking the bait.

"I know," he responded cheerfully. "I've seen you. But I like doing this," he told her, putting out his hand to her. "It makes me feel like a gentleman."

The wooziness retreated. Lila wrapped her fingers around his hand with confidence. Maybe she was worrying for no reason.

"Then I guess I'll humor you," she said, "seeing what an asset you were yesterday and today."

His smile sank deep into her very soul as he helped her out of the vehicle. "Whatever works."

Closing the door behind her, they crossed to the restaurant.

The homey, family-style restaurant was beginning to fill up, but there were still a number of empty tables available. The hostess seated them immediately and gave them menus.

"Do you come here often?" Everett asked Lila when they were alone.

"Often enough to know that they have good food," Lila answered.

Everett nodded. "Good, then I'll let you do the ordering," he told her, placing his menu on the table.

That surprised her. "Well, you certainly have changed," she couldn't help observing. When he raised an inquisitive eyebrow, she said, "There was a time when you took charge of everything."

He couldn't very well argue the point. He remembered that all too well.

"I've learned to relax and take things light," he explained. "Somebody once told me I'd live a lot longer that way—or maybe it would just seem longer," he added with a laugh.

As their server approached the table Lila asked, "Were you serious about my doing the ordering for you?"

"Very."

Lila proceeded to order. "We'll have two servings of chicken Alfredo," she told the young woman. "And he'll have a side dish of stuffed mushrooms."

"And you?" the young woman asked, her finger hovering over her tablet.

"No mushrooms for me," Lila answered.

"And what would you like to drink?" the server asked, looking from Lila to the man she was sitting with.

"I'll have a glass of water," Lila answered, then looked at Everett, waiting for him to make a choice himself. She remembered he liked having wine with his meals, but maybe that had changed, too, along with his attitude.

"Make that two," Everett told the server, then handed over his unopened menu to her.

Lila surrendered hers after a beat.

"I'll be back with your bread and waters," the server told them.

"Sounds more like a prison diet than something from a homey-looking restaurant," Everett commented.

"That's probably what she thought, too," Lila said. "She looked like she was trying not to laugh." She looked around the large room. More patrons had come in moments after they did. "Certainly filled up fast," she observed, saying the words more to herself than to Everett.

"Worried about my being seen with you?" Everett asked, amused.

"No." She was actually thinking about how all those bodies were generating heat. "Does it seem rather warm in here to you?"

"Well, when you have this many bodies occupy a relatively small space, it's bound to feel somewhat warm," he speculated. And then he smiled. "You remembered I liked mushrooms," he said, clearly surprised.

"I remember a lot of things," she said, and then the next moment regretted it. "Like quadratic equations," she added glibly.

Everett laughed. And then he looked at her more closely. There was a line of perspiration on her forehead, seeping through her auburn bangs and pasting them to her forehead. "It's not warm enough in here to cause you to perspire," Everett observed.

"Maybe you make me nervous," Lila said flippantly.

"If that were the case, then you wouldn't have agreed to dinner," he pointed out. The woman he knew wouldn't do anything she didn't want to.

Lila shifted in her chair, growing progressively more uncomfortable. "It seemed impolite to turn you down after you went out of your way to be my white knight."

Her terminology intrigued him. "Is that what I am? Your white knight?" he asked.

"Did I say white knight?" she asked, as if she hadn't heard herself call Everett that. "I meant Don Quixote, not white knight. I always manage to get those two mixed up," she said.

"I've been called worse," he said with a tolerant laugh.

Their server returned with their glasses of water and a basket of garlic breadsticks. "I'll be back with your dinners soon," she told them, placing the items on the table and withdrawing.

Everett noticed that Lila immediately picked up her glass of water. Drinking, she practically drained the entire contents in one long swallow.

Seeing that Everett was watching her, Lila shrugged self-consciously. "I guess I was thirstier than I thought."

"I guess you were," he agreed good-naturedly. Something was up, but he wasn't about to press. He didn't want to ruin their dinner. Spending time with Lila like this was far too precious to him. Having taken a breadstick, he pushed the basket toward her. "Have one. They're still warm."

He watched her take a breadstick, but instead of taking a bite, she just put it on her plate and left it there, untouched.

"What's wrong?" he asked. "You always loved breadsticks, especially garlic breadsticks."

"I still do," she answered defensively. And then she relented. "I guess I'm just not hungry."

Something was definitely off. "I've been with you

all day. You haven't eaten since you came in—that's assuming that you *did* eat before you came in this morning."

Lila shrugged, then grew annoyed with herself for doing it. She wished that he'd stop asking questions. Most of all, she wished that she was home in bed.

"I'm not hungry," she snapped. "What do you want me to say?"

This was *not* like her. His eyes met hers. "The truth," Everett told her simply.

"I don't know what you're talking about," Lila retorted, irritated. "I'm just not hungry. That's not a crime," she protested.

It felt as if her emotions were going every which way at the same time.

"Look, maybe we should—"

Without thinking, Lila started to get up—which was when the world decided to launch itself into a tailspin all around her. She grabbed the edge of the table, afraid that she would suddenly go down and find herself unceremoniously sitting on the floor. The table wobbled as she grabbed it and she stifled a cry, sitting down again.

Everett reached across the table and put the back of his hand against her forehead. Lila pulled her head away. She regretted the movement immediately because the spinning in her head just intensified.

Her forehead was hot, Everett thought. That and the sharp intake of breath he'd just heard her make gave him all the input he needed.

"Dinner is canceled," he told her. "I'm taking you home and putting you to bed."

"If that's your idea of a seductive proposition, you just washed out," she informed him, struggling very hard to keep the world in focus.

"No, that's my idea of putting a sick woman to bed where she belongs." He looked around and signaled to the server. The latter was just approaching them with their orders. "Change of plans," he told her. "We have to leave."

Without missing a beat, the young woman told him, "I can have these wrapped to go in a few minutes."

Everett was about to tell the woman that they wouldn't be taking the meals home with them, but then he had a change of heart. Lila was going to need something to eat once she was feeling better. As for him, he *was* hungry and he could always take the food to eat later once he had Lila situated.

"There's an extra tip in it for you if you can get it back here in two minutes," Everett told her.

Taking his words to heart, the server was gone before he finished his sentence.

"You're making a scene," Lila protested weakly.

"No," he retorted. "I'm trying to prevent making a scene. You're sick, Lila. I should have seen the signs. But I was so eager just to have dinner with you, I missed the fact that you were steadily growing paler all day."

Just then, the server returned. She had their dinners and breadsticks packed in two rather large paper sacks.

"Your salad is packed on top," she told him.

"Great." Taking out his wallet, Everett handed the young woman a twenty, then put a hundred-dollar bill on the table. "This should cover it," he told the server.

When he turned to look at Lila, his concern grew. She was almost pasty. "Can you walk?"

"Of course I can," Lila retorted just before she stood up—and pitched forward.

Thanks to his quick reflexes, Everett managed to catch her just in time. Had he hesitated even for just half a second, Lila's head would have had an unfortunate meeting with the floor.

The server stared at them, wide-eyed. "Is she all right?" she asked, clearly concerned.

"She will be," Everett told her. He had perfected sounding confident, even when he wasn't. "I think she just has the flu," he added. In one clean, swift movement, he picked Lila up in his arms as if she was weightless. Turning toward the server, he requested, "If you could hand me her purse."

The woman had already gathered Lila's purse. "Don't worry, I'll take it and your dinners and follow you to your car," she volunteered. Looking at Lila, who was unconscious, she asked again, "You're sure she'll be all right?"

Reading between the lines, Everett told her, "Don't worry, it wasn't anything she had here." Then he made his way to the front entrance.

Seeing them, the hostess at the reservation desk hurried to open the front door for them, holding it open with her back. "Is everything all right?" she asked Everett.

"She has the flu. She'll be fine," he answered crisply. "You do know how to make an exit," he whispered to Lila in a hushed voice. Speaking up, he said, "The car's right in front," directing the server who was hurrying alongside of him.

Still holding Lila in his arms, Everett managed to reach into his pocket and press the key fob to open the car doors.

The server moved quickly to open the passenger door for him, and Everett flashed a grateful smile at her. "Thank you."

The server waited until he buckled Lila into her seat, then handed the purse and the dinners she was holding to him.

"Are you sure you don't want me to call the paramedics for you?" she asked one last time, eyeing Lila.

"Very sure," Everett answered. "I'm a doctor. She's been out in the field, visiting sick people for the last two days and it looks like she came down with the flu for her trouble." Closing the door, he looked at the young woman and tried to set her mind at ease one last time. "Thanks for all your trouble—" he paused to read her name tag "—Ruth."

The young woman grinned broadly when he addressed her by her name. "My pleasure, Doctor." With that, she quickly hurried back into the restaurant.

Everett's attention was already focused on Lila. She was still unconscious. How the hell could he have missed all those signs? he thought, upbraiding himself again.

"I'm sorry, Lila. I should have realized what was wrong this morning in the parking lot."

And then it suddenly occurred to him that he had no idea where Lila lived. Getting her purse, he went through it until he found her wallet with her driver's license in it. Looking at it, he repeated her address out loud in order to memorize it.

"Let's get you home, Cinderella."

Chapter Ten

Everett was able to locate the development where Lila lived with only a minimum of difficulty.

Finding her house was a little trickier. Driving slowly and trying to make out the addresses painted on the curb, he finally drove up toward her house.

Pulling up into her driveway, he turned off his engine and then sat in the car, looking at Lila. She hadn't come to once during the entire trip from the restaurant to her house.

"Okay, I got you here. Now what?" he wondered out loud. "The logical step would be to get you *into* the house, wouldn't it?" Everett said as if he was carrying on a conversation with the unconscious woman sitting next to him. "But for that to happen, I'm going to need either a roommate who's living in your house or a key to the front door."

He looked back toward the house. There weren't any lights on, which meant that either Lila lived alone, or if she did have a roommate—which she hadn't mentioned—the roommate was out.

He opened her purse again. This time he was rummaging through the purse looking for her keys. He found a set of keys at the very bottom of her purse. There were five keys on the ring.

"You sure don't make things easy, do you, Lila?" he asked.

He decided he needed to find the right key and open the front door before carrying her out of his car. If he was lucky, she might even wake up by the time he discovered which of the keys fit the front door lock. And awake, she might be able to walk—with some help—to the house. That would eliminate some complications, like nosy neighbors, he thought.

Everett went up the front walk to her door and patiently started trying out keys.

The very last key turned out to be the one to open her front door.

"It figures," he murmured.

Everett went inside the house and flipped on the first light switch he found. The darkness receded.

At least he could find his way around, he thought.

Leaving the front door standing open, he pocketed the key ring and went back to the car.

Lila was still unconscious.

Unbuckling her seat belt, Everett found that the clothes she was wearing were all practically soaked.

"You're sweating this flu out," he told her. "As a doctor, I know that's a good thing. But I'd still feel a lot better if you opened your eyes." He looked at her, half hoping that the sound of his voice would somehow make her come around. But it didn't. "Nothing, huh?" He sighed.

The next moment, Everett took her purse and slung the straps onto his shoulder. Then he lifted her up carefully and carried her to her front door.

"If any of your neighbors are watching this, Lila, we should be hearing the sound of police sirens approaching very shortly. For both our sakes, I hope you have the kind of neighbors who keep their curtains drawn and mind their own business, at least this one time."

The wind had caused the door to close a little but he managed to shoulder it open.

Like a groom carrying his bride over the threshold, he carried Lila into the house. Once inside, he closed the door with his back, making a mental note to lock it as soon as he found some place to put Lila down.

Looking around, Everett found himself standing in a small, sparsely decorated living room.

"You never were one for a lot of possessions," he commented, scanning the room.

He saw a tan sectional sofa facing a medium-size flat-screen TV mounted on the opposite wall. Crossing over to it, Everett gently placed Lila on the sofa, leaving her there for the moment. Going back, he locked the front door and then walked around the single-story house, orienting himself. Like the living room, every-thing was in place and neatly arranged.

"Anyone here?" Everett called out, although he took the darkened state of the house to indicate that it was empty.

He continued to make his way through the house, looking into each room. There were two bedrooms lo-cated in the back across from one another. One was larger than the other. He took the smaller one to be a guest bedroom. Looking into it, he found that it was empty. There were no clothes in the closet.

Apparently, Lila did live alone.

His smile vanished after a moment. This wasn't good, he thought. She was sick and she needed some-one here to take care of her.

With a sigh, he went back to the living room. She was right where he'd left her—and still unconscious. He thought of his medical bag in his trunk.

"First things first," he told himself. Picking Lila up again, he said to her, "I need to get you out of these wet clothes and into bed." He caught himself smiling as he carried her to what he had determined to be her bed-room. "There was a time that would have meant some-thing entirely different. But don't worry, I've got my 'doctor hat' on and you have nothing to worry about."

As attracted as he still was to her, his first thought was about her health. He wanted to get Lila well again.

Bringing Lila into the larger bedroom, he managed to move aside the comforter and put her down on the queen-size bed. He took off her shoes and then began going through the drawers of her bureau, looking for a nightgown or something that looked as if she wore it to bed.

Moving a few things aside, he froze when he came across an old college jersey.

His old college jersey.

He remembered when he'd given it to her. He'd told her that when she wore it, she'd be close to him. Taking it out now, he looked at the jersey for a long moment, then at her.

"You actually kept it," he said in disbelief. "And judging by how faded it is, you've been wearing it. Maybe this isn't as hopeless as I thought," he murmured under his breath, referring to his plan to get back together with her.

Moving quickly, Everett removed the rest of her clothes and slipped the college jersey on her. Done, he tucked Lila into bed as if he was tucking in a child. He refused to allow himself to become distracted. Right now, Lila was his patient, not the only woman he had ever loved.

"I'll be right back," he told her even though she was still unconscious and couldn't hear him. "I'm going to bring in the food and get my medical bag out of the trunk."

He was back in a few minutes, leaving the to-go bags on the kitchen table for the time being. He had something far more important on his mind than food, despite the fact that his stomach kept rumbling in protest over being neglected.

Opening up his medical bag, Everett took out his stethoscope and several other basic instruments he never went anywhere without. Then he gave Lila a quick but thorough exam to confirm what he pretty much already suspected.

Her pulse was rapid, her temperature was high and, at one point, as he conducted his examination, she began to shiver.

"Chills," he noted. "And you were already displaying signs of fatigue this morning. You, Lila Clark, are a regular poster child for the flu," he concluded. Setting aside his stethoscope, he frowned. "I bet with all that running around you were doing, you forgot to get yourself immunized for the flu, didn't you?"

Mentally crossing his fingers, he looked through his bag and found that he had thought to pack some extra acetaminophen. Taking out a fresh syringe, he removed the plastic casing and gave her an injection.

"That should help lower your fever," he told Lila. He frowned thoughtfully. "But you still can't be left alone, not like this."

There was a chair over in the corner by the window and he dragged it over to her bed. Sitting down, Everett studied her for a few minutes, reviewing his options. He was due back in Houston tomorrow, but there was no way he was about to leave her in this condition.

The injection he gave her should lower her fever, but things didn't always go the way they were supposed to. If Lila took a turn for the worse, there was no one here to take her to the hospital. Or do anything else for her, for that matter.

Even if he didn't feel the way he did about her, he couldn't just abandon her.

Everett made up his mind. He might not have been there for Lila thirteen years ago, but he could be here for her now.

Stepping out into the hallway, he took out his cell phone and placed a call to one of the doctors he worked with. He found himself listening to an answering machine telling him to leave a message. He'd hoped to talk to the other man directly, but that wasn't an option right now.

"Ryan, it's Everett. I'm in the middle of some sort of flu epidemic here in Austin and I'm going to be staying here a few more days. I'm going to need you and Blake to cover for me at the office. I appreciate it and I owe you—big time. Any questions, you have my cell."

With that, he terminated the call.

Coming back into the room to check on Lila, Everett called Schuyler next. His sister answered on the second ring.

"Schuy, it's Everett. I'm going to be staying in Austin a few more days."

"Oh?" Schuyler really didn't sound all that surprised, he thought. "Did you and Lila manage to patch things up?" she asked.

He wasn't about to get into that right now. That was a personal matter and it was officially on the back burner until Lila got well.

"It's not what you think," Everett was quick to tell his sister.

"Okay, if you're not trying to romance Lila into taking you back, then why are you going to be staying in Austin a few more days?" Schuyler wanted to know.

"You know that flu epidemic I came here to help treat?"

"Yes, I got my vaccination, Ev," she told him, thinking that was what her brother was going to ask her.

"Good, but that wasn't what I was about to tell you," Everett said.

"Okay, then what were you going to tell me?" Schuyler asked gamely.

"Lila came down with the flu," he told his sister simply. "She lives by herself and there's no one to take care of her."

"My Lord," Schuyler cried. "If I saw this story on one of those movie-of-the-week channels I'd shut off the TV."

"I didn't ask for your evaluation," Everett told her impatiently. "I just wanted you to know that I was still in town—and why."

After a moment, Schuyler said, "You're serious. Then she's really sick?"

Did Schuyler think that Lila would pretend to be ill—and that he'd just blindly fall for it?

"Schuy, I'm a doctor. I know what 'sick' looks like. Right now, Lila's not only displaying all the signs of the flu, she's unconscious."

Schuyler's tone of voice changed immediately. "Anything I can do?"

He thought of Lila's car. It was still at the Foundation's parking lot where Lila had left it. He knew that Lila would undoubtedly prefer to have the car close by when she regained consciousness—if for no other reason than there might be something in it that she needed.

"As a matter of fact, there is," Everett told her. "If you and one of your friends could swing by here tomorrow morning to get the keys, could you pick up Lila's car from the Foundation's parking lot and drive it over to her house?"

"I think I liked you better when you didn't feel it was seemly to ask for favors," Schuyler told him.

He knew she was kidding. He also knew he could count on his sister.

"I'm growing as a person," Everett quipped.

"That's not how I see it," she told him. "All right, where's 'here'?" his sister asked.

He thought he heard her shuffling papers on the other end and then he heard Schuler say, "Okay, give me Lila's address."

He did, and then he said, "I assume you know where the Fortune Foundation is located."

"You know, you can be very insulting, big brother," Schuyler told him.

"Not intentionally," he told her, then added, "Thanks for this, Schuy."

"Yeah. I just hope you're not going to wind up regretting this, that's all," she told him, sounding concerned.

She was worried and he appreciated that. But there was no need for his sister to feel that way. "Schuy, Lila's sick. I'm a doctor. I'm supposed to take care of sick people."

Schuyler barely stifled a laugh. "You don't think this a little above and beyond?" she questioned.

"I'm an 'above and beyond' kind of doctor," Everett answered, doing his best to make light of the concerns his sister was displaying.

"Not funny, Ev," Schuyler informed him. "I worry about you," she stressed.

"And I said I appreciate that. I also appreciate you picking up that car and bringing it back to Lila's house for me," he said, bringing the conversation back to what he was asking her to do.

Schuyler sighed. "What time do you want me to come by?"

There was no reason to push. "Whenever it's convenient." He glanced toward Lila's room. "It doesn't look as if I'm going to be going anywhere for at least a while."

"I'll still call you first," she told Everett. It was obvious that she wasn't going to take a chance on walking in on something.

Everett was just about to end the call when he heard his sister say his name. Bringing the cell phone closer again so he could hear her, he asked, "Did you just say something?"

"I just had a last-minute thought," she told him.

"And that is?"

His sister hesitated for a moment. "I don't suppose I can talk you into hiring someone to look after Lila, can I?"

He knew she was just thinking of him, but he wished she would stop. He wanted to do this and his mind was made up.

"I'll see you in the morning, Schuyler," he said just before he terminated the call.

Putting the phone back into his pocket, he returned to Lila's bedside.

When he touched her forehead, it seemed a little cooler to him. Taking out the thermometer he'd used earlier, he laid the strip across her forehead and watched the numbers registering.

He removed the strip and put it back into his medical bag.

"You still have a fever," he told her. "But at least it's a little lower. Although not low enough," he stressed with a frown. "You can't go out and do your angel-of-mercy bit until that fever is gone and you're back to your old self again."

Lila moaned.

He knew it wasn't in response to what he'd just said, but he pretended that there was a semblance of an exchange going on between the two of them.

Lila had a small TV in her bedroom. Nothing like the one in the living room, but at least it would be something to fill the silence and distract him, he thought.

Turning on the TV, he put the volume on low, sat down in the chair next to Lila's bed and made himself as comfortable as possible.

He knew he could make use of the guest room and lie down on the bed there, but he preferred proximity over comfort. He wanted to be there for her if Lila woke up in the middle of the night and needed him. One night in a chair wouldn't kill him.

Besides, how many nights had he gone without sleep when he was an intern at the hospital? That certainly hadn't done him any harm, Everett reminded himself— and neither would spending a night sitting up and keeping vigil in a chair.

Everett doubted that he would get any sleep in the guest room anyway. He knew himself. He'd be too busy straining his ears, listening for any strange noises that would indicate that Lila was awake.

No, he decided, trying to make himself as comfortable as possible in the chair. Staying in Lila's room this way was better. He'd be right here, able to hear her make the slightest sound when she woke up. And he figured she *had* to wake up soon.

"I know you need your rest so I'm not going to worry about this yet. But I'd take it as a personal favor if you opened those big blue eyes of yours soon, Lila. *Very* soon."

The only response he heard was the sound of Lila breathing.

Chapter Eleven

"What are you doing in my house?"

The raspy voice was hardly louder than a hoarse whisper, but it was definitely unnerving and accusatory in nature. Catching Everett off guard, it made him jump in his chair and almost caused him to knock it over.

Coming to, Everett realized that he must have finally dozed off for a few minutes.

It took him a moment longer before it hit him that it was Lila who'd asked the question.

Fully awake now, he got up and stood over Lila's bed. Her eyes were open and she looked bewildered. Relief washed over him as he took her hand in his. "You're awake!"

"And you didn't answer my question," Lila responded, annoyed with herself because she couldn't seem to speak any louder. "What are you doing in my house?" she asked again.

Bits and pieces were slowly beginning to dawn on her. She looked down at herself. "And where are my clothes?" Her eyes narrowed as she looked up at Everett angrily. "You undressed me," Lila choked out. It was not a question.

Everett wasn't about to deny the obvious, but she needed to understand why he'd removed her clothes. "You had a high fever and you were sweating. Your clothes were soaked straight through."

Frustration robbed her of the little voice she had so she couldn't immediately respond. She struggled to sit up.

All Everett had to do was put his hand gently on her shoulder to keep her down, which he did. "Don't exert yourself," he told her.

Who the hell did he think he was? He couldn't tell her what to do, Lila thought angrily. Her head was throbbing and she couldn't remember anything. But one thing was obvious.

"You took off my clothes," she accused again.

"I already explained why," Everett told her patiently.

She couldn't make any sense out of what he'd told her. "But we were in the restaurant," she protested, desperately trying to piece things together. It felt as if there was a huge gaping hole in her brain and facts were just falling through it, disappearing without a trace.

Maybe if he gave her a summary of the events, Everett thought, it might calm her down.

"You passed out in the restaurant," he told her. "I

brought you to your house and carried you to your room. Your clothes were all wet, so I got you out of them and into that jersey."

She looked down again, doing her best to focus on what she was looking at. The jersey seemed to swim in front of her eyes. "You went through my things," she accused.

"Just in order to find something to put on you," he answered simply. Maybe he should have let it go at that, but he couldn't help saying, "You kept my jersey."

She wasn't about to get into that—and she wouldn't have had to if he hadn't gone rummaging through her drawers, she thought angrily.

"You had no right to go through my things," she said defensively.

This was going nowhere. He wasn't about to get sucked into a circular debate about what he'd done and why he'd done it.

"Lila, you have the flu. The best thing for you right now is to rest and drink plenty of fluids. Arguing is not part of that formula. Now I'll get you some water—or tea if you'd prefer. Your job in this is to take care of the 'rest' part."

Lila made a disgruntled face. "I don't like tea," she told him.

"Water it is," he responded, heading out to the kitchen.

A couple of minutes later Everett came back with a large glass of water. He propped her up with one hand beneath her pillows while he held out the glass to her with the other.

Lila took the glass with both hands and began to drink with gusto.

"Sip, don't gulp," he cautioned.

"I know how to drink water," she informed him, her voice still raspy. However, she grudgingly complied with his instructions. Getting her fill, she surrendered the glass.

Taking it from her, Everett slowly lowered her back down on the bed.

Lila's head felt as if it was floating and there were half thoughts darting in and out of her brain. Her eyes shifted in his direction.

"Did you enjoy it?" she asked.

His back was to her as he put the glass down on the bureau. Turning around, Everett looked at her quizzically. He had no idea what she was referring to. "Did I enjoy what?"

"Undressing me."

Her voice was even lower than it had been before and he could hardly make out what she was saying. He filled in the blanks.

"I did it in my capacity as a doctor," Everett answered.

Confusion furrowed her brow. Nothing was making sense. "Meaning you didn't look?"

Everett had deliberately divorced himself from his feelings while he'd gotten her out of the wet clothes and into the jersey. But not enough to be completely unaffected by what he was doing. However, he wasn't about to tell her that. That would have been deliberately buying trouble in his opinion.

Instead, he said, "Only to make sure I didn't rip anything."

Her eyes narrowed further as she tried to look into his. "I don't think I believe you," she whispered.

The next moment, her eyes had closed and within a few seconds, she was asleep again.

"That's okay," he whispered back, gently pushing her hair away from her face and tucking her back under the covers. "I wouldn't believe me either if I were you."

He'd gotten her out of her clothes and into the jersey as quickly as he could, but that didn't mean that doing so hadn't stirred something within him even though he had tried his damnedest to block out those thoughts and feelings.

He *had* been functioning as a doctor, but he was remembering as her lover and that image was really difficult to shake.

The next time Lila opened her eyes and looked around, she saw that she was alone.

It had all been a dream, she thought with a twinge of disappointment.

She struggled into an upright position, her body aching and protesting every movement she made.

She stifled a groan. She felt as if she'd been run over by a truck. A truck that had deliberately backed up over her then taken off after running her over again.

She struggled to focus, her head throbbing, impeding her thoughts.

How did she get here? The last thing she actually

remembered was being in the restaurant—sitting opposite Everett.

Everett had been part of her dream, she realized.

All these years and she was still having dreams about Everett. Strange dreams.

She needed to get up, she thought.

Just as she was about to throw back her covers, Everett walked into the room carrying a tray.

He smiled, pleased to see her up. "You're awake."

Lila's mouth dropped open as she stared at him. "I didn't dream you."

He set the tray down on the bureau for the moment.

"You dreamt about me?" he asked. He was practically beaming.

She became instantly defensive. "What are you doing here?"

"We went through this last night," he reminded her patiently. "Don't you remember?"

"I thought that was a dream." She was repeating herself, Lila thought. She held her head. It was really throbbing. "I feel awful."

"Well, if it makes you feel any better, you don't look awful," he told her. "But you are sick."

"No, I'm not," she protested. She tried to throw the covers off again and found that the single movement was exceedingly taxing to her strength. What the hell had happened to her? "I have to get ready for work," she told Everett defiantly, wanting him to leave.

Everett carefully drew her covers back up. "No work for you until you get well," he told her, leaving no room for argument.

Didn't he understand? "I've got people counting on me," she told him.

"And if you turn up, you'll be *infecting* those people." She tried to get up again and this time, he held down her hands just enough to keep her where she was. "Are you familiar with the story of Typhoid Mary?"

Was that what Everett thought she was? A woman who wantonly infected people? "That's not funny."

"I'm not trying to be funny, Lila," he told her. "But I am trying to get through to you. You're sick." Everett told her, enunciating every word slowly. "You have the flu."

She felt like hell warmed over, but she still protested, "No, I don't."

His eyes met hers. "Which one of us went to medical school?" he asked her in a quiet, tolerant voice that only served to infuriate her.

She blew out an angry breath. "You did," she said grudgingly.

Everett smiled. She had made his point for him. "You have the flu," he repeated.

"I can't have the flu," she insisted. She looked up at Everett, her eyes pleading with him.

This had to be good, he thought. "Why?"

Exasperation throbbed in every syllable. "Because I just can't."

Everett decided to play along as if she had a valid argument that needed exploration. "Did you get vaccinated?"

"No," Lila admitted, mumbling the word under her breath.

A triumphant look slipped over his face. "Okay, all together now: You have the flu."

Defeated, Lila sank back onto her pillow as if all the air had been suddenly pumped out of her.

"I really have the flu?" Lila asked him, silently begging him to come up with another explanation.

Rather than answer her immediately, Everett decided to back himself up with evidence. "What's your throat feel like?"

She didn't have to think before answering. "Sandpaper."

"And your head?" he asked, giving her a chance to contradict his diagnosis.

It was getting harder and harder for her to focus because of the pain. "Like there're twelve angry elves with steel hammers in it trying to beat their way out."

"Add that to the chills I observed last night and the high fever—which by the way is going down—and you have more than your fair share of flu symptoms."

"The flu," Lila repeated in despair, saying it as if it was the mark of Cain on her forehead. "Isn't there anything you can do for me?" she asked, almost pleading with him.

"I'm doing it," he told her. "I'm nursing you back to health with bed rest, liquids and I have here a bowl of chicken soup that's guaranteed to cure what ails you," he quipped.

He'd found a folding TV tray tucked away in one of the closets and he set it up now next to her bed. When he was satisfied that it was stable, he put the bowl of soup on it along with a large soupspoon.

"See if you can hold that down," he told her.

Lila looked down into the bowl of soup as if she was trying to make up her mind about it. "Chicken soup?" she repeated.

"Highly undcrrated, by the way," he told her. "Apparently, our grandmothers knew something about its healing powers that we didn't. Seriously," he told Lila. "Try taking a few spoonfuls," he urged, helping her sit up and placing two pillows at her back to keep her upright.

The spoon was in her hand, but it remained motionless for now. "Where did you get the soup?" she asked. She knew she didn't have any canned soups in her kitchen cabinets.

"I had Schuyler bring it," he answered. He'd called his sister this morning and added that to his first request. "Along with your car," Everett said.

"My car?" Lila repeated. And then it suddenly came back to her. "My car's at the Foundation." Panic had entered her voice.

"Not anymore. Schuyler and her fiancé swung by this morning to pick up the keys to your car. They already drove it over. It's right outside in your driveway," he told her.

Lila looked at him in wonder. "You took care of everything," she marveled.

Everett grinned. "What can I say? I'm an overachiever."

Lila smiled at his choice of words. "I remember that about you," she said with almost a fond note in her voice.

When she sounded like that, he could feel himself

melting. Now wasn't the time. "Eat your soup before it gets cold," he urged.

"And loses its magic healing powers?" she asked in an amused voice that was finally beginning to sound more like her.

"Something like that."

Lila nodded. "All right, I'll eat—if you tell me exactly what happened last night," she bargained.

"I already told you," he said. Seeing that she wasn't about to budge until he'd told her the whole story without skipping anything, Everett sighed. "But I'll tell you again," he said, resigned. "We were at the restaurant and you suddenly passed out."

She visualized that now and became horrified. "In front of everybody?"

"Just the people looking our way," he quipped. "I didn't take a head count," he said, doing his best not to get her agitated.

"Nobody called the paramedics, did they?" Lila asked. The last thing she wanted was for this to get around. She wanted to be able to do her job when she got back, not have to constantly be answering a lot of questions because there were rumors circulating about her. Rumors always had a way of escalating and becoming exaggerated.

The thought of having to deal with that made her feel more ill.

"Well, you frightened the server, but I told her I was a doctor and that seemed to satisfy her. So I picked you up and carried you to my car. Our waitress followed us with your purse and the dinners she packed up to go—

which, by the way, are in the refrigerator waiting for you once you get your appetite back."

"How did you know where I lived?" Lila asked suddenly. She hadn't told him her address.

"I got it from your driver's license in your purse," he told her. "Which, before you ask, is where I found the keys to your house. And the car," he added, "so that Schuyler could drive it here. Okay," he informed her, "that about catches us up."

Turning, he was about to return to the kitchen when she cried, "Wait."

Now what? He did his best not to sound impatient. "I told you everything," he stressed.

"Weren't you supposed to go back to your practice in Houston today?" she asked, remembering he'd said something to that effect.

He looked at her pointedly. Was she trying to get him to make some sort of a declaration about the way he felt about her, or was this just an innocent question? "My plans changed."

"You don't have to stay here on my account," she protested.

"Lila, right now a pregnant cat could beat you at arm wrestling with one paw tied behind her back. You have the strength of an overcooked noodle. You need to rest and you need someone to take care of you while you're resting. I'm volunteering."

She shook her head and almost instantly regretted it. Her head started swimming and she waited for it to steady itself again. "I can't let you do that."

"I don't recall asking for permission," he told her.

"I've got more vacation time coming to me than any two people in my office combined and I'm electing to take some of it now. Now don't argue with me. Eat your soup and lie back, watch some mindless TV and rest. Doctor's orders," he added when she opened her mouth to protest. "Understood?"

Looking somewhat subdued, which both surprised and worried him, Lila repeated, "Understood."

Chapter Twelve

She remembered.

Although Lila tried very hard not to, over the course of the next few days she began to remember why she had fallen in love with Everett to begin with. Not because he was so devastatingly handsome—which he still was, perhaps even more so—but because he was so kind.

Kind and thoughtful and caring.

She'd witnessed those traits in action while accompanying Everett on the house calls they'd paid together before she'd gotten ill, and now she was witnessing it up close and personal while he was taking care of her and nursing her back to health.

In essence, Everett was very quietly waiting on her hand and foot. He made sure she drank plenty of fluids.

He prepared a soft, bland diet for her, then slowly substituted food with more substance when he felt she could handle it. The progression took close to a week because he told her he didn't want to rush things and risk her having a setback.

By the end of the fourth day of her convalescence, Lila had gotten comfortable enough with him to allow herself to share a few old stories about people they had known back in high school.

Since she had left Houston thirteen years ago, he was in a far better position to tell her what some of the people they had grown up with were doing these days.

"Remember Jack Logan?" Everett asked, bringing up another name as they were sharing a lunch of soup and sandwiches in her room.

It took Lila a moment to put a face to the name. "Oh, you mean the guy who expected every woman to faint at his feet just because he looked their way?" She remembered that Jack was always telling everyone he had big plans for himself. "Whatever happened to him?"

Everett smiled, remembering how brash and abrasive Logan had been. "He still lives in Houston and works at the airport as a baggage checker."

As she recalled, that didn't exactly match up to Logan's lofty goals. "Is he still a lady-killer?"

He looked at Lila and answered her with a straight face. "Only if he fell on top of one. I saw him recently. He must have gained over a hundred pounds since graduation."

Lila tried to stifle a laugh, but she couldn't help herself. Somehow, that seemed like poetic justice. Logan had always been cruelly critical of anyone he felt wasn't as good-looking as he was. His remarks were always particularly hurtful about women he viewed to be over-weight, even if they were carrying only a few extra pounds.

"He was always such an egotist," she said when she stopped laughing.

"That part hasn't changed," Everett told her. Finishing his meal, he wiped his mouth and put down his napkin. "I think he just sees his expanding weight as there being more of him to be impressed with." He looked at Lila's plate. "Are you finished?" he asked, nodding at her tray.

"Yes." As Everett removed the tray, she told him, "You know, you really don't have to wait on me hand and foot like this."

For the time being, Everett placed the tray aside on the bureau. He could take both trays to the kitchen the next time he left the room.

"Well, I'm here and there's not that much else to do," he reasoned. "So, to my way of thinking, I might as well make myself useful."

"That's another thing," she said, picking up on the fact that he was still in Austin. "I'm keeping you from your practice."

His eyes met hers for a long moment. And then he said, "Maybe I like being kept."

Lila felt herself growing warm and she didn't think that she was having any sort of a relapse. At least not the kind that involved the flu.

She did her best to steer the conversation in the initial direction she'd intended.

"What I'm saying is that you don't need to take care of me anymore. I'm getting better all the time."

"That's because of all the excellent care you've been getting."

Lila smiled, shaking her head. Everett had always had a way with words. "I won't argue with that."

"Good," Everett said with finality. He had brought her that day's TV schedule earlier for her to look through. He picked it up now and thumbed through it. "Now what would you like to watch this afternoon?" he asked. Watching TV after lunch had become a ritual for them the last few days, something he felt that they both looked forward to. "There're some pretty good old movies on the Classic Channel and I found a station that's streaming a lot of those old sitcoms you used to like watching." He named a couple of specific programs.

Hearing them cited, Lila looked at him in surprise. "You remember that?" she marveled.

"I remember a lot of things," he told her. He had committed a great many things to memory about her, Everett thought.

Lila could feel her heart racing even though she fiercely ordered it not to. She'd been this route before and she knew exactly where it ended. Nowhere, leaving her with an ache in her heart. She did *not* want to go there, not again.

But somehow, she just couldn't seem to convince herself to turn away, to choose a different path. She tried to assuage her conscience by telling herself that this was only for a little while.

Lila shrugged in response to his question. "I don't know, you pick something," she told him. The next moment, she threw back her covers and swung her legs down. "I'll be right back."

"Where are you going?"

"I need to use the bathroom," she informed him with as much dignity as she could muster.

All the other times she'd felt the need to go, Everett had taken her arm and walked her to the bathroom as if they were out for an evening stroll. It was obvious to him that this time around, Lila was attempting to assert her independence. Not that he could blame her. In her place, he'd try to do the same thing.

Everett took a step back, allowing her space so she could get out of bed. However, he still kept a watchful eye on her.

On her feet now, he could see that Lila was still rather unstable. She took a single step and her right knee buckled.

Everett's arms were around her instantly, keeping her from landing on the floor. When he drew her back up, her body slid ever so slightly against his.

It was only for a second, but it was enough. Enough to send sparks flying between them and throwing old longings into high gear.

Everett caught his breath, silently ordering himself to remain steady instead of pulling her closer to him and kissing her the way he wanted to.

Instead of making love with her the way he desperately wanted to.

Only extreme self-control kept him from acting on the impulses that were urgently telegraphing themselves throughout his whole body.

"I know you wanted to do this alone, but maybe I should just walk with you to the bathroom this one more time," he suggested.

"To keep me from doing a pratfall?" she asked ruefully.

Her ego stood as much of a chance of being hurt as her body, so he tactfully rephrased what she'd just asked. "So you don't risk bruising anything if you do happen to fall," he told her. "So, is it okay?" he asked, waiting for her to give him the go-ahead on this.

She sighed and then smiled at him. She realized Everett was trying to spare her feelings. "Well, the old saying is that pride always goes before a fall and I don't want to fall, so I guess I'll have to just tuck away my pride and let you walk me to the bathroom one more time."

Everett laughed softly. "Good call," he congratulated her. "You'll be doing solo runs again before you know it," he promised.

Sitting on the edge of Lila's bed, Everett set aside his stethoscope. He'd just finished giving Lila her latest examination.

"Well, your fever's gone," he told her. "You're keeping your food down and your color's definitely back. And when you talk, you no longer sound like someone who starts their mornings with a shot of scotch and a cigarette. Although I have to say that I was getting kind of used to hearing that sexy voice. I might actually miss it," he admitted, smiling fondly at her.

"Well, I won't," Lila assured him with feeling. "I thought I sounded like some kidnapper placing a ransom call." She looked at him hopefully. "Does this mean that I'm being cleared for work?"

Everett nodded. He closed his medical bag and set it on the floor.

"Our little unofficial holiday is over," he told her, then in case there was any doubt, he added, "Yes, I'm clearing you for work."

Lila didn't take her eyes off him. "And you'll be going back to Houston?"

"I will," Everett confirmed. He knew he had to be getting back, but there was a part of him that didn't want to leave.

If he were honest with himself, he'd admit that he'd used nursing Lila back to health as an excuse to spend more time with her.

The last thirteen years had been filled with work, at times almost nonstop. He knew now that he had been trying to fill the emptiness—the gaping void that losing her had created—with work. Work and the occasional woman. None of them ever measured up to Lila simply because no one had ever even come close to making him feel the way Lila had.

The way she still did.

"But I'll still be coming back to Austin a lot," he told her, never breaking eye contact. "To see Schuyler and help her out with some things," he added, not wanting to scare Lila off. He paused for a moment, then, despite the advice Schuyler had given him, he asked, "Is it all right if I call you when I'm in town?"

After the way that he had put himself out for her, she hadn't expected Everett to ask permission to call her. She assumed he'd think he'd earned the right to call her any time he wanted to.

"How can I say no to the man who nursed me back to health?" she asked, trying to sound as if she was amused by his question.

"I'm not asking you to see me as the man who nursed you back to health," Everett pointed out. "I'm asking you to see me—" he paused for a moment, looking for the right phrasing "—as an old friend."

The silence between them grew until she finally said to him, "I couldn't say no to that, either."

"Glad to hear it," he told her.

He let out the breath he'd been holding. Honestly, he really hadn't known what Lila would say in response to his question. He wouldn't have put it past her feelings of self-preservation to tell him that seeing each other again wouldn't be a good idea.

But now that she had agreed, he saw that there was something far greater than self-preservation going on between them.

He could feel it.

And it was not just on his end. Nor was it just wishful thinking.

There was something tangible and real pulsating between them, ready to spring to life at the slightest bit of encouragement.

But even with all that, Everett knew he had to tread lightly. One wrong step and it could all crumble right beneath him, sending him plummeting head first into an abyss.

"Hi, are you free for dinner tonight?"

"Everett?" Lila was immediately alert. She'd answered her cell phone just as she'd walked in her front door, thinking it was someone at the Foundation working late, calling with a question.

But it wasn't.

"I didn't expect to hear from you this soon," she said.

It had been six days since she had gone back to work and he had returned to Houston.

"Well, I'm only in Austin for a few hours," he explained, "so I thought, if you're free, you might want to get together."

There it was, she thought. Her way out. He was handing it to her.

If you're free.

That was all she had to say to him. That she wasn't free. That her evening was already spoken for and she had somewhere else to be. And knowing Everett, he would accept that, murmur his regrets and that would be that.

The problem was, she didn't want to take this way out that he was handing her on a silver platter. She *wanted* to see him. The truth of it was, after seeing him every day for almost a week, she missed him.

She knew that she shouldn't feel this way. Knew that she needed to cut Everett out of her life before he became a habit. But then on the other hand, this *was* only going to be dinner. And dinner would last for a few hours at most, nothing more. She knew that Everett was far too conscientious to lie to her, especially for some ulterior motive. If he said he was only here for a few hours, then he *was* in Austin only for that time.

Those few hours might as well be spent with her, she thought in a moment of weakness.

"I am free," she heard herself saying, sealing her fate, at least for the next few hours. "We can do dinner if you like. And I promise not to pass out this time," she added with amusement, remembering the last time they were in a restaurant together.

"Oh." He pretended to sound as if he was sorry to hear that. "Too bad," he told her. "I was looking forward to playing the hero, sweeping you into my arms and carrying you to my car."

"I think being the hero once would be enough for any guy."

"Oh, I don't know," Everett speculated. "It's kind of addictive if the hero has the right damsel in distress to save."

That definitely conjured up an image, Lila thought. "I never envisioned myself as a damsel in distress," she told Everett.

"I wouldn't have thought of you as one, either," he admitted. "I guess the world is full of surprises." Then he changed topics. "Well, like I said, I'm only in Austin for a bit, so where would you like to go?"

"Seeing what happened the last time when we went to the Italian restaurant, how about Chinese food?" Lila suggested.

"Sounds good to me," he told her. He would have said the same thing if she had suggested strolling through the park, eating ice cream cones. He just wanted to see her. It had been six long days during which time he had forced himself not to call her just to see how she was doing. Or to hear the sound of her voice. He didn't want Lila to feel as if he was crowding her, or worse, as if he was stalking her.

But it hadn't been easy.

He had spent six days *with* her when she'd been ill with the flu and he had quickly gotten used to seeing her everyday. *Not* seeing her was hell now, but he couldn't behave like some privileged adolescent who was accustomed to having his every whim indulged—no matter how much he wished.

This was too important for him to risk messing up again. So he treaded lightly.

"If it's okay, I can be at your place in half an hour. Or is that too soon? Do you need more time?"

"Actually, I need less if you're close by. I just got home from work and I still look very businesslike, so I don't need to change."

He preferred the temptress look he'd seen on her, but to remain safe, he thought that it was best to go along with the business suit.

"You always look good no matter what you have on." *And sometimes even better the less you have on*, he added silently. "I'll be there in fifteen minutes."

Chapter Thirteen

Lila felt as if she had suddenly blinked and just like that, found herself going back to square one all over again. She was experiencing feelings of excitement and wariness and that in turn had created knots in her stomach.

Big ones.

But not quite big enough for her to call Everett and tell him that she'd changed her mind about having dinner with him.

Despite saying that she didn't need any extra time to get ready because she was still dressed for work, Lila impulsively flew into her bedroom for a quick change of clothes. She didn't want to look as if she was going to a business meeting. She wanted to look as good as she could possibly look.

Like a woman who was going out to dinner with a man who had once owned her heart.

Not that she planned on letting him own it again, she maintained as she quickly pulled the pins out of her hair. Instantly, the changed hairstyle made her appear more carefree. Her auburn hair cascaded around her face instead of being neatly pulled back, out of the way.

Her practical attire gave way to an attractive, form-flattering dress. She had just slipped on a pair of high heels that could have never, by any stretch of the imagination, been called sensible, when she heard the doorbell ring.

The sound instantly had her heart accelerating.

Showtime, she thought.

Hurrying to the front of the house, she stopped just short of the front door in order to catch her breath. She pulled herself together, doing her best to look as if she was totally nonchalant about the evening that lay ahead of her.

Everett would probably see right through her, she thought. Even so, she felt that she still had to keep up the charade.

Taking in one more deep breath and then slowly releasing it, she opened the door.

"When you say fifteen minutes, you really mean fifteen minutes," she said as she smiled up into Everett's handsome face.

"A man's only as good as his word," he responded. "You know, we don't have to leave right away if you're not ready yet."

"Do I look like I'm not ready yet?" she asked.

Despite her coy bravado, Lila couldn't help wondering what it was that Everett saw when he looked at her. Had he been hoping she'd be wearing something more appealing? Sexier?

Don't borrow trouble, she warned herself.

Everett's eyes slowly washed over the length of her. There was nothing but approval evident in his eyes. "You look, in a word, perfect," he pronounced.

Lila smiled at the compliment, secretly pleased although she tried her best to appear indifferent. "Then I guess I'm ready." Taking her purse, she walked out of the house, then paused to lock up.

Everett's Mercedes was waiting in her driveway.

"By the way," Everett said as he held the passenger door open for her, "I know you said we were going to a Chinese restaurant, but if I'm driving, you need to tell me the address."

She waited for Everett to get in on his side. Once he buckled up, she gave him the address, adding, "It's about half a mile past the Foundation. A lot of people from work like grabbing lunch at Gin Ling's."

Everett thought for a second. "I think I know which restaurant you mean," he told her. He remembered seeing it when he'd driven to the Foundation. "That's the one that's built to look like a pagoda, right?"

"Right."

Gin Ling's was doing brisk business when they arrived. They had to wait a few minutes to be seated.

Thinking that Everett might grow impatient, Lila

told him, "We can go somewhere else if you don't want to wait."

Everett made no move to take her up on the suggestion. "Do you like eating here?" he asked her.

She wouldn't have suggested coming here if she hadn't. That wasn't the point. "Yes, but—"

"Then we'll wait," he told her, adding, "I'm not in any hurry. I like making the most of the little downtime I get."

There was a reason why she had mentioned the idea of going to another restaurant. "I just don't want to make you late."

Everett looked at her as if he wasn't quite following her. "For what? I don't have a plane to catch," he reminded Lila. "I'm driving back to Houston."

"Doesn't all that driving make you tired?" In his place, she'd find driving back and forth between Austin and Houston exhausting after a while.

However, Everett shook his head. "On the contrary. Driving relaxes me."

Relaxing made her think about falling asleep at the wheel—not that Everett would ever admit that he was in danger of doing that. But she didn't want to think that he ran the risk of having something happen to him because of her.

"Still," she told him, "I don't want you so relaxed that you just slide right out of your seat."

"Never happen," Everett assured her. Still, her comment made his heart lighter.

She was clearly worried about him, he thought, and that felt particularly encouraging. Because that meant that there were still feelings there. Feelings he intended to stoke and encourage.

"Don't worry," he said. "I like staying in one piece as much as the next man. If I ever feel too tired to drive back, I'll rent a motel room and sleep until I feel up to driving. And, don't forget, there's always Schuyler," he reminded her.

A hostess came to show them to their table. Lila fell into place behind the woman with Everett following right behind her.

"Sorry, I was just remembering how stubborn you could be," Lila told him as they were being shown to a cozy booth.

"Not stubborn," Everett corrected, waiting for her to slide in before taking his own seat opposite her. "Determined."

Lila smiled. "Right. Determined," she repeated, humoring him.

"So how was going back to work?" Everett asked her after their server had brought them a pot of tea and then departed after taking each of their orders.

"Wonderfully hectic as always," she told him.

But Everett was more interested in the state of her health. "You didn't have any relapses or feel any ill effects from the flu?"

"No. I didn't expect that there would be," she told him honestly, smiling at Everett. "I always knew that you would be a fantastic doctor."

Everett maintained a straight face as he nodded. "I haven't mastered walking on water yet," he deadpanned, "but I'm working on it."

About to bring the small cup of tea to her lips, Lila stopped just short of completing the action, staring at him.

Everett laughed. "Well, you were making it sound as if I'd done something extraordinary," he told her. "I just took it a step further."

"You went out of your way for a patient—which was what I was," she reminded him. "Not every doctor would have stayed with a patient for almost a week because there was no one to take care of her."

"Not just any patient," Everett pointed out, "but a patient I was once nearly engaged to."

"And that near-engagement ended badly," she reminded him. Before he could say anything in response, she went on to tell him, "You had every right in the world to call the paramedics, then have them take me to the hospital while you walked away."

He inclined his head like a man conceding a point. "Okay. You got me. I'm a magnificent doctor—who was hoping for a second chance at dinner," he added as if that had been his sole motive behind seeing to it that she got well. "In order to do that, I had to make sure that you stayed alive. The best way to do that was to see to it myself." He shrugged. "I don't delegate very well."

She paused to sample the egg roll appetizer that had been brought to the table and then laughed.

"When did you get so good at twisting around words to make them back you up?" she wanted to know.

"It comes with the medical degree," Everett responded.

"No, it doesn't," Lila countered. She felt herself

verging on impatience at the way he was so dismissive of his own abilities.

"Okay, then let's just say it's an inherent talent. A gift," he emphasized. "Born out of necessity," he added. "Satisfied?" He studied her across the table.

"No," Lila answered honestly. "But I guess that it'll have to do for now."

She was rewarded with a smile that seemed to come from deep inside of Everett. She could feel her heart flutter in response.

They talked for another hour, long after the main course and the fortune cookies had come and gone and the pot of tea had been refilled.

"I think we'd better get going. It looks like our server wants the table." She looked toward the reception area and saw why. "There's a line going all out the door now."

Everett found himself reluctant to leave. "I'm sure I can find a way to make it up to him if you want to stay a little longer. Would you like a few more appetizers?" he asked.

Lila laughed. "If I so much as look at another one, I'll explode."

"Okay, that's a no," he acknowledged. "So I guess you're ready to go?"

Lila nodded. "I've got another day at work tomorrow and you, you've got a long drive ahead of you," she reminded him. "I can call a cab for myself if you'd like to get started on that drive home," Lila offered, watching Everett's expression for any indication that he did want to leave.

Everett regarded her thoughtfully. "If I didn't know any better, I would venture to say that you were trying to get rid of me."

"No," Lila denied, saying the word with feeling. "I'm not."

He grinned at her. "Good, because it's not working. I'm going to be taking you home. The few extra minutes that it'll take me isn't going to make a difference as far as my trip is concerned," he assured her. Raising his hand, he signaled to the server.

True to his word, Everett left an extra large tip on the table for the man. Large enough to prompt their server to call after them as they left, saying, "Please come again!"

Lila and Everett exchanged looks and grinned at one another just before they walked out of the increasingly crowded restaurant.

"I had a really nice time tonight," she told Everett once she was at her door.

Everett nodded, doing his best to look solemn as he reviewed their evening.

"Well, you made it all the way back home without passing out, so the way I see it, it was a successful evening," he said dryly.

Lila shook her head. "You're not going to let me live that down, are you?" she asked.

"In time, maybe," he conceded.

Key in hand, Lila stopped just short of putting it into

the lock. She knew she was stalling, but she couldn't help herself.

"Does that mean you want to do this again?" she asked Everett.

"Absolutely," Everett answered with certainly. He paused for a moment, debating whether or not to say what was on his mind or quit while he was ahead. After a beat, he made up his mind to continue. "Lila, I just want you to know that I intend to rebuild what we once had," he told her. He saw the wary look that came over her face even though he could tell she was trying to appear unaffected by his words. "I didn't say that to scare you, Lila. I want to be fair about this. I'm not going to go behind your back, or spring something on you. This is all going to be aboveboard and honest. I just really want to make the most of this second chance."

"Second chance?" Lila repeated.

The fact that she wasn't immediately dismissing what he'd just said told Everett that at least to some extent, she felt the same way he did. This *was* their second chance. Or more accurately, *his* second chance.

"I think that Fate threw us together like this for a reason, Lila, and I'm not about to ignore that," he told her.

He could see that she still looked wary.

"Don't worry," he reassured her quickly. "I don't plan on throwing a sack over your head and running off with you to some isolated cabin in order to wear you down until you see things my way. I told you that I'm patient and that's not just when it comes to getting a table in a restaurant. I will go as slow as you want me to go, but

I have a feeling that in the end, you'll agree with me that we were meant to be together."

As he talked, standing so close to Lila, he was overwhelmed by an urge to kiss her. But he instinctively knew that doing so at this moment would spook her and he couldn't afford the setback that would create. Kissing Lila might satisfy the need he had just to feel her lips against his, but it very well might cost him in the end. He'd be winning the battle but losing the war, so to speak.

So, difficult as it was, he was determined to hold himself in check and wait.

He had no other choice. He had told Lila the truth. Patience was at the very core of his psychological makeup. He intended to wait as long as he had to in order to win Lila back.

"Are you sure that you're up to driving all that distance?" Lila asked him, breaking into his thoughts.

The fact that she worried about him touched Everett again. It proved to him that he was right. In the long run, they were going to wind up together. Fate wouldn't be that cruel to him, to bring her back into his life like this only to ultimately have him lose her a second time. He just had to stay strong and keep his wits about him.

"I'm fine," he told her. "And I'm going to be back sometime next week for a day. I'll see you then," he promised. "Now go inside and lock the door so I can get going."

Lila was about to point out that she got inside her house on her own every night without supervision, or having anything happen to her, but she let it go. She didn't want to ruin the evening. Everett was being protective and there was something to be said for that, she told herself. Besides, being this close to him was practically setting her on fire, which she could not afford.

So she unlocked her door under his watchful eye and then went in, closing the door behind her.

"Now lock it," he told her after a beat, raising his voice to be heard.

"Yes, sir," Lila called back, humoring him. She turned the lock. "It's locked," she announced.

"Good night, Lila."

"Good night, Everett."

And then, after a couple of beats, she heard Everett's car starting up. He was leaving.

Why did that have such a mournful sound to her, she asked herself. After all, she *wanted* him to leave. Everett might be confident about their future together, but she wasn't.

He'd also been confident about their future when they were younger. *Very* confident. And look how that had ultimately turned out, she reminded herself. That big, wonderful future he had been so sure stretched out before them had shriveled up and died before it had ever had a chance to actually take root and thrive.

And history, she reminded herself as she went into her bedroom to change out of her dress, had a terrible habit of repeating itself.

Lila closed her eyes and shivered. She couldn't bear to go though that kind of heartbreak a second time.

She wasn't strong enough.

Chapter Fourteen

Lila had vacillated about whether or not to invite Everett to the Fortune Foundation fund-raiser for the better part of a week. And now the event was tonight. That meant it was too late for her to change her mind again and invite him.

Just as well, Lila told herself. She'd attend the black-tie gala solo, just as she had initially planned when she'd first gotten the invitation.

Before Everett had popped up back in her life.

The only problem was, she felt conflicted.

Ever since Everett had gone out of his way and nursed her through that bout with the flu, she'd been sorely tempted to invite him—just as a show of gratitude, of course. However, she felt that if they attended the function together, that would be like practically announcing to the world at large that they were a couple—again.

And it was much too premature for that sort of speculation to make the rounds.

Because they weren't a couple anymore and they might never *be* a couple.

So, as she wavered back and forth, Lila fell back on her old stand-by: Why borrow trouble?

Consequently, she was going alone.

It wouldn't be the first time, she thought. And given what her life was like, it undoubtedly wouldn't be the last.

The way she felt at the moment, Lila had a premonition that she was destined to be alone for the rest of her life. Her dreams about Everett had been just that: dreams. And sooner or later, people were destined to wake up from dreams.

To boost her spirits, Lila bought herself a brand-new dress. It was a gown really, she thought, looking herself over from all angles in her wardrobe mirror as she prepared to leave.

The floor-length baby-blue silk gown swirled around softly as she moved and made her feel like she was a princess.

A princess without a kingdom—or a prince, Lila added ruefully—but a princess nonetheless.

"At least for one night," Lila whispered to her reflection.

Taking a deep breath, she gathered up her wrap and her purse. She checked her purse one last time to make sure she had her invitation. It was right where it had been the last four times she'd checked, tucked against her wallet.

She was ready.

"Nothing left to do but drive Cinderella over to the ball," Lila murmured to her reflection.

She smiled to herself as she locked the door and got into her car.

Where are the singing mice when you need them? she wondered wryly, starting up her vehicle.

The Fortune Foundation's fund-raiser was being held on the ground floor ballroom of Austin's finest hotel. Everything about the evening promised to be of the highest, most expensive quality.

After slipping into her purse the ticket that the valet who'd taken her car had given her, Lila went into the hotel.

She didn't need to look at the signs to know which ballroom the fund-raiser was being held in. All she had to do was follow the sound of music and laughter. It was evident that the crowd was having a good time.

The sound quadrupled in volume the second she opened one of the doors to the Golden Room.

She stood there just inside the doors, acclimating herself and looking around what seemed like a cavernous ballroom. There were people absolutely everywhere.

"You made it!"

Surprised, Lila turned to her right and found herself looking at Lucie. Her friend easily hooked her arm through hers.

"I was beginning to think you'd decided to take a pass on this," Lucie said as she began to gently steer Lila in what seemed to be a predetermined direction.

"I didn't think the Foundation allowed us to take a pass," Lila answered honestly. Not that she would have. Her sense of duty and loyalty was just too strong.

"Well, I don't know about 'allowed,'" Lucie replied, considering the matter, "but I do think that there would have been a lot of disappointed people here if you hadn't shown up."

Lila laughed. "I really doubt that," she told Lucie.

"I don't," Lucie retorted. Her eyes were sparkling with humor as she added, "Especially one someone in particular."

Lila stared at her. Lucie had managed to completely lose her. Her brow furrowed as Lila asked, "What are you talking about?"

"Come." The woman tugged a little more insistently on Lila's arm. "I'll show you. By the way, I like the gown. Light blue's a good color for you. It brings out your eyes," she added with approval.

"It's new," Lila confessed, having second thoughts and thinking that maybe she shouldn't have indulged herself like this.

Glancing at the gown one more time, Lucie nodded. "I had a feeling."

"Why? Did I forget to remove a tag?" Lila asked nervously, looking down at her gown and then trying to look over her shoulder to see if there were any telltale tags hanging from the back.

"No, you didn't forget to remove a tag, silly. It just

has that first-time-off-a-hanger look." Looking past Lila, Lucie raised her hand and waved.

"Who are you waving at? Chase?" Lila asked, referring to her friend's husband. Scanning the immediate area, Lila tried to get a glimpse of the rancher.

"Chase is off talking to Graham about that pet project of theirs, the center for military equine therapy," Lucie said. She was talking about Graham Fortune, the man who not only had taken over Fortune Cosmetics but also owned the successful Peter's Place, a home where troubled teens were helped to put their lives together. "No," Lucie told her, a very satisfied smile playing on her lips, "I was waving at the person I said would have been disappointed if you'd decided not to attend tonight."

Before Lila could ask any more questions, she suddenly found herself looking up at someone she'd never expected to see.

Everett. In an obligatory tuxedo.

At that moment Lila realized Everett in a tuxedo was even more irresistible than Everett in jeans.

Face it, the man would be irresistible even wearing a kilt.

"What are you doing here?" Lila asked when she finally located her tongue and remembered how to use it.

"You know, we're going to have to work on getting you a new opening line to say every time you see me," Everett told her with a laugh. "But to answer your question, I was invited."

Lucie stepped up with a slightly more detailed explanation to her friend's question. "The invitation was the Foundation's way of saying thank-you to Everett for his volunteer work."

"Disappointed to see me?" he asked Lila. There was a touch of humor in his voice, although he wasn't quite sure just what to make of the stunned expression on Lila's face.

"No, of course not," Lila denied quickly. "I'm just surprised, that's all. I thought you were still back in Houston."

"I was," Everett confirmed. "The invitation was express-mailed to me yesterday. I thought it would be rude to ignore it, so here I am," he told her simply, as if all he had to do was teleport himself from one location to another instead of drive nearly one hundred and seventy miles.

"Here you are," Lila echoed.

Everything inside her was smiling and she knew that was a dangerous thing. Because when she was in that sort of frame of mind, she tended not to be careful. And that was when mistakes were made.

Mistakes with consequences.

She was going to have to be on her guard, Lila silently warned herself. And it wasn't going to be easy being vigilant, not when Everett looked absolutely, bone-meltingly gorgeous.

As if his dark looks weren't already enough, Lila thought, the tuxedo made Everett look particularly dashing.

You're not eighteen anymore, remember? Lila reminded herself. *You're a woman. A woman who has to be very, very careful.*

She just hoped she could remember that.

"Since your last name practically sounds like Fortune," Lucie was saying to Everett, flanking him on the other side, "maybe you'd like to meet a Fortune or two—or twelve," she teased.

He turned to look at Lila. "Is that all right with you?"

The fact that he asked surprised her. "Why would I object?" she asked, puzzled.

Bending over, he whispered into her ear. "I thought, looking like that," he paused to allow his eyes to skim over her from top to bottom, "maybe you'd want me all to yourself."

She wasn't sure if it was what he said, or his warm breath in her ear that caused the shiver to run rampant up and down her spine.

Whatever it was, it took everything Lila had not to let it get the better of her. She knew where that sort of thing led her. To heaven and then, eventually, to hell as a consequence.

That wasn't going to happen again, she silently swore.

Clearing her throat, Lila ignored the last part of what he'd said and crisply answered, "Yes, it's fine with me."

Lucie smiled. "Then let the introductions begin," she announced, taking charge.

Lucie led off with her husband, Chase. The latter was a genial man who struck Everett as being very down-to-earth, considering the fact that he was an extremely wealthy man.

It was while Everett was talking to Chase that he was introduced to Graham Fortune Robinson. Graham,

Everett was told, was one of Jerome Fortune/Gerald Robinson's eight legitimate offspring. Again, rather than behaving as if he was spoiled or indifferent, or extremely entitled—all traits that Everett had seen displayed by many of the wealthy people he'd grown up with—Graham Fortune came across as only interested in the amount of good he could do with the money he had.

The man, like so many of the other Fortunes who were there that evening, had a keen interest in philanthropy, Everett concluded.

While he was being introduced to and talking with various members of the Fortune clan, Everett found himself exploring the subject that was so near and dear to Schuyler's heart: that perhaps there was some sort of a family connection between the Fortune family and his own. Was "Fortunado" just a poor attempt by someone in the previous generation to either connect to the Fortunes, or to clumsily try to hide that connection?

Everett's radar went up even higher when, after Lucie said that her connection to Graham went beyond just bloodlines, Graham joked that it seemed like everyone was related to him these days.

Everett forced himself to bite his tongue in order to refrain from asking Graham if, by that comment, he was referring to the Fortunados.

The next moment, Graham cleared up the possible confusion by saying that he was referring to the fact that numerous illegitimate Fortune offspring had been located over the past couple of years. Apparently, many years ago the prodigious patriarch Jerome Fortune had deliberately disappeared. When he had resurfaced, he had changed his name, calling himself Gerald Robinson. And, in addition to going on to amass a wealthy portfolio of his own, Gerald/Jerome had amassed a sizeable number of offspring, both legitimately with his wife, Charlotte, and illegitimately with a whole host of women whose paths the man had crossed.

"How did he manage to keep track of all those kids?" Everett marveled, still trying to wrap his mind around the fact that one man had wound up fathering a legion of children.

"Quite simply, he didn't," Graham answered. "But according to one story I've heard, his wife—and my mother—did. She got it into her head to look up every one of her husband's progeny. Some of my siblings think she wanted to be prepared for any eventuality," Graham explained. "Supposedly, she has everything she found written down in a big binder or something along those lines."

Graham smiled. "My personal theory is that when she collected enough data to make that binder really heavy, she was going to use it to hit my father upside the head and teach him a lesson for tomcatting around like that."

Lila nodded, saying in all seriousness, "If you ask me, the man certainly had it coming, spreading his seed around like that without any thought of how this was affecting anyone else in his family—especially those children."

"Yes, but then on the other hand, if he hadn't done it, there would be a lot less Fortunes in the world and so far, all the ones I've met have been really decent people whose hearts are in the right place," Everett pointed out.

Graham smiled his approval at Everett's comment. "I couldn't have put it better myself. I've come to like every one of my siblings." He shrugged and held up his wineglass as if in a silent toast to them. "It's not everyone who has a family big enough to populate a medium-size town."

Everett touched his glass to Graham's. He felt as if he could go on talking about the various members of the Fortune family all night. But suddenly, everyone in the ballroom was being asked to stop what they were doing.

"Can I have everyone's attention for a moment?" a tall, imposing man with a booming voice said into a microphone. He was standing before a podium at the front of the ballroom. "This is the time in our evening where we all temporarily suspend the festivities and are asked to dig deep into our hearts—and our pockets," the MC added with a laugh. "In other words, it's time for us to donate to the Fortune Foundation so it can go on doing all those good works and helping all those people who are not nearly as fortunate—no pun intended—as we all are."

The man's piercing blue eyes seemed to sweep around the entire ballroom. No easy feat, Lila thought, watching from the sidelines.

"Now don't be shy," the MC continued. "Give as much as you're able. No donation is too small, although bigger is always better. But even a little is better than nothing. So, like I said, open your hearts and get those checkbooks out. Remember, it feels good to give. And when you do, you'll find that you'll get back in ways you never even suspected were possible."

Listening, Lila opened up her purse and took out her checkbook. She was about to start writing out what she viewed to be a modest amount—although it was all she could afford—when Everett put his hand on hers, stopping her.

She looked at him, puzzled. Why wasn't he letting her write the check?

"I'll take care of it for both of us," he told her. The next moment, as she watched, she saw Everett write out a check for the sum of one hundred thousand dollars.

At the last second, she remembered to keep her mouth from dropping open.

Chapter Fifteen

The MC, David Davenport, looked at the check that had just been passed to him by one of the aides collecting donations from the guests. Holding the check aloft, Davenport scanned the crowd until he made eye contact with Everett.

"Is this right?" the MC asked Everett, astonished. "Your pen didn't slip?"

Everett's mouth curved slightly as he smiled at the man in front of the room. "My pen didn't slip," he assured the MC.

Davenport, a distinguished-looking, gray-haired man in his fifties, instantly brightened. "Ladies and gentlemen, I'm proud to announce that we have a new record," he told the gathering. "Dr. Everett Fortunado has generously donated the sum of one hundred thousand dollars to the Fortune Foundation."

A hush fell over the entire ballroom. It lasted for almost a full minute and then people began clapping. The sound swelled until the entire ballroom was engulfed in appreciative applause.

Everett wasn't really sure just how to react to the applause. He hadn't made the donation because he wanted to garner any sort of attention. He'd written the check because he felt it was his obligation to share the good fortune he had always felt so privileged to grow up experiencing.

When the applause finally died down, Davenport proceeded to try to utilize the moment to the Foundation's advantage.

"All right, people, let's see if Dr. Fortunado's generosity can motivate some of you to do your fair share as well." The MC looked around. It seemed as if he was making eye contact with everyone there. "Remember, this is for those deserving mothers and fathers and children who so badly need our help in order to make it through the hard times."

Everett stood back and watched as more of the fundraiser's attendees began writing out checks. There seemed to be chatter going on all around him.

Except at his side.

From the moment he had written out the check, Everett noticed that Lila had fallen completely silent. She hadn't said a single word to him during the entire time that the checks were being written and collected on all sides of them.

Nor, he observed, did Lila say anything during the buffet dinner that followed, despite the fact that he had intentionally stayed close to her during the whole time. He had broached a number of topics in an effort to engage her in conversation and had only received single-word replies.

Finally, unable to take the silence any longer, he drew Lila aside to a little alcove, away from the rest of the ballroom, and asked her point-blank: "Is something wrong?"

Lila had been trying to reconcile the mixed feelings she'd been having ever since she'd watched Everett writing out a check for such an exorbitant amount. Because she didn't want to cause a scene or start an uproar, she'd been doing her best just to squelch the suspicions that had been growing in her head. That involved keeping her mouth shut and not saying anything, although it wasn't easy.

But her doubts weren't going away, and rather than taking a hint and keeping quiet, Everett was pressuring her for an explanation.

Finally blowing out a frustrated breath, Lila asked him bluntly, "Are you trying to buy me?"

Dumbfounded and more than a little confused, Everett could only stare at her. He wasn't even sure if he had actually heard Lila correctly.

"What?"

Lila pressed her lips together, then ground out, "Are you trying to buy my love by giving that huge sum of money to the Foundation?"

Stunned, he told her, "I made that donation because

the Foundation is a worthy cause that does a great deal of good work. I thought you'd be happy about my contribution." He looked at her, not knowing where this had come from. Not for the first time, he felt as if he was walking on eggshells around her.

"Why do you have to dissect every single move I make and search for an ulterior motive?" he wanted to know. "Can't I just be generous because I want to be? Because it makes me feel good to do something decent for people who weren't born as lucky as I was?" He saw tears suddenly shimmering in her eyes and immediately felt a pang of guilt because he knew he was responsible for those tears. "Hey, I didn't mean to make you cry—"

Lila shook her head, halting his apology. Taking a deep breath to center herself, she said, "You didn't. You're right. You did something selfless and I just took it apart, looking for hidden reasons behind your donation when you were just being a decent guy." She blew out a shaky breath. "I guess I've just gotten to be really mistrustful."

And that was on him, Everett thought. He'd done this to her—taken a sweet, optimistic young woman and crushed something inside of her all those years ago. He had to find a way to fix this, he told himself.

But how?

How did he convince Lila that his feelings for her were genuine? That all he wanted was to be able to show her that he loved her and that he was willing to make things up to her for the rest of his life?

Desperation had him making the next move in his

desire to reach her, to communicate to her just how sincere he was.

Since he had taken her away from the rest of the guests in the ballroom by drawing her into a recessed alcove to talk to her, he knew they'd be safe from any prying eyes.

Framing Lila's face with his hands, Everett bent his head and did what he had been longing to do since he had first seen her in that sandwich shop in Austin.

He kissed her.

The moment his lips touched Lila's, Everett realized just how much he had missed her.

How much he really wanted Lila.

A little voice in his head told him he should stop kissing her, but he couldn't. Instead, Everett deepened the kiss.

And just like that, the captor became the captive.

At that moment, he knew that he would have walked through fire just to have Lila back in his life the way she had been all those years ago: loving and untainted by uncertainties and doubts.

Lila's breath caught in her throat. A split second before Everett had kissed her, she suddenly knew that he would. Knew too that with all her heart she wanted him to kiss her.

And then he did.

Just like that, all those years they'd spent apart melted away. She was instantly responding to Everett just as she had back then.

Except that now Lila was responding as a woman, not as a starry-eyed young girl.

Lila could feel every inch of her body heating as she fell deeper into the kiss. She wrapped her arms around Everett, savoring the taste of his lips urgently pressed against hers.

Longings, locked away for so long, came charging out, demanding attention as they carelessly trampled reason into the dust.

Her heart was pounding wildly when he drew his lips away. She found herself struggling in order to pull air into her lungs.

She looked up at Everett in wonder, desire mounting within her.

He hadn't meant to get this carried away, to let the moment get out of hand like this. He'd only wanted to kiss Lila again, to silently communicate to her that his feelings for her were as strong as ever.

Stronger.

"I'm sorry, Lila," Everett began. "I didn't mean to get—"

But Lila quickly cut short his apology. She didn't want Everett to be sorry for kissing her. Didn't want to have him withdrawing from her. Not when she was suddenly having all these unresolved feelings ricocheting throughout every inch of her being.

She wanted more.

Needed more.

"Let's get out of here," Lila breathed.

She didn't mean that, Everett thought, even as he asked, "Now?"

"Now," she echoed adamantly.

Everett stood there for a moment arguing with himself, trying very hard to convince himself to do the right thing.

Another man would have talked her out of it, pointing out what it might look like if someone saw them leaving before the fund-raiser was over. Another man would have taken her by the hand and led her back into the ballroom proper.

But another man hadn't spent every day of the last thirteen years missing Lila so much that there were times he literally ached.

Now that there was a glimmer of hope that they could get back together, that he could win her back, he could admit that to himself. Admit that the reason that every possible relationship that had loomed before him over the years had fallen through was because all the women in those would-be relationships hadn't been able to hold a candle to Lila.

So instead of doing the noble thing and trying to talk Lila out of what she'd just suggested, Everett took her hand in his. And together they made their way out of the ballroom. And then out of the hotel.

Once outside, as the cooler evening air slipped over them, Everett looked at Lila for some sign that she'd had a change of heart about leaving. He didn't detect any, but because he absolutely wanted her to have no regrets, he asked, "You're sure?"

"I'm sure," Lila answered breathlessly. All she wanted was to be alone with him. To be with him in every way possible.

"We both drove here separately," Everett reminded her. While he feared that if she drove herself she might change her mind, he knew that if Lila left her car here at the hotel, someone from the fund-raiser would take note of that.

Questions would be asked and gossip would spread. He didn't want Lila subjected to any sort of talk or speculation as to why her car was still in the parking structure while she herself was nowhere to be found. He wanted to protect her from that sort of thing at all costs.

Although she didn't want to be more than a foot away from him right now, Lila didn't see any actual problem. "So? We can both drive our cars to my house. My driveway can accommodate two vehicles," she told him.

Lila could feel her heart hammering with every word she uttered as a tiny voice in her head, barely audible above the beating of her heart, was telling her to take her car and make good her escape.

But she didn't want to escape. One taste of Everett's lips and it was all she could do not to beg for more right here, right now.

When the valet came up to them, they both handed him their tickets.

"Bring the lady her car first," Everett told him.

The valet nodded. "Be right back," he promised, heading into the parking structure quickly.

"Think anyone noticed you left?" Everett asked her as they waited.

"If they notice anyone's gone, it would most likely be you," Lila told him. "After all, you're the man of the hour after that huge donation."

When the valet brought her car up and held the door

open for her, she handed him a tip and then slid into the driver's seat.

She looked up at Everett, said, "I'll see you," and then drove off.

I'll see you.

Her words echoed in his brain. She hadn't said "I'll see you *later*." Just "I'll see you." Did that mean she'd had a change of heart and decided that she'd almost made a terrible mistake?

Now who's overthinking everything? Everett admonished himself.

He put the original question on hold when the valet brought up his car.

"You car handles like a dream," the valet told him enthusiastically and a bit enviously as he got out of the vehicle. Backing away, he left the driver's door open for him.

Everett inclined his head, a grin curving his mouth. "She likes to be babied," he told the valet as he handed him a ten-dollar bill and got in.

The valet's eyes widened as he looked at the bill. "Thanks!"

Everett pulled away, eager to catch up to Lila's car. But it felt like he was catching every single red light between the hotel and her house.

He really hoped that by the time he got there Lila hadn't reflected on her impulsive decision and changed her mind about the night ahead.

If she did, he would have no choice but to go along with her decision. He would never force himself on her, but he decided that he was going to do everything in his power to convince her that they were meant to be together.

Because they were.

It was hard to stay focused on the road. All he could see in his mind's eye was Lila. Lila, offering herself to him. Lila, making love with him.

Lila, who was and always had been the center of his universe.

How had he allowed himself to let her go? Everett silently asked himself. He wouldn't have tied her up in the attic, but he could have tried to talk her out of breaking up with him, could have tried his damnedest to convince her to give him another chance.

Well, this is your chance, Everett, he thought as he turned onto Lila's block. *Don't blow it.*

Chapter Sixteen

What if Everett didn't come?

What if he did?

Lila pressed her hand against her stomach, trying to quiet the butterflies that seemed to be wildly crashing into one another in her stomach. She'd never felt so confused before.

Back in the ballroom alcove, when Everett had kissed her, awakening all those old feelings, she'd wanted him right then and there. But now she'd had a little time to distance herself from that kiss, doubts had begun creeping in. It was as if she was playing a tennis match with herself in her brain.

Where *was* he?

Granted she'd flown through every light and gotten home in record time, moving as if her car was being propelled by a gale, but she hadn't left *that* much ahead of Everett.

He should have been here by now.

Unless he'd changed his mind and decided to go straight to his sister's house instead.

Or maybe he'd just decided to head back to Houston from the fund-raiser instead of coming over to her house.

To her.

Had she come on too strong?

But after he kissed her like that, unearthing all those old memories, she just couldn't help herself. Any thoughts of hanging back or taking it slow had just incinerated right on the spot. All she could think of was how much she'd missed being in Everett's arms, of having him hold her as if she was something very precious.

She felt as if she was losing her mind.

Lila looked out her window and saw only her car in the driveway.

He'd had a change of heart, she thought, letting the curtain drop back into place.

With a gut-wrenching sigh, she turned away. Served her right for giving in to her emotions like some silly schoolgirl and—

She jerked her head up, listening. Was that—?

Yes, it was. It was the sound of a car pulling up in her driveway.

All those doubts that were surfacing took a nosedive and she threw open the door before he had a chance to ring the doorbell.

"There are way too many red lights in this city," Everett told her.

Grabbing hold of his shirt, Lila pulled him over the threshold and into her house, slamming the door shut right behind him.

"I don't want to talk about red lights," she said just before she rose up on her tiptoes and sealed her mouth to his.

It was more than a couple of minutes later that they managed to come up for air—temporarily.

"Right," Everett breathlessly agreed, devouring her with his eyes. "No talking about red lights."

"No talking at all," Lila countered.

As she sought out his lips again, sealing hers to them, she began to systematically remove Everett's tuxedo, separating it from his body so quickly she worried that she'd wind up ripping something.

If she did, she could fix it, she assured herself. She knew her way around a needle. But right now, she wanted to relearn her way around his body.

It had been a long, long time since she'd been intimate with him. Since she'd been intimate with *anyone*, because after she had left Everett, she'd never met anyone to take his place, or even come close to qualifying as a candidate for that position. Without love as an ingredient in the mix, lovemaking just didn't seem right to her.

As she was eagerly removing his clothing, Everett was doing the same with hers.

Lila could feel his hands moving along her body. Locating her zipper, he pulled it down her back in one swift movement, then peeled away the silky gown from her skin.

It fell to the floor like a sinking blue cloud, pooling about her high heels.

Lila caught her breath as she felt his strong hands tugging away her bikini underwear, then gliding over her bare skin, swiftly reducing her to a pulsating mass of desire.

With urgent movements, she hurried to return the compliment until they were both standing there in her living room, nude—except for one thing.

She was still wearing her high heels.

Lila quickly remedied that, kicking the shoes off and instantly becoming petite.

"Damn," Everett whispered against the sensitive skin of her throat as he pressed kiss after kiss along it, "I can't tell you how many times I've dreamed about doing this."

The feel of his warm breath sliding along her skin caused all her desires to intensify. Her mushrooming needs almost engulfed her as they seized control over every single facet of her being.

Her mind in a haze, Lila felt her back being pressed against the sofa. She didn't even remember how they got there.

Everett was taking inventory of every single inch of her body with his mouth, creating wonderful sensations as he moved.

Doing wonderful things.

She was eager to return the favor, but for the moment, she couldn't find the strength to do anything but absorb every nuance of what was happening. She was utterly immersed in the deliciously wicked feelings that were erupting all over her as his lips and tongue left their mark everywhere, branding her.

Making her his.

Lila twisted and arched, savoring and absorbing every wondrous salvo wildly echoing throughout her body.

And still he continued, moving lower and lower by pulsating increments.

Anticipation rippled through her like shockwaves as she felt first his breath, and then his mouth moving down to the very center of her core.

His tongue teased her ever so lightly, skimming along the delicate, sensitive area, all the while raising her response higher and higher, creating a fever pitch within her until finally, delicious explosions erupted simultaneously all through her, undulating over her like a series of earthquakes.

Lila cried out his name, pulling him to her until he was right above her, melting her soul with the intense look of desire and passion in his eyes.

She felt him coaxing open her legs with his knee. What there was left of her shallow breath caught in her throat.

The next moment, he entered her and they were sealed to one another, creating a single heated entity.

Everett began to move his hips so slowly at first, she thought she had only imagined it. But then the movements began to increase, growing stronger. Taking her with them.

And then they were no longer on her sofa, no longer in her house. They were somewhere else, completely isolated from the world. A place where only the two of them existed.

The only thing that mattered was Everett and this insanely wondrous sensation that they were sharing. Their bodies danced to music that only the two of them could hear.

The tempo increased, going faster and faster until suddenly they found themselves racing to the top of the world, to a place that was both new and familiar at the same time.

Lila could feel her heart slamming against his. Could feel Everett's heart echoing hers to the point that she thought their two hearts would forever be sealed together as one.

And then she felt the fireworks exploding, showering a profusion of stars all around her until that was all there was.

A world filed with stars.

She clung to Everett then, clung to the sensation that they had created together. She clung to it for as long as she could and bathed in the euphoria that came in its wake.

She held onto the sensation—and Everett—for as long as possible. But even so, it receded no matter how hard she fought to hang onto it.

Sorrow began to wiggle its way into the spaces the euphoria had left behind.

Everett shifted his weight off her, moving so that he was lying beside her.

He tightened his arm around her, exulting in the feeling of warmth generated by holding onto her. He glanced down at his chest and was mildly surprised that he wasn't glowing or giving out some sort of light like a beacon that guided the ships through the night at sea.

She was back, he thought. He'd won Lila back. And the lovemaking between them was so much better now than it had been before. The sex might have been familiar at its roots, but it had also felt wonderfully brand-new.

The woman in his arms was so much more now than she had been all those years ago.

How did he get so lucky? Everett silently marveled. Lying here next to Lila, reliving the lovemaking they had just shared, he found himself wanting to take her all over again.

Wanting her with a renewed fierceness that was impossible to ignore.

Propping himself up slightly, Everett leaned over her face and kissed one eyelid, then her other eyelid.

Then her mouth.

He lingered there, deepening the kiss until it all but consumed both of them, feeding something in his soul.

And then hers.

She looked up at him with wonder. "Again?" she questioned.

Lila saw laughter entering his eyes as Everett told her, "Honey, I am just getting started."

Something came over her.

Lila seized the moment and just like that, turned the tables on him. It was her turn to be the seducer rather than the seduced. This relationship didn't have a prayer of working if only one of them gave while the other received, she thought.

So, just as he had done before, Lila began to prime his body, ever so lightly gliding both her lips and her tongue along all the sensitive, seducible areas of his body.

Priming him until he verged on the edge of full readiness.

She moved with purpose along Everett's chest, gliding the tip of her tongue along his nipples just as he had done to her.

And then she slid her tongue along the hard contours of his chest, moving steadily down to his belly, teasing it until it quivered beneath her hot, probing mouth.

Raising her eyes, she met his. A wicked look entered them as she proceeded to work her way lower along his anatomy until she had reached his hardening desire.

With an air of triumph, she went on to make him hers by branding him.

She did it, once, then twice—then suddenly, she felt his hands on her forearms, stopping her. He drew her away and brought her back up to his level by pulling her body along his.

Arousing both of them even more.

The next second, he raised his head and captured her mouth with his own, kissing her over and over again until he had reduced her to the consistency of a rain puddle that was about to go up in the steam of a hot summer sun. At that moment, he deftly switched their places. He was above her and she was back under him.

And just as before, they united, forming one whole.

This time he moved urgently right from the start. There was no gentle increase in tempo. There were just the swift, direct movements that were intended to bring them swirling up to journey's end.

And it did.

So quickly that it stole away their breath, leaving them gasping and panting in the aftermath of the crescendo that had brought all the stars raining down on them.

As before, the euphoria that sealed around them in the aftermath was wondrous. And, also as before, it slipped away much too soon, leaving Lila exhausted and slowly making her way back to reality.

With painstakingly slow movements, Lila shifted her head so that she was looking at the man next to her without alerting him to the fact that she was.

It was happening. Happening just as she had been afraid that it would.

She could feel it.

She was falling in love with Everett all over again. And she was totally powerless to prevent it, she thought with a sliver of panic that was beginning to grow inside of her.

Why had she done this?

Why had she allowed it to happen? She could have stopped it from ever taking place—*should* have stopped it from taking place not once, but twice, she ruefully reminded herself. She had allowed the evening—and herself—to spin completely out of control and now she had consequences to face.

She didn't like this feeling, this feeling of being unable to stop her life from spinning out of control.

Lila could feel herself growing more and more afraid. Afraid of what she'd done. Afraid of where she just *knew* it was going to lead—to the same unhappiness she'd experienced thirteen years ago.

How could something that had felt so right in the moment be so very wrong in the long run?

But it was, she thought.

It was.

What made her think that just because they'd managed to recapture the rapturous happiness of lovemaking it was destined to end any other way for them than it already had once before?

Those that do not learn from history are doomed to repeat it.

And that was her, she thought ruefully. She was doomed to repeat the mistakes she'd made once. In fact, she already had repeated those mistakes.

Well, she *could* learn from her mistakes, Lila silently insisted. And she intended to start right now, before it was too late and things spun further out of control, setting the stage for Everett to break her heart all over again.

Summoning her resolve, not to mention her courage, Lila turned toward the man lying next to her on the sectional sofa.

She struggled into an upright position.

Everett shift toward her. "Want to take this to your bedroom and do it again?" he asked her with a warm, inviting smile.

"No," she said with such finality that it froze Everett in place. "I want you to leave."

The blissful happiness he'd just been experiencing broke up into tiny slivered shards. He felt as if he'd just been blindsided.

Everett stared at her. "Did I do something wrong?" he asked, trying to understand why she had made this unexpected U-turn.

"Things are moving too fast, Everett," she told him. Her tone left no room for any sort of attempts to change her mind. "You need to go."

Chapter Seventeen

Everett sat up. "You're really serious?" he asked, unable to believe that Lila actually meant what she'd just said to him.

He'd been with a number of women since he and Lila had broken up and although he'd never gotten to the serious relationship stage with any of those women, none of them had ever kicked him out of bed, either, figuratively *or* literally.

His confidence shaken, Everett had no idea how to react to this totally unfamiliar situation.

Lila had already gotten up off the sofa, wrapping a crocheted throw around herself in lieu of clothing. Her insides were quaking, but she held her ground.

"Yes, I'm serious," she insisted, her voice rising in pitch. "*Very* serious."

Well, he'd tried his best and for a little while there, he thought that he'd succeeded in winning Lila over. But obviously, he'd miscalculated, Everett told himself. He was willing to do anything to win Lila back except for one thing: he was not about to beg. A man had to have some pride, he thought fiercely.

Nodding his head, he quickly pulled on his discarded tuxedo slacks. Securing them, he grabbed the rest of his things and held the clothes against his chest in a rumpled ball of material. He didn't even bother putting on his shoes. Instead, he just picked them up and held them in his other hand.

"All right then," he told her, heading for the door. "I'd better go."

Lila stood like a statue, saying nothing.

Everett let himself out the door, leaving it wide open. As he walked to his car in the driveway, he heard the front door close with finality behind him, obliterating any hope that at the last minute Lila would change her mind and either come running after him or at least call him back into the house.

Forcing himself not to look back, Everett opened his car door and got into his vehicle. He felt so totally stunned and deflated that he could hardly breathe as he started up his car and pulled out of Lila's driveway.

He stopped at the first all-night gas station he came to. Ignoring the convenience store clerk's curious looks, he asked for the restroom key. Taking it from the man, he let himself into the single stall bathroom.

The conditions in the restroom were far from ideal, but he managed to put on the rest of his clothes. He wanted to avoid having Schuyler ask him a barrage of questions if he walked in wearing only the tuxedo slacks.

He loved his sister dearly, but he just wasn't up to fielding any of her questions, however well intentioned they might be. He just wanted to quietly get his things from her guest room and drive back to Houston.

But as luck would have it, a swift, clean getaway was just not in the cards for him.

Despite the hour, Schuyler was up and heard him coming in. Everett had barely closed the front door and walked in before his sister walked out of the kitchen and managed to waylay him at the foot of the stairs.

"What are you doing back so soon?" she asked him in surprise. "I wasn't expecting you back until around midmorning."

He offered her a careless shrug in response. "Fundraiser ended so I came back."

Schuyler furrowed her brow, as if something didn't sound right to her. "Why didn't you go get a nightcap with Lila?"

"I didn't want to drink and drive," Everett answered. He looked longingly up the stairs. So near and yet so far, he couldn't help thinking.

Schuyler's furrowed brow gave way to an all-out, impatient frown.

"Damn it, Ev, I'm trying to politely tiptoe around the subject but you're making me have to come flat out and ask." She paused, waiting for her brother to jump in and say what she was waiting for him to tell her. But he remained silent. Huffing, Schuyler asked, "Why aren't you over at Lila's place, picking things up where the two of you left off back in college?"

"It's complicated, Schuy," Everett told her.

"That's what people say when they don't want to deal with something," she insisted. She pinned her brother with a penetrating look that went clear down to the bone. "Do you care about this woman?" she asked him point-blank.

Still smarting from his rejection, he *really* didn't want to get into this with his sister. "Schuyler, go to bed."

They had always talked things out before and Schuyler apparently refused to back off now that she had broached the subject. "Do you care about this woman?" she repeated, enunciating each word slowly with intentional emphasis.

He could see that Schuyler wasn't about to let this go until she had an answer from him. So he gave her one. A short one.

"No."

Schuyler's eyes narrowed, looking deep into his. "You're lying."

Everett did his best to separate himself from any emotion. He really didn't want to shout at his sister. "No, I'm not."

"Yes, you are," Schuyler retorted. When he tried to turn away, she grabbed hold of his shoulder, making him face her. "You have this 'tell' when you lie. There's a tiny nerve right under your left eye that jumps every time you don't tell the truth."

"Then why even bother asking me?" He came close to biting off his question.

"So you can hear the words out loud for yourself," she told him. "Ev, when you first told me you were going to win Lila back, I didn't think you had a chance in hell of doing it. I thought you'd eventually come to your senses and forget the whole thing."

She shook her head, amused by her preconceived notion. "But you're not the type to forget the whole thing and you managed to bring me around to your way of thinking. A guy like that doesn't just give up out of the blue."

Taking his hand, Schuyler tugged on it, making him sit down on the bottom step. She sat down beside him, just the way they used to do as kids whenever they wanted to talk about things.

"What happened?" she asked him.

After a short internal debate, Everett gave her an abbreviated version, mentioning his donation to the Foundation in passing, but not the amount.

He told his sister about going back with Lila to her place, but left it for her imagination to fill in the details of what transpired there. He ended by telling his sister that Lila had suddenly pulled back, saying that things were going too fast and that he needed to go home.

"And...?" Schuyler asked, waiting for him to tell her more.

"And I came home," Everett said with a shrug. "Or to your house," he corrected. "I wanted to change out of this monkey suit, get my suitcase and go back to Houston."

"And nothing else happened?" she questioned, studying his face closely.

"Nothing else happened," he echoed flatly. He just wanted to get his things and hit the road, putting this night—and Lila—behind him.

Schuyler's mouth curved in a tolerant, loving smile. "You do realize that your shirt is inside out, don't you?" his sister asked. "Did you wear it that way at the fundraiser?"

He glanced down. Damn it, leave it to Schuyler to catch that, he thought, annoyed. "Yup. The whole fundraiser," he told her stubbornly.

"I see," Schuyler replied, watching the nerve just beneath his eye flutter. "Well, maybe nobody noticed," she said loftily. "Or maybe Lila did and that's why she told you things were moving too fast and sent you away." Schuyler's smile widened. "She didn't want to be associated with someone who couldn't dress himself properly."

"Schuyler—" There was a warning note in Everett's voice.

Schuyler held up her hands, warding off what he was about to say.

"I'm just teasing you," she told him. And then her tone changed. "Why don't you stay here for what's left of the night and then go talk to Lila in the morning?" she suggested. "Things always look better in the morning," she added kindly.

"No," he told his sister, his mind made up. "I need to be getting back. I've let a lot of things slide lately and I need to do some catching up."

"That's not the Dr. Everett Fortunado I know," Schuyler told him, rising to her feet when he did. "You can juggle more balls in the air than any two people I know."

"Not this time," he answered as he started up the steps. "This time those balls are all falling right through my hands."

"Want me to help you pack?" she offered, calling up the stairs.

"No, I've got this," he told her, glancing over his shoulder.

Schuyler stood there, arms akimbo, and murmured loud enough for him to hear, "No, I don't think that you do."

"That was some hefty donation that your boyfriend made on Friday," Lucie said the following Monday morning as Lila passed her open door.

Lila made no answer, merely shrugging in response as she stepped into her office.

Lucie didn't take the hint. Instead, she followed her friend into Lila's office. When Lila sat down at her desk, Lucie peered at her a little more closely.

"You look awful," she observed. Then a small smile lit her eyes. "Didn't get any sleep all weekend, huh?"

"No," Lila answered, deliberately not taking Lucie's bait. Her tone flatly denied any further dialogue between them.

But Lucie wasn't about to take the hint. "So how was it?" she asked with a grin.

Lila spared her friend a glance. Lucie was now firmly planted on the edge of her desk. "How was what?"

"You know…" But since Lila gave no indication that she did, Lucie further elaborated. "Getting back together with Everett."

"We're not back together," Lila answered, biting off each word. They all had a bitter taste, but that would pass, she told herself. It *had* to.

"Why the hell not?" Lucie cried. When Lila looked at her sharply, Lucie said, "Anyone at the fund-raiser could see he was crazy about you. When you two left early, I was sure you were going back to your place— if you made it that far," Lucie added.

This time Lila's head shot up. She was really hoping that no one had noticed them leaving the fund-raiser. So much for hoping.

"What's that supposed to mean?" she wanted to know.

Lucie sighed.

"Lila, there were so many sparks flying between the two of you that you'd make an electrical storm seem like an afternoon at the library in comparison." She gave Lila a deep, penetrating look, as if willing the truth out of her. "You can't tell me that you two didn't get together after you left the fund-raiser."

"All right," Lila replied grudgingly. It wasn't in her to lie. "We did."

Getting up off the desk, Lucie closed Lila's door, then crossed back to her desk, coming closer. "And?" she coaxed.

Lila shifted uncomfortably in her chair, but it was

clear that Lucie wasn't going anywhere until she heard all the details.

"And then I sent him away," she said, jumping to the end without elaborating anything in between.

Lucie stared at her. "You're joking."

"No, I'm not," Lila replied firmly. "I sent him away."

"Why in heaven's name would you do that?" Lucie cried incredulously.

"Because things were moving much too fast between us," Lila blurted out, frustration bubbling beneath her statement.

Leaning forward, Lucie took her friend's hands into hers. "Lila, honey," she began gently, "it's been thirteen years. After all that time, things were not moving fast. They were barely crawling by at a turtle's pace." She squeezed Lila's hands as she looked deeper into her eyes, as if trying to understand, to read Lila's thoughts. And then it must have hit her, because she sharply drew a breath. "You got scared, didn't you? He made you have all those feelings again and it scared you."

Lila looked away. Lucie had homed in on the truth.

But there was no running from the truth. She knew that now.

With a sigh, she nodded. And then she looked up at Lucie. "How did you do it?" she asked, silently begging the other woman for guidance.

"Do what?" Lucie asked.

"With Chase," Lila said, hoping that Lucie had some sage, magical knowledge to impart. Some words of wisdom that could somehow guide her through this densely wooded area she found herself stumbling through.

"How were you able to pick up where you left off with Chase?" The two hadn't just been high school sweethearts, they'd eloped and had been married—for all of five minutes.

"Very easy," Lucie answered her nonchalantly. "I didn't."

Lila stared at her. She didn't understand. "But you two were just recently married."

"Actually, we'd been secretly married as teenagers and never had it annulled, but didn't find out until recently. We had to get to know each other as adults, not as the impulsive kids we once were. And that's what you have to do," Lucie told her in all honesty. "You and Everett have to do the work and get to know each other all over again—from scratch," she insisted. "You have to take into consideration that Everett, in all likelihood, may very well *not* be the person he was at sixteen or eighteen or twenty."

Lucie circled to the back of the desk and put her arm on Lila's shoulder.

"And while we're at it, why do you assume that history has to repeat itself?" she questioned gently. "What if Everett really means what he says and wants to get back together with you not for a romp or a weekend of lovemaking, but for good?"

Lila rose from her chair and paced about the small office. She couldn't come to grips with the desperate feeling she was experiencing in her gut.

"Even if Everett's serious, even if he wants things to be different this time around, the past is still standing between us like a giant roadblock," Lila insisted.

"By the past you mean the little girl that you gave up." It wasn't a question. Lucie was reading between the lines. She knew the truth about Lila's past. In a moment of weakness, Lila had entrusted her with her deepest secret.

"Yes," Lila cried, struggling not to cry. "It still haunts me," she admitted. "Holding her in my arms and then giving her up—some nights I still wake up in a cold sweat, remembering how that felt. To have her and then not have her, all in the blink of an eye," Lila confessed sadly.

"Does Everett realize how you feel?" Lucie asked.

Lila pressed her lips together and shook her head. "I don't know," she answered. "I never said anything about it."

"Did you *ask* him if he knew?" Lucie pressed. "Or say anything at all about what giving her up did to you?"

"No," Lila admitted in a low voice, avoiding Lucie's eyes.

"Then for heaven sakes, *talk* to him about it," Lucie urged. "Tell him how you felt giving up your baby. How you *still* feel."

"I can't," Lila said. "I just can't. Lucie, I know you mean well, but just please, please leave me alone right now. It'll work out."

It will, Lila told herself as Lucie walked out of her office.

It had to.

Chapter Eighteen

"All right, I'm here," Everett declared when his sister opened her front door to admit him into her house several days later. "I got Blake to take over a few of my patients, had the rest of them rescheduled and drove right out because you sounded as if this was urgent." His eyes swept over her and she certainly didn't look as if she was in the throes of some sort of an emergency. "Now what's this all about?"

Instead of answering his question, Schuyler said, "I can't tell you here." Getting her purse, she took out her car keys. "In order to explain, I need to take you some place first."

Everett looked at his sister suspiciously. This wasn't making any sense to him. "Where?" he wanted to know.

Again she avoided giving him a direct answer.

"You'll understand everything once we're there," Schuyler told him, hurrying toward her spacious garage.

Fetching her red BMW, she pulled up next to her brother. "Get in," she told him, leaning over and throwing open the passenger door.

Since he'd all but raced out of Houston, driving at top speed until he'd reached Austin because he was extremely concerned about Schuyler, he went along with her instructions.

"You're being awfully mysterious about all this," he accused.

"The mystery will be cleared up before you know it, big brother," Schuyler promised, mentally crossing her fingers.

Everett suddenly sat up a little straighter in the passenger seat as a thought occurred to him.

Looking at her now, he asked, "Hey, Schuy, you're not pregnant, are you?" As the question came out of his mouth, he began grinning so widely, his lips almost hurt. He'd thought his sister would get married first before starting a family, but that didn't negate his happiness for her. "Wow, that's terrific. How far along are you?" he asked excitedly. "What does Carlo think about this? Have you picked a godfather yet?"

Apparently overwhelmed, Schuyler took a second to speak. "Hey, slow down," she said then. She slanted a look in his direction before turning back to the road. "So you like the idea of babies," she said, obviously referring to his exuberant reaction.

"Of course I do. How far along are you?" he asked her again.

"I'm not," Schuyler told him.

Everett looked as if his bubble had been pierced, sending him twisting in the wind. "Wait, I don't understand. Then you're not pregnant?" he asked, more confused than ever.

"No," Schuyler answered. "I never said I was. *You* jumped to that conclusion," she pointed out. "Let me have my wedding first, then we'll see about babies."

Everett slumped back against his seat. "Okay, then I don't understand," he said, confused. "What's this all about?"

Schuyler bit her lower lip, stalling. "I already told you—"

"No, you didn't," he insisted, trying to keep his voice even. He didn't like games, especially not at his expense.

"Just hang on a little longer and you'll see what this is all about."

Everett sighed. "Well, since you've kidnapped me, I guess I don't have a choice."

"I didn't kidnap you," Schuyler informed him. "You got into the car of your own free will."

That's not how he saw it. "You just keep telling yourself that," he said. Laying his head back against the headrest, Everett closed his eyes. Running around and not getting much sleep was finally beginning to catch up with him. "Wake me whenever we get to wherever it is that we're going," he told her.

"We're here," Schuyler announced not five minutes later.

"Well, that didn't take long," Everett commented.

Sitting up, he looked around as his sister got out of the car.

Schuyler had driven them to the Fortune Foundation.

Alert, not to mention annoyed, Everett glared at his sister when he got out. "Hey, why are we here?"

"You'll find out," she said cheerfully.

Neither his mood nor the look that he was giving her over the hood of her car improved.

"Schuyler, just what the hell are you up to?" he demanded.

"You'll find out," his sister repeated. She gave him what she no doubt hoped was an encouraging look. "Just give it a few more minutes."

But Everett didn't move an inch. "And if I don't?"

"Then you'll never know how things might have turned out." When he still didn't move, Schuyler looked at him plaintively. "Do it for me, Everett. Please," she implored.

"Damn it, Schuyler, you owe me," Everett snapped, finally coming around the sporty red vehicle.

Schuyler inclined her head and gave him a wink. "We'll see."

Lila was engrossed in drawing up the following week's schedule for the volunteer doctors when Lucie walked into her office.

"Save whatever you're working on, Lila," Lucie told her. "I need your full, undivided attention right now."

Surprised by Lucie's serious tone, Lila looked up. "What's going on?"

Instead of answering her, Lucie looked over her

shoulder and beckoned to someone. Just who was she summoning to Lila's office?

Totally stunned, Lila was immediately on her feet when she saw him.

Everett was the last person she'd expected to see here. After practically throwing him out of her house, she'd never thought she would see him again.

She fisted her hands, digging her knuckles into her desk to keep her knees from giving way.

She shot an angry look at her friend. "Lucie, what have you done?" she demanded.

"Saved two really nice people from a lifetime of loneliness and heartache," Lucie answered. Then she stepped out of the way, allowing a bewildered-looking Everett to enter Lila's office. But not before she gave a big grin and a high five to a well-dressed woman behind him.

Schuyler, Lila recognized.

Peering into the office around her brother, Schuyler declared, "I hereby officially call this intervention in session."

With that, she stepped away from the doorway.

Following her out, Lucie told the two people who were left in the room, "And don't come out until you've resolved this properly." And then she closed the door behind her.

"This your idea?" Lila asked Everett.

"Hell, no," he denied. "I think Schuyler cooked this up."

"Not without Lucie's help," Lila said accusingly. Furious, she let out a shaky breath. And then she turned toward Everett. She was furious. "You know you can leave," she told him.

"I know." Lord, but he had missed her, he thought now, looking at Lila. "But since I'm here…maybe we should talk."

"About what?" Lila wanted to know. "What is there left to say?" Restless, uneasy, she began to pace within the limited space. "I trusted you once and got my heart broken for my trouble."

Her accusation hurt. But this wasn't one-sided. "I could say the same thing," Everett countered.

Her eyes narrowed as she looked at Everett, stunned. "You?" she questioned. What was he talking about?

"Yes," he informed Lila. "I'd trusted you, too. Trusted that you'd be with me forever—and then you walked out. It wasn't easy for me after we broke up. I might have gone on with my studies—because that was what I was supposed to do—but there was this huge, empty, jagged hole in my chest where you used to be."

His dry laugh was totally mirthless as he continued. "I think I must have picked up the phone a hundred times that first year, wanting to call you and tell you about something that had happened in class or at the hospital, before I realized that I couldn't. That you wouldn't be there to answer the phone." His eyes met hers. "Nothing meant anything without you," he told her.

Lila stood there looking at him. The inside of her mouth felt like cotton and she struggled not to cry. She'd held her feelings in too long. For thirteen years, to be exact. Now she could hold them in no longer.

"I still think about our baby all the time," she admitted.

Everett felt her words like a knife to his heart. More than anything, he wished he could go back in time to make things right. To do things differently. "Do you regret giving her up?"

"Yes," she answered so quietly, he had to strain to hear her. And then Lila took a deep breath. "No."

She blinked hard, telling herself she wasn't going to cry. Forbidding herself to shed a single tear. Tears were for the weak and she wasn't weak. She'd proven that over and over again.

"I know that our daughter has had a good life. The people who adopted her send me letters and photographs every once in a while, to let me know how she's doing." Lila smiled sadly. "Emma's a beautiful girl and she's doing really, really well in school."

Everett looked at her in surprise. He'd had no idea this was going on. "Her name is Emma? And you've stayed in contact with the family?" he asked.

Lila nodded. "Yes. Not knowing what was going on with Emma was killing me so it took a bit of doing but I managed to get in contact with the family that adopted her. Emma's parents are good people. They understood how hard it was for me to give up the baby. As a matter of fact, they're grateful to us for giving them what they call 'the most precious gift of all,'" Lila said. "Over the years, I've kept track of her through emails and pictures from her parents."

It was a lot for Everett to take in. Numerous questions rose in his head.

"How is she doing? What grade is she in now?" Everett asked.

"You actually want to know?" Lila asked him, astonished. "I mean, after the baby was born, you seemed really eager to put the whole incident behind you and forget about it. About her."

Her words stung, but he knew they were true. He'd been young and he'd just wanted to pretend that none of it had happened because it was easier to erase the guilt that way.

"I was," he admitted. "I'm not proud of it now, but it was the only way I could deal with it at the time, to just bury it and put it all totally out of my mind." Everett put his hands on her shoulders now, looking into Lila's eyes. "I'm sorry I wasn't more understanding, Lila. I didn't realize that you were hurting. I only knew that I was."

Lila struggled to wrap her mind around what he was telling her. She'd never suspected any of this. "You were hurting?"

Everett nodded. "She was my little girl, too," he told Lila.

"Oh, Everett, I wish you had told me," she cried.

So much time had been lost because of a failure to communicate. So much heartache could have been avoided if he had only verbalized his feelings to her.

If he'd just given her a clue...

"I wish I had told you, too," Everett said with all sincerity. And then he looked at her hopefully. "You wouldn't have a picture of Emma with you, would you?" he asked.

Lila opened up a drawer, took out her purse and

pulled out her cell phone. She pressed the photo app and scrolled through a few photos until she came to the one she was looking for.

"This is Emma," she told Everett, holding out her phone to him.

Everett looked at the young girl on the screen. He could feel his heart swell as he stared at the image. Emma looked to be on the verge of her teen years and she had a mouth full of braces.

She was the most beautiful girl he had ever seen.

"She has your smile," he said, taking in every detail of the photo. And then he looked up at Lila. "I can't believe how beautiful our daughter is." With a sigh, he handed the phone back to Lila.

Lila closed her phone and put it back in her purse. "Emma's not our daughter anymore, Everett," she told him quietly.

Everett nodded. "Right. Have you ever seen her in person?"

Lila shook her head. "No. I wanted to, but I don't want to confuse Emma. One mother and father is enough for her right now at her age. Besides, her parents know how to get in contact with me. They have my cell number. Someday, when she's older, if Emma wants to meet me, they'll let me know and I'll be there in a heartbeat. But for right now, all I want is for Emma to grow up happy and well adjusted."

"You're a strong, brave woman, Lila," Everett told her with admiration. He hadn't realized until this moment just how strong and brave she really was.

Lila shrugged. "You do what you have to do in order

to survive. And you make the best of the situation," she added. "The alternative is much too dark."

He nodded. "You're right. It is." He paused for a moment before looking at her and saying, "Would it surprise you if I told you that I think about Emma, too? That over the last few years, I've found myself thinking about her a lot. Wondering where she was, what she's doing. If she was happy. If she ever wondered about her birth parents and thought they—we—gave her up because we didn't love her."

"She knows we gave her up to give her a better life," Lila told him.

"You're just speculating," he said.

"No, I know that Emma knows that because her adoptive parents told me they told her that when she was old enough to begin asking questions."

Everett was quiet for a long moment. And when he finally spoke, what he said really surprised her. "I really wish I could meet our daughter."

It took Lila a moment to fully absorb what he had just said.

"Do you really mean that?" she asked Everett, astonished to hear him voice the same feelings that had been haunting her for years.

"Yes," he told her honestly. "I do."

She pressed her lips together, thinking over the feasibility of what he had just told her. "Well, I'm not sure how Emma's parents would feel about that, but I could certainly let them know that you're back in the picture and that you would like to meet Emma whenever it's convenient for them—and for her."

He nodded. It was a difficult situation all around and he fully understood that.

"I'd really appreciate that," he told her. He paused, trying to find the right words to convey what he wanted to say to her. "Lila…" Everett started, then stopped, his brain freezing up on him. This was a great deal harder than he'd anticipated.

"Yes?" she asked, wondering what else there was left for him to say. He'd already gladdened her heart by telling her that he not only thought about Emma, but actually wanted to meet her. That meant a great deal to her.

His eyes met hers. "Can you ever forgive me for not being there for you?" he asked softly.

Lila blinked. She could have been knocked over with the proverbial feather. Staring at Everett, she realized that he was being sincere.

"Oh Everett, I really wish I had known that you were hurting, too and that you felt the way you did. It would have helped me deal with everything that happened so much better." She smiled at him, fighting back tears again. "We really should have communicated more honestly with one another."

Everett stepped closer, letting himself do what he'd wanted to since he'd walked into this office. He enfolded Lila in his arms. "You're absolutely right. I should have talked with you, told you what I was feeling. But I just closed myself off, trying to deal with what was going on. I was blind and didn't realize that you were going through the same thing, too, and could have used my support." He'd been such a fool, Everett thought, regret riddling him. "Can you find it in your heart to forgive me?" he asked again.

Now that she knew that Everett had experienced the same doubts and emotions about their daughter that had haunted her, all of Lila's old feelings of anger and resentment vanished as if they had never existed. All Everett ever had to do was tell her what he'd gone through.

Forgiveness flooded her. "Yes, of course I can," she told him.

Relief mingled with love, all but overwhelming Everett. He kissed Lila, temporarily disregarding where they were and the fact that the people she worked with could easily look over and see what was happening.

And she kissed him back.

Everett forced himself to draw back. Still holding her in his arms, he looked down into her eyes. "From now on," he promised, "I'm putting all my cards on the table."

"Are you planning on playing solitaire or poker?" she asked Everett, a smile curving the corners of her mouth.

"Definitely not solitaire," he answered. "But any other game that you want. Oh, Lila, we've wasted much too much time and we'll never get any of that time back," he told her. His arms tightened around her. It felt so good to hold her against him like this. He felt he'd never let her go. "But we can have the future."

"And by that you mean...?" Her voice trailed off.

She wanted him to spell everything out so that there would be no more mix-ups, no more misunderstandings to haunt either one of them. She wanted to be absolutely certain that Everett was talking about what she *thought* he was talking about.

"I mean that I'm planning on being very clear about my intentions this time around. I know what I want," he told her, looking deep into her eyes. "All you need to do is say yes."

But she wasn't the same person she'd been thirteen years ago. She knew how to stand up for herself, how not to allow herself to be swept away.

She surprised him by telling Everett, "I never say 'yes' unless I know exactly what it is that I'm saying yes to."

"To this," Everett told her, pulling something out of his pocket. When he opened his hand, there was a big, beautiful heart-shaped diamond ring mounted on a wishbone setting in the center of his palm. He'd brought it with him for luck—and just in case.

Lila stared at it, momentarily speechless. When she raised her eyes to his face, she could barely speak. "Is that—?"

She couldn't bring herself to ask the question, because the moment she did—and he said no—a little of the magic would be gone. And she really couldn't believe that the ring she was looking at was the one she'd fallen in love with so many years ago.

But Lila discovered that she needn't have anticipated disappointment, because Everett nodded.

"Yes," he told her, pleased by her reaction, "it is. It's the one you saw through the window in that little out-of-the-way shop that day when we were back in college. You made me stand there while you made a wish and just stared at it, like it was the most beautiful thing you'd ever seen."

She smiled, remembering every detail. "I was being silly and frivolous," she admitted.

"No, you were being honest about your reaction," he corrected.

She continued looking at the sparkling diamond in his hand, completely mesmerized. "But how did you...?"

Everett anticipated her question and was way ahead of her. "After I dropped you off home, I doubled back to the store to buy the ring. The store was closed for the night by then, but I kept knocking on the door until the owner finally came down and opened it. Turns out that he lived above the store," he told her. "Anyway, I made him sell me the ring right then and there. I hung onto it, confident that I would give it to you someday." He smiled ruefully. "I just never thought it was going to take quite this long," he confessed.

Taking a deep breath, he held the ring up to her and said in a voice filled with emotion, "Lila Clark, will you marry me? I promise if you say yes, I will never leave you again."

Lila could feel her heart beating so hard in her chest, she was certain it was going to break right through her ribs. The wish she'd made that day in front of the shop window was finally coming true.

"I don't plan to keep you on a leash," she told him, so filled with love she thought she was going to burst. "But yes, I will marry you."

Thrilled, dazed, relieved and experiencing a whole

host of other emotions, Everett slipped the engagement ring on her finger.

The second he did, he swept her into his arms and kissed her again, longer this time even though he could see that they had attracted an audience. It didn't matter to him.

Lila's colleagues were watching them through the glass walls of her office and cheering them on, his sister and her cohort in front of the pack.

He looked down into Lila's eyes. "We can have more kids," he told her. "An entire army of kids if that's what you want. And they'll never want for anything. We can have that wonderful life that we used to just talk about having."

"A better one," she interjected.

"Absolutely," he agreed, hugging her to him again. "The sky's the limit," he promised. "But there's just one more thing."

"Oh?" Lila refused to be concerned. She'd been down that route and this was a brand-new route she was embarking on—with Everett beside her. She knew that she could face anything as long as he was with her. "What's that?"

"I don't want any more secrets between us," Everett said.

"Neither do I," Lila agreed wholeheartedly. "Is there something you need to tell me?"

"More than just you," Everett answered. "If we're going to start with a clean slate, there is something else I need to do."

Now he was beginning to really make her wonder,

but she wasn't about to shrink away from his revelation. Because whatever it was, they would face it together. Conquer it together.

"Go ahead," Lila said, thinking that he was going to confess something serious to her.

Instead, Everett opened her office door and called out, "Schuyler, Lucie, would you mind stepping back in here?"

The two women obligingly filed back into Lila's office.

"Okay," Schuyler said to her brother, "make your announcement, although we both saw you put that huge rock on Lila's finger so this is going to be a little anticlimatic."

"It's not what you think," Everett told his sister.

Schuyler exchanged looks with Lucie, obviously confused. "All right, enlighten us then," she said.

"I'm through sneaking around," he told his sister. "This is what we talked about when I first came to Austin, thinking I was picking you up to bring you home."

"What is he talking about?" Lucie asked, looking at Everett's sister.

Everett turned toward Lucie. "Lucie, I think it's time I told you who we really are. Or at least who we *think* we are."

Lucie looked from Everett to Lila, her brows furrowed. "Lila?"

But Lila shrugged, as mystified as Lucie was. "I have no idea what he's talking about," she admitted.

Everett laced the fingers of one hand through Lila's hand as he went on to make his revelation. Nodding toward his sister, he told Lucie, "As you know, our last name is Fortunado."

Lucie waited for more. "Yes?"

"What you might not know, and I've recently come to find out—thanks to Schuyler's detective work—is that the Fortunado family might actually be descendants of Julius Fortune, Jerome Fortune's father," he added for clarity.

"You know," Lucie told Everett, a smile spreading across her face, "I'm not half surprised. With all of Jerome's illegitimate offspring coming to light lately, it stands to reason he learned the art of seduction from his father." She reached out and placed a hand on Everett's shoulder. "In that case, I have some people I would *really* love for you to meet."

"People who could substantiate my suspicions?" Everett wanted to know.

"Oh, more than substantiate, I think," Lucie said with emphasis.

Instead of eagerly asking her friend to make the meeting happen, the way Lila thought he would, Everett turned to look at her. She saw a wicked sparkle in his eyes. Her pulse instantly began to accelerate.

"That really sounds wonderful, Lucie, and I'd appreciate the introduction," he told her without so much as a glance her way. His eyes were solely on Lila. "But I'm afraid the meeting is going to have to wait for now."

"Oh? Why?" Lucie asked.

"Because," Everett began, raising Lila's hand to his lips and brushing a kiss lightly against her knuckles, "my fiancée and I have plans for this afternoon. Plans," he said, "starting right now. So if you'll please excuse us..."

The request was merely a formality. Everett was already leading Lila out of the office and toward the hallway and the elevator beyond. He was vaguely aware of Schuyler's squeal of joy behind them and the sound of Lucie's laughter as she applauded.

All that and more blended into the background and then faded away as he stepped into the elevator car with Lila. They had a lot of catching up to do. And he planned to start this minute by taking her into his arms and kissing her as the elevator doors closed, locking the rest of the world out.

* * * * *

LET'S TALK
Romance

For exclusive extracts, competitions
and special offers, find us online:

f facebook.com/millsandboon

⊙ @millsandboonuk

🐦 @millsandboon

Or get in touch on 0844 844 1351*

For all the latest titles coming soon, visit
millsandboon.co.uk/nextmonth

*Calls cost 7p per minute plus your phone company's price per minute access charge

Want even more
ROMANCE?

Join our bookclub today!

'Mills & Boon books, the perfect way to escape for an hour or so.'

Miss W. Dyer

'Excellent service, promptly delivered and very good subscription choices.'

Miss A. Pearson

'You get fantastic special offers and the chance to get books before they hit the shops'

Mrs V. Hall

Visit millsandbook.co.uk/Bookclub and save on brand new books.

MILLS & BOON